HASTE
to the
WEDDING

Jane Hatton

© Jane Hatton 2006
Haste to the Wedding

ISBN   0-9554508-0-2
         978-0-9554508-0-8

Published by RaJe Publications
Garth Cottage
Little in Sight
Mawnan Smith
Falmouth
TR11 5EY

A CIP catalogue record of this book
can be obtained from the British Library.

Book designed & produced by:
The Better Book Company Ltd
Forum House
Stirling Road
Chichester
West Sussex
PO19 7DN

Printed in England

HASTE
to the
WEDDING

Jane Hatton

For Bettine & Mark — with my love
Jane Hatton
xxxxxx

I

Chel and Oliver arrived home to the Helford river from London on a high after the close of Oliver's fantastically successful first exhibition of paintings, and came down to earth with a bump. During their absence, a wild November gale had swept up the river, shifted four tiles on their newly acquired roof, totally removed one, and left the guttering on the front of the house dangling pathetically across the front door.

'Well, welcome home!' remarked Oliver, but philosophically.

'And no landlord to blame,' said Chel. 'Fun, isn't it, owning our own house?' She opened the car door and stepped out into the lane, and the wind caught at her hair, blowing it straight back like a flag, and made her jacket balloon out behind her. She staggered with its force, even in the shelter of the creek. In the dim interior of the car, she heard Oliver laugh, the tiny inside light lit his face and showed her the accompanying grin.

'Real life starts here,' he said.

At that point, they didn't know about the tiles. They found this out when Chel went into their bedroom to dump their bags, and discovered a wet patch spreading across the ceiling and dripping onto the floor. She went back downstairs and broke the news to Oliver.

'Over the bed?' he asked, ever practical.

'No. Fortunately, it's in the corner by the window.'

'Worry about it tomorrow, then. It's too late to do anything about it tonight.'

'It's going *splat, splat, splat*. It'll drive us mad. And if it rains all night it'll bring the ceilings down.'

Oliver yawned.

'It won't keep me awake, and I can't stop it raining, can I? You can phone Deb in the morning and ask her for the name of a good builder. Mawgan is bound to know someone, you can't leave a historic building to look after itself.'

'If this was a boat, you'd find a way to fix it soon enough,' grumbled Chel. She reached for the kettle and filled it from the kitchen tap.

'If it was a boat, I'd have some idea how to,' Oliver returned, without heat. He picked up the accumulated post that his sister, who lived – in sin, according to her mother – at the pub in the village, had stacked tidily on the kitchen table during their absence. Chel watched him shuffling through it, throwing the junk aside carelessly, making a mess where there was none before.

'You could at least get into the loft and put a bucket under it. You can manage that, surely.' She tried to keep the edge from her voice. Oliver gave her a long look, on the brink of saying something he might regret later, but decided to leave it alone. Instead,

'Good idea.' He dropped the last of the letters on the random heap that he had made. 'Have we a bucket?'

'Of course we have a bucket – here – ' She took it from its cupboard and thrust it into his hands. 'I'll make some tea while you do it.'

When he had vanished upstairs with the bucket, she sighed wearily, and looked at her watch. There had still been lights in the Fish as they drove past, but it was a bit late to start phoning now, and no builder would turn out tonight, anyway. *Splashed* past, actually, the tide had been unusually high and the causeway at the bottom of the hill almost too deep under water to drive across. She pulled out a chair and sank into it. Upstairs, the sound of the loft ladder extending and a series of crashes and bangs charted Oliver's progress. She hoped he would be all right. Apart from his disability from horrendous physical injury two or three years ago, he was about as domesticated as a wolf in a forest, and finding himself a home-owner had done nothing to alter that.

Home.

Come to that, *owner*. The last, still slightly unreal, fortnight had ensured that they could stay here, the gamble of buying a house they couldn't really afford had paid off. She hadn't realised, until it actually happened, how much of a strain it had been, and how much was riding on the outcome.

So they had a home. All they needed to do now, was make a life.

Out in the living-room, the phone rang, and Chel got to her feet and went through to answer it.

'Chel! I thought I saw you go past.' Her sister-in-law's voice came lilting down the wire. 'Dreadful weather, isn't it? You should have been here yesterday, we nearly had the river in the bar, I had wondered why there wasn't carpet on the floor! Had a good journey?'

'We had a lousy journey. We were late leaving, Giff Thomas wanted to talk to Oliver, and then it rained all the way back, there was a pile-up on the M5, thick fog in Devon, and now we're home the gutter is down and the roof is leaking, and how long has it been blowing a hooley like this?'

'Hey, hey, slow down!' Debbie was laughing. Glad someone found it funny, Chel thought morosely. She said so.

'Glad you find it amusing.'

'You sound shattered.' That was more sympathetic. 'But it was worth it, wasn't it? Did Oliver have a sell-out in the end?'

'Pretty well. I believe there were a couple of sketches left, but Giff says they'll go as soon as he opens tomorrow.' Gifford Thomas was the gallery owner who had staged the exhibition. 'I was going to ring you, actually. I thought it was too late tonight, I was leaving it until tomorrow – but since you've rung anyway – '

'Sunday,' interrupted Debbie, by way of explanation. 'Mawgan's just closing up. His night on the bar, remember? We can spend it sort-of together.'

'Well ask him, can you, if he can recommend a good builder? One who'll actually turn up would be first choice. There must be somebody sticks bits back on the Fish.'

'I'm sure there is. Did you get some damage in the gale last night, then? It was all OK yesterday morning when I went to pick up the post for you.'

'No, we need them to dig the garden!' answered Chel, tartly. 'Deb *listen*, can't you? Oh – sorry! I'm just so tired, all I want is to go to bed and the ceiling is dripping water onto the carpet. I've sent Oliver up into the loft, but he looked at me as if I'd asked him to scrub the kitchen floor – look, come over for coffee tomorrow morning. We can have a real talk.'

'Great. I'll do that. There's loads to tell you, too. Meanwhile, welcome back!'

When Debbie had rung off, Chel looked at the winking red light on the answering machine and wondered if she had the strength tonight. Oliver was still upstairs, she pressed the button and listened. There were only two messages.

'Oliver!' said his godmother's voice. 'Look, I'm flying out to Greece on Thursday, can I come and see you tomorrow morning? Give me a ring if it's inconvenient, otherwise I'll be over about ten, OK? Longing to see you both! Oh – this is Nonie.'

'Chel, it's Susan. We need to get together, if Deb is really going to marry this chef of hers in February, there's things to arrange, like a wedding – Tom and I can come down next weekend if that's all right with you? Don't worry, Deb says we can stay at the pub. Give me a ring when you get back, can you? Oh – and great about the exhibition. Well done Oliver!'

There were one or two clicks, where people hadn't bothered to leave messages. Chel rewound the tape and stood lost in thought. Oliver came back down the stairs and found her still standing there. He put his arms round her.

'It's OK Chel. We seem to have lost at least one tile, I've tried to wedge something in the hole for now, and at least the rain has stopped. I'll go outside while you make the tea and see if I can stop that guttering banging about – I've put a towel under the drip.'

'I've spoken to Debbie,' said Chel. 'God knows when we can get someone here though – we won't be the only people with tiles off and things.'

'I'll have a proper look in the morning, when it's light,' he promised.

'You won't. Nonie's coming over. She'll want to talk about what comes next for you.'

'Then I'll have a look when she's gone. It shouldn't be beyond me, just to stop up a leak.'

'Susan rang, too. She wants to come down next weekend.' Susan was Oliver's stepsister, unlike Debbie, who was his half-sister. They didn't really get on. He sighed, dramatically.

'*Into each life, some rain must fall.*'

'Don't be like that. Anyway, she's staying at the Fish.'

'Poor Mawgan! He hasn't had the pleasure yet, has he?'

'Go and fix that gutter, if you're going to.' Chel managed to unstick her weary feet from the carpet and trailed across to the kitchen door. 'You've got ten minutes. Use them!'

But in the morning, things looked altogether better. It hadn't rained in the night, the drip had stopped, and the sun was shining. Even the wind had dropped a little. Standing outside in the blowy sunshine, instead of in the windy darkness, nothing could seem so bad. The arrival of Anona Fingall while they were still sitting over the remains of a disgracefully late breakfast further improved the day.

'You'll stay to lunch, of course,' said Chel.

'I'm counting on it. There's a lot to talk about.'

'That's what everyone says.' Chel yawned. 'If it's about painting, count me out. Go up into the studio and tell Oliver – I'm going to unpack and tidy round, settle back in. It feels as if we've been away for months, not weeks.'

'Some of it is about painting,' said Nonie. She gave them both a demure look. 'Some of it isn't. I'll tell you over lunch.'

'Let's get out of Chel's way, then,' said Oliver, getting to his feet. 'You OK, sweetheart? Nothing we can do?' He was already heading for the door. Nonie hesitated.

'Chel?'

'I shall be fine – Deb's coming over later, she said. Don't worry about me, it's easier without him!' They exchanged a grin.

'Point taken,' said Nonie, and followed Oliver outside.

Oliver's studio was over the adjoining garage, up an outside staircase. It enjoyed a magnificent view of the creek from a wide balcony, and was the thing that had really sold them the house, although that was lovely too. The first thing that Oliver did was to push the doors to the balcony wide open, letting the cool November air rush in. Nonie shivered.

'Fresh air fiend!'

'I hate being shut in,' said Oliver, apologetically.

'I'll keep my coat on.' Nonie looked around her. 'What happened to that lovely picture you did with the boats and the sea urchins? I expected to see it at the gallery, but I didn't, and it isn't here either. Did you sell it?'

'I gave it to Deb,' said Oliver. He shifted a few things around on the workbench where he did his framing, and didn't look at Nonie. 'She's had a bit of a rough time – I wanted to show some solidarity.'

'My goodness, you *are* improving!' said Nonie. He looked up then, and met her eyes ruefully. 'Selfish bastard? I know. But at least now, I can see it. Mostly I can see it.'

'More self-centred than selfish, maybe.'

'Yeah ... well, it'll have given Deb some practice. I think she's picked out another one the same.'

'I'm longing to meet her. Chel says she's like you.'

'*Is* she?' Oliver considered this. 'No, she's a blonde.'

'I don't think she meant *looked* like you, exactly,' said Nonie.

'Susan's the one you need to look out for.'

'She was a sweet little girl. Her father was a darling.'

'Her mother isn't. You know what she did to Deb, don't you?'

'Disowned her. You told me. Well, she got her come-uppance, hasn't your father left her?'

'Yeah – left her with the house and all the furniture, and no divorce.'

'Bitter for her, even so.'

'She deserved worse.'

Nonie couldn't argue with that. Oliver's mother, Helen Macken the sculptress, had once been her best friend, the dissolution of Helen's marriage to Jerry Nankervis due to the machinations of the woman who became his second wife, had meant the dissolution of that friendship too. She wondered whether to comment on the fact that Jerry and Helen had come to Oliver's private view together, and decided not to. She had managed a brief talk with Helen, it had felt strange and, she rather thought, led nowhere. The whole incident had been very curious.

She was Oliver's mentor and teacher now, as well as his godmother. Another thing that had infuriated and humiliated Dot – the Dreaded Dot, as Helen had christened her, back in the days when they were young together. She had things to talk about, relevant to his future career.

'So what do you plan to do next?' she asked him now. 'You have to build on that success, it won't carry you forward on its own.'

An hour later they were still deep in discussion, when a sudden and unexpected wailing screech from outside made them both jump.

'What the *hell* was that?' Oliver strode onto the balcony, and stopped abruptly. 'Oh God, it's you! What are you doing up there?'

His brother-in-law elect, up a ladder at the front of the house with an electric drill, doffed an imaginary cap in his direction.

'Mornin' zur. Oi be 'ere about the trouble.'

'Chel said she asked Deb to ask you for the name of your builder – not to take up your time.'

'She did, so I sent him round.' Mawgan abandoned his country bumpkin impression and grinned across at him. 'I'm up to the job – promise. I served my time in the building trade, as well as in one of Her Majesty's prisons, remember.'

Oliver decided not to go there, Mawgan's attitude to the tragic accident that had led, indirectly, to Deb's disinheritance was often frivolous to the point of being alarming. A defence mechanism, Oliver thought, but didn't know him well enough as yet to be certain how to deal with it. He called over his shoulder, 'Nonie! Come and see what I've found – a chef on a ladder!'

Nonie stepped out onto the windy balcony behind him.

'A what?'

'Deb's intended, Mawgan Angwin from the pub down the road. My godmother, Mawgan – Anona Fingall.'

'Nonie,' said Nonie. 'Hullo, Mawgan.' She smiled at him, and he gave her back a friendly grin.

'Hi, pleased to meet you.' He spun the drill in his hand with a whirring noise. 'Must get on, excuse me. See you on the ground later?' Nonie just had time to stick her fingers in her ears.

When they went back inside, Oliver shut the balcony doors, so there was some mercy.

'A native Cornishman,' said Nonie, stating a fact. 'Poor Dot – you'd think your sister was doing it on purpose if you had a nasty suspicious turn of mind.'

'It serves her damn well right – after the way she tried to treat Chel, it's poetic justice. But no, you wouldn't, if you knew Deb. She just fell in love.'

'I can see why. What a charmer! I should think the grin alone was enough to slay her at twenty paces.'

'So long as he doesn't hurt her.'

'How do you get on with him?' said Nonie, curiously.

'I don't know him all that well so far – we've both been too busy.'

'He's not likely to hurt her, is he?' asked Nonie, after a pause, and Oliver gave her a wry smile.

'Not that I know of – it's just that he's the first one of a long line she's got as far as marrying, and I want it to work for her.'

'You big softie! Who'd have thought it?'

'The last man she shacked up with gave her hell, and he was from her own world. It seems a bit risky to me to step so far out of line – background, upbringing, interests, everything so opposite, you wouldn't think they'd find a thing in common.'

'You did the same thing,' Nonie reminded him.

'That was different. And I didn't care a toss what bloody Dot thought. Deb does.'

'That wasn't different at all,' Nonie contradicted. Oliver thought about it.

'Not on one level, no, maybe you're right, but Chel didn't have a prison record. Nor was she dedicated to a very time-consuming career, she had room to manoeuvre. For us both to manoeuvre. And although Chel worked in a hotel, for some reason, Deb's loving mother finds the pub even more difficult to swallow.'

'He owns the pub, I thought.'

'He does, and you could add that it's a beautiful, historic building. It's still a pub, and he still works in it. That's

9

absolutely fine by me, but so far as my stepmother is concerned, it's the lowest of the low. She's never met him, but you know what Deb says she called him? Rubbish!'

'That sounds like Dot we all know, and love. You'd think she'd learn, wouldn't you?' Pause. 'He looks nice – fun,' Nonie offered.

'I've no doubt he's both those things. But apart from the pub, he's a very ambitious chef with his own restaurant. Doesn't leave a lot of time to be a party animal, I wouldn't have thought.'

'A man with his hands full.'

'Yes, exactly.'

'I'm sure they've talked about it, and worked something out.' It was so odd, hearing Oliver who claimed that he had no time for his family, fretting like this about one of his sisters, that Nonie had almost lost sight of the obvious reason. It came back to her now.

'Did you say he went to prison? What for?'

'Manslaughter,' said Oliver, shortly.

'Ouch! Nasty.' She hesitated. 'I'm surprised that Jerry …'

'He reckons that it was a miscarriage of justice, and is trying to build a case to appeal.'

'And you?'

'I hope he's right.'

'Your father isn't a fool, you know. And presumably, he loves your sister too.'

Oliver said nothing, and after a moment looking hopelessly at the blackness of his frown, his godmother decided to take the bull by the horns. There was already enough trouble in the Nankervis family without Oliver creating yet more.

'Oliver,' she said. 'Look – maybe I'm speaking out of turn here, but you know, you can't equivocate on this one. Your sister is going to live just down the road from you, she's going to marry that man out there. Credit her with being capable of running her own life, why don't you? If you do anything else, you'll run the risk of alienating her the way you did poor Susan, but without the excuse of being a child.'

'I didn't alienate Susan!'

'Don't change the subject. And yes, you did.' She waited, but Oliver said nothing, so she continued. 'Don't build up prejudices, Oliver. It can be habit-forming.'

The silence that followed seemed to go on for ever. Then Oliver turned abruptly and crossed the floor to the balcony door in three quick strides, wrenching it open to step back outside. He crossed to the rail, Nonie was glad to see, with no trace of the tension of a minute before.

'How's it going?'

Mawgan was about to climb down the ladder. He paused.

'Well, it's up. But I reckon it's been there near enough since the house was built back in 1907. You need to replace it, and that'll probably be true all round the house. D'you want me to do it?'

'You?' asked Oliver, taken aback.

'Why not me? It's not rocket science, ezackly, just replacing a launder.'

'A what?'

'Sorry. A gutter to you. I've put your tiles straight, but one blew off, and it broke. I've patched it for now, until I get you a new one.'

Oliver could be both stubborn and difficult, and wasn't much given to considering the viewpoint of other people, but much like his father, he was no fool.It wasn't what Mawgan had said so much, as the confrontational way in which he had said it. He recognised that what he had been in danger of doing to Mawgan, Mawgan was also in danger of doing to him, and that Nonie was right, it couldn't be allowed to happen. He leaned comfortably on the rail, and set out to arrest the process before it went too far.

'So what's this, moonlighting?'

'Just keeping my hand in.' Mawgan looked rueful. 'Truth is, I'm not used to having days off, I don't know what to do with them.'

'So this is a day off, is it?'

'Something like that.'

'Then you don't want to spend it up a ladder in half a gale. Come up here instead, and we'll have a beer and talk about it. Or talk about something else. Whatever.'

'Fine by me.'

Oliver went back into the studio, and looked at Nonie, challengingly.

'Did I do all right?'

'You sounded almost human. So, did it hurt?'

'Not so's you'd notice. Look Nonie, it isn't that I don't like the man, I think I probably do. It's just ... because it's Deb, I suppose. I do love Deb, you're right.'

'There's an admission. And it didn't choke you, either, congratulations!'

Oliver looked at her with an unexpected crooked grin.

'My father did warn me you were a very astringent, judgemental woman.'

'*Did* he? Poor old Jerry!' Nonie rose from the stool where she had been sitting. 'I'll get out of your way then, the two of you won't want me around for your male bonding session. But Oliver, be careful. That's a man who looks and sounds as if he's had just about enough, and you, of all people, know how that feels.'

'Paintable?' asked Oliver, with interest, for his godmother was a well-known portrait painter. For reply, she made a face.

'Very, but not right now. It wouldn't be fair. Anyway, I doubt if he could sit still for long enough, that's a live wire your sister has there.'

When she had gone, running down the outside stairway to the lane, Oliver went slowly over to the small caravan fridge that he and Chel had put in the studio to facilitate the evening enjoyment of the view from the balcony, but didn't immediately open it. He stood with his hand on the door, thinking. Down below in the lane he heard Nonie's voice, and Mawgan answering, the sound of laughter and the rattle of the ladder sliding onto the roof-rack on Mawgan's Volvo estate. Deb presumably was here somewhere, but she hadn't come up to say hullo. Did that mean that she, too, was feeling uncomfortable? No, amendment: had he himself created a situation with which *nobody* was entirely comfortable?

It hadn't been deliberate, of that at least he was innocent. Both he and Mawgan had been too busy over the last month to do more than nod to each other in passing, but while the pressures on Mawgan had been easing with the end of the season, giving him maybe too much time in which to think, they had been building on Oliver in the run-up to his exhibition, giving him none at all.

'Oh, bugger everything,' Oliver muttered to himself. He wasn't much given to self-criticism, and disliked the feeling.

'I second that,' said Mawgan, from the door.

'Come in,' said Oliver. He took two cold beers from the fridge, and Mawgan came in and looked about him with interest.

'Nice pictures – not that I'm a judge.' He accepted the offered can and opened it with skill born of long practice. 'That one you gave Deb – that's some beautiful.'

'I gave it to both of you.'

'Then thank you. It was generous.'

'Come out on the balcony. I take it you're not frightened of a little breeze, like my godmother?'

'Look,' said Mawgan, as they leaned on the rail together. 'If you like, we can talk about gutters and tiles, and whether you want me to make good the damage to your bedroom ceiling, and that's fine.'

Oliver drank some of his beer, savouring the cold of it as it ran down his throat, and chose his words carefully.

'We can do that, yes. Or?'

'Or you can listen to me.'

'You want to tear me off a strip?'

'No. Why should I? I just thought the boot was on the other foot, maybe.'

'I'm very fond of Deb,' said Oliver, moderating his confession to Nonie. 'If marrying you is what makes her happy, I go with that.'

'Do you, really?' Mawgan looked as if he didn't believe a word. 'Then perhaps this'll make you feel better about it. She's perfectly safe with me, I wouldn't hurt her, not physically, not even accidentally – you do that kind of thing once, it kind of cures you for ever.'

'I can see that it would,' said Oliver, quietly.

'What happened to Mike was a fluke. You do realise that? Even if it happened with Deb, which God forbid, she'd very likely get up and walk away.'

'You don't have to convince me.'

'I feel as if I do.'

'Then I can only say, I'm sorry if that's my doing.'

'I *killed* him. I can see you can't overlook it.' There was too much pain in that simple statement. Oliver, who was more used to creating dramas than dealing with them, forgot Nonie's advice and reacted straight from the shoulder.

'According to my father, you didn't. And for Christ's sake try and put it behind you, or you won't be marrying my sister in February, for the simple reason that you'll be on the funny farm!'

They stared at each other. Mawgan took a deep breath, he looked furious.

'Then what's your problem? You don't even want me around your house.'

'That,' said Oliver, 'is not true, but I don't know what I can say to make you believe me. Another beer? Or will you simply pour it over my head?'

'Oh, shit,' said Mawgan, and leaning his elbows on the rail, buried his face in his hands. Oliver picked up the two empty cans and went back into the studio to fetch replacements. The interval, short though it was, gave them both time. By the time he got back, Mawgan had turned round, leaning his back against the rail so that they faced each other.

'Sorry,' he said, abruptly.

'Here.' Oliver put the can into his hand. 'Now, shall we go out and come in again?'

'Deb asked me not to quarrel with you, and now look what I've done.'

'Oh well,' said Oliver. 'We can't always be doing what the women tell us to. Cheers!'

They drank in silence for a while, and then Oliver said,

'Chel once said to me, when I was in much the same sort of mood as you are now, *if you're not dead, you have to go on living.* The two of you were friends once upon a time. Do you think he'd be glad that you can't go on living, even when you're the one that lived?'

'No,' said Mawgan, after a pause.

'Well, then.'

Another silence, but a less strained one. Oliver drained his can and looked at his companion, thoughtfully.

'Another one?'

'No, better not. Deb tells me I drink too much, so I'm trying to cut back.'

'That's good. I wouldn't like to think of you drunk in charge of my – what did you call it?'

'Launder. And with my gift for hitting the floor just lately, I only climb ladders when I'm stone-cold sober.'

'That being understood, I'll be happy to have you fix it, if it really isn't an imposition.'

'It isn't.'

'I'll do something for you in return, one day – if you can think of anything, that is.'

'Fine.' Mawgan paused. His mood had changed, thankfully moved on. 'Paint a mural in my restaurant.'

'Hey, there's an idea! What of?'

'I'm not sure yet.'

'You were serious, then?'

'I think so.' He spoke slowly, thinking it out as he went. 'Although, considering who you are, I probably shouldn't ask you.'

'If I can ask you to mend my roof, I fail to see why not. It's all in the family, after all. Want to tell me about it?'

'It's just an idea, at present. I expect Deb has told you how I got landed with the pub?'

'She said your partner took off and you had to buy him out.'

'That's a kind way of putting it, but something like that. We bought the place between us, Edward and me. I wasn't the smallest bit interested in running a pub, and I'm still not. As a matter of fact ...' he paused. 'No, we'll save that. Has Deb shown you the restaurant?'

'Not so far. What's it like?'

'Strange – I think so, anyway. Got a pencil and paper?'

'I'm an artist, I've got them in spades. Come inside, I'll find it for you.'

They went into the studio, and Mawgan drew a long, thin rectangle on a sheet of paper.

16

'I have,' said Debbie, unexpectedly. They all looked at her, and she blushed. 'Well, it was obvious he hadn't given it a thought.'

'So, what did you come up with?' asked Chel.

'*An Rosen Gwyn*.'

Mawgan had gone suddenly still. Oliver said,

'Nice play on words, but what does it mean?'

'The White Rose,' said Nonie, immediately. 'It's Cornish – the name of a song, actually.'

Debbie looked across the table at Mawgan, almost with a challenge.

'Don't look at me like that. Your doctor told me – when you had that migraine that frightened us both to death, and I thought you were going to die on me from delayed compression of the brain, or an embolism or something.'

Unconsciously, Mawgan fingered the slanting scar above his right eye, acquired in the chaos that attended the burning of Seagulls in the summer. He said,

'Well, you have surprised me,' and left it at that. Chel looked at them curiously.

'Are you going to let us all in on the secret?'

'It's so old a story, it should begin *Once upon a time*,' said Mawgan, dismissively.

'Tell us, anyway.'

'Deb will. For one thing, I don't think I can stop her.'

Everyone looked at Debbie.

'*Once upon a time?*' prompted Nonie, smiling.

'It was only a couple of months ago that I first heard it, actually, just after Mawgan came out hospital. He suddenly had this horrendous migraine out of nowhere, he'd never had one before in his life and because I knew he'd … well, been less than honest with the hospital so he could escape quicker, I got in a panic and rang the surgery, and this nice Dr Pollard came over. Dr Billy, everyone calls him. We hadn't met before though, and I … oh goodness, it was unforgivable.' Momentarily, she hid her face in her hands. 'He said he thought it was just a migraine but he'd arrange to have it checked out to be sure, and I said …I can't believe now that I said it!'

'What did you say?' asked Mawgan, curiously.

'I said, it was good of him to come out, when he probably had no time for you anyway, just like everyone else.'

Mawgan winced.

'Nice one,' murmured Oliver.

'I was upset,' said Debbie, defensively.

'So what did he say to that?' asked Chel.

'He gave me a long, cool look,' said Debbie. 'I shrivelled on the carpet, and then he said, had I time to make him a cup of tea, he thought he'd better talk to me. And he told me this story.'

She paused, and looked belatedly at Mawgan. 'You don't mind if I tell them, do you?'

'Can I stop you?'

'Well, the year after Edward and Mawgan bought the Fish, Dr Pollard's wife – her name was Rose, by the way, you must remember that, it's part of the story – was very ill. Dying, actually, of cancer. They knew she was on borrowed time, so they were just making the best of what was left. She was going into hospital, and they were going to try and do something … but there wasn't really any hope. Anyway, she had a what d'you call it, a recession, and she was so much better that she asked him to take her out to dinner somewhere – they always loved going out to dinner, he told me, but they hadn't done it for months by then. It was dreadfully short notice, and she obviously couldn't travel far, and she probably wouldn't eat much when they got there, but he wanted to give her what she wanted because he knew it was probably the very last time they could be together like that. So he rang the Fish, because it was close and everyone was always saying how wonderful it was now, not really thinking that he would get a table … and Mawgan happened to take the call. He must have known, Dr Billy said, well, all the village knew. And he said he'd fit them in, and what did she particularly like to eat? And he saw that they had the best table, in the corner by the window, and he did everything to please her, all her favourite things in tiny portions that she could manage, and when they got to the coffee, he – him over there, blushing – came out of the kitchen to ask if everything had been all right, and he gave her a tight, white rosebud, that he had driven all the way to St Austell to pick from his grandfather's garden.'

'You could stop there,' Mawgan suggested, rubbing an embarassed hand over his face. 'Have mercy on me.'

'No, why? There's more to this story than even you know, so I'll finish it, if you don't mind.'

Mawgan gave a howl, and collapsed onto the table, hiding his face in his folded arms.

'I thought you said you loved me!'

'Oh, I do. Lots.' Debbie turned back to her, by this time, fascinated audience. 'She was thrilled and touched, Dr Billy said, and she looked at him across the table, her face all lit up like it hadn't been for months, and she said, laughing you know, what a pity they weren't in Italy, so some romantic young troubadour would come up to the table and sing the White Rose for her too, wouldn't it make a wonderful evening absolutely perfect? And he said – Mawgan said – would that really make it perfect? And she said yes, but that was just dreams, it was wonderful anyway, nobody got perfect. And Dr Billy said, he stood there, in his chef's whites and all sweaty from the kitchen, and he sang it for her – just like that. Only, this was the thing, and if you know the words of the song you'll understand why he did it – he sang it in Cornish, and she sat there with her eyes like two stars, shining, Dr Billy said he thought she fell in love, right then and there, and there were tears rolling down his cheeks because she was so happy … and everyone in the restaurant went silent, he wasn't the only one crying, and when it got to the chorus, the locals who were there began to hum the accompaniment, and the last chorus, they all joined in, some of them even with the harmony, and it was utter, complete, magic.'

She paused, but silence had fallen on the dining table here, too, and nobody spoke. After a minute, she went on, her voice quiet and not quite steady.

'Mawgan doesn't know this bit himself, but Dr Billy told me. She took the rosebud home and put it in a little vase and watched it unwrapping itself, day by day, delighted with it. But two days after their meal at the Fish, she collapsed in agony and had to be transferred to the hospice in Hayle, and the rose went with her. She could hardly speak for the pain, but she said 'The rose – where's my lovely rose?' and so they put it where she could see it. Of course, in the heat of the ward it came out fully, and as it began to drop … she died.'

Mawgan had raised his head and was looking at her in amazement. She met his eyes, and surreptitiously wiped a tear from under her own.

'The nurses said, should they throw that old rose away now, it was dropping everywhere, but Dr Billy said no, he'd take it away … and he wrapped it carefully and put it in the top of the freezer … and when she was in her coffin, he tucked it into her hands, and it was buried with her … and he said … he said …' She swallowed, and when she spoke again, it was in a voice not quite her own. 'He said, 'And you tell me I don't like that man of yours, young lady? Well, you're quite right, I don't. I *love* that man."

Into the long silence that followed, Oliver said quietly,

'Well, that was a real conversation-killer. Coffee, anyone?'

'I'll make it.' Chel got to her feet, glad to have an excuse to escape into the kitchen, where she blew her nose, hard, on a piece of kitchen paper. Debbie, she thought, probably shouldn't have done that, although she could see why she had.

Back in the main room, Nonie said, to bring the disconcerted company down to earth without creating a *non sequitur* that would be out of place,

'So you're a singer, then, Mawgan? That's a very Cornish 'thing', isn't it? Like the Welsh.'

'I'm not really. My family has a long choir tradition, so I grew up knowing all the old songs, but I was never a member of a choir myself. It just seemed the right thing to do at the time.'

'Oh, I agree with you. It was.'

'You never said you spoke Cornish, either,' said Debbie, and he grinned at her, relieved to have her uncomfortable revelation behind him.

'I don't. I just happen to know that particular song in Cornish, and like you said, it wasn't the moment to sing it in English.'

'I have this awful suspicion creeping up on me,' said Nonie. 'You said a long choir tradition … please don't tell us, on top of everything else, that you were brought up a Wesleyan Methodist, Debbie's poor mother will have a stroke!'

'I won't tell you, then.'

'But you were?'

''fraid so.'

'And you ended up with a pub,' observed Oliver, thoughtfully. 'Bet that went down a storm!'

'I already told you, that wasn't my idea.' He gave Oliver a mischievous look. 'Abstinence's never been a problem in our family, though. Dad's side anyway, Mum's lot are a bit more strict.'

'So, are you planning a chapel wedding?' asked Nonie.

'Up to Deb. So long as she marries me, I don't care where.'

'Oh, I'll marry you,' said Debbie. 'Particularly now even Susan can't call you a brainless country yokel.' She turned with an air of pride to the company in general. 'They did a scan, and he's definitely got one, they showed him a picture.'

'So he says,' remarked Oliver.

'That's true. He could be lying.' She looked at Mawgan, and there was such love in her look that her brother turned away, feeling as if he had trespassed on private ground. He realised that Nonie had prevented him from making a very bad mistake, and was grateful to her, one thing he never wanted to do was to – what was the word she had used? – *alienate* Debbie. He found that he had inadvertently met Nonie's eyes, and she was looking at him very seriously, as if she knew exactly what he was thinking.

Mawgan and Debbie left after the coffee, leaving the other three still sitting around the table.

'I feel we ought to help to wash up, but we're supposed to be going to see Mawgan's grandparents,' said Debbie, apologetically. 'So much for days off – but they asked us so nicely, we couldn't really refuse.'

'Don't worry about it,' said Chel. 'We took over a washing-up machine with the fixtures and fittings, what luxury! See you again.'

The front door slammed behind them, and a minute or two later, the sound of a car reversing announced their final departure. Nonie looked at Oliver, a challenge in her eyes.

'A nice pair,' she said.

'Is that meant to be confrontational?'

'No. A comment, merely. And she *is* like you, to look at as well.'

'As well as what?'

'That would be telling.'

Chel began gathering the plates together, and then stopped, pushing the pile away from her.

'So, what did you make of that tale of Deb's?'

'I hope she never uses it in an after-dinner speech,' said Oliver, 'There won't be a dry eye in the house.'

Nonie said,

'Whether she told it for that reason or not, it was the picture of a very compassionate man. I can't believe how he must have felt when he was responsible for somebody's death.'

'It was his brother-in-law's death, and he wasn't exactly responsible,' put in Chel.

'Oh no! How awful. Whatever did his family do?'

'From what Deb says, which is all we have to go on, they didn't know *what* to do – so they did that,' said Oliver. 'Mind you, I'm not saying I blame them. I don't know what I would have done myself.'

'And the sister?'

Chel said, with perhaps unnecessary force,

'She made trouble for the next few years, and now seems to have buggered off with some man without leaving an address. Let's not think about her! You said it wasn't only painting you wanted to talk about. So, what else? For instance, what's taking you to Greece in November, of all times?'

Nonie said, quietly, accepting the change of subject,

'I'm going out there to see Theo.'

'Serious talk time?' asked Oliver. Nonie's friend and ex-lover, Dimitrios Theodorakis, was a long-standing friend of his own, and her refusal to marry him because of unfinished business elsewhere had nearly wrecked the friendship altogether.

'Yes, serious talk time. Decision time, in fact.' She looked up at them both, almost with apology. 'If I sent you a message – would you drop everything, and come?'

'Come, for what reason?' asked Oliver, holding her gaze with his own.

'To dance at my wedding,' said Nonie.

'You're really going to do it?' Amazement rang clear in the words.

'Yes … yes, I think I really am. Are you surprised?'

'Gobsmacked, actually! What about your studio here, or will you paint out there all the time?'

'Oh, I shall keep it. I might sell the cottage, but I'll keep the studio. We shall spend some time in England, quite a lot of it I expect, we'll need a base. The rest of it in Ayios Giorgos and in Athens – we both have lives of our own, we shall need to work it out.'

'You've discussed it, then,' said Chel, stating a fact.

'Yes. When he came over for Oliver's private view, we talked for a long time. The only thing we didn't decide – I didn't decide – was whether I wanted to get married. But now, this time, I think I really do. I think I want to belong again … it's lonely, when you don't belong anywhere. Looking at those two just now kind of rubbed that in.'

'You always belong with us,' said Chel.

'Yes, I know, and I appreciate it, but that's different. You're a different generation, and you're starting a new life. I can't live through you, even if you were my children – and you're not, although it does often feel as if you are.'

'It feels like an ending …' said Chel, and sounded lost.

'No, it's a beginning. Two beginnings, mine and yours. You've real family with you now, and you're sure to get involved in all sorts of things. Those two pack some punch between them, and Oliver's on the threshold of a brilliant career. You won't have time to miss me at all.'

So what about me? Chel thought, a little desolately. Where do I come in? She said, trying to sound positive,

'And you're sure about it? Getting married?'

'Nearly absolutely certain.'

'Then congratulations, we're really happy for you.' Chel got to her feet, began to clear the table properly this time. 'But whatever you do, don't summon us next weekend. Susan would never forgive us!'

II

'**A**re we nearly there yet?' asked Annabel, for at least the tenth time.

'Half an hour,' said Susan, briskly.

'You hope.' Tom Casson, at the wheel of the car and peering into the seething dark, muttered the words between his teeth, he trusted inaudibly. The weather that they kept in this godforsaken duchy was appalling, he had never seen such rain in England! Behind him, his daughter bounced in her seat under the restraint, thank goodness, of a seatbelt.

'You said that the last time.'

'It's raining sweetheart. Daddy can't see very well.'

'He's got the wipers on.' Beside her, her brother Sebastian dozed fitfully. She poked him, hard, which fortunately, Susan didn't see. He woke up with an indignant grunt

'Don't *do* that!' He slapped her hand away, and she slapped him back.

'Oh God!' prayed Tom, between his teeth. He had had other plans for tonight, and indeed, for most of the weekend, that had not involved his family. He glanced at the clock on the dashboard, nine o'clock, near enough. At this moment, he should have been drinking wine in Mario's Trattoria, with Elaine, his PA. 'Working late', it was euphemistically called. He didn't think Susan knew; for someone so competent, she was amazingly naïve.

Susan, who knew perfectly well about Elaine but had chosen to ignore it, stared out through the sheet of water pouring down the windscreen and wished, with all her heart, that Tom would at least pretend to be looking forward to the weekend, even if it was just in front of the children. Children weren't stupid, or at least, theirs weren't, and he spent little enough time with his family that he didn't have to begrudge it quite so obviously. She had hoped that a weekend away – from Elaine, among other things – would put some heart back into what she feared, in the dark hours of the night, might be a failing marriage, but so far, it wasn't shaping up that way.

'It said Helston *that* way,' said Annabel, loosening her seatbelt so that she could lean forward. 'You've gone the wrong way, Daddy.'

'No I haven't.' Tom gritted his teeth. 'Why don't you sit back and close your eyes and go to sleep? You'll be tired tomorrow.'

'But it's only half an hour, Mummy said so, and that was ten minutes ago, so – '

'Annabel!' Sharply.

Susan shot her husband a glance in the darkness.

'Ease up, Tom, why don't you? The children are excited, it's not often they get a weekend away.'

'They had a – very expensive – holiday in Antigua not a couple of months ago, I seem to remember.'

'That was different.' As it had been, she reflected. A fortnight at an expensive holiday complex where the children were kept occupied and entertained all day, allowing the parents time to relax and sunbathe and quarrel with each other as much as they wished. There had been a redhead, who obviously had no particular respect for other people's marriage vows ...

Where did I go wrong? Susan asked herself, and came up with no answer. She had married Tom because he was suitable, and yes, she had loved him, or at least, she had thought she did, and she had tried to make it work. It was becoming increasingly difficult to believe that she had actually succeeded. If she had succeeded, she wouldn't have spent her holiday feeling like an unwanted third party. Tom said it was her imagination, but she didn't think she had that much imagination.

'Grandma says that Auntie Debbie lives in a horrid, common *pub*,' said Sebastian, at this painful moment in his mother's thoughts.

'Grandma's cross with Auntie Debbie, she would say that,' said Annabel, with deadly perception. 'She says I shouldn't be a bridesmaid, but I shall.'

'Are we going to stay there?' asked Sebastian, with interest. 'I've never been in a pub.'

'Anyway, you have!' crowed Annabel. 'We stopped for lunch, when we went to see the swans. It had beams in the ceiling, with horse things on them. Mummy, do we know, has Auntie Debbie's pub got – '

'No, we don't,' said Susan, interrupting abruptly. 'Now see if you can stay quiet until we get to Helston.'

'How long is that?' grumbled Annabel.

'Not long enough!' said Tom.

They proceeded for a short time – a very short time – in blessed silence, then Annabel said, cautiously,

'Mummy.'

'We're not at Helston yet.'

'No, but Mummy. Grandma said – '

The thought of what other things Grandma might have said were enough to bring you out in a cold sweat, and Susan jumped in with more haste than consideration.

'Grandma is upset, and she's said some very silly things. You shouldn't take too much notice.'

'Your mother will love that, when it's repeated back to her,' observed Tom.

'She said he *killed* someone,' said Sebastian. 'I heard her say to someone who came.' Susan cursed her mother in her head. How was she supposed to sort that one out?

'Well, she's wrong,' she said, firmly.

'He might be an ogre,' muttered Sebastian, nervously. He was only seven, and rather insecure. Annabel looked at him scornfully.

'Auntie Debbie wouldn't want to marry an ogre, don't be silly!'

'He might have *lured* her, and be grinding her bones to make him bread.' He paused, and his eyes grew round although nobody could see them. 'We might have to *eat* it.'

'I'm hungry,' said Annabel. 'Can't we – '

'No, we can't!' snapped Tom. 'Your aunt will have something ready for us when we get there, she said. Although, God knows what it will be, she's no cook,' he added, with a shudder.

'But it must be the middle of the night!'

'Then call it a midnight feast.'

Annabel, mercifully, fell silent after that, but Sebastian could be heard, muttering,

'Well, I shan't eat any bread.'

Susan leaned her head back against the seat and closed her eyes, listening to the swish of the passing traffic. Not only Debbie lay at the end of this horrendous journey, but Oliver too. She hadn't seen Oliver for nearly two years, unless you counted a brief, public encounter at the private view, and they had parted the last time on some hard words. Two years was a long time to bear a grudge, and she didn't think she had done that, but even so ... and there were other things, even more complicated ... She found that she felt sick, but it was the car, of course. Of course.

They had come to a roundabout. The car slowed.

'Bugger!' said Tom, with force. A little voice on the back seat murmured, very quietly,

'Told you.'

So, one way and another, by the time they finally reached Helston, the children were grizzly, the parents cross, and the rain heavier than ever. Tom, heading off to the Lizard on yet another wrong road, thought longingly of home with more warmth than he had felt towards it for some time.

'I don't know why you had to drag me along anyway,' he said.

'Really,' said Susan. She scrabbled in the glove box for the map. 'I don't think we take this road. The river's over there.' She pointed to their left. 'This road goes straight down past Goonhilly.'

'I do hate a smartarse!' said Tom. He pulled into the side of the road. 'You drive then, if you're so clever! I'm tired, it's hell with all this rain!'

'It's stopping,' said Annabel, and indeed, it was. Tom and Susan changed places, grim-faced, and they set off again. The first thing Susan did was to turn round and retrace their route, and Tom went into a great silence, ostentatiously closing his eyes.

Twenty minutes later, they were dropping through a shadowy wood towards the starlit gleam of St Erbyn Creek and the river, under a clearing sky.

'Deb said, drive straight through the village, almost out on the other side,' said Susan, and Tom grunted.

'Should be easy enough for even you to spot a pub,' he said. Susan made herself resist the temptation to rise to the bait, threading her way down a narrow village street lined with picturesque cottages and parked cars in about equal ratio. Annabel leaned forward again.

'Are we nearly there yet?' she asked, for the eleventh time, and as she spoke they reached the bottom of the hill, and there was the Fisherman's Arms, ahead of them on their right. 'Oh!' she said. 'Oh Mummy, are we really staying there?'

The road took a twist towards the river and the mouth of the creek that ran deeply through the village, and straightened out to become a causeway across the shingle foreshore. The pub, low, white and of venerable age, crouched over the causeway, its lighted windows warm and welcoming. Nearer, another wing of the building, which must house Debbie's Mawgan's restaurant, lay slantwise, parallel with the twist in the road. The windows here, too, were warm-lit, allowing a secret glimpse of the interior, where people sat over their food and wine and waiters moved among them, white shirts, black waistcoats, civilised. A sign with an arrow fixed to the wall pointed to the car park at the rear, up a narrow lane hung with brambles.

'It's like in an adventure book,' breathed Annabel, entranced.

'And it's the right pub,' said Tom, as if it might not have been. His tone was congratulatory. Susan narrowly missed hitting the corner of the restaurant.

Sebastian, his eyes like saucers, said,

'So why did Grandma say it was horrid, Daddy?'

'Because she's never seen it,' said Tom. He was already feeling better, a traditional old pub was exactly what was needed, and it was a Free House, too, better and better. Susan turned up the lane, and drove into the car park and parked the car in the first available slot. She turned off the engine and leaned back in her seat. They were here. Step one.

There was a knock on the window, and the driver's door was opened. Debbie leaned in, kissing her sister's cheek.

'Suse! I thought you'd never get here! Was it a horrible journey? I don't know what's the matter with the weather – hi kids!' She peered into the back, and then smiled at her brother-in-law. 'Hi Tom. You must be shattered, working all day and everything. Come on in and I'll find you a drink and something to eat.'

'Sounds a good programme.' Tom was already out of the car, opening the boot. 'Come on, everyone grab something – yes Sebastian, you too, you can manage the teddy bears – here.'

Sebastian, loaded with bears, looked apprehensively up at his aunt.

'Where's the ogre?'

'The what? There isn't one, what do you mean?'

'The man.'

Momentarily taken aback, Debbie exchanged a glance with her sister.

'You mean Mawgan? He's not an ogre, lambkin, he's a star. Who's been telling you stories?'

'Don't even think about it,' Susan advised. She grabbed one of the bags. 'Oh Deb, lead me to a comfortable chair and a stiff drink!'

'Come on up, then.'

Debbie led the way into the pub through the rear door, and up the stairs.

'That door on the left is the flat where we live. Your rooms are along here, I'll show you – get sorted out, and come along. The wine's been breathing, and everything's ready. I expected you before this.'

Susan arrived in the flat first. Debbie thought she looked more tired than the journey perhaps justified, but she had always had her doubts about Susan's apparently conventional marriage, suspecting that it might be too conventional for anyone's good. Impossible to say so. She held out a glass of wine.

'Here. Sit down, put your feet up, relax.'

Susan took the glass, but didn't immediately accept the invitation to sit, in spite of what she had said, she had done enough sitting for the moment. She looked around her with interest.

'Nice flat. Oliver painted that picture, surely?'

'It was an engagement present, he said. Did you know that Dad was here too, he's staying with Oliver and Chel. He said he didn't want to be left out, since he's the one who'll be footing the bill.' Privately, she thought that Jerry was hanging onto his children in case everything, not just two marriages, got away from him, and the family disintegrated. She hesitated. 'I don't suppose Mum sent any message, did she?' She spoke without hope, so there was no reason to be disappointed when Susan shook her head. 'Oh well.'

'She won't, Deb,' said Susan, but gently for her. 'You know her. The only thing that might change her is if *you* change – and you aren't going to, are you?'

'No. But it isn't fair if she's turning the children against him. That's mean.'

'I agree. I'd have stopped her if I'd been there, but I wasn't, and Maria wouldn't do anything.' Maria was the current *au pair* looking after the children. 'It's no use saying anything now, it's too late, all it'll do is ram the lesson home. You'll just have to put your faith in his winning them over. Do you think he will?'

'Well, not tonight anyway. He'll come upstairs shattered, and you must help me to protect him.'

'Fair enough.' Susan turned, as Tom came in with the children. Annabel sniffed the air, with a little too much appreciation, juicily.

'Something smells lovely, Auntie Debbie!'

'Make the most of the smell then, if Auntie Deb's been among the cookpots,' her mother advised.

'Oh, I haven't. Mawgan put it in the oven, hours ago before he went down to the kitchen. It's a sort of all-in-one lamb stew so I can't even mess up the vegetables – he told me its proper name, but I've forgotten it.'

'He's got your measure, then.' Tom accepted a glass of wine, and grinned at her. He paused. 'So, where is he?'

'Still working, I should think.' Debbie glanced at her watch. 'He'll be up in a while. Let's sit down and eat, before this child falls asleep in his plate.' She scooped Sebastian and a large teddy up into her arms and placed them on a chair at the table. 'You sit there, it'll be right up.'

Susan came into the small kitchen to help. Oliver hadn't given her a picture, and she tried not to feel resentful.

'They won't eat that much – Seb won't, anyway, he's shattered too. Tom didn't get home until nearly six, although I asked him to try.' She looked into the fragrant pot from which Debbie had just lifted the lid. 'That looks delicious, and by the way, I think it's called Navarin of Lamb.'

'Really? How posh!'

Susan picked up a ladle and began to serve out.

'Do you mind? I know what they'll eat.'

'Be my guest – oh, you are, aren't you.' They exchanged a smile. 'That's a first,' said Debbie.

'Do I save any for Mawgan?'

'No, don't bother. He never eats much when he's been working, he says cooking spoils his appetite, which isn't much of a recommendation for the restaurant when you come to think about it. He'll come up, drink about a gallon of water out of the fridge, and then just have a shower and fall into bed.'

'This happens every night? So what do you do?'

'I fall into bed too.' Debbie grinned at her, and her sister put on what Debbie called her *prissy* face. She said, primly,

'Not much of a life for you, even so.'

'He's running the bar Sunday nights, which isn't so bad, at least I can help, and all of Monday, plus Tuesday evenings are set aside for us, at least in the winter. Anyway, he's around the place all day, even if he's working, we see each other. Lots of wives see less of their husbands. And in the summer, hopefully, I'll be as busy myself. '

Susan winced, but nothing would make her admit that she was becoming one of those wives.

'Will you get quality time for each other at all?' she asked, refraining with only an effort from imagining what her mother would say if she heard Debbie was now working behind a bar – on Sundays, too.

'We're still aiming to keep Mondays free. He'll open five nights instead of four, and Sunday lunchtime, it'll give the restaurant staff a proper break, too. We've got it all worked out.'

Susan picked up the plates for the children and headed for the kitchen door.

'So, will we see him at all this weekend?'

'Well, Fridays and Saturdays are the busiest nights in the restaurant, and the weekend is busiest at the pub too – but he's swapped Sunday night with Tommy, who looks after the bars, and we're all eating at Chel and Oliver's place.' Debbie picked up two more plates and followed Susan. 'I thought tomorrow, we could take the kids to Flambards and give them a day out. Chel said she'd do tea for us all unless you wanted to take them out for a meal somewhere.'

'What's Flambards?' asked Annabel, who never missed a thing. Sebastian sat slumped, more or less asleep, with his thumb in his mouth and took no interest.

'It's a wonderful sort of adventure place, and theme park. You'll love it,' Debbie told her.

'But will we?' asked Tom, taking his place at the table. 'Wake up, young Sebastian. Your supper's here.'

'You'll love it too,' Debbie assured Tom. 'You can go on the log flume.'

'Thanks!'

'Yes you can, Daddy!' cried Annabel, who didn't know what a log flume was, but liked the idea of her father on it. Sebastian forced his eyes open and peered anxiously at his aunt. She didn't look all floppy, so maybe her bones were still there and it was all right to eat something. Debbie noticed the intent look and raised her eyebrows at him.

'What's the matter, Seb? Smut on my nose?'

'Nothing,' he muttered, and picked up his knife, avoiding her eye.

'Put the bear down now,' said Susan, trying to take it from him. He tugged it back.

'No. It's *pertecting* me!'

Debbie saw Tom's frown, and stepped in quickly.

'I tell you what, Seb, he can sit in the armchair where he can keep an eye on you.' She took the bear, which he relinquished only with reluctance, and placed him with his arms hooked over the back of the sofa by the fireplace. 'There. He can watch everyone now and protect us all.'

Annabel lifted a forkful of meat and vegetables into her mouth and spoke through it.

'He's frightened of the ogre,' she chanted.

'Not!' said Sebastian, and crashed his knife on the table.

'Oh God! Here comes a family scene!' said Tom, raising his eyes to heaven. 'Behave yourselves, both of you!'

Debbie had lifted the now-crying little boy onto her lap, cuddling him.

'What *is* all this ogre business? There's no ogres here.'

'The man what kills people,' Annabel told her, ungrammatically. 'Grandma said he lived here.'

Debbie's eyes met Susan's across the table. She was suddenly coldly, furiously, angry.

'How dared she!'

'She didn't say it *to* them, Deb. They just overheard …'

'It's called coercion,' said Tom, who thought his mother-in-law's behaviour indefensible.

'It's unforgivable to involve the children!' She saw the interest in Annabel's eyes and tried to moderate her fury. 'How could you allow it?'

'I told you, we weren't there,' said Susan, quietly. 'Deb, we had no idea, you must believe us.'

'She's mad!' said Debbie, with conviction.

'Just trying to get her own way,' said Susan. She gave her sister a hopeless look. 'You know what she is.'

'I never thought she'd go this far,' said Debbie, violently. She realised that her anger was upsetting the little boy still further, and pulled herself together. 'Come on Seb, don't cry, there's nothing here to be frightened of, it's just Grandma being silly. I expect she meant it as a story.'

Sebastian peered up at her.

'She didn't. She said we had to behave and not to make him angry.'

'Then perhaps you'd better,' said Tom, dryly.

'Shut up, Tom!' said Susan. She got to her feet. 'Give him to me, Deb, I'll take him and put him to bed, he's overtired, it's far too late for them to be up.' She gave her husband a killing look. 'Perhaps you can raise some milk and biscuits in a minute, Deb.'

'He's only a baby,' said Annabel, well away with her own plateful.

'Your turn next, madam,' said Susan, as she left the room with Sebastian and his retrieved bear balanced on her hip. Tom looked at Debbie.

'How can we apologise?'

'I don't see why *you* should,' said Debbie. 'Have some more wine. Don't let it spoil your dinner.'

Out on the passage, Susan found herself unexpectedly face to face with a solidly-built, dark man in chef's whites who had just come up the stairs.

'Hullo,' he said. 'You must be Susan, we spoke on the phone once. And this is Sebastian?'

'He's overtired,' said Susan. 'I'm just putting him to bed.' She tried to put Sebastian down in order to shake hands politely, but he clung to her, grizzling.

'Here – let me. He's too much of a weight for you.' Before she could do anything sensible, he had swung Sebastian into his own arms. 'Hey you, cheer up! You're meant to be on holiday.'

Sebastian was too surprised to say anything immediately, and Susan led the way to the door of the bedroom he was to share with Annabel. When he finally found his voice, it was immediately obvious that he hadn't associated this pleasant-looking stranger with the ogre who killed people. To him, a man in funny trousers was only one thing.

'Are you a clown?' he asked, collapsing to his knees as Mawgan lowered him to his bedroom floor.

'Probably. Your aunt seems to think so, anyway. Would that be good?'

Sebastian, feeling better by the minute suddenly, lowered his voice confidentially.

'There's an awful ogre lives here.'

'Sebastian – ' began Susan, broke off, and shrugged her shoulders. She went into the bathroom to start running the bath, her ears on the stretch for what would happen next. Mawgan had slid down to sit on the floor, nearer Sebastian's level. He looked interested.

'Is there really? Well, I'll tell you this, young Sebastian, then he hasn't been paying his bills. Should we throw him out, do you think?'

'Yes,' said Sebastian, nodding. He sat down too, snuggling close, in a way that he never seemed quite to achieve with his father. '*Can* you?'

'Nobody better at the job round here.'

'Teddy will help you.' He dumped the bear unceremoniously in Mawgan's lap. 'He's good at pertecting people.'

'I'm glad to hear it. You can never have too much pertection, with ogres about.'

By the time Susan came out of the bathroom, they were the best of friends, so much so that when Susan returned to finish her dinner, she left them reading a story together, Sebastian quite restored to calm. She re-entered the flat looking slightly bemused.

'If your Mawgan is an overweight, black-avised football hooligan, with a receding hairline and enough charm to stop a runaway train, I think we just met him on the landing,' she announced.

Debbie, Tom and Annabel, who had reached the fruit and cheese stage – just fruit, in Annabel's case – looked up in surprise.

'So what have you done with him? Did Seb run him through with the wrong end of the loobrush?' asked Tom.

'No. He's reading him a story.'

'Who's reading who a story?' asked Annabel, pardonably confused.

'A very good question. Finish that apple, my child, it's bathtime.'

Debbie got up to retrieve Susan's dinner from the oven.

'You eat, have a couple of glasses of wine and relax a bit. I'll see to Annabel. You can come in and say goodnight when they're both in bed, for a change.'

'That's not a change, that's like always,' said Annabel. 'Maria puts us to bed at home, doesn't she, Mummy?'

Debbie wanted to say, *how sad,* but thought she'd better not. She took Annabel by the hand and led her away, still chomping on her apple. In the bedroom, they found that Sebastian and Mawgan had fallen asleep together over *The Cat in the Hat Comes Back*.

'What a sweet sight,' remarked Debbie.

'*What* a sweet sight!' agreed Annabel. 'Is that him, Auntie Debbie? What did Mummy mean, *black-advised*? He looks ordinary.'

'Avised, not *ad*vised. It means, very dark,' said Debbie. 'And he is ordinary. Just an ordinary person like everyone else.'

'Then Grandma *is* being very silly, isn't she?'

'Amen to that,' said Debbie, but under her breath.

* * * * *

Later on, when both Tom and Mawgan had taken themselves to bed, the sisters sat together by the fire, drinking hot chocolate and winding down after an hour spent trying to avoid awkward topics in front of their respective men. But now, in the quiet, late hours of the evening, some of them at least needed to be confronted.

'He got the picture, you know – Mawgan,' said Susan. 'I just hope he didn't think we were responsible.'

'I'm sure he didn't. He's had one dose of Mum already, so he can't have many illusions. Anyway, I suppose it's an occupational hazard. The circumstances are a bit … awkward. Nobody can blame her for being protective.' Although for being vindictive, they could.

'You need bears for that,' said Susan, absently. Debbie stared at her.

'Say again?'

'Oh, nothing.'

Debbie sipped her chocolate and looked at her sister, considering. She still thought Susan seemed less than her usual capable, bossy self, and although Susan didn't tell her about it, it wouldn't necessarily have surprised her to hear about the battle Susan had needed to engage in to get Tom to agree to give up a weekend to her family affairs, when he would sooner have been left with a clear field and the sinuous, blonde, predatory Elaine.

'Everything all right, Suse?' was as far as she allowed herself to go.

'Yes. Fine. Just a bit tired. And it's been a bit trying back home. You know what Mummy is.'

Debbie was beginning to wonder if either of them really knew what their mother was, but she said,

'I'm sorry. It's my fault. And it's all falling on you, which isn't fair.'

'You don't need to apologise. It's your life.'

'If it makes you feel any better, Oliver hasn't been exactly all sweetness and light, either.'

'Why doesn't that surprise me?' asked Susan. 'He thinks the world of you, Deb. You didn't really expect him to welcome someone with a conviction for violence with open arms, did you?' Still less with an open mind, she might have added.

That sounded more like Susan.

'We think – Chel and I think – they had a row. They've been squaring up for it practically since they met.'

'And?' Susan prompted.

'Suddenly, it all seems to have gone away. That's why we think … well, that they must have cleared the air.'

'Good thing too, with you living so close together. Oliver can be a bastard when he tries.' Susan leaned forward and put her empty mug on the coffee table. 'Deb …'

'What?'

'Has Chel told you about Oliver's private view? You weren't there.'

'I thought it would be better to keep away,' said Debbie. 'I thought Mum might go, and it was better we didn't meet … but she didn't, of course.'

'No, she wasn't actually invited. And you haven't answered my question.'

'Then, yes. Dad took Helen.'

'Well, is that all you've got to say?' asked Susan, after a pause.

'What else *is* there to say? He and Mum are separated, he could take who he liked.'

'But *Helen*!'

'It was perfectly natural, Suse. He's their son, it was a big occasion.'

'But they've hardly even spoken for years.'

'So far as we know, anyway.'

Susan stared at her.

'You don't think – '

'No, Suse, I don't. What I think, and what Chel thinks too, is that if he hadn't dragged her there, she wouldn't have gone. It's probably just that simple.'

'Did Oliver mention it?'

'Not to me, no.'

'If Daddy took up with Helen again, Mummy would be devastated.'

'After tonight, do you expect me to sympathise?' Debbie immediately wished she had spoken less heatedly. When Susan was silent, she went on. 'Anyway, I think there's not the smallest chance of it. How could she ever forgive him – ' She broke off.

'That's not fair, Deb. We don't know what happened, after all. Mummy always says she was terribly ambitious, and that's true. We know it is.'

Her mother's spite was too raw and recent in Debbie's mind for her to take this at face value.

'Is she terribly ambitious *now*, or was she terribly ambitious *then*? Did something perhaps happen to make her more than usually ambitious?'

'Don't talk in riddles, Deb, I'm too tired. What are you trying to say?'

'That Mum likes her own way,' said Debbie, baldly. 'People who cross her – Helen, Chel, Mawgan, me – we suffer for it. Make sure you don't, or you may find out.'

'Don't be silly!' Susan got to her feet, yawning. 'We shouldn't be having this discussion when we're tired, we're going to end up quarrelling. Deb, it's lovely to see you, but I'm going to bed.'

'Flambards tomorrow,' said Debbie, and wondered, when her sister had said goodnight and gone, why she should have been left with the impression that days out with the children were not what Susan and Tom were used to.

＊ ＊ ＊ ＊ ＊

In spite of Debbie's fleeting misgivings, the family day out was a success. Chel and Jerry elected to come too, which might have had something to do with it, so that three generations of the family enjoyed the rides, the exhibitions, and the ice-creams. The sheer novelty of this carried the day forward, and stopping on the way home to collect take-away fish and chips set the seal on the day for the children.

'Although we shall have to do better than this tomorrow,' said Susan, sprinkling vinegar on her chips. 'What had you planned, Cheryl?'

'One thing I *hadn't* planned was to enter a competition with Mawgan, thank you,' said Chel, immediately. 'That man trained under a Michelin-starred chef in Switzerland or somewhere, Susan. He's even had a star of his own for some place he ran abroad. Don't even *suggest* I go there!'

'I wasn't going to.' Susan laughed. 'I wouldn't either, if it comes to that. But we must keep the family flag flying, there's no need to give him a walk-over. So long as we don't let Deb make *Coq au Vin*, we should be able to keep our end up.'

'Thanks,' said Debbie, and Annabel asked,

'What's Cockie Van?'

'Chicken stew, the way Deb makes it,' said Susan. 'Shopping tomorrow, then, Cheryl, from the sounds of it. Is there a decent supermarket?'

'There's a Tesco in Helston.' Chel gave in gracefully, not unpleased to be offered help with dinner for so many. 'Why, are you planning the full spread?'

'Of course. What do you do best?'

'You can let Deb make the coffee,' suggested Oliver. 'She's not bad at that.'

'And leave the wine to us,' added Debbie, impervious to insult. Chel got up and fetched a notepad and pen from the kitchen.

'Right, plan of campaign. Starter? Suggestions from the floor, please.'

Jerry sat back in his chair, listening to them. His feelings, he had to admit, were mixed and not necessarily happy. He had never seen his three children, one adopted, two his own, so easy together, and the reason, which wasn't far to seek, he realised, filled him with guilt. Except, if he hadn't done the things that he had done, there would be no Debbie, and Susan wouldn't be at this gathering either. Undoubtedly, they would all of them be somewhere else. Right and wrong ... difficult concepts, when you were looking at – and enjoying – the results of ... which?

'What do you think, Dad?' Debbie was asking him. 'Wake up at the back there! You weren't even listening!' He came back to earth with a start.

'Sorry, my darling. What did you say?'

'It seems to me,' said Oliver, 'that this house is going to be no place for civilised men or little children tomorrow. Where shall we take them, Tom?'

'Why don't you ask where would they like to go?' asked Jerry.

'The zoo!' said Sebastian, immediately. 'There's bears at the zoo.'

'The child is bear-mad,' remarked Susan.

'I'm not sure if they have bears there, but I suppose we can go and check it out,' said Oliver.

'Well, if they don't they'll have something as good!' Susan was certain. 'All zoos have lots of different animals, it's a constant. There's bound to be something for Sebby. Well, that gets you three and the children from under our feet – '

'Three?' asked Jerry.

'Certainly three, Daddy. You don't want to mope about on your own.'

'I thought I might go down to the pub, lunchtime ...'

'Oh no, you don't! You're going to the zoo. And *no*, Annabel, you can't stay here and help.'

'I could go with them,' offered Debbie, hopefully.

'No way. You can peel the vegetables, and wash up as we go.'

'Oh, thanks! Suppose Annabel wants to visit the ladies?'

'She'll manage,' said Susan. 'She's a big girl now.'

Tom had been surprised at how much he had enjoyed going out with his children. He was feeling expansive and happy, and had hardly even thought of Elaine all day. He glanced at his watch.

'Time we took these two down the hill to their beds,' he said. 'They were late enough last night. Why don't we all go? Have a drink in the pub together? You can talk about this wedding just as well there – probably even better.'

'I must clear away the mess and wash up first,' said Chel.

'You could do it when you come back.' Tom wanted to be off now.

'If you think I'm facing all that greasy paper after a night at the Fish, you're wrong.'

'Oh, let them go,' said Debbie. 'I'll stay and help you, we can walk down together when we've done.' She got to her feet and began gathering plates together.

It was quiet when they had all gone. Chel, ran hot water into the sink and stood watching the suds form. It was hardly worth loading the machine for eight plates, knives and forks and a few glasses. Her face was sad, her eyes blank. Debbie touched her shoulder, lightly.

'I'm sorry, Chel. You know that we all are.'

'He's so good with children, it's all wrong there can't be any of his own.'

'I know.'

'Oh well.' Chel shrugged her shoulders, trying to shrug off her sudden depression. 'That's the way the cookie crumbles, I suppose. He lived, at least, and it probably says something awful about me, that I can't just be grateful for that.'

'You could adopt. Have you thought of that?'

'We haven't talked about it. It seems to be a closed book. And now he's got his painting ...'

'My brother is a selfish sod!' said Debbie, with sudden force.

'Maybe. Changing the subject, what do you make of Susan?' Briskly.

Debbie shook her head.

'Something very wrong. Do you suppose she's taken a lover on the side?'

'Or he has,' said Chel.

'Tom? Never! He hasn't got it in him.'

'They've all got it in them,' said Chel, with conviction. 'Some woman waves her tits under their noses, they're off! Even the best of them.'

'Oliver?' asked Debbie, wide-eyed.

'I daresay, except I'd kill her before she got to first base.'

'Has anybody tried?' asked Debbie, interested.

'One. She didn't get far. Apart from Susan's friend Joanna, that is – and come to that, she didn't get far either, at least after I met him.'

'Her! We won't count her, she's history anyway.' Debbie remembered where the conversation had started. 'But Susan. There's something very unnatural there, at least, it is to me. Do you know, those children are left almost entirely for the *au pair* to bring up?'

'People do that.' Chel reminded her. She grinned suddenly. 'Your kind of people, that is, not mine. And be warned, not Mawgan's. But I'm not exactly surprised, at least it maybe accounts for Seb.'

'Seb?'

'That child is a bundle of nerves.'

Debbie hadn't meant to mention ogres. It was, after all, her own mother who was responsible for that scare and to mention it to Chel seemed like a betrayal, but the cue was too tempting.

'You're right there. Something happened yesterday.' She told Chel, and Chel, dunking plates through hot suds, listened intently. Why didn't it surprise her? she wondered. Why had she ever imagined that Jerry's walking out on the Dreaded Dot would remove her influence? Dot had never met Mawgan, probably never would meet him, but she still needed to bring him down. Superfluous in his case, she thought wryly. He had already done a pretty good job for himself.

'So, what happened when Seb and Mawgan met face to face?' she asked. 'They must have done by now.'

'They fell asleep together over *The Cat in the Hat*. It wasn't until this morning that Seb actually realised Mawgan was the horrible ogre, and by that time, fortunately, it was far, far too late.'

'So Grandma lost face?'

'Face, both ears, and a fair bit of skin off the neck, I would say.'

'Well, good. She deserved to. What a despicable thing to do – ' Chel broke off, remembering to whom she was talking.

'Oh, I agree.' It was Debbie's turn now to look miserable. 'Chel, how can it be possible to live with someone all your life, and not know them at all?I mean, I always knew she was very organising, and a bit manipulative, but surely this is … is …' Words failed her, at least, words that she wanted to use about her mother failed her.

Chel didn't answer for a moment. Phrases about cornered rats, and megalomania flitted through her head and were rejected. Finally, she said, more moderately,

'I suppose, having forced everyone to take sides, she's seeing you all siding with your father … it must be bitter for her.'

'She's *making* us side with him, and he's the one who walked out!'

Chel knew better than Debbie what provocation Jerry had been given, and also thought that barring her door to Debbie herself, for choosing to marry where her heart was, must in itself be justification enough, and so she had nothing to add. Instead,

'You've dried that same plate three times now,' she pointed out. 'Come on – the rest can dry itself on the draining board. Let's go down to the pub and get drunk.'

'I expect we'll find Suse pacing out the car park for the marquee,' said Debbie.

'What did she say when you broke it to her?' asked Chel, as she fetched coats.

'Not a lot she could say, when we'd already explained that Mawgan planned to demolish the restaurant right at the relevant time. Although, I think he's right, it will be better in the end – he's supposed to be the expert, after all.'

'It'll certainly disrupt the pub less.' Chel, who was also something of an expert in such matters, although she was beginning to wonder if anybody remembered, pulled the front door to behind them. 'Take the car, or walk along the foreshore? There's a moon.'

'Oh, walk, for me, every time. But then, I won't have to walk back.'

'This way, then.'

They made their way, stumbling a little in the dark, along the path that led over the point at the end of the little creek beside which Chel and Oliver had their home, and down onto the foreshore, coming out close to the boathouse on the boundary of Debbie's proposed new venture. To their left as they crunched over the shingle, the skeleton of the burnt building showed against the sky. Chel said,

'Have you told Tim and Lesley what you're planning to do?' Tim and Lesley, once friends of Debbie's, had tried to establish their own residential sailing school on the site during the summer just past, a doomed venture that had ended in a broken marriage, and Tim facing a charge of arson. Debbie shook her head, which of course Chel couldn't see in the dark.

'No, I haven't. But I expect they must know by this time.'
She sounded bitter. Chel, who agreed with what she hadn't
had the heart to say, that Dot would have made sure the news
got around if only to spite her, said cautiously,

'Don't you think you should?'

'Do you really think they want to hear from me, after what
happened?'

'Oh, Deb!' said Chel, with compassion. 'They did it to
themselves. It wasn't your fault.'

'Maybe not, but if you want to know, I still feel a bit guilty,
if only for profiting simply because I could raise the money and
they couldn't. They asked me ... I said no.'

'Good thing,' said Chel. 'From what I gather, only a
complete fool would have said yes.'

'Well yes ... that's true.'

'Somebody was going to profit from it. Why not you?'

The sad ruin had fallen behind them. The lights of the Fish
had appeared around the curve of the shore. Debbie said,

'Oh, I know, I *know*! If I didn't, I wouldn't be doing it. It's
just ... well, right now, everything that should be bringing me
joy seems to have a sour taste to it. Take no notice.'

The feel of shifting shingle under their feet had changed to
the solidity of concrete as they came to the causeway.

'What it is, you need a drink, and so do I,' said Chel,
speeding up. 'And let's swear a vow.'

'What vow?' asked Debbie.

'That we're not going to get depressed over it. Come on,
let's go plan a wedding! Without the children there, we may
even be able to get somewhere.'

And even that, Debbie thought, but did not say, as she
followed her sister-in-law to the door of the lounge bar, had its
downside. For good as it was to have Susan here, helping her
arrange things, it should have been her mother.

It must have been at that point, she decided later, that the rogue thought had entered her head. She almost remembered its arrival, a fleeting word, a name … but it passed through so swiftly that she couldn't be certain. It wasn't until later, when it popped unexpectedly into the discussion, that she realised that it wasn't new.

Tom and Oliver, mere ciphers in all these arrangements, had drifted away to join some of Oliver and Chel's new friends from the village, but Jerry had remained with his three girls, for as Debbie had remarked last night, he was the one who would be footing the bill and he needed to have some idea what were their plans. When Chel and Debbie arrived, he and Susan were compiling a guest list. Susan, a capable woman when her mind was on the job, turned immediately to Debbie.

'You'd better check these names – see if we've left anyone off, like your personal friends. Do we know how many there are on Mawgan's side?'

Debbie shook her head, accepting the list.

'He has a large family, but as for friends … I don't think even he knows how many he has left, after what happened. He hasn't been back to see.' She looked at the paper in her hand. 'Will *all* these people want to come? It's a long way west for most of them.' And for other reasons. She felt a stab of misery. Surely a wedding should be an entirely happy occasion?

'Bridesmaids,' Susan was saying. 'I suppose you're having some? Apart from Annabel and Candy, because someone'll have to keep those two under control.'

'Pen.' Debbie held out her hand. 'Bridesmaids? Oh yes – Allison, she's one of Mawgan's sisters, and Lindsey from the office. We had some good times together, Lin and me. They'll keep the rabble in order.' She wrote on Susan's list, *Chel's parents.* It was at that moment that the rogue thought reappeared and emerged as a single word through her uprepared mouth. 'Helen.' She gulped, where had that come from? 'You haven't got Helen on this list.'

'*Helen?*' asked Susan, surprised.

'Yes. I like Helen.' Debbie didn't, in fact, know Oliver's mother that well, but Helen had said nice things about her, which Chel had repeated just when they were needed. It was obvious that Helen certainly liked her.

'But Deb – ' Susan broke off.

'Why not?' asked Jerry. He tried to keep his voice casual, and was annoyed to realise that his heart had thumped once and begun to race. 'She wasn't invited to Oliver's wedding, it seems just, in a way. If Deb would like her, she should have her.'

'Mummy'll be terribly upset.'

'I'm sure that Helen was, too,' remarked Jerry.

'She was,' said Chel, but too quietly to be heard.

'Anyway, Mum has already said that she wouldn't come if I begged her on my knees,' said Debbie, dismissively, but the hurt showed in her face. Chel looked down at her hands, and Susan looked startled.

'She didn't!' Nobody answered her, so she added, more contentiously than she had meant to, 'Presumably Mawgan can find someone to be best man?'

'Oh, I'm sure *someone* will have survived the wreck,' said Debbie, in the same tone of voice, and broke off, biting her lip. 'Sorry. Let's not quarrel.'

'What about the wedding cake? It'll need at least three tiers, looking at that list.' Chel poured oil on the troubled waters. 'You need to get it ordered now, if it's going to be properly boozy.'

'Mawgan'll make it, he said.'

'I keep forgetting.' Chel smiled at her own absurdity. 'Will he decorate it too?'

'I have no idea. But if it isn't one of his skills, he'll know someone who will.'

'Then all that needs sorting out for now, is the catering.' Susan took the notepad back from Debbie and closed it firmly. 'We can talk about that tomorrow night.'

'There certainly won't be a chance earlier.' Debbie gave an unintentionally tremulous sigh. 'I can't believe this is my wedding we're all talking about.'

Susan narrowed her eyes. Separated off from Tom and the children – with whom, Debbie now realised, she wasn't often seen except at family occasions such as Christmas – she was still the old Susan.

'You're not having second thoughts?' she asked.

'No.'

'There's plenty of time to change your mind. Mummy will understand.'

'I said, *no*!' Debbie exclaimed, indignantly. 'Don't you think poor Mawgan is going through enough trauma right now, without me dumping him? And I *don't* want to – and to be honest, I don't care if you don't like him. I never thought that much of Tom …' She let her voice tail off. 'Oh goodness.' There was no point even in apologising. A silence fell on the group, emphasised rather than eased by the background noise around them.

Susan sat without moving, her face, she hoped, giving nothing away. It occurred to her, for the first time that she had ever acknowledged, that she was jealous of Debbie, and now she came to think of it, of Chel, too, and she wasn't proud of herself. Both of them had had stimulating, interesting careers, both had now formed alliances in which there was true partnership, adventure, a life … She herself, a bright and intelligent woman, had never even had a real job, let alone an adventure, she had married at twenty-one and had Annabel, a honeymoon baby, the same year, and that had been that. Settled. Tom had never been exciting, his idea of an adventure was a fortnight on a holiday complex in Antigua with everything organised. Oliver had sailed professionally all over the world, Mawgan had cooked all over Europe. Tom had studied accountancy at University and gone on to become a text-book accountant, firmly based in his home town of Embridge. He made good money, he expected her to entertain his clients, he was having an affair with his secretary. How much more banal than that could you get? She wondered, for a horrible moment, if she was going to burst into tears over her own wasted life then and there, in front of everyone.

Chel, too, sat perfectly still. She had been visited, in the past, by curious knowledge that seemed to come out of nowhere, psychic experiences, she had learned to acknowledge only with reluctance. They seemed to come when she was stressed, she now recognised, and at the moment her life was so stress-free and boring as to resemble tinned rice pudding. Nevertheless, she felt the familiar, scary cobwebs on her skin now, and three words slid into her mind.

Come and dance!

She wanted to say to Susan that if anyone ever said those three words to her, she should go with him joyfully, but how could she? For one thing, Susan would think she was mad, for another, Susan was married. She had children. She couldn't just run away and dance for joy, she had responsibilities. Probably, she wouldn't even want to do it. She said nothing.

Jerry moved first. He sat forward and reached to gather in the glasses on the table.

'I'm going to get in one more round, and then I think it's time we went home,' he said. 'Debbie and Susan, shall we take it that neither of you said any of that?'

Debbie put her hands up to her flaming face as her father left the table.

'Suse, I'm sorry, and I didn't mean it.'

'I didn't, either.' Susan tried to smile. 'Sorry Deb, I do like him. I'm just tired.' Liking Mawgan, in fact, was probably the root of the problem. He was immediately likeable, and his handling of Seb had been sheer genius. She wouldn't have wanted to marry him, or anyone remotely like him, but he was great fun. If Tom had ever been fun, he certainly wasn't now, and she couldn't actually remember that he ever had been.

'You two …' she said, almost against her will. 'You're both so lucky.'

'You too,' said Debbie, helpfully. 'Goodness, look at you! Two gorgeous kids and a lovely home – all I've got is a flat in a pub, and Chel …' She broke off, and could have kicked herself. Chel said,

'Isn't it funny how, whenever families get together, there's always a squabble? Mine is exactly the same.' She kept her voice light, and was glad to see Susan relax. She was, she found now, actively worried about Susan, which was such an unexpected discovery that she hardly registered Debbie's incipient *faux pas*.

Jerry had stopped on his way to the bar to have a quick word with Tom and Oliver, and Tom got to his feet and came back across the room. He sat down, as if casually. Chel saw, out of the corner of her eye, that Oliver was winding up his conversation and preparing to follow.

'Well then,' said Tom. 'Got it all organised, have you?' His joviality sounded false, and Susan gave him a dark look.

'It's easy to see you've never organised a wedding, if you think it's that simple,' she said.

'Sorry.' He looked penitent. 'I expect you'll get more sense out of Mawgan, he must have organised a few in his time.'

'You make him sound like a serial bigamist,' said Debbie indignantly, and Chel gave a snort of laughter.

'Nice try, Tom, but it's a good thing you never had any ambitions for the diplomatic service!'

Jerry and Oliver, arriving not exactly together but at the same time, both looked relieved to see everyone laughing. Jerry placed the round of drinks on the table and drew up another chair, Tom had taken his. Time for a change of subject, he reckoned.

'So tell us, Debbie,' he said. 'Where have your plans for the sailing school got to?'

III

One way and another, a strange evening, Chel thought, trailing in the wake of Susan and Debbie around the supermarket the next morning. She had never, that she recalled, ever spent time *en famille* with the Nankervises before, and she could see exactly why, they had obviously had little practice at family life. Put them too near each other, and their natural reaction was to fight, later if not sooner. She wasn't sure if this was inborn, or was learned behaviour, and felt a certain amount of relief at the thought that tonight, she would have the moral support, at least, of Mawgan. Mawgan, she was pretty sure, came from a normal family background much like her own, or at least, it would have been normal before he had landed in a rockery on top of little sister Cressida's estranged husband, and it would be interesting to see what he made of these three contentious wildcats. Poor old Jerry obviously had no idea how to handle them. Coming the heavy father simply didn't work.

She wondered momentarily what was happening at the zoo, but the animals there, she decided, were, if anything, probably under better control. It was to be hoped that Tom and his children could keep Oliver and his father from each other's throats for a whole day; she wasn't sure that Susan's bright idea of adding Jerry to the party to get him from under their feet had been one of her best.

'Come on, Cheryl,' said Susan, briskly, 'there's no time to dream, there's a lot to do!'

Chel sighed, and hastened down the aisle to join her sisters-in-law. Susan had more or less taken over the dinner tonight, although she herself was still to be allowed to cook the main course – burgundy beef casserole with walnuts, her dinner-party favourite and one she knew she did well, so, had said Susan, that was probably safe. Debbie was to be allowed to heat the soup – spiced parsnip out of a carton, with added cream and sprinkled with chopped parsley – so long as she promised not to boil it. Susan herself had undertaken the pudding.

'It's important not to be over-ambitious,' she had said, rightly, but why, Chel thought now, did Susan *always* have to be right? 'If burgundy beef casserole is your signature dish, then that's what we'll have, you can be sure it'll come out right.'

'Has Mawgan got a signature dish?' Chel had asked, idly, but Debbie, to whom all cookery books were closed books, simply looked blank.

'I suppose so, don't all chefs, but I have no idea what it is.'

'Then we'll just hope it's not burgundy beef casserole,' had said Susan, making Chel feel instantly about gnat-high.

Susan was running her eye along the shelves.

'I don't suppose you have leaf gelatine at home, Cheryl?' she said, in the voice of one who had already decided, it was hardly even a question. Chel sighed.

'I don't suppose I've even got one of those little packets of crystals, and Susan, I wish you'd stop calling me *Cheryl*. You and your mother are about the only people who do these days.'

Susan paused, her hand hovering over one of the little packets, and looked at Chel in surprise.

'I thought only your friends called you *Chel*,' she said. She sounded confrontational, but Chel was shocked. *Had* Susan thought that, and if so, what did that tell about her? There was no time to think it out now. She said,

'Exactly. So quit the Cheryl thing.'

Susan said nothing, but she turned an unexpected dull red, and Chel saw Debbie looking at her sister in surprise. They moved on then, with the result that Debbie had to be sent running back from the checkout to retrieve the forgotten packet of gelatine.

Susan's threat that Debbie would be the kitchen gopher proved so accurate that, halfway through the afternoon, she quit. Dumping her damp tea-towel on the draining board, she said firmly,

'It's half-past three, I'm going down the hill to see if they've finished in the kitchen.'

'Surely Mawgan can find his own way up here,' said Susan, busy with orange cheesecake and disinclined to lose the washer-up. 'He looks to me like a man who definitely knows his way around! In every sense.'

'He probably can, but believe me, he's more likely to fall asleep in front of the football on the telly. In fact, I shall probably let him, for a bit, but at least I'll be there to wake him up again.'

'Surely, he can manage the first bit on his own,' Susan said, but Debbie simply laughed at her.

'Come on Suse, weren't you ever young and in love?' she teased. Susan sighed.

'I'm really not sure any more,' she said, unexpectedly, and Chel and Debbie stared at her. She pulled herself together, saying firmly, 'You just wait until you have children, Deb – you'll forget your own name!'

But not the *au pair*'s name, presumably, Chel thought but didn't say. Debbie, still laughing, had grabbed her coat from the sitting room sofa where she had casually slung it when they came in, and headed for the front door. Chel was left with Susan, just the two of them and the orange cheesecake. The burgundy beef casserole was already safely in the oven.

It was, Chel decided, a not entirely happy feeling. She and Susan had had times when they had got on quite well, they had also had some absolutely flaming rows, after the last of which Chel and Oliver had taken off for Cornwall and not told anybody where they were going, or even, for the next six months or so, where they had gone. This was the first time that she and Susan had been alone together since, and a feeling of unfinished business couldn't help but hang unspoken in the air. However, it now seemed nothing was further from Susan's thoughts than that far-distant winter day.

'Do you think Deb is doing the right thing?' she asked, into the silence that followed the cheerful slamming of the front door.

'I think Deb is having a ball,' replied Chel, honestly. 'Look at it, Susan – she loves the man she's going to marry and he thinks the world of her, she's starting up her own business doing what she loves best, she's going to live in a beautiful place – why should you think she's doing the *wrong* thing?'

'Mummy thinks – ' began Susan, but Chel wasn't prepared to listen to the gospel according to the Dreaded Dot.

'Susan, your mother jumped to a conclusion, she doesn't *know* anything at all. You can't judge by that – you've met Mawgan. Does he strike you as an acid-bath murderer?'

Susan looked startled at this picturesque question.

'Of course he doesn't, Cheryl – Chel – don't be silly! Nobody ever said he was a *murderer*!'

In fact, at the time they had, but Chel didn't point this out, it seemed best.

'Well, then. Anyone can make a mistake.'

'Pretty devastating mistake,' said Susan. 'It cost a man his life.'

'No need, though, why it should cost *two* men their lives, is there? That's what Oliver says. And anyway, from what I can gather, it was pretty much the other man's fault.'

'So *Mawgan* says,' said Susan, and sniffed.

'Well, he was there,' Chel pointed out.

'Yes – the only living witness! How convenient is that?'

'Actually, no,' said Chel, apologetically, and Susan looked surprised. 'There were two others. Your father is trying to trace them. You haven't even talked about it with him, have you?'

'Well ... no.'

'Perhaps you should,' said Chel, and Susan was silent.

For a while, they worked in silence, Chel loading the dishwasher and Susan grating orange rind. Then Susan said,

'I like him. Nobody could help it – but that's half the problem, isn't it?'

'No,' said Chel. 'Anyway, that's not true. Tim Howells didn't like him.'

'Only because he wanted Debbie for himself.'

'Come on, Susan, he was a married man! Anyway, I think it was rather more than that.'

'It just seems ... well, risky.'

'Everything worth doing is risky,' said Chel.

'You sound like Oliver.'

'That's why he and I get on.'

Susan let go of her orange and it rolled across the table. She reached for it and went on grating, apparently unaware that she was now sending juice spraying all over everything near her.

'Will his sister be at the wedding?' she asked.

'Two of them will. The eldest one, who's married and lives abroad, and the one who's going to be a bridesmaid.'

'Not the one whose husband ...' Susan realised what she was doing. 'Oh God, look what I've done!'

'I shouldn't think so, for a moment,' said Chel. She was certain, in her own mind, that Cressida Stanley was dead, but only Debbie knew that. She hoped that Cressida's lack of communication with her family wasn't going to cast a blight over the wedding, but there was nothing to be done about that. It was simply one of those things that she wished she didn't know. 'He's a lot older than Debbie,' said Susan, still contentiously. Since this was true, Chel merely asked,

'Does that matter?'

'She'd be better with someone more her own age. She must be ten years younger!'

'Nine,' said Chel. 'Things like that aren't important, Susan.'

'They are. When you add it to everything else – his background, his job, his prison record -'

'Exemplary, I understand,' remarked Chel. Susan glared at her.

'Oh well, if you find it *funny*!'

'I don't. And Susan, neither does Debbie. Or Mawgan, come to that. Or Dad, or Oliver, or anyone. But things like age, jobs, background – what on earth do they matter?'

'Oh, so you *do* think a prison record matters?'

'Well, of course it does. I just don't think it should be allowed – given the circumstances – to dictate your attitude. Or your mother's, come to that.' That was fighting talk, and Susan took a deep breath, but whatever she had been going to say was fortunately interrupted by the return of the zoo party, and the dangerous moment slipped away.

Chel, going out into the living room to greet them all, and to hear an ecstatic account of the outing, was left with an uncomfortable impression of an imperfectly hidden jealousy of Debbie's happiness that must have its roots in some very bitter soil.

Susan and Tom, Chel soon discovered, were fairly inadequate where their offspring were concerned. The children had arrived back tired and over-excited, to which Tom's reaction was to lose his temper and Susan's to order them to go and play outside, both of which Chel felt to be inappropriate, particularly since it was beginning to rain. Oliver, who might – just possibly anyway – have been more helpful, had vanished up to his studio without even coming indoors, and that on its own set Chel to wondering.

'Where's Auntie Debbie?' demanded Annabel, throwing herself into a chair and giving her mother a defiant look.

'She'll be back later.' Chel exchanged a look with Jerry, wondering how much help she could expect from him. 'How about we play a game until she comes back? Look, we've got a pack of cards here, we could play snap, or something.'

'I want to watch the telly,' whined Sebastian, his lip sticking out dangerously.

'Television,' said Susan, automatically. 'Speak properly, Sebastian, please.'

The lip began to tremble. Chel said, bracingly,

'Well, that's fine. We've some children's videos somewhere –'

'They shouldn't watch television all the time –' Tom began.

'Maria lets us,' muttered Annabel, but fortunately under her breath, so that only Chel heard her.

'Tom, come on!' Chel was already searching in the bookcase. 'It's a wet Sunday afternoon, they've been out all day, and they've no toys or books with them, ease up.'

Susan turned on her heel, opting out.

'I'm going to make a pot of tea,' she said.

Optimistic! First find the teapot, Chel thought, but did not say. She came back to Sebastian with two videos in her hands, they had been bought last Christmas to entertain her own niece and nephew.

'Look Seb, we've got *Peter Pan* and *The Jungle Book* – that's got a bear in it, would you like that?' She saw Annabel's lips part to say that she wanted to watch *Peter Pan*, and silenced her with a look. Seb's incipient tears cleared magically.

'Yes please,' he muttered. His thumb slid into his mouth as he curled tightly into his chair in anticipation.

'Sebastian, take – ' began Tom, and broke off, catching Chel's eye. 'I'll help Susan,' he said.

Chel started the video, then wriggled in beside Sebastian and settled down with him on her lap, he seemed to her to be in need of cuddling. Annabel swung her legs for a minute, watching them, then went and planted herself firmly on her grandfather's knee. Jerry gathered her in, and the four of them sat watching Mowgli's antics in contented peace. Susan and Tom had not returned from the kitchen, still hunting for the teapot, Chel concluded. She didn't care.

Henry's grandchildren, Jerry thought, his arms full of Annabel and her curls tickling his cheek. Would Henry think he had done a good job with them? Would he approve of the way his daughter had been brought up? Jerry had liked Henry, although Dot's first husband had been considerably older. He had died of a heart attack in his sixties, before Susan was even born, which was sad for them both, and presumably for Dot too, although she had never said so in any way that Jerry found really convincing. Dot had used Henry. It was all a long while ago now.

Thinking of Henry, and then of Dot, brought him by uncomfortable stages to Helen. Helen, there was no doubt, did not approve at all of the way in which her son had been brought up, and looking at Susan's ineptitude with her own children, Jerry began to understand why. You passed on what you had learned as a child to your own children, he had heard it said, and if that was true, what he and Dot had passed on to these two, via Susan, consisted of some very harsh lessons. Like lack of any real interest, and maybe a bit too much *for-your-own-good-dear* bullying. He sensed that all was not well with any one of Susan's little family.

Jerry wished suddenly that he could rewind his whole life as expertly and quickly as Chel had just rewound *The Jungle Book*.

It was six o'clock before the main reason why this wouldn't be an answer breezed back through the door, by which time Susan had grumpily produced mugs of tea made with teabags and accompanied by milk, sugar and a disdainful sniff, and Mowgli had come to the end of his adventures. Debbie and Mawgan had obviously had a more than satisfactory afternoon, and were in a holiday mood, which swiftly and fortunately rubbed off on the rest of the company. Both children immediately jumped up and ran to them, Annabel flinging her arms round her aunt's waist, and Sebastian running to slip his hand into Mawgan's, and perhaps only Chel noticed Susan's face.

'We thought you were *never* coming!' cried Annabel.

'Well, we're here now.' Debbie moved forward with difficulty, it felt as if she was wading through a sea of Annabels. 'What have you been up to?'

Sebastian spoke with his head muffled in Mawgan's arm, thumb in place.

'We saw Mowgli and the bear.'

'Did you indeed? And how was the zoo?'

'The zoo was *wonderful!*' said Annabel. 'They didn't have bears and Sebby cried, but they had a crimson squirrel and that made him stop. Do you think it was dyed, Auntie Debbie? He had an orange underneath to his tail!'

'Sounds very dodgy to me,' said Mawgan, and Sebastian giggled.

'I'll go and put the potatoes on,' said Chel. The giggle had got to her, she realised. She didn't know Susan's children at all well, but she was certain she had never heard Seb, at least, giggle like that before. It was an endearing sound.

Debbie followed her into the kitchen.

'I'm sorry we're late, Chel, they did about a million lunches, and he was knackered.'

'What I so much like about you, is your pin-sharp accuracy,' said Chel. 'And he doesn't look at all knackered now.'

'Well, no ...' It was Debbie's turn to giggle. 'You could say that.' She reached for the cartons of soup and began to prise the tops open ready to pour into a saucepan. 'Chel, is it just me, or is this turning out a most peculiar weekend?'

'It's turning out a most peculiar weekend. You said you were bringing the wine, where is it?'

'Oh God, we left it in the car!' Debbie flew to the door. 'I'll get it now.'

'And give Oliver a call while you're there, the swine ducked out! Tell him to come and fix a drink for everyone, be a proper host I think the party may need a bit of help.'

But in the end, the party was surprisingly successful. Mawgan had brought over a folder of menus and prices, which Debbie brought in with the wine, and that immediately gave Susan a focus for her attention and kept her out of the kitchen too, which was all to the good. Oliver, coming in with a glass of wine for his wife, found her working among the cooking pots, humming to herself.

'Hullo, is this a cop-out, or are you simply taking refuge?'

'If we're to talk of cop-outs …' said Chel, accepting the welcome glass. 'I'm just making the most of it – Susan is so bossy she makes me flustered, and Debbie simply gets under your feet. Annabel would be more use!'

'Shall I send her in?' Oliver kissed her on the nose. 'What makes Suse think you can't manage your own cooking, anyway?'

'An awful fear that I'll let you all down in front of a real chef, even though she thinks it's a terribly working class sort of job to have.'

'You sounded almost as if that wasn't a deadly insult to you,' Oliver remarked. He propped his back against the worktop and took an appreciative sip from his own glass. 'Whatever class he comes from, he's at the top of it when it comes to wine. Dad is almost purring.'

'Oh, I don't mind Susan.' Chel paused, listening to that, wondering if it was true. 'I think I'm a bit sorry for her, actually. She seems to have lost her way somewhere.'

'Not her! She has it marked out for her with little arrows saying *this way to the social summit*. She always has done.'

'You should be kinder to her,' said Chel, and made Oliver choke over his wine. 'Anyway,' she went on, 'he may have started out working class, but now he's less working class than I am – except for the Cornish accent, I suppose, and I rather like that. And it only matters to Susan.'

'Perhaps he'll end up as one of these celebrity chefs on TV. I can see that, you know – he's a real showman, if you hadn't noticed. What's up?'

Chel had nearly dropped the saucepan of soup. She said,

'Don't say things like that! Your stepmother would *really* have a fit then!'

Oliver gave her a curious look.

'I never know with you, whether what you say is really what you mean.'

'Oh, thanks!' Chel adjusted the heat under the potatoes and turned for the door. 'We'd better go and socialise. I needn't put the vegetables on for a minute or two.'

'There'll be about seventy or eighty people at the wedding itself, I think,' Susan was saying, as they came out of the kitchen together. 'Can we do a proper sit-down lunch? If it's going to be a buffet for the big party in the evening, that would be best.'

'No reason why not, it'll only be a stone's throw from the kitchen anyway.' Mawgan had fallen into Chel's vacated armchair, comfortably sprawled; Sebastian was now hanging over the back of the chair, breathing into his ear, which must have tickled. Tom, the child's father for goodness' sake, stood aloofly beside the fireplace with his glass of wine. 'Mind you,' Mawgan added, 'the head chef will be off that day. You have thought of that?'

Susan almost laughed, but straightened her face before the laughter finally escaped.

'I'm sure you can find a way round it.' She found that he was grinning at her, and realised she was being teased. It was an odd feeling, one that she wasn't used to. She wondered if she liked it or not.

'How many in the evening?' asked Debbie, peering over her sister's shoulder from where she sat on the arm of her chair.

'There's hundreds on the list,' said Susan, thus proving that a tendency to exaggerate ran in the family. 'We can't really estimate yet, we need a few definite figures on the groom's side, and of course, not everybody will come.' She looked across at Mawgan. 'What about music? Is there someone who could do an evening disco, or something, round here? I don't suppose there'll be room for a proper band.'

'We can come up with someone, I expect.' He wasn't teasing her again, was he? She gave him a suspicious look.

'Well, make sure they don't play any of this Acid House rubbish.' Susan had got out her notepad again, and made a note. 'We'll leave that with you, then.'

'*And they all wrote it down on their slates,*' Debbie murmured. She looked across at Chel. 'Time to put the soup on? We shouldn't eat too late for the children, I suppose.'

Dinner was an unqualified success, from the spiced parsnip soup right through to the cheese, and although Susan watched beadily for any signs of uppishness in Debbie's undoubtedly plebeian betrothed, she saw none, indeed he seemed to become quiet and introspective as the meal proceeded, fading into the background – a place she had a feeling was unfamiliar ground to him. Over the coffee, the telephone rang. Chel got up to answer it.

'Hi, Chel,' said a familiar and very happy voice at the other end. 'You on for Friday week?'

'You're really going to do it?' Chel could hardly believe it. 'Oh, *wonderful*! Yes, we'll be there, you can bet on it – so long as we can get a flight, that is, and I don't see a problem in November.' She looked across at Oliver. 'Nonie. She's taking the plunge – all this marrying business must be catching!'

'*Nonie* is getting married?' Jerry's face was a study. 'What, Theodorakis?' He couldn't believe it. Helen's parting words when he had last seen her thundered in his ears.

Nonie will never marry this Theodorakis any more than she married any of the others ... Oliver is still to some extent disabled. He and Chel will never have children. Dot will always be Debbie's mother, and you and I, Jerry, have no future together.

One wrong, Helen. Three, well yes, unalterable. But if one can be wrong ...?

If Nonie Fingall had decided to marry after all these years, surely nothing was impossible. He saw Chel looking at him curiously, and said, to cover the sudden turmoil in his thoughts,

'Give her my congratulations, won't you.'

'Jerry sends his congratulations,' said Chel, obediently, cutting into Nonie's instructions as to where they should go when they reached Athens. 'Yes – they're all here, the whole family. Susan's trying to sort out Debbie's wedding, but she's about as much chance of plaiting fog!'

'Not dear Dorothy, I take it,' said Nonie, dryly.

'No. Did you have to ask?'

'Sadly, no. Can I speak to Oliver a minute?'

'Sure, I'll put him on – and Nonie, you couldn't have told me anything better, it's brilliant news! Tell Theo he's a star!' She held out the phone to Oliver. 'She wants to speak to you.'

Oliver took it, and Chel sat down. She explained, in case there was anybody who hadn't got the picture,

'Oliver's godmother is getting married, out in Greece. She wants us to go to the wedding.'

'That's the lady we met the other day?' asked Mawgan. 'Good for her, then.'

Jerry said, 'Dimitrios Theodorakis is a very brave man!' Oliver had put down the phone, Jerry rose to his feet, raised his glass. 'Maybe this is a good moment for a toast to all those taking the big step of getting married! Good luck to 'em, and all happiness!' And he smiled at his natural daughter as he spoke, so that Susan's response to the toast was only moderate.

* * * * *

After the eventful weekend, the rest of the week was in danger of falling rather flat, Chel decided on Tuesday. Susan and Tom and the children had left the Fish very early on Monday morning so that Tom would be in time to go to work, and the children to school – not that she could see them doing any good there, tired out as they were sure to be – and Oliver had gone straight back to his studio. Reluctant to interfere with Mawgan and Debbie's precious day off, she had mooched around the house on her own, clearing up the debris and putting the best china back in its cupboard, and then had sat and watched the rain falling down, feeling loose-endish and depressed. On Tuesday, the rain having eased, she took herself in hand and walked up to the village shop.

It was a strange thing about clairvoyance, she afterwards thought, that it never seemed to work for herself. Walking back down the hill from the shop, she decided to stop at the Fish and see if Debbie was by any chance making herself a mid-morning cup of coffee that she might like to share, and she had no warning that it was a decision that was about to change her life.

Shirley, the girl who worked in what passed for reception, looked up from her desk as Chel came through the door.

'They're both out,' she said. 'Debbie's gone to Truro about her sailing school, and Mr Angwin went up to the surgery.'

'Damn.' Chel lowered her shopping to the floor to give her arms a rest 'I was hoping to cadge a cup of coffee before I went back up the hill.'

'I can make you one,' offered Shirley, but before Chel had time to reply, the rear door through to the car park thumped open, and Mawgan came through. Chel had a swift, fleeting impression that he almost didn't notice her, but he broke stride halfway to his office and came to a stop.

'Chel, hullo. Deb's out. Gone to see an architect, or something.'

'Yes, Shirley said. I was just about to go.'

'Don't – if you've got a minute, that is. Let Shirley fix us some coffee and come and talk to me – no, leave that. Shirley can put it under her desk.'

Meeting Shirley's eyes, Chel shrugged her shoulders.

'Do you mind?'

'No. I'll see to it, Mr Angwin.'

Chel abandoned her shopping and following Mawgan into his office, accepted a chair. He had sat down behind his desk, and for a moment said nothing, leaning on his elbows with his hands folded over his mouth, as if he wanted to hide something. Chel began to feel uneasy.

'Is something wrong?' she asked. 'Shirley said you'd just been up to the doctor ...' Her mind was seething with uncomfortable speculation, and a horrible, unspecified fear for Debbie's happiness.

He came back, she thought, from somewhere a long way away, removed his hands and smiled at her, but it was only a token smile.

'No. Or yes. I've just been landed a bit of a facer, be honest.'

'Do you want to tell me about it?' asked Chel, cautiously.

'I don't know ...' He looked at her. 'Yes, maybe I do. Shirley said where I'd been, you said.'

'She did. I take it, the doctor is this Dr Billy that Deb told us about?'

'Yes. I didn't tell Deb, I made an appointment ... I was beginning to worry about myself.'

'Why?' asked Chel, realising that the conversation was going nowhere if she didn't help it along.

'Because I was getting to be such a mean bastard, if you want to know. Jumping on people for no reason, picking faults, shouting ... God, I even picked a fight with Oliver, or tried to. Did he tell you?'

'No, he didn't.'

'He wouldn't fight back.' Mawgan rubbed his cheek as if it itched. 'He said something that rocked me back on my heels, got me suddenly seeing myself as I must look to other people. So I thought I'd better check it out.'

'And?'

Mawgan spoke carefully, as if he was repeating a learned lesson that meant nothing to him.

'He said – Dr Billy said – go right away for a month now, put your appeal and everything connected with it completely out of your mind, leave the business, don't worry about it or speak about it or even think about it, or accept the consequences.'

'And you said?' prompted Chel.

'What do you think I said? I said, don't be daft, there's Christmas and New Year coming up, and the redesigning of the restaurant, how the hell can I bunk off for a month?'

'And he said?' This was like drawing teeth. In fact, drawing teeth might be easier.

'He said, fine, I'll just make a note that this patient prefers six months off in the middle of the summer to one month before the busy season begins. Which, if you want to know, was so close to what Oliver said that all I could find to say was *oh*.'

At this inopportune moment, Shirley arrived with the coffee, but by the time she had gone, Chel had had time to think.

'So what are you going to do?' she asked, trying not to be provocative. She had been in this situation with Oliver, she recalled, when whatever she said was going to be wrong, it brought back some very unpleasant memories.

'I simply do not know,' said Mawgan. He looked tired.

'Talk it over with Debbie,' said Chel, quietly. 'Tell her you're going to have a particularly prolonged honeymoon. She won't mind. She'll be happy, if it'll make you well again.'

'Deb's trying to launch a new business. She can't be away neither.'

Chel considered this.

'I don't see that it will make that much of a problem for her, actually,' she said, after a pause. 'She's got no premises to worry about, she hasn't even got planning permission yet – and Roger or Carl can deal with any correspondence and get things ready for the season, and either one of them would probably be better at keeping an eye on the builders than she would, if they've even got that far by then. They're meant to be her partners, after all – and if she takes her laptop with her, she won't be out of touch.'

'The bottom line is still that I can't leave the Fish for as long's a month. A fortnight, just maybe, but it don't run itself.'

'Then,' said Chel, 'someone will have to do it for you. Aren't there relief managers for this sort of emergency?'

'This isn't a brewery pub. It's mine.'

'So? Surely in the circumstances – ' She broke off. Mawgan looked at her for a moment, his expression difficult to read. She thought, however, that this time his mind was properly in gear, and simply waited.

'Chel ...' he said, after a long pause. 'I was going to ask you anyway, when a good moment came up ... Deb says you worked in catering. Could you run a pub, do you think? This pub for instance?'

'You mean, as a temp while you're away?' Chel sounded doubtful.

'No. I mean, as a permanent job. I can't go on trying to do both single-handed, I'll kill myself – so I'm now told. Someone has to work with me and run the Fish, why not you?'

'Oh, goodness ...' The suggestion, although it shouldn't have been completely unexpected, nevertheless had taken her by surprise. She said, 'I never went to catering college. I went to evening classes and on day release, and I learned the ropes by working through the different departments – my boss was very supportive. He encouraged me, he wanted me to be his assistant – but I married Oliver instead, and then it all went pear-shaped on us ...' She paused.

'Come to that, I never went to catering college full time neither, so that would make a pair of us.' The grin he gave her, although wry, was more like the usual Mawgan. 'What d'you reckon? The lame leading the blind – that's a classic combo, isn't it?'

'If you get married at the beginning of February, that gives you just under three months to teach me everything. God!'

'It wouldn't be that bad. Tommy looks after the bars, mainly, and my housekeeper is pretty efficient. But neither of them will take final responsibility, and nobody but me touches the books.'

'You'd want me to do that?'

'If I'm gone for a month, you'd have to. Oh God!' He covered his face with his hands. 'Surely I can't sink no further'n this?'

'Hit the bottom, you've something to bounce back from,' Chel offered, and he laughed.

'Thanks for that, it's cheered me no end!' He removed his hands and looked at her. 'I took a week off last winter, damn near killed myself, and a day off with Deb and I woke up next morning in hospital, a couple of Mondays off and I'm fit to be tied. What'll happen to me, in a whole month, for God's sake?'

'Hopefully, you'll heal.' Chel picked up her coffee and sipped at it thoughtfully. 'What about the restaurant? It won't be open, that's one thing, but you'll have the builders in, even if Deb doesn't.'

'Reckon that'd be down to you, too.' He looked at her. 'This is all too much to ask. You've got a life of your own.'

Chel shook her head.

'Oliver spends most of his time painting, and you wouldn't want me to work shifts, not like in a hotel. All the jobs but yours already belong to somebody.'

'It'd mean working the odd shift in the bar, maybe. Would you mind? Apart from that, you'd likely need to work the hours I do for the Fish – dawn until lunchtime. I suppose. You could start and finish later'n me.'

'Suppose we wanted to go away? Oliver will want to go back to Greece in the spring, I expect.'

Mawgan was calming down, she was glad to see. Faced with a solution to his problem, he was looking for ways to make it succeed, not falling into despair, so there was hope for him.

'Don't see as it'll make much difference. I've run the place on my own near on two years now, a few weeks here and there won't kill me. If you work full time, you're entitled to a holiday. Just don't go in August.'

Chel thought about her present unaccustomed lazy existence, nothing to do but the housework, no one to see but the odd friend for lunch somewhere. She thought about Susan, and her ladies' charity lunches and the emptiness of her life, her sad little children with their *au pair* to look after them. Not for her, never for her, if she persuaded Oliver to adopt a whole orphanage, which was unlikely. She looked at Mawgan.

'OK. Drink your coffee, while I write down the number of the Queen's for you. You'd better check that I can do the job, hadn't you? You can't just throw all caution to the winds.'

'Why not? Sounds a good idea to me.' He looked suddenly moody, but pushed a pen across the desk towards her, and a pad of post-it notes. To her surprise, when she had written the number, he reached straight away for the telephone.

'You can't ask him while I'm sitting here!'

'Why can't I? What're you afraid he'll say?' He was already pressing out the numbers. Chel, who hadn't meant him to do exactly this, watched him and had time to wonder what she was getting herself into.

Far away in the south coast town of Embridge, the telephone rang on the reception desk, a much grander affair than Shirley's cubbyhole at the pub, in the foyer of the Queen's Hotel, and the junior receptionist picked it up.

'Queen's Hotel, how may I help you?' She listened. 'One moment.' Turning her head, she looked at the head receptionist, who shared her shift. 'Jeanette, there's a man on the phone wants to speak to Old MacDonald. He wants to take up a reference.'

'Whose?' asked Jeanette. 'If it's about Maeve Stubbs again, he'll have an apoplexy, he hates having to give bad references, particularly on the phone.'

'I don't know.' The girl was in the first week of her first job after leaving college.

'Well, you should have asked.' Jeanette leaned over so that she could read the number on the caller ID. 'Oh! Ask him to hold, I'll see if his eminence will give an audience.'

She knocked on the door of the Manager's office and went inside. Mr MacDonald, who had long ago been re-christened Old MacDonald by his irreverent staff, looked up, irritated.

'What is it, Jeanette? I'm very busy.'

'There's a phone call – Sarah didn't ask who – '

'Well, she should have done. Tell her to ask now, and don't bother me – '

'No, wait a moment.' Five years ago, when Chel herself had been head receptionist, Jeanette hadn't said 'boo' to a goose, but time moves on. 'He wants to check a reference, whoever he is, and the code and the first three figures of the number are the same as Cheryl's new one.'

'Keep in touch, do you?' Old MacDonald grunted. He had been fond of Cheryl, a good worker and a sensible, intelligent, girl, the best he had ever had in charge of the desk. He had been sorry when she left, for her departure as well as for its circumstances. He had often regretted the waste. 'Find out his name, and put him on. And if it turns out it's about Maeve Stubbs again, I'll dock your wages.'

Fortunately, Jeanette herself asked for the required information, for the name *Mawgan Angwin* might well have stumped Sarah, and very soon Mawgan found himself connected to Old MacDonald. They spoke for a few minutes, then he held out the phone to Chel, sitting there and trying not to listen.

'He wants a word.'

'Oh.' Chel took the phone. 'Hullo, Mr MacDonald.'

'Cheryl!' Old MacDonald sounded so familiar she felt the years run backwards. 'So you think you can manage a pub, do you?'

'He does. I'm not sure about me. What about you?'

'I told him, I think you'll be very good at it. So long as you haven't forgotten all I tried to teach you.'

'I hope I haven't.'

'Licensed Trade is a little bit different, but you'll soon pick it up. It's good to hear of you again, I was beginning to think you'd got smothered by domesticity.'

That made Chel laugh. Old MacDonald knew as well as anyone whom she had married.

'Some chance!'

He was laughing with her.

'Well, you mind you don't let me down with this Mr Angwin, whoever he is, after I've just painted you in glowing colours.'

'I'll try not to.'

'Good landlord, is he, do you think?'

'He can best be described as The Reluctant Landlord, I think. He's actually a rather good chef.' Falling apart, but rather good all the same.

'Hmm, sounds like the title of a book. I just might drop in to see you one of these days, so mind you do me credit.'

'I'll do my best. And thank you.'

'Put him back on, will you. Just one more thing.'

Chel handed back the phone.

Mawgan took the phone, listened for a moment, and then laughed and said goodbye. He switched off and looked at her, thoughtfully.

'He wanted to say, I'd come to think of this as my lucky day. Nice thought.' There was no mirth in his face. Chel said,

'It'll get better. We'll get you through Christmas and New Year somehow, and after that it's all downhill. Well, do I get the job?'

'Oh, please! When can you start? Now?'

'Had I better just slip home and tell Oliver first?' Chel smiled at him.

'Tomorrow, then – yes, before you say it, I know you're off to Greece, week after next. That's understood.'

'Tomorrow.' She got to her feet. 'I'll leave you to break it to Debbie – and Mawgan.'

'What?'

'Be honest with her, won't you? I know I caught you by surprise, but when you've had time to think, don't go minimising it.'

'I won't. All right.'

'That's a promise, mind.'

Mawgan looked at one of his two blank computer screens, as if asking its opinion.

'Do I really want this bullying woman working for me?'

'Yes,' said Chel. 'Goodbye for now.'

When she had gone, Mawgan sat for a while, staring at the blank computer without bothering to move. He had fought delegating responsibility for so long, that having made the decision to do so at last made him feel almost lightheaded. He had an odd feeling, just for a second, that not just the Fish, but a hundred other heavy burdens too, had slid from his shoulders and left him floating, out of contact with the ground. Then it passed, and sweeping the two empty coffee mugs to one side, he reached for a mouse and brought up the screen.

*****

Debbie came down to the little creek late in the afternoon. Chel had been half-expecting her.

It was a peculiar thought, but Chel knew Susan, at present anyway, better than she did Debbie, and she had been uncertain how Debbie would react to the news that she was about to marry a man dangerously near to a breakdown, although surely Debbie must have realised it was a possibility. Debbie came in quite obviously in a state of shock.

'I knew he was depressed, of course I did,' she said. 'I live with him, for goodness' sake! But I thought it was getting better. I don't know what to do.'

Chel said, gently because she had been where Debbie was now, 'I don't think clinical depression is something you actually recover from. You have it, you keep it. And Mawgan tends to drink a bit – that will make it worse.'

'I've tried to talk to him. On the whole, he doesn't listen.' Debbie threw herself into a chair. 'I love him to bits, Chel, but what am I doing?'

Chel ignored this, obviously rhetorical, question. Debbie knew quite well what she was doing by this time.

'Where is he now?'

'In the restaurant kitchen, with the gas oven!' Debbie put her head in her hands. 'What do I do? I don't know. I think he was trying to get away from me, and I was half-scared even to leave him there.'

'One thing, I'll promise you,' said Chel. 'I don't think putting his head in the gas oven is an option here. He's had a scare this morning – so have you – but I think that's probably what it's intended as.' She sat on the arm of Debbie's chair, laying a comforting hand on her bowed shoulder. 'Somebody had to get his attention, I think Dr Billy Pollard just did. That's all.'

'He said you were going to manage the Fish for him.' To Chel's relief, Debbie raised her head and sat up.

'Yes, and that's a big step forward. He's never made any secret of the fact he didn't want to do it himself, and it hasn't helped. You've got to be positive here.'

'What does Oliver say?'

'Something along the lines of *I told you so.*'

Debbie said, almost to herself, but with deep conviction.

'This family is such a *mess.*'

'Nonsense. It's getting more normal every time you look.'

'Do you really think so?' Debbie looked at her in patent disbelief.

'You just all spent a whole weekend in close company with each other, and it didn't turn into The Night of the Long Knives, did it? When was the last time that happened?'

'There were some dodgy moments.'

'There always are, in families. Mine too. To be fair, I've never seen yours behaving so well.'

'Oh.' Debbie thought for a moment, and then sighed. 'I've always secretly wanted a family like anyone else's.'

'How sad,' said Chel, before she could stop herself.

'Yes, isn't it?' Debbie laughed at herself, but uncertainly. 'Chel, Oliver had a breakdown – what should I do? Please tell me.'

'You could decide where you're going for your honeymoon,' said Chel. Oliver's breakdown had been a lot more spectacular than this, which with luck would simply fizzle like a damp squib and die without even a pop, so long as everyone rallied round. One thing of which Mawgan could not be accused was an artistic temperament, Debbie should thank God for it. He was simply an overworked man with too much on his mind. Debbie had said nothing.

'Speak to me,' said Chel.

'Bugger!' said Debbie. 'Well, we seem to have cut out all the exciting things, like skiing down Everest or going on safari in an unmapped jungle, don't we? Sounds like a sun-soaked month in Tenerife to me, lying on a sunbed. Yawn!'

'There's my girl! Bite the bullet, or whatever it is you're supposed to do when it hurts.'

'Tenerife doesn't exactly *hurt*, but I know of more interesting places. Only probably not in February, if you want to just relax and let the world go by, and without travelling for days. And there's probably too much cheap booze around, too.' She looked gloomy.

'Poor old Deb!'

The front door banged, and Oliver came in, bringing with him a faint suggestion of turpentine and oil.

'Well, if it isn't Deb! Left home, have you, or hasn't he broken it to you?'

'He's broken it to me,' said Debbie. 'One of us over-reacted, and I don't think it was me.'

Chel gave Oliver a frown, but he took no notice.

'Don't make too much of it, is my advice,' he said. 'He's grieving, Deb – about his friend, about his sister, about his family. He's probably only allowed himself to do it since he met you, you'll just have to ride out the storm. Just remember, you can't quarrel with someone if they won't quarrel back. Chel's told you she's going to start a new career as a pub landlady tomorrow? I'd love to see your mother's face when she hears. Coffee?'

'*Oliver*, behave!' said Chel, but Debbie was already getting to her feet.

'No, he's right. It was silly to let him rile me – and I did. If you don't mind, I think I'll go back, there's no point in trying to run away and hide anyway.'

'Is that what you were doing?' Oliver sounded interested.

'Yes – no – probably. Sorry to bend your ear like that, Chel. See you tomorrow, I expect.'

She was gone, and Chel and Oliver looked at each other.

'Had to happen sometime,' said Oliver.

'What did?'

'That first, horrible quarrel. Come on Chel, where's your clairvoyance! It was written all over her.'

'Poor Debbie!'

'Nah – she's a grown-up. She'll live. And we don't want her making a habit of running to us every time her love-life goes over a little bump, now do we?'

'Do you really think she would?' asked Chel. Oliver, seeing her expression, laughed.

'No. But the principle remains.'

Debbie, not feeling at all grown up, but more like a chastened little girl, made her way back down the hill. Shirley had long gone home, and the hall of the Fish, on this November evening, was completely deserted. The restaurant, dark behind its closed doors, was lifeless, dead, closed. Taking her courage in both hands, she went through the door into the kitchen passage. There was a line of light under the kitchen door, and she opened it cautiously.

Mawgan wasn't doing anything particular, just leaning on one of the worktops, turning the pages of a book, not really looking at it but simply going through the motions. He looked up as she came in.

'Hullo,' said Debbie.

'Hi.' He turned another page.

Debbie went to stand beside him, just not touching, and he straightened up to look at her.

'Sorry Deb. I just feel such a fool.'

'Yes. Never mind.'

'But I do mind. You hadn't done anything. Like everybody else I've yelled at this past month, it's a wonder the lot of you haven't walked out.'

'I thought Chef shouting in the kitchen was one of the great culinary traditions.'

'There's shouting, and then there's shouting.' He moved towards her and put his arms round her, holding her close. 'Sorry,' he said again.

'They'll all forgive you. They think the world of you.'

'Huh!' She could see he didn't believe her, but it was true just the same. She put her own arms round him and they stood there, locked together, for a long moment.

'Tomorrow,' said Debbie, with a desperate lack of originality, 'is another day.'

The great, empty kitchen was quiet about them, a curious sort of peace with faint suggested echoes of its usual frenetic activity. The moment seemed to go on and on. After a while, Debbie relaxed her arms and looked down at the worktop.

'What's this you were looking at?' She turned up the front cover, idly. '*War in the Helford, 39-45.* What brought this on?'

'It's interesting,' said Mawgan. He took the book from her, and searched for a page. 'Here – there was a fishing boat in the river during World War II, called the *White Rose*, I never knew that, did you?'

'Well, no. I'm a stranger in these parts. How did you find out?'

'Tommy told me. We were talking about naming the restaurant – I liked your choice, but not the reason.' He grinned at her, with something of his usual wickedness. 'Things like that are best forgotten.' It was a good try. Debbie followed his lead.

'What did she do – the *White Rose*? There were some pretty dodgy doings in the Helford, weren't there? Espionage, and all that.'

'Oh yes, she was one of those all right. One of the little ships, too – Dunkirk and back. Brave men, most of them from this village. She went down off the Lizard in 1944, collided with a floating mine, they were all heroes. What d'you think?'

'I think it's got to be just about perfect,' said Debbie. 'They must have drunk in this very pub!' She liked the idea of those distant, brave fishermen being remembered, part of the village again. She thought that the village would, too. And everyone would remember that story she had been told, whether he wanted them to or not.

Mawgan still had an arm around her. He drew her close against him once more.

'All right now, bird?'

'Yup.' She twisted her head to smile up at him, and he kissed her, lightly but with tenderness.

'That's good then. And now I'd better go and open up the bars, or we'll have 'em all queueing up outside.Coming?'

'I thought you were meant to be easing up a bit?'

'OK. I'll leave you to run around and gather up the empties.' He rested his cheek against hers for a second, and Debbie felt her heart move with love. She slid her hand in his, picking up the book in her other one. They left the kitchen hand in hand, and the door swung to behind them.

IV

When Jerry learned that Mawgan was showing signs of strain, he found himself not in the least surprised. By this time, having spent nearly three months picking over the bones of the case, he had reached the unshakable conclusion that the conviction for manslaughter was unsound, and he was fairly certain that Mawgan must be equally well aware of it. Yes, Michael Stanley had died, and yes, Mawgan had been involved, yes, they had been fighting at the time, but that, Jerry thought, might be less shocking than it perhaps appeared to one from his own background. In the course of his enquiries, he had discovered that his son-in-law elect had started life on a council estate; the pair of them, Mike Stanley and Mawgan Angwin, although not exactly contemporary, had grown up in the same street and gone together to the local comprehensive, which had been pretty rough by Jerry's standards, and Mawgan at least had left at the earliest opportunity and worked five years in the building trade, which wasn't a soft option either. These things added together, Jerry tried to convince himself, made up a picture which might understandably explain the fact, that the court seemed to have found so difficult to understand, that the two of them had come to blows over little sister Cressida's immature behaviour, which in itself, Jerry considered, although he wouldn't say it to Mawgan, had been enough to drive any sane man to violence. He didn't really see that it mattered much which of them had started it, although much had been made of the fact that Mawgan couldn't – or wouldn't – confirm this at the trial.

Even as he thought these thoughts, he knew that he was rationalising. It was somehow specious, too simple. There were people to whom such stereotypical arguments might apply, but was Debbie's streetwise, continental-trained chef really one of them? But if not, it was inescapable; there was something missing in the evidence, that although he claimed he wasn't, Mawgan was holding something back.

What, then?

Take a second look.

Mike Stanley had stumbled and fallen, and in the process pulled his friend down with him. He had fallen unluckily, he had hit a vulnerable point on his head on the garden rockery, and so he had died. Jerry, who was coming to like Debbie's choice of husband very much, even if not precisely in that role, felt that that was enough punishment; Mawgan would have to live with it for the rest of his life. That was what had happened, and personally, Jerry defined it as an accident. The circumstances that had blown it up into a charge of murder and ended in a three-year sentence for manslaughter were surely so many lies, so much hysteria, on the part of three silly, immature schoolgirls – he included sister Cressida in the classification although she had been a widow in her twenties – who had quite simply lost their heads, mislaid their brains, and allowed their mouths to talk them into a corner. Mawgan, who would have learned to accept the fact of accident, had been cast in the leading role in a nightmare adolescent fantasy, and that, Jerry perfectly understood, was a lot harder. Little sister had made hints about an unnatural relationship, incest, to be precise. Questioned by the police, she had backtracked and said she hadn't meant it, and it hadn't formed part of the prosecution. Even so, thanks to her loose tongue it had been, to an extent, common knowledge, and in that respect it could be said that a fair trial within the boundaries of Cornwall was impossible. The two girls who had witnessed the incident from a tree in the adjoining garden had told a horrific tale of a man's head being bashed deliberately against a rock, a tale not borne out by the medical evidence, and which they had failed to justify in court, one of them telling two different versions and the other breaking down and refusing to give evidence at all.

And yet, in spite of all this, Mawgan hadn't appealed against the conviction. He said it was due to family pressure, *don't put the poor child through it all again*. Sometimes this seemed understandable, sometimes it didn't. Jerry would have been happier had his own daughter not become involved. Once again, Mawgan had nothing helpful to add.

Moreover, he had been a fool to himself. Released from prison on parole at the end of eighteen months, he had adopted an attitude of spit-in-your-eye defiance that had alienated most of the village in which he had chosen to live, and stubbornly taken on, single-handed, the running of two businesses, either one of which was a full-time job, which was a singularly foolish way of trying to handle things. His prison record, on the other hand, was suspiciously good. He had been a model prisoner, steering meticulously clear of trouble, and causing none, and had earned his release at the earliest possible moment. Jerry, ever a cynic, wondered what it had cost him, and was certainly never going to ask.

And in the middle of all this, while he was still serving a year on parole, he had met Debbie under dramatic circumstances, fallen in love, plunged into a burning house to rescue Lesley Howells and nearly lost his life thereby, been hurtled headlong into a totally different world, and reached, only a short while ago, the end of his probably undeserved punishment – and there was Deb wondering why he was beginning to lose the plot. Jerry himself thought that he would have been a lot more worried if he hadn't, and he had told her so.

He had an enquiry agent hard on the trail of those two girls, Amy Strong and Angela Bartlett, whose evidence had been so damning, and, so he was convinced, so inaccurate. Little sister Cressida, on the other hand, he wouldn't have touched with a ten-foot pole. Little sister Cressida was in a different league altogether when it came to lying. She was so totally away with the fairies that in his opinion, she was actively dangerous.

There were obvious gaps in the story – Jerry wasn't certain that he wanted them filled. Little sister Cressida might fill them. It was as simple as that.

Jerry sighed, and picked up the whisky glass that stood at his elbow, taking a sip with his eyes only half-focussed on the room in which he sat. It was a pleasant enough room, if a little bland and frilly and rather painfully genteel. He had bought the penthouse flat of a new complex, a fully furnished show flat, to give him somewhere to go when he left Dorothy, a step that had finally become inevitable: nobody, he had come to believe, could go on living with such a callous, self-seeking shrew, when in any case their marriage was only a façade by this time. His own, far more masculine, possessions, his books and pictures and his big mahogany desk with its accompanying heavy leather chair, looked completely out of place, but then, he reflected now, they had looked out of place in his previous house, too. He didn't notice that he had failed to call it 'home'. And the flat had several advantages, one of which was that he had it to himself. Being the penthouse flat, nobody passed the door to bother him. And it had the most spectacular view from its balcony, recessed into the sloping roof and thus blessedly private. Directly below was the marina, where he kept an elegant thirty-five foot traditionally-built wooden cutter, and beyond, the whole beautiful expanse of the harbour. The Embridge Harbour Yacht Club, of which he was Vice Commodore, and where he could claim many good friends and pleasant acquaintances, was only just along the road. Yes, living alone had many compensations. Even loneliness itself was a pleasant novelty at present.

But family … whatever you did, wherever you went, you couldn't escape the responsibilities that went with a family. It wasn't only Debbie causing him heartburn, there was Susan too. Susan's marriage, Jerry knew, was in trouble, but he wondered if she knew it herself. There was always somebody to tell you things, and he knew all about his son-in-law's blonde piece, his secretary or something, Jerry thought. He had even seen them together. They hadn't seen him, and he hadn't made himself conspicuous, it wasn't his business to bring things to a head if there was any chance at all that the affair – and it was definitely an affair – would die a natural death. Poor Susan.

Odd really, now he came to think about it. The only one of his family about whom he wasn't worried at present was

Oliver, after God knows how many years in which Oliver had been the one to cause ninety per-cent of the worry. If ever he had a coronary, Jerry had always thought, it would be entirely due to Oliver.

For the fact that things had changed, at least in that respect, he had to thank Nonie Fingall. Or to be more accurate, Nonie Fingall and Gifford Thomas, two names from a past that had become very painful to remember.

How on earth, Jerry asked himself now, had he allowed himself to be such a fool? To be so fooled, be honest. How had he let himself believe all that Dorothy said, when Nonie Fingall had been constantly trying to hammer home the truth? The truth being that he was allowing an outsider to wreck his marriage to the woman who, better face it, he had continued to love to the present day.

He had ended up disliking Nonie, his conscience, and it was humiliating to discover that he had transferred that dislike from himself, in order to excuse his own behaviour. And after he had driven Helen away, he had ended up marrying Dot, who had stage-managed the whole sorry show, because it seemed the sensible thing to do, thinking they would be giving a proper home to two children who now found themselves in single-parent families, and what a disaster that had turned out to be. Who had it made happier? Not Dot, he was fairly certain; as is often the way, having got what she thought she wanted, she found she didn't really want it after all. The standing her marriage had given her, yes, she had wanted that – the man who went with it, no, not really, it was only that she hadn't been able to bear him being the one who got away. Who, then? Definitely not himself, either. Oliver had reacted by becoming dangerously delinquent, and Susan … Poor Susan.

That was the second time he had thought that.

Jerry got to his feet, and although the night was cold, threw open the french doors and stepped out onto his balcony. In front of him, the harbour lay like a sheet of black glass, lights twinkling out here and there around its edge like beads in a necklace. The shadowy shapes of the yachts in the marina immediately below, semi-illuminated by the security lights, were, for the most part, deserted at this time of year, only the occasional warm, curtained glow showing behind a cabin window where some hardy soul was still living. Jerry wished, momentarily, that he was one of them, that he could do as Oliver had done and simply sail away ... but he couldn't. He had come to realise that there was something that he must face, and that trying to run away would never be an option. It would go with him wherever he went, dragging at his spirits, spoiling his life unless he could resolve it.

Helen.

It was useless to try to rationalise it by saying that, if he had stayed with Helen, there would be no Debbie. If there had been no Debbie, he would never have known, never have missed her, unthinkable though it might seem from where he stood now. There might have been other children who now would never be born. You couldn't rewrite history, not however much you tried. There was Debbie, but she wasn't part of the argument.

The last time he had seen Helen, which was recently, they had ended up quarrelling. He had kissed her, he remembered, and he thought that she had come within an ace of blacking his eye. Well, what had he expected?

If you loved someone, and they let you down so badly that you felt you could never trust them again ... then could you be near them? See them? Be friends with them?

He had deserved all that, he knew he had. It had been her answer to his question, *do you still love me?* and what bizarre instinct had made him even consider asking her that? What she had intended him to read into it, God knew, maybe, but he didn't. He wished he did, but he wasn't so conceited these days

A question in reply to a question didn't constitute an answer. He had still received no answer, but he had no right to expect anything other than *no*.

Nonie Fingall was getting married. Back in the days when they had all been friends, Helen had been with Nonie all through the terrible time that had followed the death in a plane crash of her friend and lover, the artist Matthew Sutton, and since that day, he knew, and Helen knew too, Nonie had walked alone. Helen would like to know that that was to change. He ought, too, to warn her that Debbie wanted her at her own wedding.

Two excellent reasons for contacting Helen, or two sad excuses for the same?

Perhaps it was time to be honest, *more than* time to be honest, and admit that he didn't really care which it was, he was going to do it anyway, and for the simple reason that he wanted to, which was perhaps the best one of all.

Helen, when she answered his call, was at home, yes, but obviously not home alone. There were sounds as of a cheerful party in the background, she sounded happy. Why Jerry should have found this hurtful, he had no idea.

'Hullo, this is Helen Macken,' she said. The note of laughter in her soft Scots voice, he thought fancifully, was like flying birds.

'Helen! Jerry. Have I chosen a bad moment to call?'

'Oh, it's you.' He heard the falling inflexion, but at least she didn't hang up on him.

'I wanted to speak with you, but if you're busy ...' God, he sounded about seventeen!

'I am, rather, as you can probably hear.' There was a shout of laughter in the background, and someone had put on some music. Jerry felt inordinately jealous of all those merry people. He said,

'I won't take up your time. Maybe I could take you out to lunch when you're less tied up?'

'I don't see why,' said Helen.

'For old time's sake?'

'I wouldn't cross the street for *their* sake. And how is dear Dot?'

'I neither know, nor care,' said Jerry.

'I can sympathise – with both of you.'

Ouch!

'Look, Helen, can we stop sparring? I've two pieces of news, neither of which I want to give you when you're not really listening. That's all.'

'Write me a letter, then.'

'I would, if I could be sure you wouldn't just tear it up.'

Helen paused at that. After a moment, she said,

'Well, I won't say you wouldn't deserve it, but am I really so unreasonable?'

'Look, I know I probably deserve everything you choose to throw at me, but can't we, for once, be civilised?'

'I never know where civilisation is going to lead, with you.'

That sounded better, for some reason. Jerry said,

'If I promise to behave, will you meet me?'

Helen's voice seemed to have gone a long way off.

'I've heard your promises before.'

'Shit!' said Jerry. 'Will you quit this, Helen? I'm asking you to lunch with me, so that I can give you two pieces of good news, I'm not proposing to ravish you.'

'*Good* news? You're sure it's good news?'

'The best.'

'So, when's the funeral?' asked Helen, cynically.

'The funeral?'

'Dot's funeral. I thought you just said she was dead.'

Jerry was tempted to hang up, but didn't. Both he and Dot had probably deserved that.

'Helen …'

'Oh, all right.' She paused. 'That was a bit unnecessary, I'm sorry. How about Sunday, one o'clock, in the pub down the road? It's called the Black Bull, they do a carvery, if you want to eat.'

'Fine, I'll see you.'

Helen rang off without saying goodbye, and Jerry slowly replaced his phone on its rest. Helen had a gift for rubbing him up the wrong way these days, but he suspected that it was mutual. When they were first married, she had never been so abrasive. Did that mean that he had taught her? He seemed to have been responsible for teaching too many people too many lessons that nobody should ever have to learn. He had a fear that there was no way back from them. He wasn't proud of himself, and if Dot should take some of the blame, well, who had let her in?

Suddenly introspective, Jerry picked up the whisky bottle and was about to pour himself another glass, when something that his daughter Debbie had repeated to him, in the context of Mawgan's illness, about drink and depression came back to him, and he put the bottle down again. If he was depressed, then he had probably earned it, and anyway, there was always Sunday.

* * * * *

There must be numberless pubs more or less equidistant between his flat in Embridge and Helen's Surrey home, Jerry reflected as he pulled into the car park of the Black Bull, but Helen had, presumably deliberately, chosen the one that would make him travel the maximum distance to see her. God, she could be an awkward bitch! Did she think he had nothing better to do?

Then he saw her, sitting on the bench outside in the sunshine, waiting for him, and knew that she was right if so, he hadn't. She rose and came to meet him as he got out of the car, but he resisted the temptation to greet her with more than a swift peck on the cheek, and even that was probably risky.

'Hullo, Jerry.' She didn't return the kiss, but at least she didn't draw away too obviously. 'How are you? You're looking well.'

Jerry wanted to tell her that she was looking beautiful, but he said lightly,

'You too. Shall we go in out of the cold?' He took her arm as they walked towards the door of the inn, and felt his heartbeat start to accelerate. He had been twenty-five when he first met her, he remembered, and although he was a lot closer to sixty now, he felt twenty-five again. Where did all the time go? It hardly seemed to have touched Helen at all.

They found a table, and he bought drinks and carried them back to her.

'What did you want to tell me?' Helen asked, as he sat down.

'Don't you want to eat?'

'Later. Tell me about your weekend in the bosom of your family, if you must spin it out. Did you survive in the jungle?'

Jerry had already worked out that this was a more delicate subject than either of the two excuses. He said, slowly,

'Yes ...'

'Amazing! I thought Susan and Oliver would have torn out each other's throats at the very least.'

'Well, they didn't, so you're disappointed.'

'Ah,' said Helen.

'What is *ah* supposed to mean?'

'Itching powder,' said Helen, and gave him an innocent look out of her wonderful dark blue eyes. Jerry bit his lip.

'*Itching powder?*'

'Makes everyone scratchy and irritable,' said Helen, and sipped her whisky and spring water delicately. She looked far too angelic to mean what Jerry suspected she meant. He looked at her suspiciously. Her eyes widened. Jerry began to worry for his blood pressure.

'Oliver and Chel are very well,' he said. Helen smiled at him.

'I know. I saw them, remember? More important, how was poor old Deb? So Victorian! *Go, and never darken my doors again*! You'd think she was toting an illegitimate baby at the very least, and the Good Queen was still on the throne!' She paused. 'I suppose she isn't? Pregnant, I mean?'

'God – no! I don't know. I shouldn't think so, she's planning on running a sailing school -' Jerry realised that Helen had fished for him and caught him, and felt himself go hot. 'Helen, would you mind not being so controversial?'

Helen laughed, quietly.

'All right, tell me about him instead – this man there's all the fuss about. What's his problem, two heads?'

'He's nearly nine years older than Deb, speaks with a Cornish accent, was born on a council estate, runs a pub, and has a prison record.'

'Oh, bugger!' said Helen, inelegantly. 'I could almost feel sorry for Dot! Did Deb do it on purpose? I could believe it of Oliver, but not Deb.'

'No. Deb saw someone quite different, and I have to hope she's right.'

'Obviously, or you wouldn't be sitting there looking so smug about it.'

Jerry, who had no idea that he was looking smug, hurriedly rearranged his expression.

'Go on, then,' said Helen. 'What's he really like?'

Jerry said, feeling his way towards the answer to a question that, in fact, he wasn't sure about,

'Actually, he's not unlike Oliver,' and was pleased to see that he had startled her, it was her turn.

'Like *Oliver*? In what way, for God's sake?'

'Well, not to look at. He's one of those dark, tough, round-headed types, looks a bit of a thug. And yes, he's a Cornishman, although he's spent some years in Europe – but he's certainly not ashamed of his roots, and why should he be?' Jerry paused, knowing that he was talking too much, and half of it to convince himself, giving Helen time to say,

'Only Dot would think so.' She paused too, to let this sink in, and then added, 'They don't have pubs in Europe – well, not many. What was he doing?'

'He's a chef.'

Helen shook her head, as if to clear it.

'Why do I get the feeling that I've missed a couple of chapters? What has Debbie been up to?'

'Let me explain,' said Jerry, and did so. Helen listened intently, and when he had finished, said,

'It all sounds very suspect to me, Jerry. Are you really happy about it? I think I should be asking a lot of questions, if it was me.'

This was so much his own view, that Jerry found himself at a loss as to how to reply, because he had asked the questions and received no sensible answers at all, and where did a concerned father go from there, when his daughter was so patently head over ears in love and determined to go her own way? He could hardly put his foot down. Dot had tried that, and look where it had got her. Helen, reading his expression, told herself firmly that it wasn't her business, she shouldn't get involved. Debbie was Dot's daughter, not hers. She said, curiously,

'So, why did you say he was like Oliver? Goodness knows, Oliver has done some pretty un-smart things in his life, but he never got himself into a mess like that!'

'He has the same wide vision, and lack of conformity. He's another that follows his own road and drives his family nuts.'

'Then from the sounds of it, he needs to get himself a better map!' said Helen. Jerry looked at her steadily.

'And Oliver?'

'OK. Point taken.' Helen was silent for a moment. 'So, let me get this straight. He's going to run his restaurant, and Chel is taking over the pub? Have I got that right?'

'Yes. And Deb will run her sailing school, and Oliver will paint and, if she has her way, teach navigation on the side, although the jury is still out on that one just at present.'

'Well, you've robbed me of words,' said Helen, inaccurately. She cocked her head to an enquiring angle. 'And do they all get on?'

'Looked like it to me. They even got on with Susan.'

'Gracious!' She realised that she had allowed herself to be beguiled into having a sensible conversation with Jerry, and cast about for something with which to wind him up. 'You see what can happen, when you get rid of Dot? Miracles!'

'Helen, don't rub it in, will you? I did my best, can we leave it at that?'

'With the mess *you* made,' Helen pointed out. Jerry said nothing to this, and after a minute, Helen went on. 'I said at the time that you should have left Oliver with me.' She sounded bitter.

'That's an old argument. And don't you think he might have missed me just as much as he missed you?'

'If he did miss me.'

'Oh, he missed you.' He paused. 'Helen … we can't turn back the clock, but can't we … well, rescue something from the wreck?'

Helen drained her glass with an abrupt movement, and got to her feet.

'Let's eat, shall we?' she said. 'Then you can tell me why we're here. And yes, I'd love another drink thank you. Wine. And no, I'm not driving, and if I get too pissed to walk – which is possible if you go on like that – then you can drive me home. Can't you?'

'Oh, sure,' muttered Jerry, and followed her up to the bar.

Over the roast, she became businesslike.

'So what is it that you couldn't write to me?' she asked, briskly.

'It was your reading, not my writing, that was in doubt,' Jerry reminded her, wryly.

'Fine. So what is it?'

Jerry chose his words carefully. Today wasn't shaping up quite as he would have wished, but he hadn't abandoned hope entirely.

'Do you remember saying to me last time we met, *Nonie will never marry this Theodorakis?*'

Helen stared at him.

'She never is! When? Where? *Why*, for God's sake?'

'Saturday, in Athens. Chel and Oliver are flying out on Thursday, just for the weekend. Why? Your guess is probably as good as mine.'

'Well, you have surprised me!' Helen looked pensive. 'So what does Chel's new boss have to say to that? She's barely got her foot in the door!'

'I believe he said words to the effect of, *bon voyage*,' said Jerry. Helen said, on a bubble of laughter,

'D'you remember when she ran off with Oliver? She nearly got the sack!'

'The circumstances were rather different. And I imagine Mawgan is more flexible than Ronald MacDonald anyway.'

'Where did he get a name like that?' Helen wondered. 'I couldn't believe it when I saw it written down. Or can't they spell in his family?'

'He was named after a Cornish saint, I believe.'

'Ooh! Bad choice.'

'They couldn't know,' said Jerry, but Helen's laughter had been infectious. He smiled at her. 'Don't change the subject. As to *why*, I suppose she loves him.'

Helen was silent for so long that they had both almost finished their main course before she spoke.

'She loved Matt. I thought it was for always, one of those once-in-a-lifetime things.'

'Is there such a thing?'

Helen sighed then, wistfully.

'When you're young, you hope so. But no ... probably there isn't.' She took a delicate mouthful and chewed it thoughtfully. When her mouth was empty, she said sadly, 'I never thought, when we were all young together and oh, such friends, that Nonie would get married, and me not there – she was my bridesmaid.'

They were on dangerous ground, Jerry felt it shifting under his feet. He said,

'You could be there. We could fly out to Athens too.'

'We are not invited,' Helen pointed out, precisely.

'That doesn't mean we wouldn't be welcome. Nonie is probably as confused as you are, meeting again like that after all the years.'

'I'm not confused. If she wanted us – me – she would have said.'

'OK. I'm not sure that you're right, but OK. But I'll tell you who *does* want you – Debbie.'

'*Debbie*?' Helen stared at him, her introspective mood completely shattered. 'But surely, Dot ...? She won't carry things *that* far! Not to be at her own daughter's wedding ...' She saw Jerry's face. 'She will. The cow!'

'Dot told Debbie that she wouldn't go if Deb asked on her knees,' said Jerry, and as he said it, a fresh wave of anger against Dot swept over him icily. 'Helen – '

'That woman is *abominable*!' cried Helen, furiously. 'What's the matter with her, for God's sake? Deb is a darling, and her own daughter, too! Her own woman, come to that!'

'I think Dot is hoping she may see sense, if enough pressure is applied.'

'And will she?' Helen looked at him. 'Jerry? Are *you* really happy about this?'

Jerry hesitated before he answered.

'I'm her father, Helen. I want what's best for her, I want her to be happy.'

'What's that supposed to mean?' asked Helen, but she asked it kindly. Jerry shook his head.

'I suppose ... this marriage isn't what I would have picked out for her. I can't put it more plainly than that. I think that he's a decent man, I believe that he loves her. I *don't* believe that he killed his friend in any way deliberately. I have no sensible reason for objecting. And I don't think I can stop her, anyway.'

'But,' said Helen. 'I can hear *but* in your voice, Jerry.'

'All right then, *but*,' said Jerry. 'I'll go over it again. He's a year older than Oliver. He's from an entirely different background. He's very, very ambitious.'

'Doesn't sound like grounds for playing the heavy father to me.'

Jerry had pushed his plate aside in order to lean his arms on the table to get closer to Helen. He hadn't realised how much he wanted to talk this over, not just with Chel and Oliver, but with a sensible person of his own generation, and it didn't occur to him that *sensible* wasn't an adjective that he had ever thought went with the name *Helen* very happily. He just knew that he wanted her opinion.

'There are so many things that can quite justifiably be said against him as a husband for Deb, that I don't even know which one it is that's particularly bugging me. Or if anything is, come to that. I just *feel* there's something I'm not being told.'

'You like him, though. I can hear it in your voice.'

'Oh yes – I like him very much. But I like a great many people that I wouldn't actually want my daughter to marry.'

'Just bear in mind,' said Helen, 'that it *is* your daughter who's marrying him. She's always been a one-off. Oliver too – there are some very strange genes in your family, Jerry Nankervis, if you ask me! Your father is another one who broke the mould and fled.'

'I love Deb …'

Helen looked at him with surprising kindness. 'Jerry, it can't be that Dot's snobbishness has rubbed off on you, can it? You're only one generation removed from a Cornish farmyard yourself, I ought to remind you.'

'I don't think so.' Jerry frowned, trying to work it out, but with no more success than he had already had – which was to say, none. 'Maybe it's that I feel he's just a little too streetwise … prison, and everything – or maybe it's just that fathers are over-protective towards daughters. You tell me.'

'I can't,' said Helen. 'I've never met him.' She too had leaned forward over the table, almost without knowing it. Her face was very close to his, her breath sweet on his cheek, and Jerry felt his heart betraying him again, banging against his ribs. He said, not meaning to,

'I loved your hair when it was long. I wish you hadn't cut it off.'

Helen drew back.

'Don't start, Jerry, please!'

He caught her arm, holding her to the table.

'Helen – do something for me. Dot ought to do it, but she won't.'

'Let go!' Helen drew her arm away and rubbed it where he had gripped it. 'Like what, exactly?'

'Come down to Cornwall with me. Tell me what you see.'

102

Helen sat right back in her seat, her face a study.

'Jerry, are you totally out to lunch? I wouldn't go as far as Guildford with you, never mind Cornwall!'

'Please. Just as a friend, have a look at Oliver's studio, say hullo to Chel ... you don't have to stay under the same roof, even, Deb will put you up at the Fish. I'll treat you to dinner in the restaurant, if we can get a table. You'll be impressed.'

'Bribery, now?' Helen dropped her hand from her arm, which she had still been rubbing. 'Jerry ...'

Jerry said, stonily,

'Dot's history, Helen. Surely we can be friends at least, if only for Oliver's sake.'

'I think it's a long time since Oliver even cared,' said Helen.

'Oh, Helen.' He was so sorry for her, suddenly, that if he had been a sentimental man, he would have wept. 'There's nothing I can do – I'm so sorry.'

The silence between them seemed to go on for ever, so full of unspoken, unspeakable tension that it seemed to thrum with it. Helen broke it.

'All right,' she said. 'I'll come with you.'

Her capitulation was so unexpected that Jerry nearly choked on a too-sudden breath. When he had finished coughing,

'What did you say?' he managed.

'I said I'd come, but I didn't mean to kill you, exactly.' Helen looked at him with concern. 'You've gone all red.'

'Shock,' said Jerry.

'You go white with shock.'

They looked at each other. A step had been taken, Helen realised, that might be difficult to retrace. Did she want to retrace it? She honestly didn't know. If Nonie Fingall could marry Dimitrios Theodorakis – although she hadn't quite done it yet – who knew what could happen? But there was no need to go overboard. She turned her wrist to look at her watch.

'Time I was going, I'm afraid, Jerry. Thank you for lunch.'

Jerry rose to his feet with her.

'And thank you, too, for meeting me – and for everything. Do you want a lift?'

'I'll walk, thank you.' She held out her hand, and he took it, resisting the impulse to hold it just a little too long.

'I'll give you a ring.'

'I'll wait to hear.' She smiled. 'Goodbye Jerry.'

He watched her walk away. He wasn't sure what had happened, if it was a step towards tolerance, or a step towards … well, what? What did he want? Not to get married again, of that he was absolutely sure, twice was enough for any man.

These whom God hath joined together, let no man put asunder … The old words of the marriage service rattled around in his head like peas in a drum. He practically felt them, hard as hailstones.

It wasn't until she had finally walked out of sight that he realised he had no idea whether she would actually come to Debbie's wedding or not.

On the whole, that was probably up to him.

Jerry took a breath that, this time, didn't choke him, and went out to his car. Never over-egg the pudding. It was time to go home.

V

Chel slipped into the life of the Fish as easily as a frog into water, she even felt that everyone had moved over to make room for her, greeted her arrival with relief. Tommy, the barman, put it into words, as he took her through the stock in the bar.

'Should've done it a year gone, stubborn bugger,' he said, and added, to her surprise. 'It's good the Fish should be family-run again.'

Family-run? Chel supposed she knew what he meant, but even so, thought that the wife of your half-brother-in-law, or if you looked at it the other way, the husband of your half-sister-in-law was a tenuous sort of relationship, hardly meriting the term, and particularly before the conjoining marriage had taken place. Perhaps in a family as full of tenuous relationships as the Nankervises, it would pass. She said, diplomatically,

'You've all made me feel welcome. I wondered if I might be stepping on anyone's toes.'

'Bloody glad to see you, truth be told,' said Tommy. He grinned at her. He and Mawgan were friends, Chel had found, as well as employer and employee. Tommy would be outspoken, where the rest of the staff were more circumspect. She hoped that she wasn't making use of the fact, but she found his confidences helpful in a situation where Mawgan, making heavy weather himself, tended to leave her to sort the job out for herself as often as not, relying, she thought, too heavily on Old MacDonald's recommendation. She hoped she wouldn't let either one of them down.

By the time that she and Oliver were driving to Bristol to catch the plane for Athens, she had plenty to think about, some of it privately alarming. She hadn't mentioned it to Oliver, and he never asked her to discuss Mawgan's business on principle, but she found that a talk she had had with Debbie a couple of days earlier, together with its more recent sequel, was crowding her thoughts to the exclusion even of looking forward to seeing Greece again, and under such joyful circumstances too.

Debbie had stuck her head round the office door, while Chel was trying to make sense of an accounting system set up, so far as she could see, by an accountant with a marked sadistic streak.

'Hi,' she had said.

Chel looked up from the screen, with such a scowl of concentration on her face that Debbie recoiled.

'I see I've chosen a bad moment!'

Chel made a brow-mopping gesture, but laughed as well.

'You could say that. He just gave me the password first thing, asked if I understood the system, and left me to get on with it – went tearing off to Porthleven after fish. Did you want something?'

'Just to ask if you'd like to come and join me for lunch when you knock off. I can just about manage a sandwich, if Oliver isn't expecting you back.'

'I can soon make sure he *isn't* expecting me back.'

'Do that, then. Must dash – busy!'

Me too, Chel thought, with a despairing look at the screen. Oh well, perhaps five minutes break would clear her head. Mawgan had said he would take her through it when he got back, if she couldn't make sense of it, but she placed no reliance on that. He appeared, she had decided, to have dumped the Fish in her lap with a sigh of relief and abnegated all responsibility thereafter. It was the undoubted measure of the … well, the nuisance, she supposed, that he had found it. It was a shame, it was a lovely pub, and deserved better.She had concluded after a week that had proved to be a steep learning curve, that he had run it efficiently but without any of the flair he applied to his restaurant, and its potential was beginning to interest her. But it was early days.

Making her way up to the flat later, she discovered Debbie similarly occupied to herself, that is, sitting at the dining table staring into a computer screen as if she was trying to discern the holy grail, but in her case, it was filled with words.

'Oh God,' said Debbie, when she saw her. 'Is it that time? Sorry – I got this e-mail in from Carl, and I was just …' She broke off, and smiled. Chel sighed.

'OK, I'll make the sandwiches, shall I?'

'I'll do it – just let me set this to print.'

In the end, they did it together.

'What will you do, when you want to hold a dinner party?' asked Chel, with interest, as they sat down to eat. It was a fair question, the table was full not only with Debbie's laptop, printer, and a scanner borrowed from the office, but with piles of paper and photographs.

'I've nowhere else to work,' Debbie explained. 'My office is still a twinkle in the architect's eye – and a scowl on the planning department's face, come to that. Mawgan said to use the table, but I wish it wasn't round. Everything falls off the sides.'

This was already obvious by the amount of paper on the floor, but Chel didn't mention it. Instead, she said,

'How's it all going?'

'Well, it's going. Slowly. They've accepted the general idea, thanks to the Parish Council, but they're being a blight over the plans. They seem to think we should put up something that resembles the original house, I ask you! What use is that?'

'So who's going to win?'

'The architect says, persevere. The only good thing is that the demolition men move in to clear the site next week. I think I may feel better about it when the ruins have gone.' She leaned back in her chair with a sigh. 'Don't you just hate computers? I thought I'd got away from them down here – if I'd known it was going to figure so largely in my plans, I don't think I'd have made them, but it's the only sensible way I can keep in touch with Roger and Carl.'

Chel nodded towards the table.

'Carl seems a bit wordy.'

'That's because he's a journalist.' Debbie set her sandwich aside and got to her feet again to collect her finished printout. 'I mean, not a tabloid journalist, he writes for the yachting magazines and things like that. He's doing all the publicity – he's written this article, that he's hoping he can arrange for one of the magazines to publish to coincide with the Boat Show – here.' She gave Chel the sheets from the printer. 'Have a read, while you eat.'

The article was entitled *A Phoenix from the Flames* and told, briefly, the sad story of Seagulls and then, in detail, the new plans for the future. It was illustrated with pictures of people enjoying themselves the previous year, sailing, lying on the foreshore in the sun, rigging boats. It was full of optimism and enticement. Chel read it carefully, and then placed the sheets on the arm of her chair.

'You do realise that Tim will probably see it?'

'Yes.' Debbie met her eyes. 'You can see that Carl has been very careful. Nowhere has he said anything that even involves Tim – just that two of the instructors, that's me and Roger, have taken over the premises and plan to start again. But I know what you mean ... as a matter of fact, after what you said the other night, I was wondering if I ought to go to see Tim.'

'It might not be a very good idea,' suggested Chel.

'I'm sure it would be a terrible idea ... it just seems more honest, somehow.'

'He knows it was you who bought the place when the bank foreclosed, doesn't he?'

'I suppose so. Chel, I already told you, I don't actually know. That's what bothers me.'

Chel was silent for a minute, considering this.

'Are you fishing for my opinion?'

'Probably.'

'Then, I think it might be better if you wrote. I really don't think you should see him again, and I think your father would agree with me.'

'It seems so cold.'

'Exactly. And cold is exactly what you need to be. He wrecked his marriage over you, Deb. Get real!'

'He didn't burn the house down over me, and that's what matters.'

Since this was something about the rights and wrongs of which nobody – except Tim, obviously – was certain, there didn't seem anything to add to it. Chel said,

'I agree it must be cleared up, but don't jump in with both feet, Deb. It's a bit of a thing of yours.'

Debbie stared pensively at the remains of her sandwich, her face was sad.

'Goodbye, then, isn't it?'

'Yes,' said Chel, firmly. 'There's no future in anything else – particularly since you've already told us that he and Mawgan can't stand the sight of each other. So enjoy what you've got and let Tim go. You can't do anything for him.'

'Except play fair with him.'

'Then write.'

'OK, I'll write. How're you getting on with the Fish?'

'I think I'm getting it sussed – it wasn't badly managed, or anything, so it's only a matter of taking over something that's up and running – building on it, maybe. But I wish Mawgan would stand still long enough to answer questions.'

'His family say he was always hyperactive. You'll get more sense out of Tommy and Mrs Solomons and Shirley.'

'He kept an awful lot to himself, though,' said Chel. 'A real one-man band, is your Mawgan.'

'The word you're looking for is probably *secretive*,' said Debbie. 'Myself, I always wonder what he's up to.' She lifted her brows enquiringly, but Chel wouldn't be drawn. She had deduced, from her morning on the computer, that either Mawgan himself or his accountant was both devious and clever, but probably stopped short of being actively dishonest, but it wasn't for her to say. 'Oh well,' said Debbie, giving up. 'How do you get on with them all? The staff?'

'With Tommy, fine.'

'Oh, anyone could get on with Tommy!'

'With Shirley ... she resents me a bit, I think, but she's coming round. Mrs Solomons is hard work, she treats me like an interloper.' Mrs Solomons was the housekeeper.

'Yeah, well ... so long as there aren't complaints, Mawgan doesn't take any great interest in housekeeping. And she's very protective towards him, she probably feels you're in her territory.'

'She seems to think the world of you.'

'Me, maybe, but a whole shoal of nubile young women invading the Fish and taking over may be a bit different. What about the rest of them?'

'The bar staff ... they're fine, they take their cue from Tommy. I don't have anything to do with the restaurant.'

Debbie laughed, unexpectedly and happily.

'The restaurant staff have declared Be Kind to Chef Week. I think they've suddenly got the picture, the significance of your sudden appearance must have been quite hard for them to miss. After all, they've been the ones in the firing line.'

'And Mawgan? How's he coping?'

'He's not exactly off the wall yet, but he's sliding gently down it. Two consecutive days in the week without having to work himself to death might have something to do with it. You really are the answer to a prayer, Chel.'

'Well, the job is a godsend to me, too. Quite apart from the money, Oliver and me aren't exactly good at living in each other's pockets. If I'm really honest, it gets on our nerves a bit – even last year, when things were going well, there were a couple of occasions at least when axe murder was on the cards. And I loved my job at the Queen's, I really missed it.'

'I can see that. If I didn't have all this to organise – ' Debbie made a sweeping gesture that took in the room ' – I should probably be higher up the wall than poor old Mawgan is.' She sat forward suddenly. 'Chel, can I bounce an idea off you? It was Roger's, actually, but it seems to me a good one … I haven't had the courage, to be honest, to take it up with Mawgan yet, perhaps you could do it better.'

'Me?'

'Well, if you're running the Fish, it would concern you, too. More, even.'

Chel looked at her warily.

'What is it, then?'

'Well, as you know, we're planning to build in facilities for visiting yachtsmen – people who hitch up on the moorings in our creek – showers, fresh water, fuel, that kind of thing. And a chandlery *if* we ever get permission for a sensible building. What we can't provide, of course, is meals.'

'The Fish does bar lunches,' said Chel.

'I know it does, I've eaten a fair few of them – and very good they are, too. But apart from the Kosy Kafé up the village, there's nowhere else. And that closes dead on half-past five, even if it wasn't the ultimate naff caff.'

'*Up the village*,' murmured Chel. 'You're naturalising, Deb Nankervis, that's what you're doing.'

'And it isn't just the visiting yachtsmen,' Debbie continued, ignoring this with a passing grin. 'If any of our students are B&B-ing in the village, as they probably will be, there's nowhere to eat in the evenings unless they get in their cars and drive somewhere – which is fine, as far as it goes, but if we're going to have lectures in theory and navigation, and the racing rules and all that jazz, in the evenings, we don't want them scattering all over the Lizard. They'll half of them never come back in time – if at all. Mawgan's posh eatery is almost too successful for its own good already, and if he gets his wish, it'll get worse, there's no way anyone is going to get a table there unless they book it when they book with us – that's even if they want to afford it. And even if they did, that's only one night in fourteen possibles.'

'So?'

'The original Fish building has a perfectly good kitchen of its own, and it only does breakfast for a few residents when there are any, and the bar lunches. It's a total waste in the evenings.'

'You want him to do bar food in the evenings?' Chel pondered for a minute. 'It's an interesting idea – setting up in competition with yourself.' She looked sceptical. Debbie shook her head.

'It wouldn't be like that. The restaurant is a completely different animal, believe me. You haven't eaten in it yet, but you will, and then you'll see. What Roger and I had in mind was steak, chips and salad, home-made pasties, fish and chips, cheesecake, apple pie and cream, that kind of thing.'

Chel immediately saw both the possibilities and the problems.

'It'd have to be the best bar food for miles around – it'd be riding on the reputation of the existing restaurant.'

'Surely not!'

'Yes, it would. That's probably why he's never done it.'

'According to Tommy, Edward – that was his original partner – did. He used the snug, where they serve the breakfast.'

'That was then. This is now, and anyway, I think you'll find that things are about to move onwards and upwards.'

'But do you think he'd consider it?'

'God, Deb, surely you know that better than I do!'

Debbie was silent, and after a moment, Chel said,

'OK, I'll raise it with him – if he ever stands still for long enough, I'll raise it with him. But I can't just throw it at him, you must leave me to pick a good moment. Right now, your man is on a very short fuse, I'm not playing with any matches.'

'Who're you telling?' Debbie had asked, and given her a rueful smile.

But that wasn't what was filling Chel's mind now, as they tore up the M5 headed for Nonie's wedding. What had kept her awake last night, and was monopolising her thoughts this morning, was Mawgan's reaction when, an opportunity naturally arising the very next day, she had seized it and asked the million-pound question.

'Do what you like,' he had said. 'It's your pub now, you're the manager – just don't lose me money.'

'What?' Chel stared at him. He looked at her, as if surprised.

'Come on, Chel – you're an intelligent woman, and it's already obvious you know your job. Are you going to tell me that you don't know I've barely kept the Fish ticking over? Why will nobody believe me, when I say *I didn't want the place?*'

'It's made a good profit,' said Chel, because it had.

'Anyone can sell beer, if they're the only pub in the village,' Mawgan had said, dismissively, and gone on to the next thing with barely a pause for breath.

He was selling himself short, Chel thought now. To succeed, as the Fish succeeded, a pub needed more than beer, a picturesque building and a steady flow of summer visitors, it also needed its local trade. It therefore required high standards and sympathetic management, which he had supplied, however grudgingly, and a friendly, welcoming atmosphere, which Tommy had provided. Tommy, Chel had very soon realised, was the Fish's biggest asset. As for Mawgan, he hadn't wanted the Fish, but he hadn't exactly let it down. What he hadn't done was to recognise its possibilities.

If he had been entirely himself, Chel knew, he wouldn't have dumped it in her lap wholesale the way he had. But he demonstrably *wasn't* entirely himself, and so here she was, left holding the baby – and a baby that was squalling loudly for attention. Mawgan had, quite simply, walked away.

It wasn't, Chel admitted to herself, quite what she had expected, or certainly not after just over a week spent working for him. What on earth could Old MacDonald have said to him?

Oliver, aware that she was deep in thought, drove without trying to talk to her. He wasn't much of a one for talking for the sake of it anyway, Chel thankfully thought. He would listen though, if she chose to tell him anything, and she wondered how much she could say without breaking any confidences. Certainly, Mawgan had always been open on the subject of not wanting the poor Fish, and it would be good to bounce a few ideas off somebody. Debbie would have been first choice, but Debbie wasn't here. With Oliver, you could never second-guess his reaction to anything.

'Oliver,' she said, tentatively.

'Hullo, so there is somebody home! Does this mean you're ready to tell me what's on your mind?'

'Yes.' Chel took a sudden decision. 'I had a bit of a ... not a shock, exactly. I don't know how you'd describe it ...' He said nothing, merely waited as they screamed up the fast lane of the motorway, concentrating on handling the car and leaving the pace of the conversation for her to set. She said, 'Mawgan's given me a completely free hand with the Fish.'

'Oh?' Oliver sounded interested, but not surprised – which was interesting in itself, she decided. 'Did you expect something else?'

Had she? It had all happened so quickly and suddenly, she realised that she hadn't even had time to think specifically.

'I thought he'd want to keep control ... have some sort of input. He doesn't.'

'That's good, then.'

Was it? Well, yes, Chel supposed it was, in a way. She said,

'It took me aback.'

'Ah. Sails shaking, everything loppy, how do we get sailing again from here?'

'Exactly.'

'I'm sure you're equal to it.'

'I wish *I* was,' said Chel, feelingly.

'Oh, you are. And if he hadn't thought so, Mawgan would be breathing down your neck, believe me. I take it, he isn't?'

'I hardly see him. He spends all his time either cruising the countryside checking out new local suppliers, or working in the kitchen, the only time I catch him is if he's in the office in the morning, keeping the restaurant's affairs up to date – and then I only have half his attention. No, make that a quarter.'

'Just like home, then,' said Oliver, with a grin.

'Mawgan's got his own agenda,' said Chel, thinking. 'I just wish, sometimes, that I was sure he was firing on all four – no, eight in his case, probably – cylinders.'

'He wants me to paint fishing boats on his wall,' said Oliver, casually. 'Did he tell you?'

Chel's jaw had gone slack with surprise, although Oliver, his attention on changing lanes for the junction, didn't notice.

'What?' It came out in a strangled gasp.

'I offered. In return for him fixing our gutters.'

Chel found her voice.

'Does he realise just *what* you offered?'

'I don't expect so, for a minute. He's not much into art, I don't think. But after all, what's a picture, between friends? And anyway, I'm not a hundred per cent sure what *he* offered, either.'

'But – ' Chel broke off. She let out a long breath. 'That'll send up the value of his restaurant building,' she said.

'It's only a mural, for God's sake!'

'Yes. And look what Michelangelo did for the Sistine Chapel.'

Oliver reacted to that with a snort of irreverent laughter.

'You're drawing comparisons?'

'Posterity might,' Chel pointed out. 'Why fishing boats? I thought Deb planned on calling it – what did she say? *An Rosen Gwyn?*'

'She did. She does – they do. It's the reason that's changed, that's all.' He told Chel about the *White Rose*. 'He showed me some pictures. It's a subject after my own heart, much better than bloody roses! She's – she was – a chunky little Cornish trawler, lightly disguised as a French fishing boat for dubious purposes, full of character. I shall enjoy immortalising her – or at least, until somebody repaints the wall.'

'They wouldn't dare!' said Chel, with conviction.

'Mawgan probably won't, I agree with you. He'd dare, all right, I don't mean that – just that he won't do it.'

Chel stretched out her legs, and yawned. She was feeling better, she found. Oliver's calm acceptance of her news, as if he had never considered anything else, had a soothing influence, and three or four days away from the Fish, she now thought, would bring it properly into focus. She voiced, instead, another concern, one that she shared with other members of Oliver's family.

'Do you think Deb will be happy?'

'No, I think Deb is *already* happy. Anyway, you're supposed to be the one who's clairvoyant, why're you asking me?'

'To hear your opinion, I suppose.'

'Sounds fair. Why, do you have any doubts?'

'No. No, I don't. I think, as much as you can be sure, she's headed for a good marriage. I like Mawgan, he's ... well, a stable person, I suppose.'

Oliver's laughter this time was a shout.

'Several tables short of a restaurant, I thought you just implied.'

'Oh, that's just temporary.' Chel thought about this. 'If he was a boat, I suppose you'd say, he'd just limped into harbour after a storm. A few running repairs, a coat of paint … and heading out again, stronger and better than ever.'

'And a new crew,' said Oliver. 'Isn't that where we came in?'

'Yes,' said Chel. 'I suppose it is.'

* * * * *

Nonie's wedding – very Greek – was everything a wedding ought to be, although a small and private occasion. The groom was obviously unable to believe his luck, and Nonie herself looked radiant, the fact that it was raining and grey outside didn't have so much as a slightly dampening effect on Theo's friends and relatives, and very little even on Nonie's, whose brother and sister-in-law, although present, quite obviously weren't sure that they approved of this strange foreign marriage, and so late in life too! Impossible not to think of Matt Sutton, Chel found. She had thought, no doubt fancifully, that she felt a stranger at her side during the ceremony, but Nonie's happiness was unmistakeable and she believed that if he was there at all, it was to wish her well.

'Your father-in-law sent us a card to wish us happiness,' Nonie said to her later, and pulled an expressive face. 'Poor Jerry, he really doesn't like me, bless him. I've always been the cricket on the hearth to him.'

'He needs a good shake-up,' said Chel, without thinking.

'Helen, too,' said Nonie, although whether she was referring to Chel's comment or her own previous one was debatable. She sounded less certain. 'She sent us a present – a beautiful piece of hand-engraved crystal, all the flowers of Cornwall. I …' She blinked. 'Oh God, did getting married make you all sentimental, Chel darling? It's having a terrible effect on me!'

A softening effect, Chel thought, as they flew home. Something had melted in Nonie when she married Theo, some residual piece of ice deep inside her that had first frozen back in the long-ago sixties. She had at last put the ghosts from the past behind her.

'What are you thinking about?' asked Oliver, idly, but she laughed and didn't tell him. Instead, she said,

'I was just thinking, what has that Mawgan Angwin been doing with my pub while I've been gone?'

'*Your* pub, is it now?'

'Poor, unwanted Fish. It's ice-cream immaculate, but it needs hanging baskets, and tubs of flowers – no, even better, big, square, wooden tubs of growing herbs that he can pick for his cooking, and ...' She thought for a moment.

'Karaoke nights?' asked Oliver, his eyes agleam.

'You're joking – I hope. *No*, definitely not karaoke nights. A bit of thought and time spent on it, loads of TLC. I can't think how Edward, whoever he was, could bear to walk away and leave it. It's a film-set pub, and it's old – it must have centuries of history. I wonder if anyone knows any of it?'

'Ask Mawgan.'

'He won't know. He's from St Austell.'

'How parochial of you!'

'No, correction – how parochial of *him*!'

The seat-belt lights flashed, they were approaching Bristol Airport. A few more hours, and they would be home. Chel found that she was looking forward to it with a pleased and personal anticipation that, she realised, she hadn't felt for too long. Three difficult, endless years spent helping Oliver through his bad time, and now her life, not just her time, was her own again. Had she ever wondered how she would fill it? She couldn't believe it now.

'I can't wait to be home,' she said, and even the word *home* sounded unfamiliar in the context of herself and Oliver, and yet as warm and welcoming as a log fire on a cold night. A real change in perspective, she wondered, or just for now, until something different turned up? But she pushed the weasel thought away from her. She had chosen to marry Oliver knowing what he was, and if she feared in her heart that painting in itself would never serve to keep him in one place, well, that was her own secret.

* * * * *

By the time that Chel and Oliver had returned home from Greece, Jerry had realised that he had, to a certain extent, painted himself into a corner over Helen. It wasn't, no, it certainly wasn't, that he didn't want to go away with her for a couple of nights, even if it was not just in separate rooms, but under separate roofs. Everything had to start somewhere. It was how to explain it to Debbie, to Susan, and probably even more, to Oliver. Particularly to Debbie and Oliver, who would be asked to put them up – no, make that particularly to Susan, who would take it as a personal affront – oh God, what on earth had he been thinking about?

When you once start making a fool of yourself, Jerry concluded, the effects can go on for a lifetime. He had sent Nonie and Theo a card on their wedding day, and kidded himself somehow that if Nonie could get married, everything else could fall into place too.

Not so.

Telling Susan would be only a short step towards telling Dot. He winced at the thought of Dot's reaction, but if he didn't tell Susan, then *her* reaction, when she found out as she undoubtedly would the moment she spoke to Debbie … No. Unthinkable. Susan was vulnerable enough already; of all of the three of his children, Jerry had always known, she was the least resilient in spite of her abrasive shell. She was, in fact, in many respects very like her father, the late Henry Worthington. Shrewd, intelligent, and hopelessly soft in the centre. Look at Henry's performance, marrying Dot, over thirty years his junior, because she needed a husband of her own before he married Helen in order to salve her pride, and he was easy game. Jerry had eventually worked this one out. His own mistake, as Nonie Fingall – no, Nonie Theodorakis now, how odd that sounded – had frequently told him, had been in not telling Dot, in no uncertain terms, to stay away from him, that a residual friendship wasn't on the cards. It would have been perfectly possible, men did it every day to obsolete girlfriends. It might not be admirable, but, as Jerry had learned to his unbearable cost, it was wise! Learned too late …

He had to resolve this problem, he had already left it long enough. So far as he could see, he had two choices. He could tell Helen, who wouldn't be very surprised, or even, he sadly suspected, upset, that he had changed his mind after all, or he could face the music and phone Susan. Get it over with. Why it had to be Susan first, he wasn't sure, it would be all the same in the end.

On second thoughts, he wouldn't phone her, that would be a cop-out, and his life already held enough of them. He would go and see her, face to face. He couldn't look on it as taking her into his confidence, under the circumstances, but at least he would be being honest with her. Susan would value that, he hoped.

Although, in the end, he wasn't entirely honest with her.

'I'm driving Helen down to Cornwall at the beginning of next month,' he told her, which was true enough. 'I thought it was only fair to tell you.' Not the best way to put it, he immediately realised. Susan stared at him.

'Why?' Her voice was sharp, her attitude contentious. Well, what had he expected? Jerry suddenly felt that it would be a great mistake to say that he wanted Helen's view on something that, arguably, had nothing to do with her. He said, instead,

'I'm hoping that now, after all this time, it may be possible to reconcile her with Oliver.'

'Why is that your business?' asked Susan, pertinently. 'I would have thought it was between the two of them.'

'Left to the two of them, the present Mexican stand-off will last for ever,' said Jerry, dryly. It was all true, of course. He resisted an impulse to fidget with his feet on the carpet.

'I still don't see why you have to hold her hand,' said Susan, with just the suspicion of a sniff.

Jerry looked at her more closely, suddenly. Susan didn't look her usual organised self, he thought vaguely. There was a ... he could only call it a *fuzziness*, as if her normal sharp edges had blurred. She looked, somehow, as if her clothes were a size too big, although they weren't, as if she had maybe lost weight. Diminished. Did she know, then, about Tom's blonde? Jerry felt a pang of pity, followed immediately by a sick feeling.

Had Helen looked like this once, and he not noticed?

'Susan ...' he said, and stopped, helplessly.

'Oh, you'll do what you want, I have no doubt,' she said, misunderstanding. He gave it up. Daughters were a mother's province, let Dot handle it. It was all she had left herself to handle, after all. He said,

'There's nothing sinister about it, Susan. I shall stay with Chel and Oliver, and Helen will stay at the Fish. Don't look for innuendoes, please.'

Or you might find them ...

Susan shrugged her shoulders.

'I just think you might have more consideration for poor Mummy. What's she going to think, if you go straight back to Helen as soon as you leave her? How's she going to feel?'

'Much as Helen felt, I daresay,' said Jerry, and wished that he hadn't. 'Anyway, it isn't like that,' he added. Susan didn't rise to the bait. She merely said,

'I suppose, what you're saying is that what you do is nothing to do with me any more.'

Jerry couldn't let that pass.

'Susan, you're my daughter. I've taken the trouble to tell you, haven't I?'

'Adopted daughter. It was convenient at the time, when you married Mummy.' She didn't sound as if she cared. She sounded listless, if anything. Jerry became acutely aware that she was very unhappy, and he didn't know what to do, had no idea what to say to her.

'Why don't you come down too?' he asked, on impulse, and wondered immediately afterwards what had possessed him. But he persevered. 'Have a break, get away, see Deb. There must be lots you need to talk about.'

Susan gave him a long, cool look.

'No thank you, Daddy,' she said. 'I wouldn't want to be the unwanted third, thank you.'

Well, it had always been difficult to put one over on Susan. Jerry was about to speak when she went on,

'Certainly not in triplicate.' Something, some great hand, was squeezing her heart out, as if it was a sponge. If Daddy went back to Helen after all this time, Oliver and Debbie would belong to them, but not she. She wanted to cry out to him, painfully, *Nobody wants me, I don't belong anywhere*, but couldn't do it. The prospect was too awful even to start a row over it. There had been enough rows already. She felt as if life was slipping right out of her control and there was nobody she could turn to. She couldn't speak to her mother, whose own separation was so recent. She had too much pride to talk to her friends. Her sister was too full of her own happiness and her own plans, Chel didn't even like her much. She felt horribly alone.

'Well then ...' said Jerry, wishing she would confide in him. He couldn't be sure what she knew, it could be as simple as time-of-the-month blues and/or resentment over Helen. He felt totally helpless. Susan glanced at her watch.

'Daddy, it's been nice to see you, but I have an appointment, I'm going to have to go out in a moment.'

So, that was that. Jerry drove away and Susan, who had no appointment, and who had wanted so much to throw herself into his arms and cry her heart out, went upstairs to the bedroom she nominally shared with Tom, where the *au pair* wouldn't seek her out, and sat on the edge of the bed for a long time, simply staring into space and watching her world crumbling about her.

* * * * *

The inevitable sequel, of course, was an infuriated phone call from Dot.

'Jerry!' she began, without preamble, the moment he picked up the phone. 'What's this Susan's been telling me? You're going away for the weekend with *Helen*? I don't believe it!'

'I expect there are things in the past that Helen didn't believe, too,' said Jerry. He wouldn't say to Dot, as he had to Susan, that there was nothing in it. 'We're separating. What is it to you?'

'Separated isn't divorced,' said Dot, forcefully. 'What will people say? I shall be a laughing stock all over town!'

'Is that all you care about, what people say?'

'But that woman! After all she did, walking out and leaving me to bring up her child just because she thought her silly clay modelling was more important!'

One way of looking at it, certainly. Had it been Dot's way? Genuinely Dot's way? Jerry could never be sure with Dot, and he knew, neither could Nonie. Only Helen had been absolutely certain as to her ultimate motives. On the other hand, Helen's *silly clay modelling* had, in Jerry's estimate, probably made her a millionaire by this time, so it had been important. More important, certainly than he had ever realised but not, he would dispute with Dot, more important to her than Oliver.

That had been his own fault.

His hesitation had given Dot time to realign her guns.

'Susan is terribly upset! She thinks you're going to abandon her along with me and make a new family with Helen and those other two.' This wasn't exactly what Susan had said, but it served for Dot to make Jerry feel a bastard. Jerry, in Dot's book, *was* a bastard, in fact, viewpoint is everything.

'One of *those other two* is your own daughter,' said Jerry. Dot's behaviour over Debbie had been the final straw of a huge and growing pile, his continuing anger showed in his voice.

'Not while she continues in her determination to marry that criminal,' said Dot.

'He's not a *criminal* – ' Jerry began, but Dot interrupted him.

'*Criminal: one who commits a crime.* Consult your dictionary, Jerry. I'm sure you have one in your office among all your law books.'

'He's a decent man, Dot,' he said, knowing it to be useless.

'Oh yes, very decent! A working class oaf, who can't control his temper! I'm surprised *you* haven't sent him packing! Deborah is your daughter, even if she is no longer mine. Have you thought that he is almost certainly after her money?'

Jerry thought about the beautiful old building of the Fish, sprawling snow-white and prosperous along the causeway, and the prices of the wonderful dishes in the adjoining restaurant, that was always full to overflowing. He didn't think Mawgan had much stake in Deb's trust fund.

'I don't think so. He owns two businesses.'

'Yes, a public house and a café! I've been told.' Scorn you could cut with a knife.

Really? If she had been told, she certainly couldn't have listened. Jerry wondered if it was any use trying to explain, and decided that it wasn't. They seemed to have come a long way, very quickly, from Helen. Jerry said,

'You're quite wrong, Dorothy, about just about everything. You should take the trouble to meet him before you form your opinions.'

'Thank you. His antecedents, his record, and his choice of – I won't say *profession*. Job, then – all tell me everything that I need to know about him. Susan says he's very charming and persuasive, easy to see then how Deborah has lost her head.'

'Well, just be careful how you speak about him among your friends,' said Jerry.

'Threats now, Jerry?'

'A friendly warning. And as to Helen – '

'Oh *stuff* Helen!' cried Dot, and slammed the phone down.

If it had been anyone but Dot, Jerry would have sworn she was crying, but no – Dot was too sure that she was in the right to have anything to cry over.

Or was she?

Payback time all round, it would appear.

* * * * *

When it came to speaking to Oliver, only honesty served. There was no way, Jerry decided, that he was really going to try to effect a reconciliation between Oliver and Helen, that would happen, or it wouldn't.

'I'm not at ease in my mind,' he confessed. 'I thought that your mother, as an outsider … well, she might have a different slant. I feel too close to the problem.'

'This is Mawgan, we're talking about?' Oliver asked. 'I think he's only a problem to himself, you know, but I can see your point of view. Although I don't see how Helen will make it any better.'

'Helen was always very wise,' said Jerry.

'You mean, she saw through the Dreaded Dot?' asked Oliver, derisively. 'Much good did it do her!'

There was a shift in attitude there, if Jerry could only put his finger on it. He let it go.

'She saw through all the prejudice over Chel,' he said, which silenced Oliver for a moment, but only for a moment. Oliver said,

'So how are you going to explain it to Deb? She won't thank you for calling her choice in question – she loves him. He loves her. However ill-matched they seem to you and me, they work as a team. It sounds to me as if you're maybe sailing a bit close to the wind.'

Jerry couldn't believe that he hadn't thought of this. His mind went into overdrive, there had to be a third excuse, surely.

Luckily, there was.

'I understand that Nonie and Theo will be in England by the time we come. It's high time that the bodies were decently buried. I thought perhaps you and Chel could give a dinner party and we could all be civilised.'

'*Ouch*!' said Oliver, and was about to add that he thought that was a really bad idea, when he reconsidered. An awful lot of water had gone under the bridge, surely it had scoured out the channel by now. Nonie, he knew, regretted the loss of her friendship with Helen all those years ago, although he had no idea how Helen might feel. It sounded like the dinner party from hell on the surface, but was it?

Jerry, who had spoken off the top of his head, winced in sympathy. He must be losing his grip to suggest such a risky plan. To his surprise, Oliver said, after a pause,

'Were you planning to include Debbie and Mawgan in this beanfeast?'

'At a weekend?'

'Come on Dad, think it out!' Oliver sounded, for a second, almost like the normal, ordinary son he had always wished he had, which is to say, slightly pitying for the frailties of the older generation, and genuinely affectionate. 'If you want Helen to suss Mawgan out for you, the weekend is the very last time.

Quite simply, she'll hardly see him – and when she does, he'll either be manning the bar on Sunday evening, or very likely, fast asleep in front of the telly! Even if he's awake, if you ask me, she's on a hiding to nothing, so don't make the job impossible. On a Monday, he'll at least stop still long enough for her to say hullo – and their presence might help things along a bit.'

'You don't blame me, then – for wondering?'

Oliver paused for so long that Jerry thought he wasn't going to answer, but finally he said,

'No. I don't see how I can. But on the other hand, I don't think you need, either. Is that OK?'

'So you think he's genuine?'

'Genuine what?' asked Oliver, with a laugh in his voice. 'Look, we got off to a rather shaky start, Mawgan and I, and yes, it was for a similar reason to yours, but when we sorted that one out, we saw each other differently. I think, if you want to know, that he's a diamond – maybe a rough one, but a diamond for all that. But that's only my opinion. Chel, if it matters, thinks he's on the beginnings of a roll, but that's another story. Does any of that make you feel better?'

Did it? Jerry didn't know. He said goodbye to his son and rang Debbie, with whom he had to be highly diplomatic, having said one thing to Susan and two different ones to Oliver. Lying, he concluded, was a job for experts. Then, check that his engagements for the whole of Monday, and Tuesday morning could be re-scheduled or allocated elsewhere, and back to Helen to fix a definite date without giving her the sub-plot. Nonie and Theo, he thought thankfully, were best left to Chel and Oliver. He wondered what on earth he had been thinking about to get himself into such deep and troubled waters, and if he had done anything that could turn out to be illegal, such as incitement to violence, or breach of the peace.

The bottom line was Helen. If lying himself green in the face to his children was the only way to see her, then green was the colour he would choose to be.

* * * * *

The last person to be informed of the treat in store was Chel, whom in a very important way, it most concerned. She looked at Oliver with the expression worn by working wives the world over when faced with a dinner-party for eight out of the blue, on a working day.

'Are you barking mad? I'll be at the Fish until early afternoon, at *least*!'

'Well? Look Chel, Dad asked. How could I say no?'

'You just place the tongue against the teeth and round the lips into a rosebud shape,' said Chel, demonstrating. '*Nnnno*, like that. God, Oliver, do you have to behave so like a – a *husband*?'

'Deb'll help. You managed it before.'

'With Susan, who's used to entertaining large numbers – Deb's about as much use as a sick headache! You're not, I hope, suggesting that we serve Cockie Van to everyone?'

'Can't you do the preparation on Sunday afternoon?'

'Oh God!' said Chel, to the ceiling. 'What have I done to deserve this?'

She got more sympathy the following day, when she told Debbie, despairingly, over a quick cup of coffee in the office. Sympathy, however, is one thing.

'Poor you!' said Debbie.

'Gee, thanks!'

Debbie sighed.

'I'll peel the vegetables. I had a lot of practice at that, back in the summer.'

'Peeling vegetables is nothing. Come to that, I can go to Tesco or somewhere and get them ready prepared. But what am I going to cook? I've already done my party piece, and anyway, I'm no good at the sweets. My mousses always separate.'

'Then serve something simple. Apple pie and Cornish cream.'

128

'I think,' said Chel, quailing, 'that this guest list calls for a little more than apple pie and cream. It's a real killer, your dad must be out of his tiny mind!'

'Then how about some rather good cheese?' asked Debbie.

'As a main course, are you suggesting? And I suppose there'll have to be a starter, and I can't get away with soup out of a carton a second time. I can't do this off the top of my head, Deb, and the swine *knows* it!'

'Then do it off the top of somebody else's head, whatever it is,' suggested Mawgan, coming through the office door right on cue. 'What's going on, children? We can hear you in the kitchen!'

Debbie burst into a peal of laughter.

'Chel's getting hysterical. She just invited us to dinner – '

'No, *Oliver*'s just invited you to dinner!'

'So? What's the problem?'

'The problem,' said Chel, between her teeth, 'is the guest list from hell, and the little matter of, without Susan to help me, four people, six when the wind's behind me, is about my limit. This is *eight*! And on a working day, too!'

Mawgan, to whom dinner for eight, she thought crossly, was probably just the equivalent of most people's boiled eggs and marmite soldiers for the kids, looked amused.

'Would a day off help any?' he asked.

'To be honest,' said Chel, 'a day off would probably just give me that much more time to screw up. I'm an OK cook, when it's just plain stuff for the family, but this is … is just a disaster in the making. Roast chicken and Paxo simply isn't going to do.'

'Dad's coming down for a couple of days, and bringing his ex-wife – that's Oliver's mother,' Debbie explained.

'Dodgy.'

'That's only the beginning! You just wait – he wants Chel to invite Nonie and Theo, and Nonie and Helen have hardly spoken for more than twenty years! You and I,' she added kindly, 'are to go along to create a diversion.'

'And that's before you even start on Oliver's relationship with Helen,' said Chel. 'Or Jerry's to Nonie, come to that.'

'Come home Susan, all is forgiven?' asked Mawgan, with a rather scandalised grin. 'I know you said your family was different Deb, but surely this is going a bit far?'

'Yes, it is, and poor Chel's got landed.'

'Theo owns a *taverna*!' said Chel, on a wail, 'and that's before we even *start* on you!' This was too much for Mawgan. He burst out laughing.

'It's all right for you!' said Debbie, punching him on the arm, not gently. He caught her hand and held it.

'All right, joke over. When is this nightmare function to take place?'

'Monday week!' said Chel. 'I'm going to leave the country, I warn you!'

'No, don't do that. Just call in the Fish outside catering service,' said Mawgan.

'The what?' Chel stared at him.

'Me. I'll do it for you.'

Chel and Debbie were both staring at him now.

'But it's your day off,' Chel objected.

'Chel, dinner for eight *is* a day off. Debbie can help if she wants – only if she wants.'

'My usual menial position at the sink, no doubt,' said Debbie, and made a face. Chel stared at him.

'Have I got this right? *Did* you just say you'd cook the dinner for me?'

'The least I can do, I would have thought, considering what you're doing for me. Just tell me what you want.'

'I don't *know* what I want,' said Chel, helplessly, and Debbie grinned.

'How about if *you* tell *her*?' she suggested.

'Fine. Italian suit you?'

'What?'

'I do a mean Italian, but not here in Cornwall. Make a nice change.'

'He ran a restaurant in Italy,' Debbie put in.

'No, I was in charge of the kitchen, be accurate.'

'Don't split hairs! Chel? *Chel*?' She waved her hand in front of Chel's face. 'Wake up!'

Chel had just been imagining a master chef working culinary magic in her kitchen for her nightmare dinner party. She said, weakly, as if it mattered,

'We've got a Rayburn.'

'No problem. A Rayburn is good,' said Mawgan, kindly.

'She's in shock, poor girl,' said Debbie. She got to her feet and gathered up the coffee cups. 'Right, I'm off to see what's happening up the road. I've been listening to the crash and rattle of falling masonry and the merry shouts of your father's bully boys all morning, it's time to check it out.Have you got ten minutes to spare to come with me, my darling?'

'Yeah, why not. I could do with some air.' Mawgan went with her to the door, turning back to look at Chel, trying to pull herself together at the desk. 'Cheer up, Chel. It'll be all right on the night!'

But would it? Chel asked herself, when they had gone, but clairvoyance never seemed to be there when she really wanted it.

She could only trust that he was right.

VI

Sitting in his car beside Jerry, driving down to Cornwall, was the oddest feeling she had experienced in a long while, Helen decided. She had, as yet, no idea of the delights in store for her when she got there, but Jerry himself was enough to be going on with. It was like being caught in some bizarre time-slip, and she wasn't certain if the feeling was entirely pleasant.

This was something that she had long-ago promised herself that she would never do.

Once bitten, twice shy. She couldn't trust him, that she knew. Dot, who she thought possibly *didn't* know, couldn't trust him either, although in this instance, she couldn't find it in her heart to blame him. Helen had friends and contacts in Embridge, she hadn't broken them all when her marriage failed, although it had been tempting. She knew at least some of the things that Jerry had got up to over the years, just as she thought he probably knew some of the things that she had done. The differences were twofold. Jerry was married, even if it was only to Dot. She herself had been divorced, and therefore free to do what she liked.

It wasn't helped by the recollection that the last time she had driven down to Cornwall had been to see Nonie, while she herself had still been married to Jerry, and only a matter of a few weeks before her world shattered to fragments. She remembered, too, catching the sleeper from London, all in a rush, on that terrible night when they had heard of Matt Sutton's death, heavily pregnant with Oliver and only thinking of one thing, her dear friend's pain. She and Nonie had been so close, how had it all happened? Until they had met, awkwardly, at Oliver's private view, they hadn't seen each other for a quarter of a century. The reason had seemed overwhelming at the time: Nonie and Jerry had kept from her the fact that her old and once dear boyfriend, Daniel Peachey, had phoned her on her wedding day before committing suicide. At this remove it seemed perfectly understandable on their part, even if she still wished they had been honest with her that was only her own view. The years had shown her that only Dot's involvement had ever made it anything else. At the time, Dot had seemed to poison everything, but how much had that been her own fault?

Damn age! Damn wisdom! Why weren't they there when you were young, and really needed them?

Jerry, no thought-reader even on a good day, picked this ill-chosen moment to say,

'Oh, by the way – I forgot to tell you. Nonie and Theo are in England, Chel invited them for tomorrow night, too.'

A statement that would very much have surprised Chel. It surprised Helen, too – if *surprised* was the correct word.

'*What did you say?*'

'I said …' Jerry found that he hadn't the courage to repeat it. 'You heard,' he said, instead.

'I was hoping I hadn't. Jerry, is this your doing? For I'm damn sure Chel wouldn't do anything so – so *disastrous*!'

'It won't be disastrous,' said Jerry. 'Don't you think it's time you two buried the hatchet?'

'We have buried it. That doesn't mean we want to dance on its grave. Anyway …'

'Anyway, what?' asked Jerry, when she had paused for too long.

'Anyway, I'm jealous of Nonie, if you really want to know. I … oh, never mind!' She sat for a moment contemplating the awfulness of meeting Nonie at a family dinner party, of all things, and after a minute, Jerry said,

'Why on earth should you be jealous of Nonie?'

'Because it's she, not me, who gave Oliver back his heritage,' said Helen. 'Is that clear enough for you?'

It was Jerry's turn to pause. Helen's relationship with their son had been strained to breaking point for years, and he now saw that Nonie had, yes, usurped the position. Even so, he couldn't let it pass.

'Helen, keep a sense of proportion here. Even had things been different, it would never have been you. Oliver is a painter, not a sculptor. He never showed the smallest wish to follow in your footsteps.'

'Is that supposed to make me feel better?'

'You chose her as his godmother.'

'You wanted Dot,' Helen reminded him.

'It seems to me,' said Jerry, slowly, 'that if you aren't careful, you're going to let Dot louse up your entire life.'

'She already has, wouldn't you agree?'

'You don't look very dead, to me,' said Jerry.

Helen sat in mortified silence for a while. When several more miles had passed under the wheels, she said,

'It isn't possible to go back, Jerry. What's done, is done.'

'I think I told you once before, *back* isn't a place I plan to go.'

'I should ask you to put me off in the next town with a railway station,' said Helen.

'But you won't.'

It was an added mortification to have to admit, only to herself of course, that he was right. Helen, who had been sustained throughout the last quarter of a century by a burning resentment against Dot, who had taken her husband and wrecked her personal life, finding herself now sitting beside that same ex-husband was left without a word to say. She had no idea what it was she wanted, if anything at all, from Jerry, but looking back over her life she saw it as two distinct bands, white and then black. With the removal of Dot, would it – could it, even – turn back to white? She didn't think so, but a weasel thought that it would be nice if it could drifted into her head and out again. Even just a quiet shade of grey would be good … but no. There was too much baggage to carry forward into any renewed life with Jerry.

And then there was Nonie.

Dot had this inexorable way of organising life to her own specifications. Helen had married Jerry, Helen had to go. Nonie criticised the new arrangement, Nonie had to go. And last of all, Deb threatened her mother's status, so Deb had to go, and surely that last was pathological behaviour even if the rest was not. Just because one woman wanted everything her own way.

Did Dot have any idea at all just what she was doing? What she had done?

To be completely fair, Helen found herself thinking, Dot wasn't wholly to blame for the rift between herself and Nonie, that had been almost entirely her own work. Their friendship had been little more than an incidental casualty in the path of Dot's ambition. Dot got her own way, that was the constant. Damn anyone else.

'Jerry,' she said, suddenly uncomfortable.

'What?'

'About Deb ...'

'Yes? What about Deb?'

'If Dot – '

'Ah, no, Helen. Let's give Dot a rest, shall we?'

'I don't think, even now, you've got the measure of her,' said Helen. 'Just listen, will you? If Dot finally decides that Deb isn't going to marry this Mawgan of hers, looking at her past track record, what do you give for their chances?'

'Deb seems to be pretty determined,' said Jerry. 'I don't think you need to worry about that.' Although, as to whether this was good or bad, the jury was still out.

'I wasn't thinking of Deb,' said Helen. 'If Dot wants Deb crawling home with her tail between her legs, she won't alienate her irretrievably, don't think it. But how about Mawgan?'

'He looks like a stayer to me.' Sometimes he almost thought this to be a pity, but he suppressed the recollection hurriedly.

'If she decides he has to go, and *then* he stays, he'll be the first.'

'Nonsense. Chel stayed.'

'No, Chel didn't stay. She and Oliver both ran away, they didn't face it out. And it wasn't so important to Dot, either. She never cared about Oliver. Getting them out of the way like that was almost a victory.'

Jerry couldn't deny it, but he wasn't going to admit that to Helen.

'I wouldn't give much for the chances of anyone who tried to eliminate Mawgan Angwin. You're being silly, Helen.'

'I hope so.'

Another few miles passed in silence, while they both thought about what Helen had just said. Jerry found himself wondering, against his will, if this was root, branch and flower of his own problems with Mawgan. Not that he would hurt his daughter, but that she would get hurt through him. He was everything that Dot held in dislike, tailor-made, you could say, to antagonise her. If ever she found a way to do it, she would see him off without a second thought. But was there a way?

Jerry found himself hoping that, if there was, Dot would never hit on it. He might not be overjoyed at the prospect of the marriage, but only Debbie had the right to call time on the event.

No, Helen was just trying to wind him up. She always did. She always had.

All the same, the difference between being embroiled, however passively, in Dot's schemes yourself, and sitting on the outside with a ringside seat, made a prickle run up the back of his neck.

Helen hadn't intended to wind him up, not this time. It was simply a thought that had come into her head, born of bitter experience, and she wished that she hadn't had it. She would be all the more interested now to see this man who had dared to woo and win Dot's beloved daughter – Dot's most beloved daughter, because she was also Jerry's. The prospect almost made her forget the other pitfalls that these next two days would hold.

The meeting wasn't to be immediate. Chel had suggested that, since Sunday was Mawgan's duty night in the bar, Jerry should bring Helen straight to the creek and she would feed them both. They could all, then, go down to the Fish after they had eaten, take Helen's luggage up to her room, and maybe have a drink together. It happened therefore that the first time Helen set eyes on Dot's current *bête noir*, he was pulling pints behind the bar.

'So which is he?' she asked, as they sat down at a table, beside the log fire that burned hospitably in the old fireplace all winter long. 'The slim, handsome gingery one, or the dark blokey one with the angry eyebrows?'

'The gingery one is Sunday Sam,' said Debbie, who had come to join them. 'He's a teacher, moonlighting. His girlfriend walked out.'

'Is that cause, or effect?' Helen asked, while thinking that she was glad to hear it. Sunday Sam was certainly good to look at, but he would be roadkill in no time if he came anywhere within spitting distance of Dot. The other man, now, he was different. Surprising, in the context of Debbie, but different anyway. And then he looked across, caught Debbie's eye and smiled, and Helen was no longer surprised. All the same, she wasn't sure yet where her money would be if it came to a shoot-out – just that it would probably take a little longer, and perhaps be a little messier.

Jerry and Oliver collected orders and moved away to the bar to get the drinks, and Helen stretched a cold hand towards the blaze on the hearth. The cold, she thought, went deeper than the frosty November night. Finding herself under Oliver's roof had been a novel experience, and not one that she had found entirely happy. Face to face like this, there was an uncharted sea of awkwardness between them that wasn't apparent when they simply spoke on the telephone or met casually on neutral ground. There was an intimacy to being in her son's house that she hadn't expected. Jerry and Chel had needed to work too hard to keep the conversation afloat.

Things like this wouldn't do. Jerry was right, it was conceding points to Dot. She got no further than this in her thoughts, when Chel said, with interest

'Why did you say *angry* eyebrows?'

Helen had spoken off the top of her head. She took a second look to see why she had said what she did.

'Very black and heavily defined,' she said, but it was more a description than an explanation. She had just thought, in that first second before he saw them, that he looked angry, but it had only been an impression. He was serving a customer at the far end of the bar now, talking pleasantly enough at this distance, but without that flash of warmth that he had directed to Debbie, and Sunday Sam was seeing to Jerry and Oliver.

'Dear of him, he's no oil painting,' said Debbie, affectionately. 'Particularly since he got that scar. Susan called him a hooligan.'

Helen thought, fleetingly, that she saw Susan's point for once, she wouldn't like to get on the wrong side of him, he looked like a man who might know how to play rough. Dot had never come up against a real heavyweight. The trouble with her immediate circle was that they were all too well brought-up, they none of them knew how to wallop her into the ground. This Angwin, rather unfortunately, had already proved that walloping people into the ground was something he was good at, but the discovery could have had an inhibiting effect.

If only he would do it to Dot! If only she would give him the opportunity!

Although, come to think about it, that would hardly be of help to Deb. Rather the reverse, in fact.

At this point in her thinking, Mawgan finished serving his customers and moved along the bar to speak to Jerry and Oliver, their heads close together. They laughed, as if he had told them some joke, and Sunday Sam, heading for the till with the money, had a grin on his face. They came back to the fire still smiling, and Oliver, seemingly casual, took the seat beside Helen. She moved to make room for him, conscious of the warmth that radiated from his nearness, an unexpected lump in her throat. She shouldn't have come, she felt like a trespasser. To cover the feeling, she turned her attention to Jerry.

'So, are you going to share the joke?'

Jerry grinned. He looked about Oliver's age when he did so, and her heart clenched.

'Certainly not. It was extremely sexist, and we're outnumbered here. How's it all going, Deb? Are you winning?'

'We've cleared the site,' said Debbie. 'I expect you saw that – I think it helps. Without the remains of the house there to remind them, maybe the planners will listen to us. Our architect seems to think so, anyway. But we're obviously going to have to start the season giving our evening talks in the snug, here, there's no way we can have everything done, not now.'

'That's fine, isn't it? Nobody objects?'

'I've talked to the manager about it,' said Debbie, and grinned across at Chel. 'When it gets warmer, and things get busier here, we can use the boathouse if we have to. So, no problem.'

'Isn't that called, keeping it in the family?' asked Helen, amused.

'You'd be amazed at what we keep in the family these days,' Chel told her. 'Has Oliver told you about the mural? Or come to that, the guttering. Or tomorrow's dinner, if you get right down to it.'

'You're not letting Deb cook it!' said Jerry, in mock revulsion. 'That's carrying family feeling too far!'

'Wait and see,' said Chel.

It was the weirdest thing, Helen concluded, watching them all. Her casual remark about keeping it in the family had touched a chord that was yet another unexpected thing among so many of this strange evening. Because it was true, they were behaving like a family. Like Nonie before her, she speculated that it was due to the subtraction of Dot's influence, but surely it was more than that. Chel, she decided, was one factor. She had never been welcomed in the family circle, indeed, Helen knew, Oliver himself had helped to keep her apart from them all, but here, everything seemed to have changed, and her probably unconscious influence was felt. Chel very possibly couldn't even spell the word *dysfunctional*.

The bar wasn't busy tonight, and another person who almost certainly couldn't spell *dysfunctional*, or even define it, had left the bar to the care of Sunday Sam and the girl in the public bar adjoining, and was heading towards them with the amiable intention of putting another log on the fire. Debbie reached out as he approached.

'Mawgan, come and say hullo to Helen.'

'Hullo, Helen,' said Mawgan, and held out a welcoming hand. Helen took it, and received the full blast of a friendly grin. A real charmer, this Angwin, and no mistake about it.

'Hullo, Mawgan,' she said. 'Oh – and congratulations. You don't need me to tell you that you've picked yourself a winner, I don't suppose.'

'Not sure that Deb has,' said Mawgan, with a wry smile. 'Just look at us – Beauty and the Beast!'

'Ah, but you have a lovely nature,' said Debbie, sententiously, and he laughed, turning away to pick up a log from the hearthside and wedge it onto the glowing fire.

Helen, watching him, began to revise her too-hurriedly-formed opinion, you'd have thought she'd been listening to Dot! Probably, even if he couldn't spell *dysfunctional*, he could define it, and in close up, he wasn't so much angry as tired, with dark shadows under watchful eyes, golden-hazel with thick, straight black lashes. Not a tall man, he was a good three or four inches under Oliver's six feet, but powerfully built with dark, close-cropped hair that was already on borrowed time, his rather formal working attire of white shirt, tie and dark trousers looked like fancy dress on him. Definitive bloke, yes, but with loads of too professional charm and probably, unexpected depths. She thought that once maybe, say around three years ago, the charm had probably been less calculated, and the reflection saddened her. But if Dot was thinking along the lines of *uneducated, working class oaf*, she might be in for a shock, and the idea was heartwarming. This was one very attractive man, and far from being a fool, whatever his education.

'Have you got a minute to stay and talk to us?' asked Debbie. 'It's not exactly packed out tonight.'

'Five minutes, then.' Mawgan perched on the arm of her chair and put his arm around her, and the way she cuddled in towards him for some reason made Helen feel fiercely protective of them both. Debbie wasn't her daughter, the daughter she might have had had never been conceived thanks to Debbie's mother, but she felt for a second there as possessive as if she had been.

Beside her, the son that she had conceived, borne, and then lost to circumstances, stirred, and spoke for the first time since he had sat down.

'Have a swift one with us, then. I'll get it, you stop there –' He was already on his feet, moving away to the bar. Helen watched him go. She hadn't seen Oliver more than once since the incident that had left him disabled, and at the private view there had been so much going on that she hadn't taken in more than the fact that he was on his feet and behaving like anyone else. Now, watching him crossing the floor, she realised that he loped more than walked properly, moving from the hips rather than from the knees, and felt tears sting behind her eyes. Oliver had been so beautiful, so physically perfect. She looked hurriedly down at her hands. This visit was so full of the most exquisite pain, she must have been out of her mind to agree to come.

Never go back. Going back was impossible anyway. But, like Debbie and her sailing school, was it possible to rebuild? On a different plan, maybe?

Sadly, Helen concluded, it probably wasn't, but for the first time she openly admitted to herself that she wished it was. They could be mistaken for a real family, sitting here – herself and Jerry, Oliver and Chel, Debbie and Mawgan. Except that, thanks to Dot, they had no shared history.

Jerry had asked another question about the proposed sailing school, which allowed Helen to pull herself together before Oliver returned and resumed his seat beside her. Debbie and Chel had begun a discussion that was nearer to an argument about bar meals, which dovetailed naturally into an enquiry about Mawgan's restaurant and its proposed redecoration, and Helen heard, for the first time, about the mural, as all four of … well, the children, she supposed, wryly, told her about it together. She caught an expression on Jerry's face that was almost laughable, any minute now the four of them would sit down and start playing Monopoly – or perhaps not quite that, but they were behaving in such an ordinary way that it was breathtaking. Or heartbreaking. Or something.

'I haven't shown you my studio yet,' said Oliver, turning to her unexpectedly in the middle of it all. 'You're coming over after breakfast, aren't you? I'll show you then, and the sketches I've done for the mural too. You can tell me what you think.'

Not that he would take a blind bit of notice of anything she said, Helen knew, but even so it was heartwarming to hear. She blinked hard, and hoped nobody noticed. This was either nightmare or a miracle, she wasn't sure which.

'Of course,' Mawgan was saying, 'we need to be sure where the beams are before we decide exactly what's going on the wall – but the sketches are good. Not that I know anything about it.'

'You!' said Debbie, punching his thigh with a small, hard fist. 'You're a complete moron, don't try and kid Helen, we all know!'

Mawgan grinned at her, unoffended, and as a group of people came in through the outside door, got up to go.

'Me, I'm only a simple Cornish boy,' he said.

And if you believed that, you would believe anything.

Lying alone in her comfortable bedroom above the restaurant later on, Helen wasn't sure if she wanted to think or to switch off completely, except that switching off didn't seem to be an option. There had been so many threads, this evening, that had teased loose from the tight pattern that Dot had woven for everyone over the years that it was difficult to know where to begin. What was all too apparent was that there were four people, herself, Jerry, Oliver and Debbie, who had each taken their own route to survival and pulled apart from each other so that they lived almost entirely separate lives by this time, and who were now being thrown together – temporarily or permanently, Helen had a feeling that might be for themselves to make a specific choice. Of those four, she herself had found it too easy to splinter off from the main group, since she had been pushed out and thereafter largely ignored. Jerry, she now saw, had tried to do his best with the situation that he had, himself, helped to create 'for the sake of the children' – that awful phrase that caused so much unhappiness for so many people. Had he been horrified by what he had allowed to happen? Helen didn't know, couldn't begin to guess. Back in the sixties, men were still a superior species, or had been brought up to think that they were; no doubt he had thought he knew best. Finding that he hadn't after all must have come as a considerable shock.

If he had ever accepted it.

Oliver had rebelled from the start, and gone on doing so – would be doing so now, Helen had no doubt, if it hadn't been for that horrific incident three years ago. Effectively, now, he and Chel had opted out. They had their own life, their own friends, had even found a completely different set of close relatives, and things were happening around them as they always had. The mould into which Oliver had been cast, or maybe forced, was set like concrete now, he would never be a son, not to her, not to Jerry. But tonight, she had wondered, might he become a friend?

Debbie's situation was more ambiguous. Dot was her mother, up until now, although she had obviously been a witness to the family's internal strife, she was so much the youngest that it couldn't have directly involved her. All of them, Dot, Jerry, Oliver and Susan would have to an extent conspired to protect her. When she was grown, she had flown the nest and gone to London to seek her fortune, and until she came to St Erbyn, had stayed there. There was nothing in that, not in itself, to appear unusual, lots of girls did the same. So that Debbie's attitude to Dot wasn't predictable. That Dot's rejection had hurt her bitterly was obvious, but she had compensations, considerable compensations. She had the prospect of running her own business, and above all, she had Mawgan.

As Oliver had Chel.

It was those two who were making the difference, Helen was aware without being able to work out exactly why. Maybe it was because they were stable, where the other two were volatile.

If they were volatile – and they were – the common factor between them was Jerry. Oliver undoubtedly got it from her as well, but she couldn't claim responsibility for Deb. Jerry's own father, she had pointed out herself, had done exactly as Oliver had and broken away from his family – had run off, indeed, and never got in touch again, and until Oliver and Chel turned up by chance on the family's doorstep, nobody back in Cornwall had known if he was alive or dead.

She had never, Helen suddenly realised, known Jerry without the influence of Dot in the background. The only time that she had ever known him to kick over the traces was when he had ditched Dot for herself – however he chose to wrap it up, that was what he had done. One impulse in his whole life, and in the end, Dot had got him back and he had settled into stodgy middle-age.

'For the sake of the children …'

But the children were grown and gone. Oliver – and Chel – had run away, Deb had been disowned, for heaven's sake! They were re-grouping, remarkably they were making like a real family. What would Jerry do now?

I don't want to know. I don't want to be hurt again. I don't want to spend my whole life, however much there is left, wondering when Dot will shoot me down again. There's no going back, and I don't want to go forward. I should never have come here.

But she had come, and in coming, she had opened a door.

If she was invited, would she walk through it?

No!

* * * * *

Jerry walked down to the Fish to collect Helen in the morning. It was a fine, clear, cold day and perfect for walking, and he felt that he needed to clear his thoughts. Like Helen, he had found himself with a lot to think about last night, and in his case not for the first time. It was impossible to overlook the fact that there was something different about his children in this environment. For the only time that he could ever remember, first all three of them, and now just the two, were interacting like normal siblings, and it couldn't be dismissed by saying that they were grown up now. They had been grown up for a long time, all three of them. The truth of the matter was that they were simply being themselves, and nobody was coercing them and pulling the strings.

Blame is a very heavy thing to shoulder. Jerry felt the weight of it, bowing him down. He would have liked not even to have to think about Helen, but there she was, sitting outside on the forecourt in the sunshine, waiting for him.

He had brought her here himself, into this shifting quicksand of re-aligning relationships. How far would that re-alignment go, and did he even dare to think?

'Hi!' he called cheerfully, as he stepped off the causeway and walked to join her. 'Did you sleep well? Where are the children?'

'Like a top,' Helen lied. 'The children, as you call them, have gone tearing off in a car on a foraging expedition. I believe they've been elected in charge of tonight's dinner, which sounds promising to me. Chel's in the office, if you wanted her.'

'I've seen Chel already, thank you.' Jerry sat down beside her, not too close, and felt sweat break out on his forehead as if he was a lovelorn teenager, or possibly a man walking naked into a cage with a hungry lioness. 'Warm in the sun, isn't it?' He mopped the sweat away with his handkerchief. Helen gave him a cynical look, like a woman who wasn't deceived, but all she said was,

'You need to spend more time at the gym, if walking downhill on a November morning brings you out in a sweat.'

'Ha!' said Jerry, meaninglessly, and it would be impolite to say that Helen sniggered. She had always had a strange effect on his metabolism, he recalled. These days, she also affected his blood pressure, perhaps she was right and he did need to make changes in his lifestyle. He stole a glance at her lovely profile and thought of one change that he would like to make above all others. He changed the subject. 'So, what do you think?'

'Think?' asked Helen, whose mind had been miles away.

'About Debbie's Mawgan.'

'Goodness!' said Helen. 'I hardly met him. He can handle a beer engine, but is that a recommendation?'

'A man should be good at his job,' said Jerry.

'It isn't his job, apparently. It's Chel's.'

146

'You must have reached some conclusion,' Jerry pressed. 'Should I forbid the banns, for instance, do you think?'

This time, Helen laughed outright.

'I wouldn't bother. It looks to me a bit late for that, since they're already living together.'

'They seem to do that these days,' said Jerry, regretfully.

'You poor old thing! Shall I fetch your wheelchair?'

'If you don't desist, *I'll* fetch *you* a clip round the ear!'

'Oooh, violence!' She took pity on him then. 'First impressions. He's very, very attractive. Bright – sharp, even. Streetwise, cosmopolitan, and out of his depth in something that isn't, strangely, your family. On the evidence available, it's more probably his own. Not quite as straightforward as he would have you believe. Will that do to be going on with? Any help?'

'Shall we say, it doesn't add anything to the sum of my present knowledge.' Jerry sighed. 'He's also seriously depressed, which you seem to have missed, Sherlock, but no prizes for guessing why.'

'Yes, that figures. It all figures. Why are you worrying about it so much? To a very large extent, what you see with that one is probably what you get. I liked him, I imagine most people will.'

Jerry pulled a rueful face.

'My daughter Deborah is the apple of my eye, the core of my probably foolish heart. Fathers are like that with their girls, so I'm told.'

'And mothers with their boys,' said Helen, more tartly than she had intended, and bit her lip, hard. Jerry said nothing. After a while, she went on. 'Perhaps you'd find it easier if you looked around him, rather than straight at him. You can't put people under a microscope. You won't ever find them perfect.'

'What do you mean?'

'I mean, the four of them are a group. They interact with each other. How people affect other people is a very important part of who they are, I would have thought a solicitor needed to know that. And some of what I saw last night – even very briefly – was very interesting indeed.'

'I know what you mean,' said Jerry, slowly. 'They're different, aren't they – Debbie and Oliver? Different with each other, different to me. It was the same when Susan was here.'

'Now that *does* surprise me,' said Helen, thinking about it. 'Well, well ...'

'Shall we start walking up the road?' asked Jerry, getting to his feet.

They walked in silence for a while, each of them busy with their own thoughts, then Helen said,

'Debbie and Mawgan are obviously very much in love. I don't think you can argue with that, Jerry. They can't take their eyes off each other, and as soon as they're close, they touch each other, they don't even know they're doing it. They can't believe it's happening to them, they're not just on Cloud Nine, they're up there on Cloud Eleven or Twelve. And he isn't going to swallow her up, he's too busy himself for that. But he has time to be as interested in her business venture as she is, he's part of it. That is both valuable, and amazingly rare.'

'I tried to be like that with you.' said Jerry, defensively.

'Yes, and we both know when you stopped,' Helen retorted, and was momentarily silent. 'But we're not talking about us. Look further. Look at Chel.'

'Chel?'

'Chel has always stood one step behind Oliver. Put herself second, allowed him to be the dominant one. It suited them both, *then*. But being creative is a solitary occupation, it isn't shareable. It's not like sailing, where there's space to move up and make room for someone else. Life with an artist isn't a flotilla in Greece. You know that. We're selfish, we don't mean to be, it just goes with the territory. I was afraid for

Chel, as a matter of fact, I thought she might turn into one of these women who allow the children they can't have to fill their whole horizon, only worse because she knows she only need leave Oliver to have them – but look what's happened! She's a different person, sparkling with life and enthusiasm, raring to go, full of plans, she can't wait for the winter to be over and the season to start, you can see it all over her. And whose doing is that? Not Oliver's, he didn't even notice she was being left out, is my guess.'

'It was fortuitous,' said Jerry.

'That doesn't matter. It stems from Mawgan – like Debbie's shining happiness. Think about it. And that's not even the bottom line …' She paused.

It was cool under the trees as they walked uphill. On their left, the cleared site of Debbie's new venture allowed an open vista through to the river, the few moored boats, the further shore. On this autumn morning, the damp, fallen leaves were soft underfoot, the colours around them warm, like fire, but muted in this western part of the country where heavy frost so seldom came. Their footsteps were muffled on the leafy tarmac.

'So what is the bottom line?' asked Jerry.

'Oliver,' said Helen. Where Debbie was closest to her father's heart, Oliver, her beautiful, talented only son, only child, was as dear to her as her own life – dearer, and she knew him so little. 'Did you notice Oliver, last night?'

'Not particularly, no. He was just Oliver, I thought. Sitting back, keeping his distance, never a joiner.'

This was such a perfect description of the social behaviour over which Oliver's mother had always grieved, believing it to be both unnatural and learned, that she spoke with unintentional force.

'And did you notice, when they were all arguing and laughing together, how many times Mawgan knocked him off his perch?'

Jerry hadn't noticed. He had seen what he always saw, because he expected to see it. Now, he thought back, and his memory presented him with a revised picture of a coherent group of four young people, laughing and teasing each other, not three and one quiet, separate onlooker. He said, unwisely maybe, but out of a sudden blinding realisation,

'A brother would have been the salvation of Oliver.'

'A real family would have been his salvation,' said Helen, crisply. '*Mawgan* had no brothers.'

Jerry stopped. Because he had linked his arm through hers as they climbed the hill, Helen had to stop, too. He put his hands on her shoulders and turned her towards him. For a minute he looked into her dark blue, angry eyes, and then he said.

'Helen, I'm not going to go on and on saying I'm sorry. I know what I did, I know how it happened, I know what came of it What I don't know, is why you feel it so necessary to keep banging on about it. I can't undo it. What do you want me to do?'

'I don't know,' said Helen, and to her own horror and surprise, began to cry. Jerry said nothing. He took out his already crumpled handkerchief and gently dried her tears, before linking his arm once more through hers and continuing up the hill.

They came to the little lane that descended steeply to the creek, and had turned down it before either of them spoke again. Then Helen said,

'Jerry, I'm going to say this, and then I'm going to shut up about it for ever, so will you please listen?'

'OK.'

'She forced us apart, and she's kept us apart for a quarter of a century. She's brought up three children, and each one of them is a separate entity – until now, that is. Not only separate, come to that, forever at odds with each other which is worse. If all that's over, for whatever reason, then I don't know what to do. I don't know what I should do, I don't know what the options are, I don't even know what I want to do. I just don't think that … well, you can wave a magic wand and say, goodbye Dot. Because I don't think she'll go that easily. And Jerry, I can't go through it all over again. That's all.'

Jerry was silent, feeling after a subtext that he felt sure was there somewhere. Finally, he said,

'Are you saying, that if you thought I *could* wave a magic wand, or somebody could, that you …' He broke off.

'I'm saying,' said Helen, quietly, 'if you were listening, that I just don't know.'

'Do you want to know?' asked Jerry, after a pause.

'I don't know that, either. I just know that I'm fifty-five, and my life is empty, and that it feels very … bleak. And has done for a long time.'

Jerry had said he wouldn't say it, but he did.

'I'm sorry,' very gently. She shook her head, and sniffed, inelegantly.

'My fault too. You're quite right, if you can blame somebody, you don't fight, you just sit back and let it all happen. I could have married again, even had other children. It's my fault, not yours, or hers come to that, that I didn't.'

The thought of Helen married to someone else was unexpectedly repugnant. Jerry said,

'I hope that one day, I may be glad that you didn't. You too.'

'I can't see how,' said Helen, and then they were at the house.

There was, of course, nobody home. Oliver was up in his studio, Chel back at the pub, being a manageress. Debbie and Mawgan could be anywhere by this time. Jerry picked up a newspaper that lay on the table.

'You go up and have a chat with Oliver. I'll just catch up on the news. After that, I thought we might go out somewhere, what do you think?'

Helen knew that there was nothing more to be said, and that what happened next was in the lap of the gods. At least, now, Jerry understood the rules, she hoped.

'Sounds good to me. Any ideas where?'

'I'll give it some thought while you're gone. Up the steps at the side, you'll find the way.'

Helen went outside and stood, for a moment, at the foot of the stone steps that led up to the studio above the garage. Ever since the break-up of her marriage, it had been Oliver who had, often with obvious reluctance, come to visit her out of a sense of duty, never the other way about, not until last night. Although it had occurred of late years because he was a wanderer, and had no settled home, she nevertheless knew that it was wrong, had no idea how to put it right, it just felt completely alien to be standing here. It took a conscious effort to set her foot on the first step. She reached the top and knocked on the door, and Oliver opened it after a minute or two, an abstracted expression in his eyes and a brush laden with greenish paint in one hand. When he saw her, his expression changed, became wary.

'Hullo,' said Helen, and added, foolishly, 'may I come in?'

Oliver opened the door wider so that she could step past him. She took three paces into the room and stopped.

'Oh, wow!' she said. 'Oliver, what a marvellous place, what a find! It's perfect!'

'Deb found it,' said Oliver, speaking for the first time. He closed the door and walked to the kettle on the workbench at the back of the room, balancing the brush beside it. 'Coffee?'

The universal panacea in difficult situations, *have a drink*. They both thought the same thing at the same moment and exchanged rueful smile.

'Yes please,' said Helen, and added, since it was obvious what they were thinking. 'It gives one something to do with one's hands.' They both laughed. While he fiddled with mugs and coffee, she walked through onto the balcony, and after a moment he came to join her. She sensed his apartness from her almost as if it was tangible.

'Lovely view,' she said. Oliver said, ignoring this,

'Tell me, should I attach any significance to your coming here with Dad? Only, it might make things less awkward for you if you told me. For me, too.' There was nothing in his voice to give her a lead. Helen said, slowly,

'It was an impulse. There wasn't any significance at the time, it was just something I said – to shake him up, I suppose. He was being ... presumptuous. I don't know why I said it.'

'And now?'

'Now, God knows. I wish I hadn't come. It feels like ... well, an intrusion actually. And I shouldn't have said that, either.'

'It's something about this balcony,' offered Oliver. 'People lean on it and start talking, and all sorts of weird things come surging to the top. Most of them, believe me, are better out than in. I blame the view, myself.'

Helen said, without quite intending to,

'It's a great view, but it's restricted, the headland hides most of the open sea. It won't make you stir-crazy, will it?'

Oliver was silent for so long that she thought he wasn't going to answer. In the end, he said,

'The kettle's boiled,' and turned away.

It was chilly on the balcony, and after a moment, Helen followed him back into the studio, wandering round looking at the pictures that hung against the wooden walls. Oliver was good, she already knew that. What disconcerted her anew was the breadth of his canvas, the visual scope of his experience. She paused in front of a picture that contained almost nothing but sea, endlessly tossing to a limitless horizon with two tiny black sailing yachts silhouetted against the white disk of a low sun. There was wind in the pale sky, a suggestion of more to come. She looked at it for a long time, and after a while, Oliver came to stand at her shoulder.

'Here.' He handed her a steaming mug. 'Only instant, I'm afraid.'

'Actually, I like instant,' said Helen.

'Fine.'

A stilted silence hung between them. Helen sipped her coffee and Oliver contemplated the steam rising from his, and when they spoke, it was together.

'I think – ' began Helen, and Oliver said,

'You know – ' They both broke off and exchanged wry smiles.'

'You go first,' said Helen.

'We're strangers,' said Oliver, with unexpected directness. 'Don't you find that rather sad?'

'I was going to say almost the same thing.'

'So long as we both understand.' Oliver relaxed, balanced his mug on his painter's trolley among a tidy array of paints and brushes, and opened a drawer to take out a folder. 'Here, have a look at these.' He spilled some sketches and old photos out onto the trolley. 'When people in the village heard what Mawgan had in mind, they came up with all sorts of material, Deb's been running some of these through the scanner, bringing them up clearer and enlarging them to make a montage to hang behind the bar, or somewhere. We've got just about the whole crew here, and the ship.' He paused. 'And yes, in answer to your question, I daresay it will.'

Helen's fingers froze onto the photograph in her hands. She swallowed.

'So what will you do, when it does?'

'Remind myself how much worse it could have been,' said Oliver, quietly. He picked up another photo and held it out. 'Look, this is the whole crew, outside the pub. Their faces are clear – I wondered if I could put them aboard, or how people would feel about that.'

'I expect they would like it,' said Helen. 'I mean, it's not exactly a memorial, obviously, but it's like … well, bringing them home. If the restaurant is named for the ship, it's named for them, too. And their courage. It's not reverence, it's more a celebration, isn't it? Here we are, remember us? We drank in this pub, sailed out of this river, we're here among you still.'

'I thought I'd put out a few feelers here and there, see how people react.'

'Good thinking. I expect they've been missed, but after all, it isn't as if it's recent. After fifty years, maybe it's right … but you could sail a boat, couldn't you? You can drive a car.'

'I can't lift, or haul, or take any heavy strain, the only car I can drive is an automatic. What you see is a patch-up job, not the original me. So yes, probably – on a nice light day, with some good self-steering gear and electric winches – an automatic boat, in fact. Bugger, isn't it?'

'So, will you do that?'

'If I could answer that, I'd know if half a loaf really is better than no bread – and I've always had a sneaking suspicion that maybe it isn't, always. Perhaps you just die more slowly of starvation.'

'This is the trawler?' Helen looked at the picture she still gripped in her hands. 'She's been around, hasn't she? Will you paint her like this?'

'It's how she was. Mawgan is in favour, and I agree. Where's the point in smartening her up?'

'You could, of course, change the flavour of the bread,' said Helen. She laid the photo of the *White Rose* back on top of the pile. She said, feeling her way, 'You could help Debbie with her sailing school, pass on your knowledge and experience to other people. She said she had asked you to teach navigation.'

'Yes, she did.'

'And will you?'

For answer, Oliver turned away, and crossed the studio to stand in front of the picture that had caught his mother's eye earlier. The empty sea, the declining sun, the two tiny ships caught in its rays, all these belonged in a free and adventurous past, irretrievably gone. He looked at them without speaking for a long moment. Then,

'Probably not,' he said.

Helen moved with him, to stand at his shoulder.

'Oliver, don't blow it. If one way of enjoying what you loved is taken away, find another. It's a great mistake not to, and I should know.'

He turned then to look at her.

'And did you?'

She met his eyes steadily.

'That's how I know it was a mistake. You're thirty-three, give or take a week – there's a long time left. Painting can't be enough for always. Now, it's new, but in the end, if you do nothing else, your outlook will narrow and your memories will be sterile and the spark that makes your work so different will be gone.'

'You know that, too?' asked Oliver, and the satirical note in his voice made her flinch.

'Yes, since you ask. People need outside stimulation, they need other people. I know you believe that you don't.'

Oliver said, not meeting her eyes,

'I feel as if I'm as much in prison as Mawgan ever was.'

'Then just make sure it isn't solitary confinement. For Chel's sake, if not for your own.'

'Chel's OK. She's in her element with the Fish.'

'I think that's probably the most selfish thing I have ever heard you say. In fact,' said Helen, calmly, although her heart was hammering, 'you sounded just like your father. *Helen's got her sculpting, she'll be all right.* As if that was *it*.'

'I – '

'Shut up, I haven't finished. Whoever told you that life is one-dimensional? It isn't. You're a clever, intelligent man, you

156

can't possibly believe what I think you just said!' She took a deep breath. 'There's the river out there. It still leads to the sea. For Christ's sake, Oliver, wake up!'

Oliver turned away to gather up the empty mugs, and made a great play of sluicing them under the tap of the tiny sink. It meant he could turn his back to her, and after looking at it for a while, Helen said,

'I didn't mean to quarrel with you. It's still true.'

'You think I should teach navigation?' He sounded interested, but his back was still turned.

'I don't see that it would hurt you. That's all. Whether you do it or not, *when you've actually thought about it*, is up to you, of course.'

'Ooh, nasty!' He turned round then, his expression bland, giving nothing away. 'All right, *Mother*, I'll actually think about it. Will that satisfy you?'

He had never called her anything but *Helen* since he was a very little boy, and Helen's smile in response was therefore stilted. They had succeeded, she thought, in the space of a scant quarter of an hour, in upsetting each other to a considerable depth, which wasn't bad for two people who had readily admitted to being strangers. It was time to leave.

'Jerry is planning to take me out somewhere,' she said, as lightly as she could manage. 'I had better go and join him, or he'll be pacing the floor. Love the sketches. I'll see you this evening.'

'And you hope I'll be in a better mood?' He almost smiled, at least it was an attempt. 'Have a good day, then. *Ciao*.'

She almost ran down the steps.

* * * * *

The day having got off to such a bad start, Helen's misgivings about how it would end could only grow stronger. Being out for the day with Jerry didn't help, she found it was too easy, increasingly so, to slip into their old easy, bantering relationship, just as if there had never been anything come between them, and the effort to keep fighting to prevent it was exhausting. She didn't tell him about her exchange with Oliver, but the temptation to do so was almost irresistible. Debbie was the one they were supposed to be worrying about, she told herself firmly, not Oliver, who was surely big enough to take care of himself. Walking along the beach at Gunwalloe, lunching in a pleasant roadside pub, standing on the point of the Lizard, buffeted by an exhilarating wind, her estranged son filled her thoughts. Jerry, who naturally thought she was worrying about meeting Nonie tonight, began to wish that he had never had his bright idea. You couldn't force people to be reconciled, as he very well knew. It never worked. Therefore, for their separate reasons, they were both in a subdued mood when they returned to St Erbyn at teatime.

The instant they entered the house, all that changed. The first thing they heard was laughter.

At the sound of the front door opening, Chel came from the kitchen, still giggling, with a teatowel flung over her shoulder.

'Deb says she can't face it,' she announced. 'She's just found out she's marrying a man who makes his own ravioli!'

Debbie appeared at her shoulder.

'Ravioli comes in little plastic pockets in the supermarket, or in a tin, if you sink that low' she said, firmly. 'If life is too short to stuff a mushroom, like somebody said – I don't remember who – then it has to be too short to *make* ravioli! Don't go in there, Dad – he's doing something with pork fillet and toasted almonds that's probably a prosecutable offence!'

'Sounds as if dinner will be worth eating, then,' said Jerry.

Mawgan had followed them out. More relaxed and informal than last night, jeans, T-shirt, and a blue and white striped butcher's apron tied around his waist made him look like a godfather's minder about to man the barbecue, but it was more his style, Helen decided.He wasn't a man on easy terms with formality, in fact, if you wanted to be rude, the phrase *a bit of rough* sprang readily to mind.

'Don't listen to them,' he said. 'And they have the sauce to call *me* a moron!'

'Any chance of a cup of tea?' asked Helen, smiling – it was impossible not to smile at them, they were having such a good time. 'Or is that a tactless question?'

'The kettle is about the only piece of my kitchen equipment he isn't using,' said Chel, diving back towards the kitchen door. 'And talking of sauce, Deb, weren't you meant to be stirring something?'

'I moved it,' said Debbie. 'I did – ow!' She wriggled clear of Mawgan's attack, and all three of them disappeared again.

'I think Chef is having problems with the kitchen staff,' remarked Jerry, grinning. 'Where's Oliver, do you think?'

Chel, appearing on cue, said,

'He's been sent down to the Fish in search of some semolina. He was the one we decided was most expendable, but it's to be hoped he knows it when he sees it.'

'I'm not even going to ask,' said Helen, on a wondering note.

'I wouldn't! We haven't – it went something like, *blast, I forgot the semolina*, and we decided to leave it at that. I wouldn't expect semolina pudding, though. Milk and sugar? In your tea?' She vanished again, returning in a few minutes with three mugs on a tray.

'No biscuits?' asked Jerry, regretfully.

'Biscuits will spoil your dinner,' said Chel. 'All four courses of it – just wait and see.' She sank into a chair with her tea. 'He's threatening to make her do the ravioli – I'm keeping out of it.' And she took a grateful sip.

The front door opening again announced the return of Oliver, carrying a packet marked, conspicuously, SEMOLINA.

'Well done,' said Chel, without getting up. 'The kettle's just boiled, if you're interested.'

'Shirley found it for me,' said Oliver, heading for the kitchen door. Shirley Pengelly worked in the office doing what she was told, which was mainly typing letters and checking invoices. Chel was slowly training her to be more generally useful, something that Mawgan, with his one-man-band mentality, hadn't bothered to do. If Shirley was capable of doing things on her own, Chel reasoned, then not only would she be more useful and more likely to stay, but her own freedom, and Mawgan's too by inference, would be all the greater. It certainly wasn't that the girl was stupid, far from it, and there was a great deal she could do without breaking any confidences. It was all, she thought now, in the difference between having been involved in hotel management, and being a chef, albeit a superlatively good one, who found himself running a pub. Mawgan, quite simply, had no idea how to delegate outside of his own kitchen. Looked at like that, and taking everything else into account, it was no wonder he was stressed.

Oliver returned, without the semolina, and headed back for the door.

'I'll be in the studio, if anyone wants me.' Slam. Gone. Chel made no comment, but was aware, out of the corner of her eye, of Helen looking down at her hands as if she didn't know quite what to do with them. After a moment, Helen said,

'It's a great studio. Did the exhibition generate a lot of work?'

'Several good commissions,' said Chel. She placed her empty mug on the hearth. 'And a man out in America who wants him to put on an exhibition in New York next year sometime. I don't know if he will.'

'What does Gifford Thomas say?'

'Go for it, but you know Oliver.'

Helen said nothing to that, for the truth was that she didn't know Oliver, not at all, and it was Jerry who answered.

'What's his objection?'

'Big cities, and being lionized. Two things he hates. Oh well, there's time.'

'If he did, could you go with him? Now that you've a full-time job?'

'Mawgan says yes, so long as it's off-season.'

'You want to reckon that it's the kind of thing that's going to happen now,' said Helen. 'If Oliver wants to take his place among the greats, he's going to have to do a lot of things that he doesn't want to do. These days, publicity is all, and the collective memory is short. People will forget, very soon, that he ever sailed around the world unless he allows it to be hyped, and himself with it.'

'They wanted him to appear on an Arts Programme on BBC2,' said Chel.

'Then tell him that he must.'

'You don't *tell* Oliver.'

'He needs to pull himself together,' said Jerry, and heard himself, sounding so like a father, with something approaching horror. Oliver always did this to him, always had. He got to his feet.

'Think I'll go for a stroll,' he said, and made his escape. Helen gathered up the empty mugs.

'I'll take these out of the way, shall I?'

'Be careful,' advised Chel, settling herself more comfortably. 'You'll be up to your elbows in suds if you're not in and out quick.'

'Not me!'

Mawgan and Debbie were involved in the ravioli, Debbie carefully placing little heaps of filling at intervals on a large sheet of pasta, and Mawgan, so close at her shoulder that he was nearly leaning on her, criticising her skill, teasing her.

'Keep them *even* for heaven's sake, it's not hard! And try not to scatter it about like seagull-shit, or they won't seal properly

– ' They looked up as Helen came in, their two laughing faces close together, one vividly attractive, gypsy dark, the other golden-fair and beautiful. The contrast between them was striking, their closeness strangely moving. Helen rattled the mugs into the sink without ceremony and headed back for the door. She felt as if she had intruded.

Somewhere between the sink and the door, a fear that she had tried to voice to Jerry crystallised into something real. She said, as she rejoined Chel,

'Those two scare me. They're so happy in each other.'

Chel could have said that it was a strange thing to say, but she didn't.

'I know what you mean,' she said. 'But why should they scare you? We were all like that, once.'

'That's exactly why. It makes you vulnerable while it lasts. If Dot has made up her mind that it isn't going to happen for them ... well, you and I have both been there.'

'I don't see what she can do,' Chel objected. 'She's had a go, but it hasn't worked, has it? Deb didn't fall for it. What else can she do? She got to you, and to me, too, because we were *there*. By disowning Deb, she's snookered herself. Deb isn't there any more.'

'The only way you can make yourself safe from Dot, when she thinks she's right and you're wrong, is to do what you and Oliver did – vanish. Those two aren't going to vanish. They can't.'

'Even so, I still don't see what she can do.'

'Jerry says I'm paranoid about her. Maybe he's right, but nobody I know of ever stopped her in her tracks.'

'Pity he isn't paranoid himself,' said Chel. 'I'm sure it's much safer.'

'Jerry is as stubborn as Oliver when he doesn't want to see something,' said Helen. 'He said, you know – Jerry said, that is – that Dot's saying that Mawgan is after Deb's money.'

'Nah.' Chel thought about it for a moment. 'He hadn't the faintest idea she had any until after they were well and truly engaged. And if he'd known, I don't think he'd have cared a toss, do you? He's hardly short of a bob or two himself, even Dot must see that.'

'Dot hasn't looked. Also, she knows people's weaknesses, that's how she's so dangerous.'

'Well, take heart, I doubt if that's one of Mawgan's.'

'Nonie Fingall always used to say, the dangerous thing about Dot was that she always acted with what seemed to her to be the very best motives. I never believed her then, but when I look back, I think maybe she was right – Nonie, that is. Only, you can never be sure.'

'You can be sure that she's a fat, meddling cow!' retorted Chel. 'Whatever her motives.'

'Debbie's her daughter. She must have already tarnished her happiness.'

Chel recalled Debbie, after her return from Embridge to visit her mother soon after she and Mawgan became engaged. She shook her head, as if to clear it.

'Deb was distraught, of course she was. But Susan …'

'What, about Susan?' asked Helen, when she didn't go on.

'I don't know. Just that, I never do know, with Susan, just like you said about her mother. She couldn't make it right, who could, but she somehow managed to make it bearable. And she's being brilliant over the wedding. Poor Deb – she wants her mother to be there, who doesn't? But Susan is doing a good job as big sister.'

'I hardly know Susan,' said Helen. 'She was a dear little girl, and her father was really nice. Much too nice for Dot. She gave him an awful time, running after Jerry, in fact I think that was quite possibly one of the causes for his coronary …' She broke off. 'Oh well, that's old news. And to get back to where we began, and I can only say this to you, so please listen – I don't see what Dot can do, you're right – but I'm damn sure it won't be nothing. And that, Chel darling, is why those two scare me.'

* * * * *

It seemed as if none of Jerry's plans for the weekend were going to bear fruit. Helen had nothing to add to his own estimate of Mawgan, she most certainly hadn't become reconciled with Oliver, and although the dinner party, against all the odds, was a success, that didn't achieve its object either. Miracles, this weekend, were not on the menu, unless, that is, you included the food, which, from the moment Nonie and Theo came through the door and Nonie cried, 'What a wonderful smell!' rather took over the occasion. In this, it was ably seconded by the efforts of Chel, Oliver, Debbie and Mawgan, who were all determined that there should be no awkward moments, and by some excellent wines.

Jerry realised straight away, over a wonderful fish soup generously dotted with mussels and accompanied by home-made focaccia studded with rock salt crystals and scattered with rosemary, that the occasion was against him. Nonie, Theo, Oliver and Chel all knew each other too well, they had too much to talk about among themselves, too many amusing Greek stories to entertain the rest of the company. Mawgan's ownership of the pub had made him socially adept, even without a natural gift for mixing with people that Oliver would do well to emulate, Debbie was so bubbling with happiness that she lit up the room. Helen had slipped naturally into the position of observer, speaking when she was addressed, self-contained, proving, if nothing else, where Oliver got it from.

Around the slightly irregular circles and bumps of wild mushroom ravioli in fresh tomato sauce with oregano, Jerry conceded that this was just going to be a bloody good evening, thank you, and settled down to enjoy it. By the time the stuffed pork fillet with apricots and the tossed salad had become a memory, the company had coalesced without achieving anything other than undirected goodwill.

'What sort of a restaurant are you planning on?' Nonie asked, with interest. 'An Italian bistro?'

'What, in St Erbyn?' Mawgan grinned at her. 'Can't see it going down a storm, can you? No, near as I can I want it to be Cornish – good ingredients, sourced locally, and presented simply, based on traditional recipes with maybe a bit of a twist …' He let the sentence die, fiddling with a fork.

'What, no fancy stuff?' asked Helen.

'Occasionally, maybe, by way of a change. Not sure people want that in a place like this. If they do, they c'n have it. The punter is always right.'

'Is that what you've done in the past?' Jerry speculated.

'Not exactly, no. It's what I've *wanted* to 've done, but that's not quite the same.'

'Are there enough truly Cornish recipes to make it work?' asked Jerry, with interest. Mawgan looked at him, a glint of a smile in his eyes.

'You'd be surprised, time I've finished.'

Theo, who had been listening with interest, nodded in agreement.

'Is good plan. This is a beautiful county you have, special. A shame to make it all McDonald's and foreign bistros.'

'A shame to make it all pasties and heavy cake, too,' Mawgan remarked. 'Not that I've anything against either.'

'Cornish *cuisine*,' Nonie mused. 'Great idea. Hope you can make it work!'

'Watch me.'

'Oh, I will. With great interest.'

'What I want to know,' Helen said, as Chel got up to clear the plates, 'is what he wanted semolina for. It doesn't seem to go at all with the feast we're eating here.'

'Tell you this, you won't believe it,.' said Chel, who already knew the answer.

'School dinners?' Nonie speculated, and then they all had to explain English school dinners to Theo until Chel returned from the kitchen bearing a light-as-a-feather orange cake drenched in orange syrup and still warm from the oven, and accompanied by generous dollops of home-made ice-cream, speckled with the dark dots of vanilla seeds and tasting of heaven.

'Heavenly!' said Nonie, on a sigh, as she scooped up the last deliquescent spoonful of ice-cream and leaned back in her chair. 'Belt-loosening wonderful!' A murmur of agreement ran round the company. Mawgan, twirling a half-empty wine-glass between his finger and thumb, accepted their congratulations easily, but he was going quiet, Debbie noticed, as the levels dropped in the bottles, becoming moody and sliding down into the all-too-easy depression that, these days, seemed to lie in wait around every hidden corner. She wanted to reach out to him, but it wasn't the moment. She looked away, and found herself meeting Helen's eyes.

'And to be honest,' Helen said, driving home with Jerry the following morning, 'that's the only thing I can find to wonder about. Well – two things, I suppose. He's a workaholic, and he drinks too much. But it isn't grounds for divorce, or even disengagement. Deb seems to cope.'

Jerry shook his head, his eyes on the road.

'There are times I feel he's an alien, newly landed from planet Zog,' he admitted. 'It seems to work well between them – and then, at other times, it spectacularly doesn't, or shouldn't anyway. I tell myself, it's the circumstances, and I try to believe it.'

'I honestly don't think he'll ever hurt her. That's what really worries you, isn't it?'

This was too true to need an answer. After a moment, Helen said, out of the blue,

'Have you met his family?'

'No. Not so far.'

'Shouldn't you?'

'They're in the middle of moving house, Debbie says. They moved to Launceston after … well, the trouble, but now they're moving back. When they're settled, then we'll meet.'

'You should make it soon,' said Helen. 'Families tell you a lot about people. It might make you feel better.'

'So, what do my family tell people about me?' asked Jerry, still with his eyes fixed ahead.

'Yours? Right at this moment, God knows,' said Helen, and lapsed into a silence that he didn't feel it necessary to interrupt.

A strange weekend, Jerry thought. Strange, because of Helen, because of the luminous quality in his beloved Deb, because of the moody, charismatic culinary genius on whom she had set her heart, because of his continuing ambivalent relationship with his son. But they had survived it, and maybe it had been a start to something different, new and better. He had to hope so.

A weekend she should have avoided, Helen thought. She had fallen out all over again with Oliver, she had been unwillingly ensnared in the problems besetting Debbie, for whom she had a great affection, she had allowed herself to spend too much time with Jerry.

Dinner had been wonderful.

And she had managed not to come face to face with Nonie, without actually cutting her dead and Nonie, she had noted, had done the same.

But never again. Sorry, Jerry.

Definitely not.

VII

The knowledge that Jerry had taken Helen to Cornwall with him hung over Susan's spirits like a pall. It wasn't simply that it seemed to drive a further wedge between Jerry and her mother, she was realist enough to know that there was no hope there anyway, and hadn't been for a long time. It was far more the feeling of being shut out from all the fun and laughter that, she knew from her own recent experience, would be the background to the visit. In Cornwall, things were happening, her half-brother and sister and their respective partners were establishing a new pattern of association in which she had no part. Less than no part. She had a certain importance to Debbie over the wedding, but she didn't try to kid herself. Once the wedding was over, she would come back to Embridge and be the outsider again, as she had always been. Helen was just one more factor that would make sure of it.

'You may as well make up your mind to it,' had said her mother, with a disdainful sniff. 'Once Helen Macken gets her foot back in the door, it will be goodbye to you and me.'

Susan had never felt so alive as she had felt in St Erbyn, or not since she grew up. The easy acceptance of Chel, and even more of Mawgan, had served to negate even Oliver's confrontational attitude towards her, she had felt, for the first time, as if she belonged in a family group, mattered to somebody. Listening to Debbie's plans, hearing about Mawgan's brilliant ideas for his restaurant, master-minding the wedding, had given her a sense of involvement that, she told herself, had been wholly illusional. It was all the harder, then, to come back to life as lived in Embridge, and to her mother's bitter, ill-concealed resentments.

'I shall be late tonight,' said Tom, not for the first time. 'Meeting over the Lawley Engineering accounts, can't be helped. Don't wait dinner, I'll probably go out for a steak with Mark and old Hetherington, go on talking when the client isn't there. You don't mind?'

The question was rhetorical, Susan thought. If she said she did mind, it would start an interminable row about her not caring about his work, always putting herself first, etc. etc. She knew very well that Mark, his associate, and Mr Hetherington, who was his boss, translated either sooner or later into Elaine, his assistant. It was beginning to feel almost understood between them, although they had never discussed it.

Not for the first time, she asked herself the question, did Tom know that she knew? Once again, she had no idea of the answer.

'It's Parents' Evening at school,' she reminded him, without hope.

'That's all right. You can manage all that kind of thing much better than me.'

It was all so predictable. When he had gone out of the house, swinging his briefcase and whistling happily, she went upstairs and sat in front of her dressing-table mirror, looking at herself. Elaine was slim, tall, blonde, sleek, sexy ... how could she compete with all of that? Nature had made her sturdy and curvaceous, given her curly dark brown hair and brown eyes, to her own eyes a no more than pretty face, broad across the cheekbones and with a blunt nose that had freckles scattered across the bridge. The luck of the draw had endowed her with the fortune that had bought this house, to an extent maintained their lifestyle, leaving Tom free to spend much of his salary on golf, sailing ... Elaine ... She was the mother of two children, at present being driven to school by Maria the *au pair*. It would, she thought miserably, be more appropriate for Maria to go to the Parents' Evening than either herself or Tom.

How had it all happened? Until recently, she had been so satisfied with her life.

She tried to imagine that satisfaction now, but failed. When had she begun to set so much store by charity coffee mornings, shopping, tennis, dinner parties, the operatic society, concerts, and all the rest of it, and lost touch with her children? Let's face it, with herself? When had she turned into this sad lady who lunched?

When Sebastian fell and hurt his knee, or had a nightmare, or was bullied at school, it was Maria he cried for. That was dreadful. She had only realised how dreadful it was when she had seen him running to Mawgan, a stranger, rather than to his own father or mother, and felt a deep twist of jealousy in her guts. Mawgan who had, in the space of about two minutes, soothed and healed the fears at which his own parents had – no, not even laughed. Been irritated, dismissive.

Uninterested.

Surely not.

A hot tear trickled down her cheek, she wiped it away with her finger, looking at her swimming, mirrored eyes in helpless misery.

So here she was, thirty years old, with children who didn't know her and whom she didn't know, a husband who preferred a younger, racier model, and a full, but nevertheless empty social life, and the bitter knowledge that, unless she took the initiative, her husband took her so much for granted that he was perfectly happy with the situation in which he and Elaine had placed her.

She wondered what would happen if she confronted Tom, and knew, with a sense of deep humiliation, that he would agree to anything she suggested to preserve his comfortable lifestyle and keep hold of his children, and then go off and continue doing exactly as he pleased, but with more circumspection, and that she would remain the lonely, neglected, unwanted wife for as long as she chose to put up with it.

Another tear welled up, and she pressed the heels of her hands against her eyes to hold it back. Crying had never solved anything.

'I did try to be a good wife,' she said, aloud.

Treacherously, there came into her mind the picture of her sister's happiness, her radiance, her complete faith in a fulfilling future. Hard on Debbie's heels came Oliver and Chel, fighting shoulder to shoulder to build hope out of despair, success out of disaster. She had never had anything like that. She had got married because that was what one did, and Tom was there. She had thought she loved him at the time, but what did anyone know about love if they didn't know anything about life? And she hadn't, she was twenty-one and she had kept herself for Mr Right, according to her mother's plan for her, and ended up married to Mr Wrong. It was just that it had taken her a long time to admit it.

There was nothing particularly dreadful or even unusual about Tom. He was a well-meaning man, in his way, no better and no worse than a million others. A stereotype, almost.

But dull. There was none of Oliver's genius and courage, none of Mawgan's vigour and ambition, in Tom. There never had been. Tom was a plodder, with a good job within his abilities in which he would probably rise very little further, didn't even wish to. If a skinny blonde threw herself at him, he would have an affair. He probably wouldn't leave his wife and children, that was for the wife to choose. It was how men were.

Not *all* men, surely?

Downstairs, the slam of a distant door announced the return of Maria. Scrubbing her palms across her wet cheeks, Susan pulled herself together. There was no future in sitting here giving way to despair, whatever decision was to be made would be for her. Life-changing decisions were not within Tom's province or capability, and anyway, there were the children to consider. As she thought this, the front door bell chimed and the telephone rang, almost at the same moment, and she got to her feet to go downstairs. Even the wonderful Maria, she thought sourly, couldn't be in two places at once.

This was unfair to Maria, a pleasant Polish girl with a warm love for children, and in many people's estimation a treasure, but jealousy had always been Susan's besetting sin, fostered in her childhood by her mother's attitude, and for the moment Maria could do no right. Not, thought Susan piously as she ran down the stairs, that she would be unfair. Perish the thought! She just couldn't help the way she felt, even while knowing it was mean-minded.

I am not a very nice person, Susan decided. I don't deserve that anyone should love me.

The phone was still ringing, Maria had gone to the door. Susan snatched it up.

'Hullo, Susan Casson.'

'Hi, Suse,' said Debbie's happy voice, just as their mother crossed the threshold. The black labrador that lay under the hall table staggered to his feet and strolled across to sniff at her, yawning, and Dot flapped at it. Dot didn't like dogs, couldn't understand why Susan wanted one, horrid, smelly things!

'Get the dog, Maria,' said Susan, 'Deb – bad moment. Can I ring you?' Right at this moment, she didn't know which of the three of them she wanted least, her mother, Maria or her sister. She would settle for the uncritical comfort of the dog, no question about it. Her impatience sounded in her voice, and Debbie heard it.

'Oh – sorry. It's nothing important, I just wanted a chat, I thought the kids would be at school and you'd be alone.'

Susan could guess what about. Helen's visit would be as unsettling to Debbie as it was to herself – or Oliver, probably, come to that. She said,

'I'll ring you back. Mummy has just arrived.'

The phone went down at the other end with a shocked click, and Susan, flustered now, turned to greet her mother.

'That was Deborah, I take it,' said Dot, presenting a powdered cheek for her daughter to kiss. Maria, sensing an atmosphere, dragged the dog in the direction of the kitchen.

'I bring coffee,' she said, before she could be asked – no, ordered, to do it. Mrs Casson was in a mood, her mother always did this. Maria didn't like Dot, she had listened to her talking in front of the children about sister Deborah's young man, and had longed to interfere and hadn't dared. She hadn't dared to tell Mr and Mrs Casson either, and had been ashamed of herself. This was an unhappy house, she told herself firmly, and a sensible girl would leave, if only it wasn't for that poor little boy. Brash Annabel would manage, not little Sebastian. The kitchen door slammed, but it might have been due to the dog.

'That girl is becoming impertinent,' said Dot, sweeping uninvited into the drawing-room, for the dislike was mutual. She looked around her with her usual approval, Susan had excellent taste and had listened to her mother's guidance. She sat down.

'She's good with the children,' said Susan, still standing. Dot looked at her impatiently.

'She spoils them, and she is defiant. You should be firm with her, or she'll take advantage.'

Susan felt like saying, why not, everyone else does, but didn't. You didn't say things like that to Mummy. Instead, seeing no help for it, she sat down too.

'I wasn't expecting you,' she said, and realised that she had sounded abrupt.

'I wanted to talk to you. I take it this *wedding* –' she spoke the word with distaste, ' – is still going forward.'

'Well … yes. Why shouldn't it be?'

'I wouldn't waste too much time on it,' said Dot, and sniffed disdainfully. 'In the end, it will not take place.'

'Oh, I think it will,' said Susan, before she could stop herself..

'Really? Come, Susan – you've met the man! He won't do.'

'Yes, I've met him.'

Dot fussed around, placing her handbag and gloves just-so on the table beside her. She didn't meet Susan's eyes.

'I'm having his financial affairs investigated. I believe that Deborah has fallen victim to a glib fortune-hunter, and I will not have it.'

'You can't do that!' Susan was too astonished to be tactful. 'People's financial affairs are private!'

'Really,' said Dot, for the second time, but with a different inflection.

Maria came in with the coffee on a tray – cups and saucers and the *cafetière*, not nice friendly mugs. She placed it with care beside Susan and withdrew, shooing the dog ahead of her. The interruption gave Susan time to think.

'Have you talked about this to Daddy?' she asked, knowing the question was tactless but having to ask it anyway.

'Your father!' said Dot. 'He seems to be as taken in by this man as any of you! You would have thought that he would follow every avenue to prevent Deborah marrying a jailbird, but apparently not. That leaves it to me – and to you.'

'Oh no, not me!' said Susan, immediately. 'No, Mummy – count me out. There's nothing that I can do anyway.' She said this with thankfulness, believing it to be true.

'You can tell me about him,' said Dot. She accepted a cup of coffee delicately. '*Know thine enemy.* What is he really like?'

Susan had liked him, she had fallen under the spell of the whole St Erbyn scene. She couldn't say that to her mother. Come to think, there were a lot of things she couldn't say to her mother these days. She said, not entirely truthfully,

'I only met him briefly, one evening. He works very hard with his restaurant.'

'A hick from the sticks, I understand,' said Dot, with distaste.

Not a good description. Susan wondered how she could best modify it, but it was hopeless. You couldn't do anything with such deep-rooted preconceptions. She was more concerned, in any case, with her mother's interference in Mawgan's private affairs, she couldn't feel it was wise. Pleasant and easygoing though he appeared, she had sensed a hardness in him, underlying the charm. His reaction, if he ever found out, could be unpredictable. It was true about the jailbird bit.

'When you say you're investigating his financial affairs, you don't mean you're employing a private detective!'

'Oh, very discreetly, I made that quite clear.'

Susan gulped her coffee and burnt her mouth. She choked.

'Mummy, you really can't do that.'

'Thank you, Susan, I have already done it.'

Susan had thought that life couldn't get any worse, she now saw that she was wrong.

'I really do think it's unwise.'

'I'll make a note of your opinion.'

It must have been an instinctive, desperate attempt to change the subject that surged up, unsought, from the depths of her subconscious. Susan heard herself saying,

'Tom's having an affair with his secretary.'

Dot raised her eyebrows.

'I wondered if you knew. I hope you're not planning to do anything silly.'

'*Silly?*' said Susan, unable to believe her ears.

'Men do these things. Your father is a prime example.'

'He's *sleeping* with her!' It suddenly seemed far worse than it had before. Susan almost shouted the words.

'They generally do. If you behave with dignity, it will be over all the quicker.'

'*Dignity!*'

'Come, Susan, there's no need to be hysterical. Women of our class don't make scenes about such things.'

'*Scenes*!'

'Is there an echo in here?' asked Dot, with a humorous little smile. 'Now Susan, pull yourself together, I expected better from you, it's silly, ill-bred girls like Cheryl who behave this way. Think of the children.' She reached out to pat her daughter's hand. 'I rely on you to set an example. After Cheryl's disgraceful carrying-on, and now Deborah – well, it's up to us to show that we know how ladies should behave.'

Susan latched onto one phrase in this brisk speech.

'Did you and Daddy think of the children?'

'Of course. That, and the fact that divorce is against the teachings of the Church.'

Susan wanted to say *stuff the Church*, but didn't. It wouldn't help. She thought about her childhood instead, her adolescent years, her young adulthood. Constantly feeling inferior to Oliver, constantly at odds with him whenever he condescended to appear, constantly caught in the crossfire of his relationship to their parents. It was a picture that made *think of the children* a singularly empty phrase. Debbie, she thought, had always been the favourite of both parents, for Jerry because she was his natural daughter, for her mother because she was Jerry's. Where she herself belonged in this complicated family structure was something she had never worked out. As with her marriage, she had tried to be good, in this case, a good daughter, sister. But surely none of that had any relation to Annabel and Sebastian?

The iniquities of the fathers are visited upon the sons, and then something about generation unto generation, she thought confusedly, and felt sick with guilt. But it hadn't been her iniquity, not in the first instance. She didn't have to pass it on.

She had been silent for so long that Dot concluded her wise words had found their mark. She smiled approvingly.

'There, you see, it's easy to handle these little upsets when you follow the rules,' she said, so piously that Susan suddenly wanted to slap her; she twisted her hands together, tightly. 'There's no need to make a silly fuss, and we need all our wits about us to see off this bully boy of your sister's.' Dot nodded, satisfied and smiling. 'I know I can rely on you.'

For what? Susan asked herself. Life was suddenly full of impossible questions, and Deb, yet again, coming before herself..

'Another cup of coffee?' she offered, as tepid as the coffee itself, but Dot was ready to go. She reached for her gloves, still smiling.

'No, I must be off, I have an appointment with my hairdresser.' She picked up her bag. 'We've had a useful little talk. If you should hear anything that may be relevant, I rely on you to tell me.'

She patted her daughter's cheek affectionately as she left. Dear, good, Susan. She would never cause the rumpus and contention of which the other two had shown themselves capable. For the first time for many years she gave Susan's father a fleeting thought. Dear, good, Henry. He would be proud of her.

When she had gone, Susan hesitated. She knew that she ought to ring Debbie back, but between old resentment and her new, guilty knowledge, she didn't think that she could face it. Her mother, she thought confusedly, had no right to interfere with Deb's life like this, no right to pry into Mawgan's affairs. It was unforgivable, and she shouldn't be a party to it herself.

And then, she came face to face with the Dot conundrum, not for the first time in her life. *If* their mother really thought that Mawgan was after Deb's money, then she was perfectly justified in checking him out, it was what any concerned parent would do, and in that case her father should be doing the same. It was true that Mawgan had to be putting a big investment into the renovation of his restaurant, and that his decision to do so appeared to have come hard on the heels of his meeting Debbie. Ask yourself, Susan thought, do you want your sister made the victim of a fortune-hunter? And the answer had to be a firm negative.

But … He really loved her. Or if he didn't, he was the world's best actor and had missed his vocation. The quality of the love between those two was yet another thing that made her sick with her own situation, her own life.

Her mother had never met him. If she did, would she think differently? But that was another of *those* questions, and Susan abandoned it. Instead, she thought, if he believed there were any grounds for concern, Daddy *would* have done the same as Mummy. Perhaps he had, and not told her so as not to put her in an awkward position. Thankfully, she seized on this way out of the dilemma. She would ask Daddy.

There was no way she could do so right now. He was in court today, she knew, and she would have to wait until this evening, but she could drop by and leave a note with his clerk to say that she was going to the flat after the Parents' Evening. He would let her know if it was inconvenient, and Tom would be out anyway. Going to her desk, she wrote the note, collected her coat and her car keys, and called to Maria that she was going out. It was a relief to be away from the house.

* * * * *

Jerry, reading the note, concluded that Susan wanted to talk to him about the wedding arrangements, and sighed resignedly. Poor Susan, he couldn't turn her away, but he really had been looking forward to a quiet evening catching up with some work. He was confident that most of the practical arrangements could safely be left with Mawgan and his staff anyway, it was only the guest list and the invitations that really concerned Susan. Wedding dresses and bridesmaids and all that faff were outside a father's brief, thank God, at least until the bills came in, and since Debbie was down in Cornwall and likely to stay there, outside Susan's too. Maybe he could plead pressure of work and get rid of her very quickly.

But when Susan arrived, and he heard what she had to say, he knew that he couldn't. It was too serious, and Susan should never have been involved in it.

'Mummy is worried about Debbie,' she had begun, and Jerry said,

'Oh, God! Do we have to, Susan? This isn't new.'

'Yes Daddy, I'm afraid we do. She thinks it may be Deb's trust fund he's got his eye on, and she's paid to have Mawgan investigated.'

'She's done *what*?' he asked, not sure that he had properly understood.

'She's got a detective prying into Mawgan's financial situation,' Susan repeated, more succinctly. Her father's first reaction was exactly the same as her own.

'She can't do that!'

'Apparently, she can. I don't know how they go about these things, but I suppose you do.'

Jerry knew at least some of the avenues open to a determined investigator, and checking somebody's credit, at least, was these days as easy as kiss-your-hand. He found himself wondering if Mawgan had anything to hide and hoping that he didn't; if Dot found anything, anything at all, the resulting row would be spectacular. He felt tired at the very thought of it.

'Why can't your mother ever leave things alone?' he asked, hopelessly.

'The thing is,' said Susan, Dot's daughter after all, 'if there's anything to find, then oughtn't we to know?'

'It isn't always wise to know too much,' said Jerry, speaking from a wide experience.

'But this is Debbie we're talking about, not some dubious client of yours. And there's no denying, Daddy, he hasn't got a very good track record. He's been in prison, remember.'

'Not for fraud.'

'Aren't our jails supposed to be a great training ground for crime of all sorts?' asked Susan. 'And we do know, he had to raise a large sum of money while he was inside to buy his partner out of the pub.'

'Oh *God*!' repeated Jerry. 'Don't say things like that, Susan, please! Let me think.'

It occurred to him that Chel was handling Mawgan's accounts, at least as they related to the Fish, but he dismissed the thought. Apart from the fact that he couldn't ask her to betray her employer's secrets, he thought that if she had come across anything doubtful, she would have told him anyway and packed in the job, simply because of Debbie. The reflection was only partly comforting, for Mawgan had another business in which Chel had no part. If he did have anything to hide, he was unlikely to let any of Debbie's family run loose in his files, so it naturally followed if there was anything to know, then it wasn't about the Fish.His original business had been the restaurant, so logically, that's where any bodies were more likely to be buried. None of these reflections was comforting.

Not quite as straightforward as he would have you believe. Thank you, Helen!

Susan, he realised, was looking at him curiously.

'Daddy?'

'A bugger, isn't it?' said Jerry, with a wry smile. 'It goes very much against the grain to investigate a man behind his back, but we didn't instigate it. If we tell Mawgan, or even Debbie, we'll never know if there was anything to hide, because he'll cover his tracks – if he hasn't already, and if there were any in the first place. And if there isn't anything to find, then it doesn't matter anyway. There'll be no harm done.'

'You could talk to Mummy,' Susan suggested. 'Perhaps she could call off her private eye.'

'On the 'Ignorance is Bliss' principal?'

'If Deb ever finds out, she'll never speak to any of us again, and I shan't blame her!'

'What did *you* make of him?' Jerry asked his daughter, wanting to know. Susan was nobody's fool, and he was still uneasy.

'Goodness!' She looked thoughtful. 'I liked him. He's the sort of person you can't help liking. I think he genuinely loves Debbie, and if that's the case then does all this matter anyway? But ...'

'Ah,' said Jerry. 'You think *but* ... as well. Any ideas as to why?'

'Oh yes,' said Susan. She made a grimace. 'It won't help. I think that he's probably capable of things that we – that's you and me, or Debbie, or Oliver – are not. He grew up against a different background, and he has a different mind-set. If he's pushed, he'll probably push back – hard. But that's not to say that I think he's dishonest.'

This was a new idea, and one that hadn't occurred to Jerry. It gave him an odd prickly feeling at the nape of his neck. There was so much that they didn't know ... even more that Susan didn't know, and certainly not Dot. He dreaded to think what Dot would do if she ever got wind of the incest thing. It would probably end in a lawsuit, and Susan was on the right lines, Dot would be minced if she wasn't careful. Much as she might deserve that, the price would be too high – not just to her, but to Debbie and Mawgan too. Perhaps, he thought with relief, his omission to tell Dot the worst was the measure of his own confidence in its falsity. He did hope so. And it wasn't in the written record, so with luck her detective would never stumble on it.

This was the proper line of thought for a solicitor?

'*Damn* Dorothy!' he said. 'Sorry, Susan, I know she's your mother.'

'The thing that gets me the most,' said Susan, slowly, 'is how little she seems to be thinking of Debbie in all this. Debbie doesn't want to be rescued from a fortune-hunter. Debbie wants to marry Mawgan, to have her own business – to have a life, be happy. I don't think the money has even entered her head, or that she would care if it did. Whoever wanted to be saved from themselves? It's just another way of saying, *do what I want –* ' She broke off, and looked down at her hands. The movement hid her expression, and Jerry looked at her curiously.

'You said that almost as if it had a personal application,' he observed.

Susan shook her head, as if to clear it.

'It's old history. Forget it.'

'No, tell me. Did she ever do that to you?'

Susan's head jerked up, she looked at him almost angrily.

'You know she did!'

'No. I don't. So tell me.'

'It doesn't matter. Anyway, I got married.'

'Ah.' Jerry looked at her. How could he have forgotten? Poor Susan! 'This is about university.'

'I wanted to study law.' She spoke it like a challenge.

'Yes, I remember. But you chose not to. I often wondered why …' He allowed the sentence to trail into silence, tempting her to continue, but she didn't rise to the bait.

'I told you, it doesn't matter.'

Jerry recalled it all more clearly now. He had been disappointed, he remembered – not as disappointed as he had been when Oliver elected first to waste his time at university studying political science and then to run away to sea: even if not precisely shipping before the mast as a cabin boy, it had amounted to exactly that. He spoke the thought that he had had at the time, absently, as he remembered.

'It would have been good if one of my children had wanted to follow in my footsteps, and my father's. I would have liked that.'

An old hurt reared its head, unexpectedly.

'It wouldn't have been the same,' said Susan. 'I'm not really your child.'

Jerry stared at her.

'Whoever told you that?' And then, as Susan blushed fiery red, he said, 'No, don't bother to tell me! It was her, wasn't it – Dorothy?' Her silence answered him. 'How could she!'

Susan's colour had receded as suddenly as it had risen, she looked pale.

'She was right, wasn't she? I'm not a proper Nankervis, I'm just adopted.' She was obviously quoting.

'*Just adopted* …' Jerry was so angry that he had difficulty in speaking sensibly. 'Is that how she put it? Is that how you see it?'

Susan shook her head, not meeting his eyes, and didn't answer. The conversation had gone right off the rails, she didn't know where it was heading any more. She felt the weight of an old misery added to her present one, an integral part of it. Jerry took a deep breath, feeling the importance of the moment and afraid of making a mess of things.

'Susan,' he said, gently. 'Susan, look at me.' He waited until she had done so. 'Now listen. Your own father died, you know that, and before you were even born. He was a friend, a man I very much liked. When I married your mother, I asked her to let me adopt you and to take his place as far as I could, and so far as I'm concerned, that made you my daughter. That's how I have always thought of you. I promise.'

'As much as Debbie?' asked Susan, with difficulty. There was a lump in her throat. She swallowed. Jerry lied without hesitation.

'Quite as much as Debbie. Don't be a silly girl, now.'

'That isn't true,' said Susan, but she gave a lopsided smile. 'But thank you for trying. And thank you for wanting me, too.'

It seemed a good moment to take her in his arms, so Jerry did that, holding her close, feeling the soft curls of her hair brushing his cheek. They held each other without speaking for a long moment, and Jerry found himself remembering things that he hadn't thought about for many, many years, simply because Susan was so much a part of his family, and that, at least, he could say with his hand on his heart. Dot had made a bargain with him when he adopted little Susan Henrietta Geraldine Worthington, a bargain that, in one very definite way, had robbed the child of her heritage. He had thought that he had been giving her a new heritage, but it now began to seem as if Dot had robbed her of that, too. The things that Dot had wanted forgotten had seemed reasonable at the time and in the circumstances; now, suddenly, they didn't. She had, he knew, meant it for the best. That was Dot, and in fact, this time he had agreed with her unequivocally.

Then ...

He found himself wondering if bloody interfering, sit-in-judgement Anona Fingall – Theodorakis – *her*, anyway, had known about Henry. Helen certainly had, and he wondered if she remembered. He wondered if she knew that Susan *didn't* know: probably not, there was no reason why she should ever have been told, at the time they had hardly been speaking. He wondered all sorts of things, among them whether, if he ... no, not exactly broke a promise, but saw to it that the cat emerged from the bag with its whiskers twitching and its ears pricked, it would be a good thing or a bad thing. Time, after all, is famously a great healer.

At this point he realised that his daughter was shaking with sobs, and came back to the present with a jerk. For one reason and another, he didn't know Susan that well these days, in fact the weekend in St Erbyn was the first time he had spent any appreciable time alone in her company since he could remember. After her marriage she seemed to have drifted away and made her own life, but he was damn sure that weeping all over the place wasn't her usual behaviour. He had no idea that she might be feeling her world disintegrating around her, but he knew deep distress when he heard it. It shook him. Susan was always so much in control of everything, herself included.

'Hey, Susan,' he said, distressed. 'What's all this? What's the matter? Come here.' He cradled her head against his shoulder, stroking her hair. Bloody Tom and his shenanigans with that blonde piece! That had to be at the root of this. He wondered what he could say, and knew that the answer was, nothing unless she told him. If he had guessed wrong, he would only make things worse.

After a while, Susan stopped crying and sat up, drawing herself out of his arms as she did so. She sniffed, juicily.

'Sorry Daddy, don't know what came over me. Got a tissue?' Sniff.

Jerry went to his kitchen and took a handful of paper towels off the roll. It gave him time to think. He carried them back to her and she blew her nose, hard, and mopped at the tearstains on her cheeks.

'God, what an idiot!' she said, sounding more like herself. 'Sorry. Must be time-of-the-month, or something.' Oh, what a useful excuse that was!

Jerry hadn't gone back to his seat beside her on the sofa, he remained standing where he could see her properly. It unsettled her. She began to fidget with the crumpled ball of paper in her hands.

'Susan,' he said. 'Going back to what we were just saying, I *am* your father, all the Dad you've got, if you like to look at it that way. If there's anything wrong, surely you can tell me?'

How could she tell him she feared to be pushed out, to lose them all? Come to that, how did you tell your father that your husband was playing the field? After her mother's reaction, she wouldn't even want to try. She shook her head.

'It's nothing. Just Mummy, I suppose, and everything.'

It was Debbie – or Mawgan, rather – that Dot was gunning for, not Susan, so that was an obvious lie, Jerry thought. He tried another tack.

'Everything all right at home? Your own home, I mean, no problems with the children? Tom?'

He thought she flinched a little, but couldn't be sure. She looked down at her fingers, now busy tearing little pieces of paper from the main ball and rolling them into pellets. She said,

'Of course.' She swallowed, visibly. 'Maria is a treasure. The children adore her.'

Jerry gave up. He couldn't nag her to death. He said,

'Have you had anything to eat? I know you said that Tom was out.'

'Not yet. Actually, I'm not that hungry.'

'Then how about an omelette with your old dad? I haven't eaten yet, either.'

'Thank you, Daddy. That would be nice.'

She came into the kitchen to help him, expertly making *vinaigrette* dressing, tossing salad, gathering cutlery from the drawers. While she did this, she talked cheerfully about Annabel's progress at school (Sebastian, it appeared, hadn't made any), about the arrangements for the wedding, anything impersonal, and Jerry listened to her and wondered.

They shared the omelette and salad, followed it with some cheese and fruit, and the conversation got no further than the number of guests on the Angwin side of the equation – a surprising number, if they all came, said Susan, the family alone seemed to go on for ever. It would be a full church.

'I wish that your mother ...' Jerry began, and stopped. Susan said,

'Well, she won't. But we can make it into a great day without her, since that's the way it has to be.'

Neither of them added, *if it ever takes place*, but the thought was in both their minds.

* * * * *

After Susan's visit, Jerry spent a wakeful night. It had triggered memories that he had long ago shelved at the very back of his mind and set him thinking. These memories even took precedence in his head over Dot's unforgivable meddling in Debbie's affairs, and when he rose in the morning, stiff and sore and bug-eyed from a night spent tossing and turning, almost the first thing he did, after a refreshing shower, was to go and stand beside his phone, fighting with his inclinations.

Helen would remember. Everything that had happened then must be graven on her memory, as it now appeared it was graven on his. It hadn't concerned either of them at the time, but even so, she would remember, she had liked Henry as much as he did. More than anything, he discovered, he wanted to talk with her.

Their weekend in St Erbyn together had only been a moderate success, the children, intentionally or no, had outflanked him; he supposed most parents got used to that, but it had been a novel experience for him. Helen had told him, when he took her home, not to expect her to do it again. She had smiled as she said it, and thanked him anyway, but she had meant it. She didn't want him to pursue her, if that had been his intention.

Failing Helen, of course, he could talk to Nonie – but no. He could just imagine what she would say if she heard what Dot had made him agree to, and indeed, at this distance and after last night, it didn't look too good. You shouldn't use a child to manipulate another person into doing what they knew was basically wrong. And where had that gem of insight come from? He hadn't thought like that at the time.

Was everyone right, and had he let Dot wind him around her thumb?

He didn't want to think that, it altered too many perspectives. He left the phone where it was.

It may, however, have had some bearing on his decision, later on, to ring Dot – not about Henry, certainly not, but about what Susan had told him last night.

'It's way out of order,' he told her. 'You mustn't do it. Debbie is an adult, she can make her own choices.'

'And you'll just go ahead and let her,' said Dot. It was a statement, not a question. 'Do you have not one reservation about this – this publican of hers? I won't believe you if you say you haven't.'

That was the trouble with living with someone for any length of time, Jerry reflected. The other person came to be able to predict what you might be thinking. On the other hand, he didn't think that Debbie's money had anything to do with his own doubts. He said so.

'Dot, I know what you're saying, but believe me, his capital may be tied up – in two good businesses, I might add – but his income has to be more than adequate. I promise you. I'm not a fool.' He realised that he had called her *Dot*, where *Dorothy* had become the norm over the years. That was where reminiscence got you.

'I'm glad you consider yourself not to be a fool,' said Dot, satirically. 'I'm only taking perfectly natural precautions. For all you know, the man is mortgaged to his eyeballs – yes, I'm quite sure you haven't asked, for all it's your right as Deborah's father.'

He hadn't, it was true. It hadn't seemed to be his affair when Debbie was twenty-five years old.

'I don't think that's among a father's privileges these days,' he said. 'The days when a suitor was sat down in the study and grilled as to his prospects and his ability to support a daughter have long been gone.'

'I understand that this one didn't even have the courtesy ask,' said Dot. She didn't sniff, but the sound was inherent in the words. Jerry said, defending Debbie and Mawgan as much as himself,

'He might have, if circumstances hadn't got in the way. Probably would have, in fact.' Although he wasn't sure about that.

'Ho!' said Dot, in disbelief.

They seemed to have wandered far from the point, Jerry realised. He got back to it, *pronto*.

'However that may be, it doesn't give you any right to pry into his affairs behind his back.'

'I am not *prying*,' said Dot. 'I'm simply making sure that our daughter – *your* daughter, Jerry – isn't *used* by this opportunistic young man. *Whatever* his antecedents, which we neither of us know, I would point out.'

'Debbie's money is allocated to her own business, with the approval of her trustees,' Jerry reminded her stiffly, for he was aware that in that last respect, Dot – and Helen – were in the right. He should have at least checked out the family. It would have involved nothing underhand, after all, simply expressing a wish to meet them, a perfectly reasonable request.

'And what interest does *he* have in that?' Dot asked, pertinently.

'Well ...' said Jerry, and hesitated. In fact, the interest was tenuous – so far. The licensee of the Fish, which at present wasn't even Mawgan, would also hold the licence for the sailing school club bar. If it went further, he didn't know it. Of course, if the appeal was successful ... His hesitation confirmed Dot in her suspicions.

'I see. Well, it's a good thing that Deborah has a mother at least with her wits about her. What is it about this man? Even Susan seems to have fallen under his spell! And *Oliver!*' She almost spat the last name. 'Tim and Lesley Howells tell a different tale, however.'

'Listen Dorothy, I didn't ring to quarrel with you. I'm warning you, if he finds out about your private detective, you could be in trouble. That's all. And don't expect me to help you, I think you're in the wrong.'

'Well, that told me.' Dot sounded unconcerned. 'I suppose, if that happens, you'll be acting for him?' He suspected she was laughing. 'That will be interesting. Goodbye Jerry.' She rang off. Jerry replaced his own phone, carefully. Dot, when she tried, could be almost as irritating as Helen. He sat for a minute or two, wondering if he ought to ring Mawgan and warn him, but that would look as if he thought there was something to find. He decided to leave it for now.

It would be nice to hear Helen's views on the subject.

He managed to fight off the temptation until he found himself at home, alone, that evening. His children's affairs were, arguably, none of hers, with the obvious exception of Oliver, that is, but he might get more sympathy from her than from Dot, and the need to discuss the Henry question was becoming more and more insistent the more he thought about it – and he couldn't seem to stop thinking about it. Finally, almost without his own volition, he picked up the phone.

'May I take you out to dinner?' he asked, without preamble, when she answered the ring.

'Oh God, it's not you again! No, Jerry, you may not. I thought I had made that clear already.'

'I've got problems,' pleaded Jerry. 'I need to talk.'

'See a solicitor, then.'

'Oh, very funny!' He paused. 'Seriously. I need your input, there isn't anyone else.'

'You poor thing!'

Jerry took a deep breath.

'Helen, do you remember Henry's funeral?'

She was silent for so long that he thought she wasn't going to answer, and thinking back, he wouldn't blame her.

'Oh yes,' she said, at last. 'Dot was unforgivably rude and hurtful to poor Nonie, and then you went and sat in on the birth of her child without any reference to me.'

'That,' said Jerry, forcefully, 'is a gross distortion of the truth.'

'Oh, I'm not saying it was all your fault,' said Helen, with all the bitterness of a long-festering wound. 'She only had to whistle and you'd come running, I know that.'

'Helen!' he protested.

'Don't drag me into her affairs now, please,' said Helen. She felt better for that small outburst, as if she had just squeezed a persistent zit. 'Now, will you ex – '

'Don't you dare hang up on me!' said Jerry.

She didn't hang up, but she didn't say anything either. He waited, to give her the chance, and then said,

'Please, Helen. This isn't about you and me, or Dot even. It's about Susan.'

'Susan is no concern of mine. She's Dot's child.'

'And Henry's.'

'Exactly.'

'Helen, I really need to talk to someone. I can trust you.'

'*Trust* me! You're an optimist, what do I owe you that you should *trust* me?' Another surge of release. She must stop this, or she would begin to enjoy herself, and worse, begin to feel eased, and who knew where that might lead? Jerry said, steadily,

'I could always trust you. You are … full of integrity. I know that I didn't give you the same.'

'Let us not go there, Jerry. It's desert land.'

'Then come with me to an oasis, and we can eat dates together.'

The peal of her laughter was music. He hadn't heard her laugh like that for … well, a long time. He waited.

'Not dinner,' said Helen, after a pause. 'I'll meet you for lunch. Sunday, in the Black Bull.'

'No way. It's your turn to travel. Sunday in the Ravenscourt Arms.'

She hesitated. The Ravenscourt Arms was in a village not far enough away from Embridge.

'Someone will recognise us.'

'So? We were married, we're allowed to have lunch together.'

'You're married to Dot now.'

'Separated.'

Helen wanted to tell him to stop being childish, but she found that she was smiling instead, and not even at the prospect of some busybody tattling to Dot, but with the sheer pleasure of seeing Jerry again in one of their old haunts.

'All right. Twelve thirty, if I've got to drive back. I'd prefer to do it in daylight.' This time, she did hang up. Once again, Jerry hadn't expected her to agree, he had been, if he was honest, trying it on. He, too, was smiling as he replaced his phone.

VIII

Debbie had made one more attempt to contact Susan during the day, after allowing time for her mother to leave, only to be told by Maria that she was out. She had supposed that Susan might ring her back, and when she didn't, concluded that she must have had an appointment and put the whole problem on the back burner. Susan would ring this evening, or if she didn't, then Debbie decided that she would try again herself. When she did, of course, it was only to learn that Susan was out once more.

'She has gone to have supper with your father,' said Maria, a little sniffily, for she was supposed to have some time off this evening which had now been shifted to another day. Urgent family affairs, Mrs Casson had said, but she didn't repeat that to Mrs Casson's sister, naturally presuming that she would already know.

Debbie didn't, of course. She contemplated for a few minutes the idea of catching Susan with her father, but rejected it. What she wanted to talk over with Susan was no more appropriate in her father's presence than it was in her mother's. It would have been interesting to review present developments with her sister, but it could wait.

Mawgan was working this evening. With the burden of the Fish largely removed from his shoulders he was coping better, but he was volatile under pressure, and she was glad she wasn't in the kitchen. Everyone was going to be relieved when the year was safely over. At a loose end, she switched on her laptop and tried to focus on her own affairs, but her mind wouldn't concentrate, and after a while she switched it off again and sat with her chin on her hands, thinking.

It wasn't, she told herself, that she had any particular objections to her father and Helen getting together, she liked Helen, and her father's marriage to her mother had been history for a lot longer than the time elapsed since it had officially ended. To see two people that you cared for making each other unhappy over a long period of time, as her parents had done, was a depressing experience anyway, and she had left home so long ago now that it hardly had a practical bearing on her own life, so that wasn't an issue either. If it had been any other woman, she would probably have even been quite pleased, she decided. It was the Helen aspect that was somehow disturbing,

Why this was, she was reluctant to think about. Helen and her father had deep-rooted, shared history, of which Oliver was the living legacy. As in all families, there was a certain amount of folklore current – mainly among connections of her paternal grandmother – that had formed a half-understood, whispered-in-corners background at family gatherings throughout Debbie's growing years, particularly when Oliver, as so often, was causing trouble, which, although she had heard nothing specific, nor taken much notice, had always left her with an uneasy impression that there was antagonism towards her own mother; that Dot had, in some way unspecified, caused the break-up of that original marriage. Well, these things happened – but the fact that Helen and her father appeared to be drifting together again was obscurely upsetting. Debbie put it no higher. She didn't wish to plumb the depths that she suspected might exist beneath the obvious, didn't even see how she could do so.

All the same, it would have been nice to talk to Susan.

Restlessly, she got to her feet and headed for the door. Susan was out, she had established that, so she couldn't talk to her, but she certainly wasn't going to sit here brooding. She had two alternatives, she could drop in to see Chel and Oliver – and after Oliver's reaction the last time she had done so, she hesitated over that – or she could go down, as she sometimes did, and give Tommy and Denise a hand in the bar, where she knew she would be welcome. Any company was better than none when your thoughts were trying to stray into forbidden territory.

It was now early December, and visitors in the Fish were a rarity, particularly in the evening. The drinkers in the bar were almost entirely locals, which made for a cosy, friendly atmosphere that Debbie rather liked. In spite of her upper-middle-class upbringing, she found that living in a pub was good fun a lot of the time, there was always something happening. Her mother, she thought, would have been deeply shocked to hear her say so, and made derogatory remarks about the smell of beer and cigarette smoke pervading everything, but in sober fact, it didn't really. The Fish might have its faults, she concluded, but it was no spit-and-sawdust dive as her mother seemed to imagine, and since Chel had taken over the management, even after so short a time, it was becoming subtly different again. So that it was with a feeling of pleased anticipation that she pushed through the door behind the bar counter. Tommy looked up, and nodded to her, smiling.

'None too busy tonight, but a hand is always welcome,' he said. Debbie gave a quick look round the bar; mostly regulars, she saw, no doubt there were more round the other side in the public bar. A couple of strangers sitting beside the fire, middle aged, comfortable looking. She had an orange juice, he had a half. Tommy saw her looking at them speculatively, and moved closer to speak to her.

'Touring round, they said. Seems a funny time for it.'

Something about the way he spoke made Debbie turn her head to look at him.

'So? We get 'em, you know we do.'

'Ask a lot of questions, them two.' Tommy looked disapproving. 'I told Denise not to tell them nothing.'

'Visitors always do ask questions. They want to know things.'

'Not them sort of questions. You watch 'em.' Tommy moved away to serve a customer, and Debbie looked at the couple by the fire with more interest. They looked innocuous enough, but even just one season in the catering trade had widened her horizons considerably, and she knew too that Tommy was nobody's fool. So that it was with some curiosity that she watched the man toss off the last of his half and come across the room, specifically towards herself.

'Good evening,' he said, smiling genially. 'Another one, if you please. And how about something for your pretty self?'

Smarmy git! Debbie, *fiancée* of the landlord, sister-in-law to the manageress, found herself, almost instinctively, giving a sweet-village-maiden simper.

'Thank you sir, later maybe.' She took a clean glass from the shelf. 'Which one was it?'

'Ah ...' He ran his eye along the line of pumps. 'Think I'll try a different one this time. What do you recommend, little lady?' He nodded at the glass in her hand. 'There's no need to make washing-up. I can use the same glass.'

'The landlord would kill me,' said Debbie, removing the used glass to the top of the washing-up machine. He grinned.

'Tough employer, is he?' He nodded towards Tommy. 'That him? He looks quiet enough.' He winked – oh God, he actually *winked*!

Debbie smiled, and waved the new glass over the pumps, an enquiring expression on her face.

'Which, then?'

'I think I'll try the Doom Bar this time,' he smiled.

Tommy had only just put the new barrel on, and it came out foaming. Debbie set the first glass aside and took up a pint glass to pull it again. The man leaned on the bar watching her.

'I see you've done this job before,' he said.

'A time or two,' said Debbie. She set the second glass aside to join the first. It was clearing now, she picked up another half pint glass and tried again, setting it down to settle half way. Just her luck, to catch the beginning of the barrel *and* this patronising, sexist plonker!

'Nice little pub, this,' he said, settling his arms on the counter as if he meant to stay for a bit. 'Worked here long, have you?'

Debbie began to see Tommy's point. She picked up the glass and topped it up a little, setting it aside again and using the small activity to avoid answering.

'I'd heard the landlord was somebody called Angwin,' he said, casually. 'I see that's not the name of the licensee, so perhaps I was misinformed.'

Debbie said,

'Here you are, sir.' She topped up the glass and set it beside him, mentioning the price as she did so. He felt in his pocket, coming up with a five pound note.

'I'm sorry, I don't seem to have anything smaller.' He smiled widely. 'Are you sure you won't have one with me?'

'Your wife is all on her own,' Debbie reminded him, heading for the till, throwing a smile over her shoulder as she went. As she sorted the change, Tommy came to stand behind her.

'Still asking, is he?' he muttered, quietly.

'Not anything desperate, but yes – he's asking. Fishing, anyway.'

'Don't tell 'n nothing. I don't trust 'n.'

'Why, what do you think he is?'

'Spy for the weights and measures, I shouldn't be surprised,' said Tommy, darkly. He moved away, and Debbie went back with the change. The man was sipping his beer appreciatively.

'Good drop of stuff, this.' He took his change, but left it lying on the counter as if he planned to drink his way towards a refill. His wife, Debbie noted, was sitting quite contentedly, her orange juice on the table beside her. She had an air about her as if, at any moment, she would be taking out her knitting. Someone else was heading towards the bar, Debbie excused herself and went to serve them. When she had finished, he was still standing there, smiling and nodding at her. She decided, on impulse, to string him along a little, see what came of it.

'We don't see many visitors around here in December,' she said, casually.

'We're just touring round. The wife hasn't been well, she needed a break.'

Debbie didn't like men who called their wives *the wife*. She said,

'Wouldn't somewhere warmer be better? A bit of sun?'

'Oh, we love Cornwall.'

'How lucky that you were able to take the time off,' said Debbie. He had emptied the glass, she held out her hand. 'Another one?'

'Please.' While she pulled it, he sorted out the change on the counter and pushed the money towards her. She asked, as if casually,

'So what do you do? What's your business?' concentrating on the pump as she spoke.

'Me? Oh, a bit of this and that – you know.' He winked again. 'I bet this place is heaving in the summer, isn't it?'

'It gets pretty busy, yes.' She wondered if Tommy would think she ought to have said that, although it was hardly a secret, but it was too late now. She couldn't take it back. He nodded, but seemed only casually interested. He said,

'You live around here, I take it, Denise?'

'Denise is the girl in the other bar,' said Debbie, with a smile. One of the regulars came up, pushing his glass across to her, she turned to him.

'Fill 'er up, Deb, there's a good girl. Short round this time, miserable buggers!' He nodded to the man beside him. 'Evenin', mate.' He took the refilled glass. 'On the slate, I'll settle up later.' He went back to his seat beside his friends.

'So you're Deb,' said the man, smiling. He picked up his half-empty glass. 'Sorry for the mistake, my dear. Better get back to the wife, I suppose, she'll be grumbling about me chatting up the pretty girls.' Nod. Leer. Wink. Gone.

And that, thought Debbie, could be taken as very interesting indeed, if you had a nasty suspicious mind. He would chat up Denise – and he must have heard the name mentioned to be using it – but for some reason, he wouldn't chat up Deb. She wondered about the inferences for a minute, but decided that she was being paranoid. He was just a creep who had realised he was on to a loser, surely.

'Got rid of 'n then, good girl,' said Tommy, half as a question. He had been within earshot, Debbie wondered if he had been listening, and if so, what he made of it.

'Yes ...' she said, slowly, but in fact, she hadn't. He had gone on his own. Tommy looked at her quickly.

'What's wrong, my lover?'

Debbie gave herself a shake, as if to shake the man out of her head.

'Nothing. But what a slimy toad!'

Tommy turned his back to busy himself among the mixers, pulling fresh bottles forward on the shelf.

'Tried to book a table in the restaurant, he said. Couldn't get a reservation, was asking why it was closed half the week, 's if it was any of his business. I told him, winter opening times. He asked me, was business bad in the winter then.'

'So what did you tell him?' asked Debbie, after a pause.

'I didn't,' said Tommy. He shot a sideways look at her. 'Might be an idea to mention it to the boss, d'you think?'

'No.' Debbie thought for a moment. 'No, he's got enough on his mind. It's probably nothing. You might run it past Chel though.'

'I'll do that. She's no fool, isn't that Chel.' Tommy moved away to serve, and then a cheerful group came through the door, and settled around the bar, and that was the end of private talking. The man, Debbie noticed out of the corner of her eye, was trying to chat up one of the regulars now, full of cheerful *bonhomie*, but it looked as if he might be getting a disappointing response. He left shortly after, accompanied by his wife, and the group around the bar being in a party mood, Debbie forgot about him.

Not so, the wily Tommy. As soon as Chel came into the bar the following day to have their usual morning review of the stock, he mentioned it. Chel listened in silence until he had finished, then she said, much as Debbie had done,

'It could just have been simple curiosity. You know what some people are like – quaint Cornish customs, and all that.'

'Maybe.' Tommy looked unconvinced. 'There's things I can't help remembering, like Mawgan has them as bears him a grudge, them as'd like to see him in trouble.'

'Anyone particular in mind?' asked Chel, as if casually. Like Debbie, she had respect as well as liking for Tommy, and he had, she knew, been a loyal friend to Mawgan when the chips went down.

'Like, for a start, that sister of his and her friends. I often wonder about that rumpus we had in the bar here back in the summer, and if it was somehow down to her – night before the house went up, along the road there, that was before your time, but Deb'll not have forgotten. Then there's Mike Stanley's friends – can't help thinking, the family's moving back home, stirring it all up again. Might not be good.'

'You're thinking, this man might be after a story? Newspaper, maybe?'

'Could be. Or just someone trying to get him in bad with the law. People do that, make up some fault to report, hope as something comes up when they come around. Been done before, and nobody's perfect.'

'It sounds a bit far-fetched.' Chel hesitated, but she knew that Tommy was right, and such things had been done. 'Tell you what, if he appears again, give me a buzz. If I'm not down here, I can be here within ten minutes. I'll check him out, see what I think.'

'That works,' said Tommy, after a pause to think. 'He likely won't know about you. That's one thing gets me thinking, reckon he did know about Deb. Backed off, soon's he heard her name. I don't like it. She didn't neither, tho' she didn't say.'

On reflection, Chel voted with the majority, she didn't like it either. She returned to the office she now shared with Mawgan, very thoughtful, and sat for some time staring at a blank computer screen.

* * * * *

On Sunday, Debbie remembered her abortive attempt to speak with Susan and tried again, with more success this time, for what good it did her. Susan appeared to have something on her mind that Debbie got the impression was other than Helen and their father, although she didn't say what it was. Her contributions to their talk were crisp and short, Susan at her most big-sisterly.

'I don't see that what Daddy does is any concern of ours any more,' she said, in answer to Debbie's first, speculative comment on the visit.

'That's not what I meant,' Debbie pointed out. 'I like Helen, it isn't that. It's ... well, I get to wondering about what really happened – you know?'

'No, I don't know. I might, if you'd talk English.'

'All those years back, when Helen walked out. Most divorced wives won't give their husbands the time of day, in my experience, or the other way about. They certainly don't go away together for the weekend, years after. So what I can't help wondering is, what really happened?'

'What really happened when?' asked Susan, densely her sister thought.

'When they fell out. Did you ever know?'

'No. I was only about two at the time, how could I?'

'You might have heard things. You're older than me, I know that people like Auntie Anne and Auntie Ellie used to talk to Grannie, but when I appeared they always shut up.'

'What Grannie talked about with Dad's sisters needn't have had anything to do with Mummy *or* Helen. Don't be so paranoid!'

'I just wondered, that's all.' Debbie heard herself, sounding defensive, and took a deep breath. 'There *was* something, Suse, you know there was.'

Susan's hackles rose at the thought that her mother might have done to Helen what Elaine was doing to her, and she repudiated the mere idea. Sympathy, her mother might have withheld, but loyalty was deep-rooted and couldn't be withdrawn in a single moment.

'Debbie, you're talking rubbish!' All the easier to say since she didn't want it to be true. She knew that, at the very back of her mind where the bad things lurked, but chose to pretend otherwise.

'No, I don't think so. Look how she's behaving over Mawgan – Mum. It's ... well, it's unreasonable. Don't you think?'

But the way that their mother was behaving over Mawgan was even more dangerous ground. Susan said,

'Deb, you're being ridiculous. She only has your interests at heart, you know she has.'

Debbie said, in a lost voice that unexpectedly touched her sister's conscience,

'I can't help wondering if it's her own interests that she has at heart. That's all.'

'Well, Daddy's on your side. I wouldn't worry. Maybe she'll do a U-turn.'

'I just think, it'll be a first if she does.'

It was necessary to alter the direction of the conversation. Deeming it unwise to change it completely, Susan asked,

'Would you mind – if Helen and Daddy got back together?'

'They won't, will they?' Debbie had avoided thinking directly about this, not really knowing how she would feel. Susan shrugged, although Debbie couldn't see her.

'They might. That's the second time they've been seen around together. The second time that we know of, anyway. It might be a regular thing.' She allowed a challenge to creep into her voice. 'Maybe it's been going on for ages. Maybe that's the real reason he left. We don't know, do we?'

It wasn't a pleasant thought. Debbie wriggled uncomfortably on her chair.

'No, I won't believe that.'

Susan, who didn't really believe that either, said contentiously,

'The whole point is, *we don't know*. We never have known. So it's useless to start speculating about it now. There's damn-all we can do about it, anyway.'

'How would *you* feel?' asked her little sister.

Betrayed. Lost. Lonely. Shut out. Susan couldn't say any of those things.

'It wouldn't be anything to do with me. Deb, stop going on like a temperamental teenager, please! Behave like a grown-up!'

'It's all right for you,' said Debbie, inaccurately. 'It's my wedding she's spoiling. If she can do that – well, what else has she done?'

It takes an Elaine to spoil *my* wedding – my marriage, anyway, Susan thought, and almost said it. But Debbie was right, she already had enough to contend with and their mother was definitely out of line here. So she said, instead,

'Deb, you just have to believe it'll be all right on the night, and get on with it.' And if you do believe that, you'll believe the moon is made of green cheese too.

'I want her there. I don't want this rift between us.'

The thought was in both their minds then, perhaps Helen hadn't either. They both spoke at once.

'Want will get you nowhere, that's the way it is,' said Susan, and,

'Oh God, I didn't mean to moan!' cried Debbie, ashamed at the childish wail she had just uttered.

'Deb –' Susan began, but was interrupted by the purposeful entrance of Maria. The guilty knowledge of her mother's unforgivable behaviour made her seize on the excuse . 'Oh sorry, Deb – I've got to go. Look, I'll speak to you later in the week. And cheer up!'

She was gone, and Debbie switched off her mobile and slung it irritably onto the table. Mawgan, at that moment walking in through the door from his stint with the Sunday lunches, raised an eyebrow.

'You look cross.'

'Just been talking to Susan. She's in one of her I-am-always-right moods, I think we just fell out.'

'Not hard, with that one, I imagine,' said Mawgan cheerfully, and this was so true that Debbie laughed.

'Do your sisters ever get like that?'

'Mine? No. I've got the big advantage, I was the only boy.'

'It never worked for Oliver,' said Debbie, already feeling better.

Mawgan had gone into the tiny kitchen in search of a cold beer to take into the shower with him. His voice came to her muffled by the wall.

'His problem. He should've trained you better.'

'Yes, I can just see you training Anna and Allison,' scoffed Debbie. She winced. The unspoken words *or Cressida* hung in the air, so solid they were almost visible. Mawgan headed for the bedroom door with his can and she threw herself into the corner of the sofa.

The trouble was, of course, that little sister Cressida was one of the reasons why Mawgan was so stressed out, and Debbie was well aware of it. She hadn't communicated with her family since the end of August – three months, by this time – and although she was reputed to have gone off with a friend of her late husband's, not even a postcard had arrived to say that she was all right. With Christmas looming up, and after it the wedding, this omission was causing the whole family concern – concern that would, before too long, metamorphose into distress. Mawgan, rightly or wrongly, felt responsible, although in Debbie's view little sister Cressida should take most of the blame on her own shoulders.

Chel, she knew, thought that Cressida was dead, but she could hardly say so, certainly not to Mawgan. She wasn't even certain that she believed it herself, although at the time that Chel had said it, it had been convincing enough. But clairvoyance? Who believed in that? *Really* believed in it, that is. Weirdos and idiots!

One of the reasons? Debbie found herself thinking. She was *all* of the reasons! Directly or indirectly, Cressida had stage-managed the original fatal confrontation, she lay behind her brother's arrest for murder and the prison sentence that, Debbie was certain, had changed him irrevocably, she was the reason that he consistently overworked, that he was on, let's say dodgy, terms with his family, and that his relationship to most of his old friends seemed to be irretrievably damaged. And that was before you even started on the relationship that had been between the two of them and now lay in tatters.

The really lousy part of it was that she had probably never meant any of it to happen in the way that it had. Events had got away with her, as they had with Mawgan, leading her deeper and deeper into the morass she had herself created, and if she had simply opted out and made a run for it, intending to cut her losses and never confront any of them again, Debbie could quite see why. How did you set about repairing such damage? You couldn't, was the short answer to that, and Cressida's reputation wasn't that of a person who thought too deeply, or had moral courage; if that had been the case she would have stopped the whole thing before it fairly started, and she hadn't. Cut and run would be just her style.

Only, unless she got in contact, nobody could prove it, and if she had cut and run, then obviously she wouldn't get in contact. And if she didn't, nobody would ever know whether Chel was right or wrong.

So what could you do about any of that?

Nothing. And the bugger of it all was, alive she would make things worse, dead she would only compound it all. So no winners there.

People had no right to mess up other people's lives like that, thought Debbie, and came full circle, back to her mother, her father and Helen. No right to do it, but they did it just the same. So, what was the truth, and would anyone ever tell her, and had she any right to ask them anyway? What useful purpose would it serve if she found out that her mother had, as she was beginning to suspect, deliberately forced herself between her father and his first wife? None!

Except that it would give an uncomfortable insight into her mother's relentless methods, and perhaps be a salutary warning to herself. Did she really want to believe that?

No, she didn't. And there was nothing worse than being totally disowned that her mother could do to her, anyway. The situation had been made very clear, unless she changed her mind about marrying Mawgan, then her mother never wanted to see her again, which was bitter, but more bearable than the alternative, which was where Dot had made her mistake.

'You look miserable,' said Mawgan. 'What's the matter, bird? Sunday afternoon blues?'

Debbie jumped. She had been so immersed in her own thoughts that she hadn't heard the bedroom door open, and she looked up to find him standing beside her, damp from the shower, wrapped in a towelling bathrobe.

'I was just thinking about my mother.'

'Ah!' He sat down beside her and gathered her into his arms; she rested her cheek against the rough towelling and felt comforted. When he was close to her like this she had no doubts that she had made the right choice, no fears that anything would come between them.

But the man was back in the bar that evening.

Sunday was Tommy's night off, Mawgan's night on. Even with Chel managing the Fish, he liked to work in the bars occasionally to keep his finger on the pulse, usually at lunch time, but Sunday evenings was a regular shift, allowing Tommy to spend the afternoon and evening with his mother and to escort her to the chapel. He could have asked Chel to take the turn, he knew, but it hardly seemed fair, so he kept it on. Often, Debbie helped him, together with Sunday Sam, at least during this winter season, and she spotted the man as soon as he came in.

This time, he was alone. It fell to Debbie to serve him, both Mawgan and Sunday Sam being already occupied.

'On your own tonight?' she asked, almost by rote. It was pointless to upset the punters, even if you didn't like them, as Mawgan had been at pains to point out – in the context of her friend Tim Howells and himself at the time, but the rule held good. The man smiled at her, as if she was a fellow-conspirator in something.

'Can't have the wife around all the time,' he said. 'Cramps a man's style. I'll have a half of that excellent liquor that I had the other night, thank you, young lady.' He looked around him, expansively. 'Landlord's night off, is it?'

The landlord was, at that moment, drawing a pint of draught Guinness, while listening to a probably scurrilous story being recounted by one of the fishermen. Debbie smiled, but didn't immediately say so. She began to pull the half of Doom Bar. The man leaned on the bar, his head too close to her own.

'When the cat's away, eh?' Debbie looked up then and met his eyes.

'I beg your pardon?'

He winked.

'Sunday staff, part-timers, never know what they get up to. Leave you in charge, does he? I'd keep my eye on that dark one.' He nodded in Mawgan's direction, just as a burst of testosterone-rich laughter rose uproariously from the group around him at the bar. Debbie said, with satisfaction,

'He *is* the landlord,' and turned to serve the next customer, thus missing the suddenly narrow stare he gave her before turning to take a second look at Mawgan. Tommy would never have missed it, but Tommy was singing hymns in the chapel at the other end of the village, and helping his mother sort through her small change for the collection plate.

The next time she saw him, he had worked his way through into the public bar and was talking to Sunday Sam. She had come through with a tray to collect empties, and there was nothing she could do about it, even had she had a real excuse. It did feel, though, almost as if he was sifting through the bar staff to find out who was who, and then ... well, talking to the lesser fry, actually, but what could there possibly be in that?

She found the opportunity later on to ask Sam what the man had been saying, if he had been asking questions, but Sam didn't even remember him.

'Come on Deb, you know we talk to lots of people, every evening. How can I remember just one?'

'This one was a stranger,' said Deb, but Sam only replied, logically,

'They're all strangers to me, Deb. Get real!'

Which was as near true as to be unarguable, Sam lived in St Keverne.

Since by this time the man had left, Debbie couldn't even point him out. She had to leave it at that but, she told herself, if nothing memorable had been said – asked – then that was probably all right. Not having been party to Tommy's confidences to Chel, she put it out of her mind, with a mental reservation to tell Tommy when she saw him.

That, of course, wouldn't be until Tuesday, since Monday was now Mawgan's day off.

* * * * *

It was the woman who came in on her own at lunchtime on Monday, ostentatiously toting bags full of shopping, telling anyone who cared to listen that, ooh, it was good to take the weight off her feet!Unobtrusively, Tommy sent one of the lunchtime kitchen staff to the office with a scrawled note for Chel.

She's back. No sign of him. T.

At first, the woman seemed happy to settle herself into a corner with a glass of orange juice, sorting through her bags as if gloating over her purchases, but when Chel unobtrusively slipped in behind the bar, she sat up. A new face, a pretty redhead, what luck! Andy would be so pleased. She tottered to her feet as if her shoes pinched, and shuffled up to the bar.

'I think I might like a nice sandwich, dear, while I'm waiting for my hubby,' she said.

'Certainly.' Chel reached for a bar menu. 'If you like to choose, I can take your order and bring it to you.' She smiled ingenuously.

Mary Barlow, who was neither so old nor so mumsy as she appeared, nor anyone's wife, for that matter, took the menu and perused it short-sightedly while the pretty redhead waited with her smiling face.

'Ooh, it all looks very nice. What do you recommend, dear?'

'If you'd like a sandwich, the roast beef is very good today. Or the pasties are home-made on the premises, if you want to be more adventurous.' Chel reached for a pad and a pencil and waited. She didn't make the mistake of believing that the show was for real, although, without Tommy's warning, she admitted to herself that she might have. Mary mumbled indecisively for a minute or two, and then settled on a roast beef sandwich with English mustard.

'So much nicer than that French kind – De-john, or what do they call it?' she said, and waited while Chel put the order through to the kitchen – the pub kitchen, of course, in this case. When Chel turned back, she was still standing there, so she naturally asked,

'Can I get you anything else? The sandwich will be a minute or two, they're always freshly made to order.'

'That's nice. I do so hate those little plastic triangles, don't you?' Mary Barlow hesitated, as if making a difficult decision. 'I think I'll have a nice ginger ale.' She perched herself on a bar stool, looking hopelessly out of place, like a duck on an eagle's nest. 'I'll just sit here if that's all right? My hubby isn't here yet. Don't take any notice of me.'

'Please,' said Chel. She fetched the bottle of ginger ale and poured it foaming into the glass. 'Ice?'

This one, Mary found, was more than willing to chat. Yes, certainly, her luck was in today.

'Are you down here on holiday?' the redhead asked, in a friendly way quite different from that stuck-up blonde the other night. Fancied herself, that one, Andy said. The client's daughter, and engaged to the landlord. The client wanted it stopped, well, Andy was good at finding things out about people that they wanted hidden so that was a foregone conclusion. He said, it was no wonder, the man was a peasant, apparently, and the client thought herself no end of a lady, although he had his own views on that, no question. As these thoughts went chasing through her head, she smiled back at Chel.

'I've been ill, you know, bronchitis. My doctor said, get out in some good clean air in the country somewhere, so we thought we'd just have a week in Cornwall. We spent our honeymoon here, you know.' She leaned forward, embroidering freely on the cover story. 'Down in the far west, that was.'

'Really?' said Chel, widening her eyes. 'Where would that be?'

Mary hurriedly searched a map of west Cornwall in her head for somewhere sufficiently obscure, and made an unlucky guess.

'A little place called Trelewan, not far from Land's End. We stayed in a dear little whitewashed pub, with roses round the door and everything, so romantic! Much smaller than this one, of course. Do you know it at all?' She put her head on one side, like a robin asking for crumbs.

Chel knew the Cornish Arms in Trelewan very well; had, indeed, spent many a merry evening in its bar. She therefore knew that a.) it was built of granite blocks, b.) it had no roses round its austere door, and c.) it didn't let rooms, but she kept all this interesting knowledge to herself.

'That sounds lovely.' She moved a cautious pawn across the board, temptingly. 'Of course, this pub was much smaller than it is now, when it was first built. It's very old.'

'It must take a lot of upkeep,' said Mary, making her eyes round. 'But then, I expect it's very busy in the summer.'

'Oh, simply seething,' said Chel. She had to turn away then to serve someone, but Mary Barlow was pleased to see she came back afterwards to go on chatting. One of *those* sort, more interested in talking than working. Perfect!

'We wanted to have a meal in the restaurant here,' Mary confided, as her sandwich arrived, plump and tasty-looking, on its plate. 'We couldn't get a table, it was so disappointing. My hubby promised me, 'Mary, I've read some good things about that restaurant, I'll take you for a meal there,' he said. 'Nothing's too good for you.' But then, there wasn't a table for two weeks, they said, and the place is shut half the week, too.'

'Well, it's winter time, isn't it?' said Chel. She had been about to add, everyone deserved a break after working all the hours God sends all summer long, but decided against it. Let the woman ask, if she wanted to know.

'Not so many people around,' said Mary, nodding sympathetically. 'Well, there's no point in paying people to do nothing, I suppose.'

Mawgan, Chel knew, could open his restaurant eight days a week if there were that many, and still fill it respectably each night. She held her peace. It seemed to her that the conversation was taking a definite direction, she moved out another verbal pawn.

'A lot of catering businesses in Cornwall do find it difficult to break even in the winter. A lot of the trade is very seasonal.'

'Ah, yes.' Mary nodded, wisely. 'It must be very hard for those that have mortgages to keep up. Quite a worry, I daresay.' She added, innocently, 'I hope the landlord here manages to break even, my dear. It's such a beautiful place! It would be a shame if it went the way of so many village pubs these days and had to close. Then you'd be out of a job, and I don't suppose there's too many of those around here.'

That was far enough, Chel decided. She had a picture now, although she couldn't tell if it was the right one.

'Oh, I don't think there's much fear of that,' she said. 'Let me take your sandwich to your table for you? You'll be much more comfortable there, and you can keep an eye on all your parcels.' She came round the bar and picked up the plate without waiting for a reply. 'Have you had a lovely day, shopping?'

Mary found herself back at her table, without quite knowing how it had happened. She nodded to the couple at the table nearby.

'What a sweet girl,' she said, keeping in character.

'Ah, she's a nice woman, is Mrs Nankervis,' said the man, watching Chel with approval as she returned to the bar. 'Come in to manage the place, she has, while Mr Angwin makes changes to his restaurant. Going places, is this old pub, it seems.' He nodded, and returned to his companion.

Mary Barlow was surprised – no, shocked might be a better word. But one unexpected nugget of information she had, at last, obtained. Changes meant money being spent. Andy would be pleased, and there was no need, after all, to tell him that she had been talking too freely to the manageress, and certainly not to mention her very unusual name – unusual to Mary, anyway. It was the first real lead they had come across, and totally by chance. She ate her really excellent beef sandwich with enjoyment.

'What d'you reckon?' Tommy asked. Chel looked thoughtful.

'She was asking a lot of questions about the amount of money the place made – no, not asking questions exactly. Speculating. I've no idea why, but I can think of a few reasons just like you can.'

'Trouble, then.'

'I don't know …' Chel thought back over the conversation she had just had. 'It was all a bit strange for someone who wanted to cause the obvious kind of trouble.'

'Tell Mawgan, then. We should.'

'No. There's nothing really to tell, and it would only worry him. He doesn't need that, as no doubt you realise.'

'I guessed,' said Tommy. He gave a grimace. 'All right then. But keep your ear to the ground, and so will I.'

The man and his 'wife' were never seen in the Fish again, they took their enquiries elsewhere with no idea that they had, to a certain extent, been rumbled. But only to a certain extent. Neither Chel nor Tommy knew what Mary Barlow had learned by chance, and it wouldn't have told them anything if they had.

After a while, it was almost forgotten, dismissed as a bad case of galloping paranoia.

IX

'Y ou said you wanted to talk about Susan,' said Helen, 'And I want to put on record, before you start, that I think it's Dot's business, not mine, and perhaps you should discuss whatever it is with her.'

'That's the trouble,' said Jerry. 'I can't, I know what she'll say. And I'm starting to believe that she's terribly wrong, and always has been.'

'That's a first,' Helen murmured, into her wineglass. Jerry pretended he hadn't heard.

'Tell me, what did you know about Henry?'

'*Henry?*' Helen stared at him. 'My goodness, that's digging up old bones! Henry ...' She thought, frowning. 'Henry was an investment broker? He was fool enough to marry Dot? He was Susan's father? What else is there to know? He was a nice man, if that matters. Too nice for her.'

Jerry said,

'Henry was a widower. Did you know *that*?'

'Yes, I think so. I hadn't really thought about it.' Helen paused. 'Yes, of course I knew. His sons and his daughter were at the funeral. I remember, because they were our age, and had children and everything, and it seemed so strange when Dot ...'

'Was pregnant with his child? He didn't want any more children, did you know that?'

'He should have been more careful then.'

'He let Dot persuade him, because she was young and she told him it wasn't fair to deprive her of her birthright as a woman.'

'She had a point. On the other hand, she didn't have to marry him in the first place. It was always a risk, he was nearly forty years older than her.'

'Not so much May to September as April to November, I know.' A silence fell between them, while both of them thought about Dot marrying Henry and the reasons she might have had. Their thoughts were slightly different, but essentially the same too. Jerry thought that Dot had married out of disappointment and chagrin over his engagement to Helen, Helen thought that Dot had been determined to beat her to the altar to prove that she didn't care. They didn't exchange these ideas, it was a barren subject.

'She didn't love him,' was all that Helen allowed herself to say.

'I wouldn't know about that. She cared about him.'

'So did you and I,' Helen pointed out. 'Anyway, why are we talking about him now? How does he affect Susan? He never even knew her.'

'Nor do they,' said Jerry.

'What?' Helen stared at him. 'Nor do who? What are you saying?'

'Henry's children. They don't know her. And so far as I'm aware, she doesn't even know that they exist.'

For once, Helen was left without a ready answer. She finished her wine and held out the glass.

'Get me another one, please. I need to think about that.'

By the time he returned, she had got her breath back and her thoughts in order. As he sat down, she said,

'Was I not concentrating properly, or did you just say that Susan doesn't know she has more brothers and sisters than just Oliver and Debbie?'

This was putting it more specifically than Jerry was ready for.

'There were reasons.'

'Christ! I hope they were good ones! She's got nieces and nephews – *great* nieces and nephews by this time, probably, God knows what in the way of cousins, and *she doesn't know*?'

'No.'

'Explain, please.'

'Of course, you left the funeral early,' said Jerry, choosing his words carefully.

'Too right I did. After those terrible things she said to poor Nonie – and after Nonie came all the way up from Cornwall out of misplaced fellow-feeling to be there for her, and you know what it must have cost her.'

'Helen – '

'She said,' said Helen, recapitulating, 'that she didn't know why Nonie had bothered to come, that she wasn't a friend, and that Matt had been a pervert. She said it loudly, and in front of everyone.'

'I'm not denying it. *Or* excusing it, before you set about me. A lot of people heard her, including Henry's daughter. She wasn't impressed.'

'Good. She sounds like a nice woman!'

'She was – is, no doubt. On the other hand, you have to bear in mind that none of his children was in favour of their father's second marriage. In fact, they blamed his coronary on Dot.'

'Harsh, but probably fair. She did take it out of him – and take it out *on* him, too.'

'Helen, I know you don't like Dot – '

'If *that*'s what you think you know, I have to tell you that you don't know anything! I *loathe* Dot, Jerry, and I think I'm about to loathe her some more. You'd better tell me, what did she do? Quarrel with them all?'

'What happened at the funeral didn't exactly help, and then there was some unpleasantness about the will – as so often.'

'Henry was loaded, I thought.'

'They claimed that Dot had exerted undue influence to exclude their children in favour of her own child.'

'Ah. But her own child was *his*, too. And fatherless, as it turns out.'

'That's all true. And Henry had treated all the children equally – he set up a trust fund for Susan – of course, he didn't know it would be Susan, but for his unborn child – equal to the bequests to the children of his first marriage. And a generous bequest to Dot, of course. But only keepsakes to his grandchildren. Valuable ones, but nonetheless …'

'Sounds quite reasonable to me. It was up to them to provide for their own children, I would have thought.'

'I thought it was reasonable too, when I drew up the will for him. But Dot had managed to create a lot of bad feeling, and I told you … they blamed her – some of them did. One of his daughters-in-law is a practising barrister, and a right snotty bitch into the bargain. She postulated that Dot should have been placed on a par with his children, and Susan with the grandchildren. She had a point – of sorts. There was no real case to answer, of course, but there was a lot of mud thrown – well, you can imagine.'

'I'm sure Dot threw a lot of it,' Helen murmured, interrupting. Jerry frowned.

'However that may be, it ended, they wouldn't speak to her again, and she turned her back on them. Family life in the raw.'

'God, and I thought *your* family had problems!'

'You know what they say, where there's a will, there's trouble.'

At this point, the waitress came to tell them their table was ready in the restaurant – the Ravenscourt Arms didn't do a carvery – and the discussion had to be shelved while they carried their drinks through and took their places. Then Helen said,

'Of course, the truth is that their family problems and yours stem from the same cause. Dot doesn't know how to be conciliating if she wants something.'

'She was within her rights on this occasion.'

'Her trouble is, she always is. You can't go through life being that inflexible, other people have a right to a point of view. But they were wrong too, to take it out on Susan. She was their sister, after all. It wasn't any of it her fault.'

'I wouldn't like to swear that they did,' said Jerry, slowly.

'Really,' said Helen. She picked up her spoon to start on her soup, leaving the word hanging in the air, not quite a question. After a moment, Jerry spread toast with *pâté* and crunched the first mouthful. By the time he had emptied his mouth he had won himself space in which to think.

'The thing is,' he said, 'by the time I married Dot, Susan was three or four years old. I don't know what had happened during that time, Dot never said. I adopted her – Susan – you know that?'

'I heard you had. I liked you for it, if you want to know,' said Helen. She crumbled her roll, reflecting. 'You were always a nice man, that was your big problem.' It was the kindest thing she had said to him in years. Jerry blinked. Helen said, 'But don't let it make you conceited.It meant you were a bloody fool.'

'On this occasion, I believe you might be right,' said Jerry, soberly.

'Tell me,' said Helen, when the pause had gone on too long.

'Dot agreed to the adoption. I wondered if she would, or if she would want Susan to keep Henry's name and maintain the connection with his family … but she was more than happy for her to take my name. Only she made a condition. It seemed reasonable at the time.'

'It always does,' said Helen, and sighed. 'Tell me the worst, then. What has she done to poor Susan? I always thought it was odd that she should escape so thoroughly.'

'Oh no, she hasn't done that – then *or* later,' said Jerry, with what seemed to Helen unnecessary force. 'Dot said that she would be happy to have me adopt Susan, but that she was never to know that she had half-brothers and a half-sister. And since there was so much bad feeling, and she assured me that she hadn't spoken to them since the big row over the will, it seemed OK to agree. Where was the point in telling her? I adopted her as my daughter, as if she was any child who didn't know its antecedents. It seemed the best thing – the *only* thing, their rejection would only have hurt her.'

Helen had known Dot and studied her methods over a long period of time.

'But she never said *they* hadn't spoken to *her.* I see. That's Dot.'

'Yes. And there's another thing, and I'm not proud of it but there's nothing I can do about it.'

'Which is?'

Jerry didn't meet her eyes as he replied.

'I never knew that I would have a daughter of my own. I love Susan – dearly, as it happens. But I know, and she knows, that Debbie is closer to my heart. You never think of it when you're surrounded by your own, but the tie of blood is very, very strong.'

'And Susan senses the lack of it,' stated Helen.

'So I think. Yes.'

'You must tell her. I don't care what you promised Dot, she had no right to ask it of you. Susan has the right to know.'

'I can't. We signed an agreement.'

'*Jerry*! And you a solicitor, too!' Helen was shocked.

'I told you. It seemed like the right thing ... at the time ...'

'And your legal conscience can't stomach breaking the agreement and risking Dot's wrath?'

'Basically, no. Do you really think she'd not tell the whole world?'

'No, she'd wipe the floor with you.' Helen had finished her soup, she laid down her spoon. 'Are you telling me you want me to do it for you?'

'I don't know what I'm telling you. I just think … what was right at the time, or seemed so, isn't right any more. I don't know why this should be, I just know that Susan is in need.' He pushed his plate away, the *pâté* only half-eaten.

'And you say you love Debbie more,' said Helen, thoughtfully. 'Want my opinion?'

'Yes – no – I'm getting it any way, I rather think.'

'I think,' said Helen, 'that you just love Debbie *differently.*'

Jerry considered this. He remembered Susan in his arms, the softness of her curly hair against his cheek, her unspoken despair.

'That could well be so,' he conceded. 'It doesn't help the present problem.'

The waitress came to clear the plates.

'Was your *pâté* all right, sir?' she asked, solicitously.

'Yes yes – fine – I'm not that hungry.' He waved her away.

'The thing is,' said Helen, 'I don't see what I can do. If Susan chose to confide in me, then yes, I'd be glad to tell her the truth. But I can hardly walk up to her and say in cold blood, hey Susan, guess what, you've got nieces and nephews older than you are, not in any language. We aren't on those terms. I can't imagine anyone who *is.*'

'I feel I have to do something.'

'Why?' asked Helen. 'I mean, why now? Susan's been legally your daughter for – what, twenty-six, twenty-seven years? What's suddenly different?'

The waitress was back with steak and ale pie for Jerry, grilled rainbow trout with almonds for Helen. She fussed with the vegetable dishes, spooned hollandaise sauce, seemed as if she would never go away. When she finally did,

'If I tell you, it's like everything else we've discussed today, in strictest confidence,' said Jerry.

'Understood. But if it's private, perhaps you shouldn't.'

'There's two things,' said Jerry. 'One of them I know to be a fact, the other is guesswork. I don't know what I should do about either of them.'

'Then give me the fact, and save the speculation for pudding,' said Helen.

Jerry hesitated. He spent time grinding pepper, sprinkling salt, concentrating on what he was doing.

'I don't know if Susan knows this,' he said, at last. 'I hoped she didn't, but I'm beginning to suspect that she does. Tom is having an affair with his assistant. He's not being very circumspect about it.'

Helen had almost guessed already, it wasn't hard.

'How tacky,' she said. 'Poor Susan.'

'Maybe,' said Jerry, surprising himself.

'*Maybe?*'

'It's been a very bland marriage,' said Jerry, as if in apology. 'Perhaps it suited her, I don't know. I do know that she isn't happy now, but there could be another reason.'

'Which is?'

'We haven't reached the pudding yet.'

'Stretch a point.'

Jerry sighed. He wasn't at all sure that he wasn't being silly here, and he knew that if he was, Helen wouldn't hesitate to tell him so. He said,

'It's Cornwall. Debbie and Oliver – and Chel and Mawgan too. You must have noticed. They're …'

'Behaving like a proper family? Yes, I pointed it out, if you remember. But it's Chel doing that, and more particularly, Mawgan. Deb and Oliver are simply along for the ride.'

'They haven't jumped off, however. In fact, Mawgan is the nearest thing to a really close friend of Oliver's that I have yet seen, and did you notice *that*?'

Helen had of course. She had even mentioned it, if obliquely. She shook her head.

'Even so, I don't see what that has to do with Susan.'

'That's the whole point. Neither, I suspect, does Susan.'

Helen thought about this. She lowered a forkful of trout back onto her plate.

'Oh sugar! Poor Susan.'

'The thing is,' said Jerry, warming to his theme, 'everything is happening down there. Debbie is starting a sailing school with her friends, she's getting married, she's got a whole new life opening up. Oliver and Chel live so close they can hardly help being involved, and Chel is managing the Fisherman's Arms anyway, now. Oliver's going to paint this mural in Mawgan's new restaurant, Mawgan – you're right – is the magnet that's pulling them all together. But Susan ... she's stuck here with – well, with what?'

'The life her mother planned for her,' said Helen, and tried not to sound sour as she said it.

'Exactly.'

'So what you're saying,' said Helen, thinking it out as she spoke, 'is that you think that Susan thinks that the other two are ... not deliberately shutting her out, they wouldn't. But doing things together without her. But she's not there, how can she think that?'

'Maybe she'd like to be there.' Jerry shrugged his shoulders. 'I don't know, I told you, it's just speculation.'

Helen put her finger onto the nub of the argument.

'Seeing you and me going down there together can't have helped. She must have felt it was just one more nail in the family coffin – the family as she knows it, anyway.'

'But it isn't,' said Jerry, and wanted to add, I wish it was.

Helen picked up her fork again.

'Well, if you're on the right track, then poor Susan. But Jerry, handing her an alternative family isn't going to help, even if it's possible, which you don't actually know. It's you three that are the family she knows – and she loves you all. I know she can be abrasive.'

'I'm beginning to wonder if that's always been down to insecurity. I'm beginning to think – Helen, I fucked up, didn't I? Spectacularly.'

'Yes, you did, a bit,' said Helen.

'It's not so easy to put everything right.'

'Impossible, I should think.'

Jerry said, *à propos* of nothing obvious,

'Bloody Anona Fingall!'

Helen sent him a look that he couldn't read, but made no comment. They ate in silence for a while. Helen spoke first,

'So far as Susan is concerned,' she said, 'I don't believe you can blame yourself. Even if she hadn't married you, Dot would have married again, probably, and he might not have been as good a father to her as you've been. He could have been a lot worse. The only thing you couldn't do, was to bring her own father back to life for her.'

'And Oliver?'

'That's another question.' Unaccountably, Helen found it was difficult to swallow. She took a sip of wine. 'But you haven't fucked up over Debbie. Debbie is great.'

Jerry didn't mean to say it, the words simply emerged from his mouth while he was feeling for Helen's justifiable bitterness and hurt over Oliver, because that, at least, was entirely his fault.

'No, but I think I may be about to.'

Helen sat perfectly still for a long moment, waiting for him to continue. Then she said,

'You can't just leave it there. What's gone wrong?'

'Nothing – yet. I hope it won't.'

'This is Dot again, isn't it?' said Helen, and although Jerry knew that she spoke out of prejudice, she was undeniably right, so,

'Yes,' he said.

'I would have thought,' said Helen, 'that this is one instance where getting her own way simply isn't an option. What can she do? She's already shot her bolt, so far as I can see, and Debbie has had the sense not to fall for it. She's in love, she's going to be married, Dot can't stop her. She can't leap up in the church and stop the marriage, she's no legal reason. The only thing she can do, if she wants to do something positive, is to back down. And she won't do that.'

'No,' said Jerry.

'What do you mean, no?'

'No, that isn't the only thing she can do. There's something else, and she's done it.'

This time, it was Helen who pushed her unfinished plateful away. She leaned her elbows on the table.

'So, tell me.'

Jerry told her. Helen listened carefully, and at the end, she said,

'And do you really think this is going to work? Do you think he only wants Deb for her trust fund? If so, you're fair and far off! Quite apart from the fact that Chel is certain he knew nothing about it, he worships the very air she breathes, he's a man who can't believe his luck – particularly when it's recently been so abysmal!'

'If Dot's detective turns up something to his discredit, all of that may make no difference.'

'Debbie has more sense! And she's got your approval. What can Dot do?'

'That,' said Jerry, 'would depend on what came out.'

Helen appeared to consider this.

'No,' she said, finally. 'No, there might, I suppose, be a teeny-tiny element of tax evasion, something like that, but he's not a *criminal*!'

It was Jerry's turn to say,

'Really?' He saw her face and relented. 'No, I know what you're saying. But it needn't be anything in that line. If it turned out he was simply in financial deep water over his head it might be enough. For one thing, a responsible father could hardly approve in that case.'

'Your Deb would want to bail him out.'

'The trustees wouldn't let her. I know, I'm one of them. Dot is another, come to that.'

'Jerry ...'

'I know, I know.' He looked at her, ruefully. 'It's just ... you know Dot. She gets her own way. And so far as I know, nobody has yet found a way to stop her.'

'There has to be a first time for everything.'

'So they say, but there's no guarantee that this is it.'

'Have you told Mawgan that there's a detective on his trail? What did he say, for God's sake?'

'No, I haven't.'

'His reaction might be interesting – informative, even. I think you should.'

'I might, if I thought that his present state of mind was anything approaching stable. It isn't. He's liable to go off like a rocket if anyone lights the blue touch paper.'

'Serve Dot right!'

'It might not be Dot that he ...' Jerry paused on the word *hits*. He added, more prosaically, 'Or of course, he might simply plunge right down into the abyss. Which might be even worse.'

'Bugger! But even so, you must tell him. You've been on about people's right to know – he has a right to know this.'

Jerry said, simply,

'I'm afraid for my daughter's happiness.'

'Not telling him isn't going to protect her. It may just do the reverse.' When Jerry said nothing, she went on. 'Jerry, pull yourself together. You're inventing bogeymen here, you know. Mawgan is depressed, he's overworked, he's overtired, he's got a right to be all those things, he obviously been through a bad time. He's a long way from *unstable*, however, get real! In fact, I know of few people with their feet more firmly on the ground, come to think. There's no way he would ever hurt Deb, and you know it! So either you trust him or you don't, and if you don't, why the hell are you footing the bill for the wedding?'

'I do trust him.'

'Well, then!'

'It's just that when you start stirring the pot, things bob to the surface – and some of them can be unexpected.'

'Dead flies and gristle?'

'Bodies ...' said Jerry, and was taken aback when Helen said,

'We know about that already, it won't come as a surprise.'

'Helen! I didn't mean – ' He broke off. He had forgotten about Mike Stanley, genuinely forgotten. Helen gave him a gimletty stare.

'Jerry Nankervis, you are a vacillating fool! You know what you should do, you always have. It's doing it that's always been your problem. Why don't you just forget that you're a solicitor, and act like a man instead?'

Jerry tried, feebly, to defend himself.

'It's just that Dot never meant Susan to tell me, I'm sure of that.'

'It's not your fault if she did, however,' retorted Helen. She narrowed her eyes at him. 'You're scared of Dot, aren't you?' She sounded so accusing, so taunting, that Jerry rocked back on his chair.

'No!'

'Then for God's sake, come out of your mousehole in the woodwork and *warn* the man!'

There was a long, pregnant pause, while they tried to stare each other out. Jerry said, finally,

'All right. I will. But I can't do it on the telephone; if I'm going to do it at all, you're right, I want to see his reaction. And you could at least have called me a rat.'

'No, you're a mouse,' said Helen. 'Good boy, Jerry. How does it feel to take a stand against the Dreaded Dot, then?'

'I haven't done it yet,' said Jerry. 'Helen …' He wanted to ask her if he really had let Dot run the whole show, but he couldn't. Not Helen, she was too deeply involved. It occurred to him that maybe, if he could resolve the question in his own mind, he might know what to do next. Might, even, rescue something worth having from the wreck he had made of his life.

His life, Helen's, Oliver's, Susan's it now appeared – but not, definitely not Debbie's.

'I'll go down next Sunday,' he said, and was surprised at the decision in his own voice. 'I can do it there and back in the day, Deb did. Want to come?'

'No, thank you. I'm glad the mouse has turned! Keep it up, you'll be a rat yet.'

'It's worms that turn.'

'No,' said Helen, with a very sweet smile. 'Worms wriggle out of it. Are we having pudding?'

* * * * *

Jerry drove back to his flat, and before he could talk himself out of it, picked up the phone and rang the Fish. He hadn't liked the suggestion of scorn in Helen's candid eyes, in her soft Scottish voice. He was surprised to find how much Helen's good opinion meant to him, even after all these years.

'It's like waking from an anæsthetic,' he found himself thinking, as he waited for someone to pick the phone up at the other end. 'Everything blurred but coming into focus, and the bad dreams fading, and pain … everything coming alive again. God, never mind Mawgan, I think I must have been having a nice, quiet breakdown of my own! How can I have wasted so much precious time?'

''ullo,' said an unfamiliar male voice. 'Fisherman's Arms.'

'I wanted to speak to Debbie. This is her father.'

'Ah – hang on a mo – *Deb*! It's for you!'

Jerry removed the phone from his ear, flinching and looked at it in amazement. The unknown man apparently hadn't bothered to move it away from his mouth before he yelled. His daughter's quieter voice on the line came as a relief.

'Hullo?'

'Hi, Debbie, who in hell was that?' Jerry's ear was still ringing.

'Tommy. Sorry Dad, we've got a bar full. What's the problem?'

'Oh God, Deb, I'm sorry, I never thought. I can't get used to this pub life of yours – would you like me to ring back?'

'Is it going to take long?'

'No. Just wanted to say I was coming down next Sunday, I want a word with Mawgan. Are you around?'

'Yeah – sure.' She sounded taken aback. 'Anything wrong? He could ring you.'

'No, I'm glad of the excuse to come and see you both, to be truthful. I miss you all. I don't suppose we can do lunch somewhere, get Oliver and Chel to join us?'

'Why not? I'll see if I can get us a table here, shall I?'

Jerry could hear the murmur of voices and laughter in the background. He said,

'That'll be great. See you, then.' He rang off after they had said goodbye. He was glad, he realised, about the bar being full. It had stopped Deb asking awkward questions.

228

Awkward questions …

Jerry stood for a long time, staring into space. A man should confront his conscience every now and then, if he wasn't to be mistaken for a mouse, or worse, a wriggling worm. In order to confront his, he would have to take a long, long walk down memory lane, but perhaps it was time. More than time.

If he left very, very early on Sunday he could do it. It was becoming more and more important, he found, to clear the ground. Of course, when he had done so, nothing might grow there, but he wanted to try. He wanted to try, he realised, more than anything else in the world.

He picked up the phone again and dialled Enquiries.

* * * * *

There is always somebody to tell you the things that you really would be happier not knowing, and in Susan's circle, there were several people who habitually started sentences with phrases like *I thought you ought to know*. By the evening of Sunday, two of them had already rung, gleeful for a gossip, to let her know that her father had been seen lunching with Helen Macken in the Ravenscourt Arms.

'I don't see why you're bothered,' said Tom, when she told him this. 'It isn't as if there's the smallest chance that your mother and father are ever going to get back together, after all.'

'But *Helen*,' said Susan.

'What's different about Helen compared to anyone else? Your father's played the field in his time before this, you must know that. Who did it hurt? Not you! And your mother always pretended not to notice anyway. She's the type – *hear no evil, see no evil* – ' He broke off. The final three words of the aphorism he considered inappropriate. He wasn't all that fond of his mother-in-law. He contented himself with saying, 'She's too much the lady,' and trying to keep the sarcasm out of his voice. The unspoken words *like you* hung in the air.

Susan flushed. This might be true – she knew it was true, in fact – but Tom didn't have to say it out loud. He looked at her, shrewdly.

'Or is this just because she's Oliver's mother?'

'Of course not!'

'Face it, Suse,' said Tom. 'It's nothing to do with you, anyway. You've never been one of them, you know it, I know it. Get real!'

'I just think that Mummy has had enough humiliation for the moment,' Susan retorted, more hurt by this remark than she wished him to see.

'That's an interesting choice of word,' said Tom.

'Yes, isn't it?' replied Susan, before she could stop herself.

Suddenly, they were no longer talking about Jerry and Dot. Between one sentence and the next, the boundaries had moved. Tom hesitated for the space of a heartbeat, then he laughed, lightly.

'Come on, Suse.' He put his arm around her. 'It's their affair – maybe in every sense. They're all grown-ups.'

'You think *affairs* aren't to be taken seriously, then?' She didn't respond to his hug, and he dropped his arm again.

'Of course I don't think that. But if the marriage is a good one, an affair shouldn't be the end of everything, these things happen after all, they mean nothing. And if it isn't a good one – and your parents' obviously wasn't – why should it matter?'

'That's an interesting point of view,' said Susan. Almost, then, she brought up the subject of Elaine – but immediately she thought of what might follow, and her courage failed. She already felt that she was losing too much, she couldn't face …

Face what? Losing Tom, too?

'What's the matter?' asked Tom, narrowing his eyes at her suddenly.

Susan sighed.

'Just that, it being Helen seems gratuitously hurtful, I suppose …'

'If you can't take it, don't dish it out, is what they say, isn't it?'

Susan knew that her mother had behaved, on the whole, highhandedly, *badly* even. Nevertheless, she obscurely felt that someone should be on her side.

'She meant well …' she said, and thought what a vapid, unsatisfactory epitaph that was to her parents' failed marriage and all the carnage that surrounded the vacated field of battle.

'Anyway,' said Tom, in an unlucky attempt to be bracing and positive, 'it's no skin off your nose. He's only your adoptive father, not your real one. Don't get yourself into such a state over it!'

Susan felt tears sting behind her eyes. Did he really have to labour the point like that? She turned away.

'Oliver won't like it, anyway. That's for certain,' she said, with an obscure wish to see someone else hurt, however vicariously. Tom only laughed.

'Your brother Oliver is such a law unto himself, I doubt he'll lose any sleep over it,' he said. 'And neither should you.'

'Yes, you already made that clear.' Susan went over to the door. There, she paused with her hand on the handle, looking back at him. He stood by the window, lounging around with his hands in his pockets, serene and untroubled. She suddenly had a wish to needle him into a reaction. Any reaction.

'You have remembered we're supposed to be going to Seb's nativity play tomorrow night? He's one of the wise men. You promised.'

'I said I would if I could, if you remember,' said Tom. 'It's a busy time, Suse – I can't promise. You know that.'

'Sebby thinks you promised.'

'I can't help that. Business is business.'

'But you'll try,' said Susan, making a statement of it.

'I said I would.' He smiled like a man who could be trusted, he hoped. 'If I can't make it, take your mother. Sebby'll like that, too.'

Susan gave him a contemptuous look, but made no reply. She left the room, closing the door behind her with a noticeable snap.

Tom, when she had gone, took his hands out of his pockets and straightened up. He looked thoughtful. That had been a warning, he rather thought. He didn't want to find his marriage on the rocks, he had too much at stake within it. His comfortable lifestyle, his children … He cared about his children. Well, he cared about Susan too, of course he did. It was just that Elaine … Well, nobody would call Susan a sex kitten, would they now? She was far too uptight.

But perhaps he had better let Elaine know that he couldn't 'work late' tomorrow. It might be safer, and Elaine would just have to understand.

X

Jerry's freedom to come and go at will was naturally constrained by the responsibilities of his working life, he had already taken one rather inconvenient day for 'family affairs', he couldn't justify another one so soon. For Andy Simpson, his working life was defined by his freedom to come and go. While Jerry, therefore, was spending his time on his clients' affairs and in court hearings, Andy continued with his client's business out in the wider world. Under such circumstances, a week can be a long time.

He was beginning to amass some curious, although not so far conclusive, information.

The first, and most obvious thread to follow had been Edward Rushton, of course. Edward Rushton had been the subject's partner in the purchase of the Fisherman's Arms and its adjoining restaurant, and having drawn almost a blank in the pub itself, Andy therefore lost no time in searching him out. His trail wasn't hard to pick up, and on the whole, Andy found, it led downwards. Edward Rushton, once landlord and part-owner of a prosperous country inn, had moved at the behest of an ambitious wife into the night club business, where he had spectacularly failed. He was now barman in a modern, brewery-owned theme pub on the outer fringes of Bristol, full circle back to where he had begun. He was a bitter man. Some temptingly placed bait soon had him baring his soul.

'Places like this!' he said, looking at his surroundings with scorn. 'They say they're the coming thing, and OK, they bring in the punters! Cater for the kiddies, you've got them hooked – but I ask you, is a pub the place for kiddies? No, it isn't, and most adults I know would agree with me!'

'People on holiday like places like this, where the kids can play safely while they have a drink in peace, and a decent meal that suits everyone, surely,' said Andy, amiably. He ordered another pint and settled himself more comfortably on his bar stool. Investigating a subject in the licensed trade was proving very much to his taste. Edward Rushton scowled.

'It's not real life,' he said. 'It's a bad copy – real life is a pub like the one I had down in Cornwall – centuries old, seen some history. Local trade and good local beers, atmosphere you can really get your teeth into. They're dying off, one by one. Sad.'

'So, why did you leave it?' asked Andy reasonably, although he knew perfectly well.

'My partner got into a bit of bother,' said Edward, but didn't enlarge on the theme. 'The wife wanted out, went banging on about guilt by association. She always wanted a more exciting life than we had down there.' His gloom deepened. 'Fat lot of good it did, listening to her. She wanted a club, dim lights and bright music and entertainments and I gave it to her. Then she ups and off with one of the entertainers, and leaves me lumbered.'

'So you sold out,' suggested Andy, quirking his eyebrows into a question.

'I went bust,' said Edward shortly. 'I never wanted the bloody place, and it went flat on its face. Knew I hated it, I always thought. I only bought it to please Amanda, and mortgaged my soul.'

'Women!' said Andy, sympathetically, and raised his eyes to heaven. After a pause, he ventured, 'So what happened to your old pub? Couldn't you have bought back in? I expect your partner would've been glad to see you back, or did he sell up too?'

'He bought me out. He wasn't likely to want me to buy back in, even if I could, which I couldn't, not after I let him down so badly. He wasn't – *isn't* a fool – not in business, that's to say.'

'So his bit of bother wasn't financial, then,' said Andy.

'No,' said Edward. He closed his lips firmly and made to turn away. Andy said, as if casually,

'That's obvious enough, I suppose, if he could raise the money to buy you out.'

Edward gave him a look, and moved away to serve a family party clustering noisily further along the bar, and Andy went quietly on with his pint. After a while, when the barman was free again, he ordered another. This time, Edward Rushton opened up a little. He seemed to want to talk now.

'Thing was,' he said, polishing a glass and not looking at Andy. 'We had a bit of luck, he and I. Came up on the pools, would you believe it? A crowd of us did – we all worked in the same place, a hotel in the city here, we formed a syndicate, you know how you do? He was the head chef, I managed the bars. There were one or two others, the DJ who did the evening entertainment, he went on to do well for himself. The assistant manager, he's in charge now. The head waitress – oh, about half a dozen of us, I suppose. The rest of them all went on to greater things.' He laughed, without amusement.

'Presumably then, you all won the same amount,' said Andy, knitting his brows. 'So how come he was able to buy you out so easily? Or was it millions you won? You lucky devils!'

'Not millions, we didn't get that lucky. I never do.' It seemed for a minute as if he wasn't going to enlarge on this, but Andy waited, and after a while he was rewarded. 'We had enough, Mawgan and me, to buy the business between us – there's a restaurant, which he wanted, and the old pub that I wanted. The pub was the most valuable property, so when we put in fifty-fifty, as we did, that meant he owned a bit of the pub too. And after a couple of years, he'd got a bit put by to upgrade the restaurant. I always assumed he must have used that. It wasn't my business.'

'But you hadn't got anything put by?' Andy queried.

'I had a wife.' Edward gave a short laugh. 'You have a wife, squire?'

'No, thank God.' Andy looked thoughtful. 'The restaurant must have done well, if he'd nearly doubled his stake in two years – I presume he had, from what you say?'

'He did OK. He's a bloody good chef and he's an extrovert – he was then, maybe not so much now. He got noticed. But no, I doubt he'd put that much by.'

'So how ...?'

'How the hell do I know? I never asked, and his solicitor wouldn't have told me anyway. I just took the money, sorted out the problems, and left. Amanda saw to that. If you want to know, I wish a dozen times a day that I'd never listened to her, but I did, and that's that.' He turned away, this time, with finality. Andy sipped his pint and thought about what he had learned.

It confirmed, rather than added to, what he already knew, but it also deepened a mystery. Angwin's solicitor, Andy knew, had handled the purchase of the Fish on his client's behalf, his client being at that time detained during Her Majesty's pleasure. There was no chink in that solicitor's armour, his office, unusually, appeared to be bombproof and therefore the only details that Andy had been able to ferret out so far had been from the subject's bank, where one employee wasn't as far above reproach as he should have been. The loan – which had not originally come from the bank – had been repaid in hefty monthly instalments to a client account managed by the bombproof solicitor. At the beginning of the current year it had been transferred to a regular business loan and presumably thereafter been repaid in entirety to the original lender, and a second loan had been authorised in the last couple of months to cover the renovations to the restaurant, which, just to complicate the issue, had up until that time been considered as a separate enterprise, and was unencumbered.

It was fairly obvious from all of this that the money had originally come from a private source. The question of the week, however, was this: who would risk such a sum when the beneficiary was in prison, his business partner was about to flit, and he was therefore very far from a good financial proposition? There could be several answers, each more unlikely than the last. The correct one would be handy to know.

It might even turn out to be *The* Answer. Prison, after all, was a place where they put criminals.

Studying the copy bank statements that he had 'acquired' in the privacy of his own office, Andy had reached a conclusion. The subject was making good money from both his businesses, to cover his loans and still be making a profit; if there was a bias in one direction or the other, then the restaurant was overtaking the pub these days – but it was borderline. He was not obviously strapped for cash, which would disappoint the client. Andy was something of an expert in these matters, which was why Mrs Dorothy Nankervis was employing him to investigate her putative son-in-law. In his opinion, cash-flow was not a big problem here. If he wanted to earn his bonus, he would have to find some different questions to ask.

The most appealing possibility, and one that wouldn't disappoint the client, was that there was some dirty work going on at the crossroads, such as tax evasion, in which regard a look at the subject's business accounts might possibly be interesting as a last resort. Or blackmail was another avenue to explore, that loan had to have come from somewhere, and Andy, like Jerry Nankervis, was aware that the subject's prison record had been unusually free from incident. He could, of course, have simply kept his head down but he hadn't, from Andy's brief glimpse of him, looked the type; so to stay out of trouble, it was possible he had learned where somebody else had buried the bodies. There were several other areas that would need to be looked into, but on the whole, he was inclined to think that the solution to the client's problem had to lie in the explanation for that original loan. The client simply wanted rid, Andy didn't think she would particularly mind about the exact reason.

So, where *had* it come from?

How to set about finding out?

In Andy's experience, nothing was ever a total secret. He wasn't even sure that this piece of relevant information was a secret, as such, at all. It might be perfectly innocent when viewed in the light of day and in the public domain, its concealment purely accidental. On the other hand …

Know thine enemy.

He set off in search of Amanda Rushton. There had been a lot of mud flying around at the time of the subject's arrest – for murder, interestingly. Andy had, of course, seen the transcripts of his trial. Before he proceeded any further, he wanted to know a little more about the man he was investigating. In St Erbyn, they had all been far too *nice* – to the point where he had sensed a deliberate barricade set up against his artistically friendly questions. Amanda Rushton, he was fairly certain, wouldn't turn out to be nice at all, and would sing like the proverbial canary, and up to a point he was right.

Like her ex-husband, Amanda Rushton had found life a disappointment. Her fling with the comedian for whom she had left him hadn't outlasted its first impulse, and she had found herself, not the wife of a night-club owner, but on her own in London and needing to earn her own living. She had ended up where her husband had first found her, still reaching after the bright lights that she craved, as a hostess in a second-rate night club in the wrong part of town. Andy found that she blamed the whole thing on her ex-husband's one-time partner.

'Stupid Cornish git!' she said, when she was asked – directly, in her case. Andy, measuring her up during an evening's observation, had concluded that the best way to access what she knew would be to tap into the resentment that he detected in her attitude, and although he hadn't given her the reason, had made no secret of his interest in Mawgan Angwin. 'Anyone with half an eye could see that little madam was trouble!'

'This is Cressida Stanley, we're talking about?' Andy said, carefully.

'Who else? She wound him round her little finger, that brother of hers!'

'You didn't like her.'

'What was there to like?' Amanda tossed her head. 'She was terminally silly. The fluffy kind that sits and cries to get its own way.' She wrinkled her nose. 'She made the men sorry for her – like a kitten in the rain. But she knew exactly what she wanted, and she always got it.'

'So, as an observer – and I can see that you are an acute one – what did you make of her relationship with her brother?'

Amanda thought she knew at once what he was asking her, and reddened a little, not meeting his eyes. She therefore answered carefully.

' Oh … *she* was manipulative, but *he* was only dumb. She was around enough for anyone to be sure of that.'

'In what way, dumb?' asked Andy, interested.

'In not telling her to push off and let him get on with his job,' said Amanda.

'He wasn't unduly partisan, then?' His antennae were twitching; he wasn't certain why.

'Not that I ever saw.' She fidgeted.

'You didn't come out and say this at the time?'

'Nobody asked me, did they?' said Amanda, with another toss of her head. 'Anyway, he killed that man – her husband. It didn't come into it.'

Oh yes, it had come into it, the subject's defensiveness on his sister's behalf was a pivotal point in the evidence. However, it was no part of Andy's brief to find evidence in his favour. He said, instead,

'I have to tell you that you are the only person who has used the word *dumb* of your ex-husband's partner. Why would that be, I wonder?'

To his amazement, she blushed fierily and looked away.

'He was only dumb about her, I suppose.'

'Family relationships are odd, quite often,' observed Andy, wondering. He paused. 'Your husband must have had confidence in him, he worked with him before, I believe.'

'For one of those big hotel chains. Edward had worked there years.' She had trouble keeping the scorn out of her voice. 'He'd have been there yet, but Mawgan was different. He was only there while he looked around for something better, he made no secret of it. He'd been abroad for years and he was a brilliant chef, much too good for that place.'

'So when they had their lucky win, they pooled their resources, and bought the Fisherman's Arms?'

'Yes – and what a mistake *that* turned out to be!'

'I understand it was doing rather well for them.'

'Oh yes – until that stupid thug lost his temper and let fly with his fists! Edward couldn't be partners with him after that, could he? Everyone was talking – he wouldn't sell, so we did. And if you want to know, I was glad to see the back of it! God, what a dump that St Erbyn place is!'

'And Angwin bought your husband's share.' Andy brought the conversation back into line. 'Do you have any idea how he did that, when he was in prison?'

'He borrowed, I suppose.' She wasn't interested, had obviously never given it a thought.

'Not so easy, under the circumstances.'

'Who cares, anyway? It let us off the hook, however he did it.'

Amanda Rushton obviously didn't like Mawgan Angwin, and the reason, Andy suspected, wouldn't be far to seek. Edward Rushton was a plodder, ultimately a loser. Mawgan Angwin, on the other hand, was ambitious – and very talented, if rumour didn't lie. A potential high-flyer, in fact. Had she made a pass at him and been given the elbow? Or had he, perhaps made a pass at her? The former, almost certainly. Giving men the elbow wasn't Amanda's speed, if he didn't miss his guess. Particularly attractive men who were going places.

There was nothing useful to be learned from her, he mistakenly thought – or nothing that his client was going to want to know, at least. The man had upset her, the reason was probably obvious, whatever she said would be laced with malice. He therefore failed to ask the one further question that he might have asked, and went away satisfied.

But what a little cow! Rushton was well rid of her.

It was interesting, however, to discover how few people really disliked Mawgan Angwin, in spite of everything – of course, you had to except the family and friends of Michael Stanley, but them apart, so far as Andy was aware, there was only one other. He didn't think that Tim Howells would have anything relevant to say, but he thought that he would like to talk to him anyway. You never knew.

Talking with Tim Howells was a more complicated issue than searching out the Rushtons and leading them on to gossip about their past life. Howells – or at least, his estranged wife's family – was an acquaintance of the client, and the client, in this instance, was one whom Andy wasn't in any great hurry to cross. A bossy woman, to put it kindly; determined, liked her own way a bit too much. Moreover, Howells was a very close friend of the daughter – had been, that's to say, even if exactly where the friendship stood at the moment was debatable. He would immediately smell a rat if anyone started making casual conversation on the vexed subject of Mawgan Angwin, so the obvious move, Andy decided, was to have the rat in full view right at the start. With this end in view, he called on the client.

Dorothy Nankervis wasn't impressed with his reasoning.

'The cause of Tim Howells' dislike must be obvious, even to you. I don't see how talking to him can help you.'

Andy spoke reasonably.

'With respect, Mrs Nankervis, no, it isn't obvious. The ill-feeling between the young man and Angwin appears to be of longer standing than the growing affection between Angwin and your daughter. The affair may have fuelled it, it doesn't seem to me that it caused it in the first instance. Howells was, to all intents and purposes, happily married when they met.'

Dot accepted that this was possibly true, but still rejected the idea that it might be of importance.

'I can imagine no way in which Tim Howells could have known anything against him, certainly that early on in their acquaintance. Apart from the obvious, of course.'

'Then what *did* set it off?' Andy asked, pertinently, but Dot didn't know.

'Don't you think it might be useful to find out?' He looked thoughtfully at the backs of his spread fingers. 'It might be informative. It's interesting, when you come to look at it, how many people that come up against Angwin subsequently have ill fortune.'

Dot looked at him without speaking for moment. That was interesting – maybe.

'Very well,' she said, conceding a point. 'I'll set up a meeting between you, if I can.'

Tim Howells was in a very strange mood these days. Caught in a limbo, out on bail between being charged with arson and tried for it, his marriage in ruins and his embryo business ditto, and the love of his life not only engaged to marry a man he heartily disliked but muscling in on what he still considered to be his territory, he believed that life had probably sunk to its lowest possible point. Debbie's letter explaining what she was planning had ended up in the fire. He lived only from day to day, the only person in the whole word who knew, or even simply believed, that he was innocent, not counting, of course, the one who was actually guilty. His wife was petitioning for divorce, he was deeply in debt, he was probably going to prison: he sometimes found himself thinking, it would be good to sail his Flying Fifteen out into the far distance and just quietly slip over the side. The very last thing he needed was a visit from Debbie's domineering mother.

'I'm deeply concerned about Deborah,' she told him. 'I'm sure that you must be, too.'

'It's her life,' said Tim. He shrugged his shoulders. 'None of my business, anyway, is it? She's made her choice.'

'You can't be happy about it. You care for her, I know.'

Care for her. Yes. Nice way of putting it.

'I have no right to care for her,' said Tim, carefully.

'But you can care about her future happiness, surely.'

'Oh yes. I do that.'

'And do you feel she will be happy with this Cornishman?'

'It's none of my business,' Tim repeated, stoically. He didn't want to be dragged into a discussion on Angwin. No, he didn't like the man, but overlying the deep dislike he felt, sometimes almost obscuring it, was the recollection of Angwin plunging into a burning house to look for Lesley, without apparently taking a second thought. At a time, too, as Tim was now well aware, when he had unexpectedly found an overwhelming reason for staying alive. He had owed Lesley nothing, Tim even less – certainly he hadn't owed them his life, but he had come within a whisker of paying with it.

'If you care for her at all, it's very much your business. What, for instance, made you dislike him in the first place? It wasn't Deborah, he didn't even know her then.'

'Actually, he did,' said Tim, being, Dot thought, unnecessarily pedantic. 'It's just that none of us realised it.'

Dot paused, while she organised her thoughts. She recognised that Tim had no wish to be involved in Debbie's affairs, but he must be made to see differently.

'I intend to bring this engagement to an end, if I can,' she said, putting her cards on the table with apparent openness. 'He's obviously completely unsuitable, but the circumstances of their meeting seem to have brought about some infatuation – pity, maybe. I don't know, I haven't met the man. But you have.'

Tim said nothing. Bloody Angwin! Plaguing him to the bitter end.

'Well?' said Dot. Tim realised that she intended to have an answer, and he couldn't summon the energy to defy her.

'I don't think *pity* enters into it,' he said, allowing himself that much.

'Very well, maybe it doesn't. But you have to agree that it's a totally unsuitable marriage.'

Tim once more said nothing. Dot said, candidly,

'I believe that it may be her money, in his case, that forms the main attraction. Would you say that was possible?'

'I know nothing about his business affairs,' said Tim. 'The place was always seething in the summer. I would have thought he was doing OK on his own. Anyway, he didn't exactly pursue her, you know. They just seemed to come together naturally.'

This was something that hurt him to say, and that Dot had no wish to hear. She said,

'Appearances can be deceptive. He has very grandiose plans, I understand.'

Including an interest in my sailing school. *Mine*! Tim tasted bitterness, but retained a stoical expression.

'Presumably Debbie is part of them now.'

'Do something for me, Tim,' said Dot, persuasively. 'For Debbie's sake. If I send someone to see you, will you tell him everything you know about this man? Your reasons for disliking him?'

'They're totally irrelevant,' said Tim. 'He's going to marry Deb. Isn't that enough?'

'Please, Tim. You can't want that to happen.'

'Look,' said Tim. He had suddenly had enough of this conversation, and there was only one way he could see to bring it to an end, give Deb's mother what she wanted. 'I don't want to speak to anyone, I don't want to be involved. I'll tell *you*, but it won't help you.' He paused. 'Angwin and I had a business disagreement. I don't see that we would have been close friends anyway, but he wantonly obstructed my application for a licence, and thereafter he was a constant thorn in my flesh. He used Lesley and Deb to make a fool out of me and whether

244

he intended it or not, he played a part in the collapse of my business, so to be honest, I hate his guts. But he's a brave man. Braver than I am. That's all I can tell you.'

He refused to speak to Andy Simpson, refused to add anything to what he'd already said, wished, indeed, that he hadn't said as much. Dot went away, not unpleased with what she had learned, although she couldn't see how it could be turned to her use. But as a character reference, it was interesting. She concluded, in her own mind, that 'brave' meant 'too stupid to see the danger' and was moderately satisfied.

She had, however, told Tim quite as much as he had told her. After her departure he spent some time thinking about her visit and telling himself it wasn't his business anyway, but he failed to convince himself. Two things kept getting between himself and his intention to forget all about it. His love for beautiful Debbie, which was deep and all the more painful for being, as he knew, quite hopeless. The recollection of Angwin running into Seagulls without a second thought when it was already well ablaze. Because of him, Lesley had escaped a terrible death. She wasn't Debbie, could never measure up to her, but she had been his wife and in one way – a different way – he had loved her.

'Bloody Angwin!' said Tim, aloud, and not for the first time in his life. He went upstairs to his room and sat, for a while, at the table beneath his bedroom window where, in happier times, he had done first his homework from school and later, his studying for university.

Lesley was alive, unharmed. Debbie loved the bastard, and it was true what he had told her mother, they did come together naturally.

He reached out and switched on his computer.

*＊＊＊＊

The letter came on Saturday, twenty-four hours before Jerry was due to arrive at the Fish. It was marked PERSONAL, so

Shirley put it aside on the pile of correspondence relating to the restaurant and placed it on Mawgan's desk for his attention, and Chel never saw it at all. Never saw the postmark, for what it could have told her. She therefore jumped in alarm when, into a period of quiet concentration on the pub's computer, Mawgan unexpectedly swore, loudly and angrily. It was all the more startling because he wasn't, on the whole, much given to swearing. A good Methodist upbringing, Debbie said, had a lot to recommend it.

The shock had made Chel insert an unintentional row of nines into the bar account. Deleting them gave her time to recover. She stole a cautious glance at Mawgan, and saw at once that he was white and angry, angrier than she had ever seen him, reading a letter. He finished it, read it again, and then crumpled it up, throwing it into the waste paper bin. A moment later, he had retrieved it, smoothing it out and reading it yet again. Chel said, cautiously,

'Problem?'

'What's the matter with the bloody woman?' Mawgan asked, rhetorically. 'She doesn't even *know* me, for Christ's sake! Here – ' He thrust the letter at her, blindly. Chel took it, she had little choice.

'Do you want me to read it?'

He flung himself down in front of the other computer, anger and, Chel thought, hurt too seemed to throb off him.

'Be my guest!'

Forgive me if you think I'm interfering in your affairs, Tim had written, without salutation. He had never called Mawgan by his given name, but *Dear Mr Angwin* was somehow inappropriate. *I don't suppose it's really any business of mine, but Debbie as you know is very dear to me, and I probably owe you anyway, for one thing and another. Deb's mother has just been to see me, asking questions that are certainly no business of hers. I get the idea that she's gunning for you, in fact I believe she may have set a private detective onto you. Don't imagine from this that I'm accusing you of anything, or believe that you have anything to hide, but I feel you have a right to know, and that I would be wrong to keep it to myself. She has no right to try to come between the two of you. The only people with any right to change your minds is you and Debbie.*

Maybe I'm wrong about this, I hope so for Deb's sake, but have to say – to you – I don't really have any doubts. Deb's mother has a reputation for getting her own way and she's set her face against your marriage. In your place, I should be watching my back as a general precaution. Hope all goes well in spite of.

Sincerely, Tim Howells.

'Oh dear,' said Chel. Her mind was reeling, with the knowledge that if she wasn't careful here, they might all find themselves in very deep water. She said, in one way almost relieved to have it in the open, but with apprehension too, 'That explains it.'

'Explains what?' asked Mawgan, in a voice she had never heard from him before. She gave him a swift glance, then dropped her eyes back to the letter. *Ouch!* She had better choose her words with care.

'There were some people down here on holiday last week,' she said, slowly. 'They came into the bar two or three times. They chatted – you know how people do. Tommy thought they asked some odd questions.'

'Then why didn't he tell me?' Spoken with force.

Chel spoke even more carefully.

'He told me. I'm supposed to be the manager. You can't fault him for that.'

'OK, point taken. So what stopped *you* telling me?'

Deep breath. There is nothing so undermining as knowing that you're at fault. Chel met his eyes candidly and took the only way open, absolute truth.

'There was nothing you could really put your finger on. Yes, they asked questions – and yes, it was strange that they didn't seem to want to talk with Deb, almost as if they knew who she was ... and he – they were a middle-aged couple – didn't try to talk to you either, when he knew who you were.'

'You mean, they were there on Sunday night? Yes, now you come to mention it, I remember a strange face ... so why didn't Deb say anything then? I take it she was in on this, too?'

Chel swallowed. It went through her mind, possibly for the first time so specifically, that Mawgan wasn't just a friend, Deb's *fiancé*, but her own employer. He paid her, among other things, to watch his interests. She had no right, therefore, to keep things from him on personal grounds.

'I'm sorry,' she said. 'You're right, I should have mentioned it. It was unforgivable.' Mawgan said nothing, but his face spoke volumes. After a minute, she said, 'I never thought of Deb's mum. Tommy thought it might be someone trying to make trouble ... for other reasons.' She took a deep breath. 'Looking back, it's obvious. They were asking questions about how well the place was doing, why the restaurant was shut half the week, things like that. We stalled them off, of course ... Mawgan, I'm *sorry*. How can I ever apologise?'

Mawgan took a breath, she thought he might be counting. Finally he said,

'Chel, let's get one thing clear here. While you work for me, your loyalties are to my business, not to Deb. You don't keep things from me: whatever you know about my personal problems, in this office they cut no ice. Any other way, and we can't work together. Understood?'

'Yes,' said Chel. There was no other possible answer.

'Good.' He turned away and switched on the restaurant computer with a final gesture that ruled a line under the discussion. Chel closed her eyes. Just for a minute there she had seen why Mawgan would undoubtedly go places, and felt sorry for anybody – like Tim, for instance – who got in the way. Not an easy-going, likeable extrovert with things in his past that were making him work himself into the ground to forget them, but a single-minded succeeder, who would clear the dead wood from around his feet without compunction if it suited him. Slash-and-burn Angwin.

Ouch, indeed.

Opening her eyes, she looked down at the letter that she still held in her hands. She took a breath to help her gather courage.

'Mawgan ...'

'What?' He had opened a website on the internet, and didn't even turn his head. Chel said,

'That being so ... and your business interests being mine, and private between us ... will you tell me, *is* there anything that Deb's mum can find and use against you? Because I have to tell you ... she will.'

For a moment, he didn't move. Then he swung round on the chair to face her. She wouldn't, Chel found herself thinking, like to play poker with him.

'What makes you ask that?' he asked. He still sounded dangerous.

'Nothing. I have no reason to believe that there is, I'm simply asking. Because I know her, and you don't. And ... on the whole ... I don't know you. Is that honest enough for you?'

Mawgan said, very quietly,

'You don't none of you really trust me, do you? Maybe it'd be best to call the whole thing off, before it's gone too far.'

Chel sat very still. She was conscious of her heart beating, so loud that she thought he must hear it. Deb would never forgive her if she blew it now. She said,

'I don't know where you get that idea from. I thought we had all given you a rousing vote of confidence.' When he didn't reply, she went on, in a voice that sounded unlike her own. 'Anyway, you don't mean that. You'd break Deb's heart, and you wouldn't exactly please the rest of us, either. Just give me a straight answer. Is there a skeleton living in your office cupboard? Yes or no. Because if the answer is yes, we need to start work.'

A glimmer of curiosity came into his eyes.

'We do? What on?'

'Digging a deep dark hole?'

'What?' He stared at her. 'You are something else! But you can save your energy, there's no skeletons.'

'Not even a spare rib, or a few old teeth?'

'Those, maybe. Nothing actionable. I take it that's what worries you?' He sounded derisive, and Chel winced.

'Concerns me, more like.' She tried to keep the relief out of her voice. 'Then you don't need to worry. There's nothing she can do.'

Mawgan spoke bitterly.

'I would've thought, I was that vulnerable anyway, she didn't need to look for no more mud to sling at me! What's she got against me, apart from the obvious? We never even met – her choice, not mine.'

'The same thing she's got against me,' said Chel, more cheerfully now. 'We're common!'

'Are we?' He gave her a measuring look. 'Well, me maybe – but she didn't set private detectives on you, did she?'

'She wasn't given time.' Chel thought back. She was relaxing now, the dangerous moment seemed to have gone, and she allowed herself to smile. 'That's been your big mistake – you should just have taken Deb by the scruff of the neck and hauled her into the nearest registry office, like Oliver did me.'

'*Did* he? Goodness!' He paused, thinking. 'But it's not the same, is it? Oliver isn't her son, as I understand things.'

'No. He's Helen's.'

He met her eyes, and for the first time in this interview she saw someone she recognised.

'I'm causing trouble, aren't I? Story of my life just lately.'

'It's almost impossible *not* to cause trouble around The Dreaded Dot. She likes to run the world.'

'It upsets Deb. I don't like that.'

'If you want my opinion, short of a titled aristocrat, almost anyone would cause the same reaction. Don't lose sleep over it.' Chel paused, hesitating, but it had to be said. 'Tim's right, you know, she does have a bit of a reputation for getting what she wants. Don't let her get to you, will you? It's what she'd like.'

Mawgan turned back to his website, muttering something that she didn't catch, and the discussion seemed to be over. Chel waited a minute, but when he didn't say anything else she returned to her own work. The thought of Dot sent its old, familiar prickle up her spine and she tried very hard to banish it. If Mawgan was sea-green incorruptible, as he claimed – and she almost believed him – what could Dot do?

Nothing. Surely.

When Mawgan had finished on his computer, shut it down and gone, Chel stopped what she was doing and sat for a moment, fighting an unworthy inclination.

She had sworn, many times, that she would never do this. She had said that it was intrusive and unforgivable, unless someone asked. She knew that she was about to do it, all the same.

Yield not to temptation! Easier said than done.

Chel got out of her chair and walked over to the other desk, scanning its clutter with her eyes. What would work best, what was most personal? The scatter of pens was communal stuff, the thing he handled most was probably the mouse. She reached out, clearing her mind deliberately, and touched it, possibly the first recorded instance of someone using modern computer technology as a medium for psychometry.

A few minutes on, she removed her hand and stood there, thinking. She should, she realised, have felt guilty – it was a bit like spying, and that was undoubtedly wrong. If you believed in it, that was. Her own ambivalence on the subject made her cautious, but ... well, lucky old Deb!

She went back to her own desk and sat down. Nobody was better aware than she was that clairvoyance was an inexact – no, not science. She didn't know what she should call it, really. She knew that it gave her the *feel* of people when she made the effort, and that the feel of a person was what she had just experienced.

Off a *mouse*? Get away!

Her screen had gone into screensaver mode, Mawgan favoured stars and planets, very pretty. Picking up her own mouse, Chel disposed of them and returned to the bar accounts. She wondered if Dot might be in for an unpleasant shock this time and was almost sorry for her.

Well, time would tell. The battle wasn't over yet.

She must remember to warn Debbie to have her defence ready over the visitors in the bar. She wouldn't want Deb to have to face that stranger that she had herself encountered.

What she now knew, that she would never pass on to a living soul, faded out of her head. She reached out for the Brewery's last invoice and recommenced work.

XI

Unaware that the gaff was already blown, and his visit therefore not only unlikely to yield the information he needed but also requiring delicate diplomacy, Jerry set off for St Ives at an early hour on a pouring wet Sunday morning that did nothing to improve his mood. Nonie had invited him for breakfast, it occurred to him as he drove that this would be the first meal he had ever eaten under a roof of hers.

Breakfast with the Borgias ...

She had given him clear directions to find her cottage, which was tucked cosily into a fold of the moorland outside the town, and, as he found, even in the rain had a spectacular view of the sea. As he pulled up on the verge of the lane outside, he found himself thinking what a pleasant idea it would be to have a cottage like this for himself, where he could escape from business, town, and all his other problems and hide out when he needed to. He and Helen had had a cottage when they first married, in a village certainly, but old and full of character like this one. He remembered it with wistfulness as he got out of his car, and in the short distance between Nonie's gate and her front door had relocated that distant home to be on the Helford River, close to his children, and mentally installed Helen, her two terriers, and her beloved cat. Well, it was before breakfast he excused himself. The result, however, was that when Nonie opened the door to him, he found he had put himself at a disadvantage and he could tell from the sardonic expression on her bright, intelligent face that she knew it.

'Well, Jerry, this is a surprise!' She held the door wide. 'To what do I owe the honour? No – don't tell me now. The coffee's hot, strong and fresh – you look as if you need it.'

She closed the door behind him and led the way into a neat kitchen, fragrant with the smell of good coffee, pulling out a chair from a table already laid for two and inviting him to sit.

'Unless you've done enough sitting for now,' she added, reaching for a mug and the *cafetière*. 'Milk? Sugar?'

'Black will be fine.' Jerry took the mug and leaned his back against the window sill; she was right about the sitting. As he got older, he found long journeys made him ache in places he had never thought about before. 'Thank you. Theo not here?'

'He's in Athens. We aren't joined at the hip, you know.' She laughed at him, she always had. Jerry unexpectedly remembered that once upon a time he had rather liked her. He found the recollection made him miserable. 'Full English?' she asked him, now. 'I get the bacon from a local farm, it's wonderful.'

'Nonie – ' said Jerry, but she cut him short, if kindly.

'Later. When we can sit down together and I can listen properly. I know it has to be really important to bring you here, but rushing your fences will only bring you down. Drink your coffee, and if you want to be useful, you can make some toast. She pointed to a loaf on a board beside the toaster, and Jerry meekly did as he was told.

The domestic task was soothing. By the time Nonie had grilled bacon and tomatoes, and scrambled eggs for the toast, he was insensibly comforted, and as they sat down he found himself able to speak to her honestly for the first time in a very long while.

'I don't really know why I'm here. I've made a comprehensive mess of everything, and I don't expect you to say anything other than *I told you so*. I just felt I wanted to talk with you.'

'Is this about Helen?' asked Nonie, pertinently.

'Helen – Oliver – Susan. Debbie.'

'And Dot,' said Nonie. It wasn't a question.

'And Dot,' Jerry agreed. He took a mouthful of scrambled egg and bacon. Nonie was right, the bacon was ambrosial. He ate appreciatively. After a while, Nonie said quietly,

'I won't say that, Jerry. There isn't any point. You know better than any of us what you let Dot do to you – to us all, come to that. But it is a bit late to want to put it right now, wouldn't you say? Like, thirty years too late.'

Jerry laid down his fork.

'If I try to explain – will you let me?'

'Yes, but keep eating. Wasting good food won't help anything.'

Jerry loaded another forkful, but left it resting on the plate. He found that he felt sick. If he tried to explain he would, probably for the very first time, find himself confronting exactly what had happened … what he had allowed to happen.

'She's so convincing,' he said, and was ashamed to hear the pleading note in his voice. Nonie shot him a sideways look from her bright brown eyes that always saw so much – too much – and he blushed.

'She never convinced me,' she said.

'No,' said Jerry, quietly. 'But then, you turned out to be the toughest of the lot of us.'

'I had to be,' said Nonie. 'There was no going back from the place where I was.' Matt, dead. However much she loved Theo now – and she did – the pain had never gone away. A world without Matt contained a permanent empty space. Unexpectedly, Jerry reached out and covered her hand with his.

'I know,' he said.

'Don't get sentimental,' Nonie ordered. She trimmed the rind from her bacon carefully, concentrating, and chose what she felt to be the least controversial option. 'What's she done to Debbie, beyond the obvious? She looks to me to be doing very nicely, thank you, and forgive me if I say this, but the loss of her mother from her life is no great one.'

'Debbie doesn't necessarily see it that way,' said Jerry.

'No … but it was Dot that forced the choice, and if you want my view, Deb made the right one.'

'I hope she did.' Jerry paused. 'I *think* she did. But I can see Dot's side, too. From where she sits, it must look as if I'm barking mad to even dream of allowing the marriage to happen.'

'Do you actually believe you could stop it?' asked Nonie, with interest.

'Probably not. But I haven't tried, either.'

'Possibly,' said Nonie, framing her sentence with care, 'Dot isn't the only one who might wonder about that.'

'Do you?' asked Jerry.

'No. But then, I've met him. He doesn't look good on paper, and that you can't deny.'

'It was an accident.And little sister Cressida is an hysteric, she was upset, naturally enough, and didn't think what she was saying, and she didn't know how to stop saying it when it dawned on her what she was doing. The miracle is that he didn't go down for murder, because if that had happened there would have been no way back. He wouldn't have met Deb, and nobody would ever have had a second look at the case, and his life and all his talents would have been wasted for nothing.' He listened to the echo of his own words, and not for the first time, felt them in some obscure way inadequate. But Nonie was speaking.

'Excuse me? What have little sister's hysterics got to say to anything?' She saw the look on his face and narrowed her eyes at him. 'Come on, Jerry. What haven't you been telling me?'

So Jerry told her. He hadn't meant to, but he had no choice now. When he had finished, she sat in silence for a full minute, before saying in a voice suddenly full of strain,

'You and I both know, Jerry, that that kind of mud can stick for a lifetime. After more than thirty years, people still wonder if Matt ...'

Jerry looked at her with sympathy.

'You and I both know, too, that the accusations against Matt were pure malice, he never fancied young girls – except for you, and that was another matter. I believe the same about the accusations against Mawgan, I have to. The sister wouldn't repeat them in court under oath; they never came into the public domain except by way of local gossip. Hopefully, they will go away, given time.'

'I suppose we have to call him lucky, then,' she said, but they both knew that the calumnies against the late Matthew Sutton had passed into folklore, and that even local gossip could be enough, and so Jerry was relieved that sharp-tongued Nonie said no more. He said,

'I don't think he sees it like that. I think that, whatever we can prove now, he's going to be haunted by it for the rest of his life, because he's basically a decent man. But that's no reason to play the heavy father. I might think sometimes that he's beamed down from another planet, but I don't believe the rest of the rubbish. I hope it has died a natural death, but only time will tell us that. I think he's a good man. I'd stake my life on that ... I'm staking my daughter's life.'

Nonie said, sensibly,

'He's the product of his background. It's as different from yours – or Deb's, come to that, as chalk from cheese, but it'll be sound enough. When you dig down under the continental veneer, you'll find that sophistication isn't even skin deep. He's the same direct, uncomplicated Cornishman that he was born, it's just that at the moment he's punchdrunk, and now you've told me the whole truth, I can quite see why. Have you met his family?'

'Not yet.'

Nonie said what Helen had said.

'You should.' She went on. 'It might set your mind at rest. They won't be your sort of people, or not the sort you've become, anyway. But unless I miss my guess, you'll find them decent, honest and God-fearing, and they'll make you welcome.'

'You're probably right.'

'I *am* right.' She looked at his face and knew that she hadn't won the point. 'Eat your breakfast. I told you, starving won't help matters. And then tell me what's troubling you.'

Jerry ate in silence for a while, but the food didn't seem as delicious as it had to begin with. When he finally laid aside his knife and fork, Nonie poured more coffee and said,

'All right, so some things never change. What's Dot done now?'

He hadn't meant to discuss Debbie's affairs with her, but now he had fairly started, Jerry found himself telling her about the private detective. Nonie listened, sipping her coffee, and then she said,

'Well, she shouldn't have done it, but for once, I can't blame her. And if there's nothing to find, she won't get anywhere. Are you saying you think that there is?'

'Susan pointed out, quite rightly, that he came by a very large loan while he was still in prison.'

'So? Ronnie Biggs and the Kray brothers weren't in Exeter jail that I ever heard.'

'Other criminals are.'

'Dirty money, you think? Come on, Jerry!'

'It came from somewhere,' said Jerry, stubbornly.

'Undoubtedly. Hadn't you better ask him where, then?'

Jerry stared at her.

'Are you crazy? What's he going to think, if I do that?'

'That you don't entirely trust him,' said Nonie, peacefully. She looked at him. 'As you don't. Do you?'

'It's just, that to find someone to lend you *honestly* what must have been quite a lot of money, when you're in prison, is quite an achievement.'

'It certainly sounds like a bit of a fiddle, but it doesn't necessarily have to be a criminal one. What about his family?'

'Get real, Nonie! His father runs a small building firm, he's not Big League.'

'Just a thought. One of his continental friends?'

'He's a *chef*, for God's sake! He isn't going to have big business contacts, and if he did, can you really see it? People don't amass large sums of money by lending them to lost causes!'

'But as it turns out, it isn't a lost cause.'

'Nobody could have foreseen that. No, it's a nice idea, but it's a horse that won't run.'

'An inside job ...' said Nonie, relishing the words. She laughed outright. 'Jerry, get real yourself! Are you seriously suggesting that the Fish was saved with the proceeds of organised crime? You've been watching too much telly!'

Jerry remembered that he had often found Nonie uncomfortably outspoken.

'So what's your explanation then, if you're so clever?'

'I can't even begin to guess,' said Nonie, equally. 'More coffee?' She picked up the *cafetière*, which was empty. 'I can soon make some.'

Making the coffee allowed the dust to settle. Talking with Nonie had always tended to talk up a storm, Jerry reflected, nothing changed. It was oddly comforting, in its way, for she had always had the gift of being close to the truth, even if this was the first time he had openly admitted it. He *would* ask Mawgan, it was the honest thing to do, although the jury was out on how he might react. Not listening to Nonie had got him in desperate trouble in the past, perhaps it was time he gave the alternative a try. This brought him insensibly to the next item on the agenda, but still not the one he was really here to discuss. He said, as he watched her,

'What did you know about Henry, Nonie?'

'*Henry?*' Nonie turned to him in amazement. 'He was a man who should have known better? A doting fool? Victim of delayed midlife crisis? What should I know about him?'

'That he was a widower?'

'Was he? Yes, I think it was mentioned. Is it important, after all this time?'

'He had children. Susan doesn't know.'

'*Jerry*!' Nonie nearly dropped the kettle. 'How did that happen?'

Jerry explained.

'It seemed the right thing at the time,' he said, when he had done, and instinctively flinched before she had a chance to speak.

'Doesn't it always?' But she sounded more thoughtful than condemnatory. 'Oh well, I suppose what you don't know isn't going to harm you, and I can at least see the reasoning – I must watch that. That's twice in one morning! But I wouldn't like to be Dot, if Susan ever finds out! Ooh!'

'The thing is,' said Jerry. 'I think Susan should be told.'

'Then tell her.' She met his eyes. 'Ho hum, don't tell me. You're afraid of Dot!'

'No –' He broke off. 'Oh, all right then. Guilty as charged. I signed an agreement when I adopted her.'

'Moral cowardice was always your besetting sin,' said Nonie. She put the *cafetière* back on the table and sat down again. 'Jerry, you're going to have to pull yourself together. Nothing is ever going to sort itself out until you knock this Dot thing on the head, once and for all.'

'I've left her, haven't I?' He hoped he didn't sound defensive.

'Oh yes – after Oliver had come close to murdering her, and Debbie had been disinherited. I must say, you have generous notions of what constitutes provocation. Does it come of being a solicitor?'

'That wasn't fair,' said Jerry, after a pause.

260

'You forget, Jerry – while you and Dot have been having your little marital falling-out, I've been at this end, catching the backlash of her appalling behaviour.'

Jerry was silent, outfaced by the simple truth. After a minute, Nonie said,

'I'm sure you're going to tell me that it's none of my business, and you're right. But although Oliver is terminally Dot-proof, remember that Debbie isn't. If Dot manages to break up her engagement, not only will she lose Mawgan, but the old relationship with her mother will be beyond saving. I don't suppose that Dot will think of that, experience will have taught her different.'

'Oh God!' said Jerry. He buried his face in his hands. 'How did I let all this happen?'

Bang! There it was. The great computer virus in the game of Life.

There was a great silence.

After a while, Nonie got to her feet and began gathering the plates into the sink, meticulously tipping bacon rinds and uneaten toast crusts into the bin. She had got as far as running hot water before Jerry spoke.

'I love her, Nonie. How the *hell* was I such a fool?'

Nonie turned off the tap. She came back to the table, and reaching out, took one of his hands and held it.

'Come on, Jerry. What's done is done. Just don't let it become worse.'

'Tell me what to do,' said Jerry, simply. There were tears running down his face.

'How can I know?' asked Nonie. 'Helen and I were friends – I suppose you could call us best friends. Dot manipulated us, too, now we're strangers. Unless you can find a way to control her, I don't see that anything is ever going to get better. Or can.'

'She's a monster!' He choked on a sob.

Nonie refrained from saying that Jerry had helped to make her that way, it would only be scoring valueless points. Moreover, it possibly wasn't even true. She had never been sure.

'She believes she has everyone's best interests at heart. She quite possibly genuinely believed Helen was a bad wife and mother, and by her standards, perhaps she was. She thought I was a bad influence, she was entitled to her opinion. She must have thought it was all for the best to keep Susan in the dark about her Worthington family, and I've already admitted I can see why. Oliver *was* a total iconoclast, or to put it more bluntly, a pain in the arse, you can't blame her for hitting back. And when in the end he needed help, don't forget, she was right there, even if she did get it all wrong. Even Chel admits that, although Oliver never will. And Debbie ... so far as Debbie is concerned, she's still acting for the best according to her lights. She sees a potentially violent ex-con who keeps a pub and wants to marry her wealthy daughter, not a complete person in his own right. She doesn't see Mawgan.'

'How can she be so narrow-minded?' Jerry sounded desperate.

Nonie shrugged.

'People are like that. Maybe we are, too. We all look from our own perspective.'

'Life is like a picture?' asked Jerry, with sarcasm.

'Absolutely. A great, big, pulsating canvas full of movement and colour.' She let go his hand. 'The problem with Dot is that she sees in black and white.'

'She doesn't take prisoners. She just goes for the throat.'

'Someone should go for hers,' said Nonie, more forcefully than she had meant. She picked up the *cafetière* again. '*More* coffee?'

Jerry waved it away, impatiently.

'God, no, I'll never sleep again as it is!' He picked up the napkin she had laid for him and wiped his eyes. 'I'm sorry. I'm being stupid.'

'No. You're being honest. Stick with it.'

Their eyes met. Something nearer liking than had been there for a long time flashed between them.

'What can I do?' asked Jerry, for the second time, but without the desperation.

'All any of us can do. Your best. Protect Debbie. Be fair to Susan. And as for Helen …'

'I never stopped loving her, you know,' said Jerry. 'I learned that too late. I don't know what to do.'

Nonie said something that she had never thought to hear herself say.

'Poor Dot.'

'We had a ghastly marriage,' said Jerry, in extenuation against the implied criticism. 'Nothing in common, no mutual ground to stand on – until Debbie was born. If I had affairs with other women, she ignored them – Nonie, she didn't even care enough to make a scene, there was no way out that way. How did we *get* like that? And all the time … all the time, Helen stayed in my head like an obsession. I ate and drank her, breathed her, dreamed her – if you think I didn't pay for my idiot behaviour, you're way out. I paid, over and over and over again.'

'And so did Oliver, Susan, and now Debbie.'

'I know.'

'And Helen,' said Nonie. 'Helen paid highest of all.' She hesitated, then couldn't resist asking, 'Did you *want* Dot to make a scene over your affairs?'

'It might at least have proved that we weren't totally dead as a couple, maybe made it worth sticking it out.'

'Is that what you would have liked?'

'You know it isn't.'

'Bugger, then. Isn't it?'

'Do you know what Helen said to me?' asked Jerry.

'Obviously not. Unlike your lovely daughter-in-law, I make no claims to being clairvoyant.'

Momentarily distracted, Jerry stared at her.

'*Does* she? Good God, I never knew that!'

Nonie realised that she had erred on the side of inaccuracy.

'No, she doesn't. But she is. Ask Oliver.'

'Oliver!' Jerry looked sceptical.

'What did Helen say?' asked Nonie, side-stepping a delicate subject, but Jerry had initially spoken on impulse, and now the impulse had passed, could find no way to tell Nonie, of all people, that Helen had stated the impossibility of being with someone whom you loved and couldn't trust. Confidences between them had effectively come to an end. He looked at his watch.

'I should be getting on. I'm supposed to be in St Erbyn before noon, and it's half-past ten already. Thank you for listening to me, I appreciate your input.' He had plenty of time in hand, but he now wanted to get away.

'I don't suppose I've been much help,' said Nonie, regretfully, fully understanding. 'Jerry, the ball's in your court. Don't just swipe at it anyhow, in your usual fashion. Take time to think about it. And be careful how you approach Mawgan. He isn't going to like it, you know.'

'I will. And thank you for breakfast.'

'You're welcome. Any time.'

He didn't believe that, Jerry thought as he drove away. Nevertheless, she had given him food for thought, Nonie with her straight thinking and sharp tongue. She had drawn from him admissions he had never thought to hear himself make, and she had shown him consequences of Dot's behaviour that he hadn't taken into account.

If Debbie got crunched under Dot's well-meaning, self-interested feet, he would throw the book at her! Enough Mr

Nice-guy. He would protect his beloved daughter to the last ditch.

He drove into the car park behind the Fish unaware that it was already too late.

* * * * *

Jerry realised that all was not well when he walked in through the rear door into the Fish and found Oliver waiting for him. He had the air of someone who had been waiting for a while, lounging around, reading the flyers in the rack on Shirley's counter. When his father appeared, he looked up, and one look at his expression made Jerry's heart sink.

'Ah …' he said. 'Don't tell me … trouble.' Even then, he didn't guess, which afterwards he thought was strange. Perhaps he simply hadn't wanted to.

'To put it bluntly, the shit has hit the fan,' said Oliver. 'Did you know that dear Dot had set a detective onto Mawgan?'

Jerry's jaw dropped at the accusation in his voice.

'I – '

'You could have warned us. Warned him, at least. How long have you known?' He narrowed his eyes. 'It wasn't your idea?'

'Good God, no! And I came here today to do just that – warn him.'

'You left it a bit late.'

'How – ?' Jerry realised that he was reduced to speaking in monosyllables and pulled himself together. 'Who told him?'

'Tim Howells, would you believe?' Oliver gave him a sardonic look. 'I think that was the final straw.'

'How did Tim …?'

'Dear Dot gave him the third degree. Fortunately – or unfortunately, perhaps, in view of the result – Tim had the decency to pass the news on. Unlike you.'

'Oliver, I already said – ' Chronic inability to finish a sentence was an indication of a guilty conscience, Jerry recalled. 'What happened?' he asked.

'Well, first of all, he wiped the floor with Chel – who, like you, had known or guessed and kept it to herself. Then it came out that Deb had been a party to the cover-up and probably because he cares about her so much, all hell broke loose. She's still crying now, Chel is up there trying to calm her down. She has no idea where he spent last night, but it certainly wasn't here, she was searching every room at three o'clock this morning.'

'Is he here now?' Jerry asked.

'Yep. Working in the kitchen. Deb says he came back early, said 'Oh, are you still here then?' and slammed into the shower. They haven't spoken since.'

'Have you seen him?'

'No. Only the results of his reappearance.'

'Oh,' said Jerry. He made a grimace. 'I see – *enjoy your meal ...*'

'In Deb's case, I think it'll choke her. Yesterday, he seems to have said words to the effect of, if that's how much your family think of me, we're on a long road to nowhere and we might as well call it a day now. And I have to agree that, if it is, he's probably right.'

'It isn't.'

'So what's the problem with that harpy?'

'She seems to have got it into her head that he's after Deb's money. And she claims to believe that the money to buy the pub was raised from dubious sources.'

'The first is bullshit, I was there when he first learned she had any. He was more startled than anything, if you want a considered opinion. As for the second ... bearing in mind that he was backed against the wall and his options at the time were limited, would that be the end of the world?'

This was something that had entered Jerry's head, too, sneakily when he wasn't looking, but he had dismissed it as unworthy of a respectable solicitor. Now, he took the thought out and looked at it again.

'What, the profits of organised crime?' He sounded like an echo of Nonie.

'So long as he didn't organise the crime in the first place, what odds?'

Jerry thought about this.

'It would mean, at best, that he had put himself under an obligation. I'm not sure I like the idea.'

'Nor me, although I don't see that we can criticise until we've been there ourselves. But perhaps he didn't. Unfortunately, we – or *you* – are now going to have to ask.'

'And if he won't answer? He's not on trial here, and arguably it's within his rights.'

'Then, we trust him, or we don't.'

'Does Chel …?'

'If Chel knows anything, she's keeping shtum. And you can't ask her.'

'*Bloody* self-righteous, effing Dorothy!' said Jerry, picturesquely.

'And so say all of us.' A group of people came through the front door headed for the restaurant, and Oliver moved away towards the stairs. 'You'd better come up. Hopefully, the storm has passed.'

Jerry had never seen his carefree, insouciant daughter look so distraught since the awful time when they had thought Oliver was going to die. She flung herself into his arms the minute she saw him and hugged him tightly. Jerry hugged her back, his heart full. It was as if she was a little girl again, crying, *make it better, Daddy*! And he couldn't.

Chel came forward, a loaded glass in her hand.

'Have a drink. We all need one.'

'Thanks.' Debbie had relaxed her arms at last, and Jerry unwound himself to accept the glass, while keeping a firm hold on his daughter. 'Now, what's to do?'

'Didn't Oliver tell you?' Chel asked, surprised. She shot Oliver a savage look, and he threw up his hands in defence.

'Of course I have. I think Dad is asking what happens next.'

Debbie sniffed, and wiped her hand inelegantly across her cheek.

'He was just so *angry*. And hurt. And I don't blame him.'

'Let's all sit down quietly,' said Jerry, leading her to the sofa. 'Come on, Debs, pull yourself together. It's not beyond repair. Here – ' He handed her his handkerchief, pressing it into her hand. The feel of it, and the way he called her *Debs*, as he had when she was a child – he and he only – was comforting. Debbie blew her nose. It was irrational to think that now Dad was here it would all come right again, but she couldn't help it.

'What can you do?' she asked, in a small voice choked with tears. Jerry said,

'First of all, you're going to get a stiff drink down you – please, Chel?' Chel moved to the table obediently, where a bottle of whisky stood sentinel among Debbie's assorted papers. 'And then,' Jerry continued, 'when you've calmed down, you're going to go and wash your face and fix your make-up, and by that time it'll be time for our booking in the restaurant.'

'But Dad – '

'Ssh. And after we've eaten, and Mawgan has finished in the kitchen, we'll sort all this out. He loves you, chicken. He isn't going to throw you out.' He gave her a hug. 'It's us he doesn't love, right now.'

'He said, if Mum was prepared to go that far, how could the rest of us feel so much different? He doesn't *understand* –'

But what Mawgan didn't understand was equally painful, and she began to cry again. 'I want everything to be right, and it isn't ever going to be!'

'That's enough,' said Jerry, firmly. He took a glass from Chel and held it out in front of Debbie's nose. 'Take this. Drink it. And dry your eyes. You look a complete sight. Suppose he came in now, what's he going to think?'

'He won't,' said Debbie, choking. 'He'll just finish downstairs and disappear again, I know he will.'

'Enough,' said Jerry. He pushed the glass into her unwilling hand. 'Get that down you. And that's an order!'

'*The course of true love*,' said Oliver, sententiously, '*will never run smooth*. Cheer up, Deb. If he won't toe the party line, Dad'll thump him. I'd do it myself, but he might thump me back.'

Debbie managed a ghost of a laugh, although it was half a sob. She took a sip of the stiff whisky that Chel had poured, and choked.

'I never thought we'd quarrel like that,' she said, forlornly, when she had got her breath back, and Oliver said,

'Who does?' and exchanged a glance with Chel.

It was touch and go whether Debbie would make it to lunch, Chel thought judiciously, but after half an hour of coaxing and cajoling, she had recovered enough to go into the bathroom and fix her face, emerging looking pale and red-eyed but at least in control, in time to go downstairs for the meal that Jerry had booked. It was a silent one, and none of them was particularly hungry, but they got through it. To their surprise, however, when their coffee had been served, Mawgan appeared from the kitchen and came over to join them. He looked, Jerry thought, very little better than Deb. Whatever he had done last night, sleeping hadn't played a big part. Unlike Debbie, who looked merely terminally unhappy, he looked ill. Without speaking, he brought a chair across from a nearby table that had been vacated and putting it between Chel and Jerry, sat down with them. Tony, the restaurant manager, came across with a pint from the bar. When he had left, there was a silence until Jerry, feeling that someone should speak, said,

'Hullo, Mawgan.'

'Hi,' said Mawgan. He looked across the table at Debbie. 'Sorry, bird.'

Debbie muttered something indistinguishable and played with the spoon in her saucer. Mawgan drank some of his pint.

'Christ!' said Oliver. 'Can't you do better than that?'

'Nope.' Mawgan took another swallow. Jerry said, quietly,

'When you've finished in the kitchen, can we talk?'

Mawgan flashed him a look.

'If you want.'

Debbie said, as if it had been wrenched out of her,

'Where were you last night?' and Chel winced for her. Bad move, Deb. Wrong question, in front of the family. Mawgan, however, replied calmly,

'Tommy let me crash on his sofa.'

'You could have let me know!' She sounded near tears again.

'Sorry.'

There was no point in letting this develop into a public showdown. Jerry stepped in smoothly with a comment on the meal they had just eaten, and Chel backed him up. Mawgan finished his pint.

'Excuse me,' he said, rising to his feet with the empty glass in his hand. 'I'll see you when I've cleared up.'

'And mind you're sober,' said Debbie, sharply. He gave her a long, cool look, nodded to the others, and left.

'Nice one, Deb,' said Oliver, and Debbie promptly burst into tears. Fortunately they were the last people in the restaurant.

Tony gave her a sympathetic look and then pretended that nothing was happening.

'Let's get out of here,' said Oliver.

Up in the flat, Debbie rushed into the bedroom and slammed the door, and Chel made some coffee to replace the coffee they hadn't drunk downstairs.

'Well!' she said, as she sat down at last. 'If I never have to sit through a lunch like that again, it'll be a day too soon!'

'Do you think he *will* come and talk to us?' Oliver speculated.

'God knows, but I hope so.' Jerry sipped his coffee. 'It seems to me, this business of Dot is the last straw, and you can see why – he's spent the last eighteen months working himself into the ground, and what was going on before that, I don't even want to know. Then on top of that he had all the worry over his partner pulling the rug from under him, and what the hell *did* he do about that? He wouldn't get a mortgage – at least, I doubt it. I'm almost afraid to ask, and I'm not joking. But I can't bear to look at Deb's face ...' He let the sentence fade.

Chel said, slowly,

'You want to know what I think?'

'We might as well,' said Oliver. 'It's a pleasant surprise to find someone who *knows* what to think.'

'We've all talked about it enough, but if you look at it in cold blood, the man who died was his friend, and that must have been a pretty terrible thing to witness, whatever the circumstances. Then the little sister ... Deb says they all made a pet of her and looked after her, they were all so much older you see, and what she did to him is as bad, if not worse, as what happened to her husband, at least that was most likely an accident. And the resulting split in the family must be like the Grand Canyon, and they were just normal, ordinary people getting on with their lives ... and now she's buggered off without a word, and what does he feel about that, I wonder?

If it's just caught up with him, and I think perhaps it has, then it's no wonder he's losing it. He didn't need the Dreaded Dot and her stupid detective.'

Jerry raised his eyebrows at this open use of Helen's derogatory nickname, and Chel blushed.

'You know what I mean.'

'Perhaps you should say all that to Debbie,' said Oliver, quietly.

'Perhaps I will, but I don't think this is exactly the moment.'

They drank their coffee in silence for a while, and then Jerry said,

'I wasn't at all sure about this engagement, you must both know, but now I see it falling apart … I just wish I could think of a way to stop it.'

Chel got up to gather the cups and wash them, and heading for the kitchen, nearly collided with Mawgan coming through the front door of the flat. He nodded as he passed her and headed for the bedroom.

'Just let me have a shower,' he said, before he vanished again. Chel came out of the kitchen.

'At least he spoke,' she said.

It was nearly a quarter of an hour before Mawgan reappeared, clean and dressed now in jeans and a sweatshirt, his face a carefully neutral blank. Debbie didn't appear with him. Although the three in the other room had tried not to listen, it had been impossible. There had been no exchange even of further recriminations.

Jerry said, cautiously,

'Can we discuss this now?'

'I don't think,' said Mawgan, 'that there's anything to discuss, is there? I just can't do this. I'm sorry.' He didn't sit down. Oliver said,

'Do what, exactly?'

'Marry Deb,' Mawgan said, bluntly. 'It was bad enough to begin with – but now she's in there, breaking her heart and won't even speak to me. I can't break up your family. It's too high a price. That's all.'

'Let's not be too hasty here – ' Jerry began, but Mawgan interrupted.

'It's no good is it? Deb loves her mum, if she feels she needs to set detectives on me, how is either of us going to live with that?I haven't got nothing to hide – but she's going to keep digging until none of us can bear it no longer. So I'm calling time, before it's too late. I don't fit anyway, Deb's best out of it. I should never have started it, first off. That's all.'

'You can't – ' said Chel. She broke off, and looked at Jerry.

'I'm sorry you should feel like that,' he said, quietly. 'Will you give us a chance to explain?'

'Explain what? It's plain enough to me.'

'But you love her,' said Chel.

'Yes, I do. That's why I can't tear her in pieces. I've done enough damage like that in my own family. Excuse me – ' He headed for the door. 'I've got work to do. Just tell her – ' The door slammed on the last few words, cutting them off.

Chel, Oliver and Jerry sat in frozen stillness for a few moments, then Jerry said,

'I can see what he means ... but perhaps when he's had time to think it over ...'

'I think he has already thought it over,' said Chel. 'I'd better go to Deb ...' But she didn't move. It was Oliver who did that.

'Bloody Dot!' he said, and got to his feet abruptly, already in motion across the floor. He slammed out of the door in Mawgan's wake before either of the others had found their breath to ask where he was going.

He had no idea where Mawgan might have gone, it was his pub, he could legitimately be anywhere within it, but that he *was* still within it was a probability, outside it was tipping down with rain and he had no coat – although that, Oliver admitted as he went downstairs, might not stop him in his present frame of mind. He headed first for the office, and crashed into Mawgan in the doorway, heading off with the keys of his car. Oliver put his hands on the doorframe to either side.

'No you bloody don't!' he said.

'Yes, I bloody do!'

Oliver said, calmly,

'If you push me around, you're liable to hurt me, so just back off will you? You aren't going anywhere until I've spoken to you, and you *certainly* aren't going by car. What do you think you're playing at, you stupid Cornish oaf?' One swift twist and he had the keys in his hand. 'Get back in there. I'm not quarrelling with you in public.'

For a full minute, Mawgan didn't move. Then he stepped back.

'Come in, then.' He slammed the door behind them and went over to his desk, sitting down abruptly and putting his face in his hands. Oliver moved more slowly to Chel's chair. He allowed time for the dust to settle before he spoke.

'You haven't thought this through,' he said, then.

'Yes, I have. You've all been very kind, and that's why I can't do it. I'm just bad news all round.'

'Right, now you've got that off your conscience, will you listen to me for a minute?' He allowed a pause, but when Mawgan said nothing, he went on. 'First and foremost,' he said, trying to keep his voice level, 'you may not realise this, but you live in a different world from the rest of us. May I tell you about it?' Still no answer. 'OK, I'll take that as a yes.' He paused. It might have been easier had Mawgan looked at him, but he didn't. 'Mawgan?'

'I'm listening,' said Mawgan, but still kept his face hidden.

Diplomacy and Oliver had never been on good terms with each other, acting as an intermediary was alien territory. He would have liked to give Mawgan a good thump and make him pay attention properly, but there were several reasons why this was ineligible, among them the fact that he had the shoulders of a rugby player and looked to be in a foul mood. Right down at the bottom of the pit, Oliver suspected, and he had been there himself, he knew what could happen there. He therefore spoke very simply and directly.

'It's pretty obvious that you come from a normal family, and that the relationships between you all are friendly and ordinary – loving, even. You get on with your siblings, your parents probably love each other, we never had those advantages. By the same token, they wouldn't disown you whatever you did, or wanted to do, and I don't want to dig up old bones, but they've already proved that. They wouldn't force your hand, either. I know you've had your differences ... but you're still a family. Am I right?'

Mawgan didn't reply, but a slight movement of his head signified recognition, at least. Oliver went on.

'The point I'm making here is, Deb and Susan and I have never had that sort of family life. Dad and my stepmother have been like strangers to each other for as long as I can remember, there isn't any one of the three of us children who has the same relationship to the others; Susan shares a mother with Deb, Deb shares a father with me – if it ever had a chance of working, it died in its infancy. You can't break us up, we were never together. So half your case goes to the wall straight away.

'Now for the argument that Deb loves her mum. Well yes, she does – did, I should possibly say. But she loves you more, for some reason that escapes me at present – so how do you think her relationship with her mother is going to look if you remove from her the freedom of choice, and just dump her?

Think about it, before you do anything rash, won't you?' A long pause. 'It would be nice if you would say something,' remarked Oliver.

Mawgan removed his hands. He went so far as to look at Oliver, but there was no relenting in his expression.

'I just can't get the hang of your family,' he said. 'I don't know what you want from me.'

'Honesty?' suggested Oliver.

'What's Deb's mum trying to do?'

'You should take no notice.'

'In my family, since you brought it up, we don't set private detectives on other people, no matter what. If we want to know something, we come right out and ask.'

'The point that you're consistently missing here, is that only Deb's mum *does* want to know anything. Don't include the rest of us, please.'

'You must think I'm a real idiot!' said Mawgan, bitterly.

'Oh, I do!' Oliver riposted, immediately. 'You're making too much of this, for one thing. For your information, she's had a go at my mother, my father, Chel, me, Nonie, the late Matthew Sutton … the list is endless. It's not a personal vendetta against you. She just has to manipulate people. You can let her, or not, it's up to you. But I have to tell you, that over this you're playing right into her hands.'

'I just don't fit. You know it, I know it. Bad luck on the hoof, that's me – you want to be shut of me, before it gets you, too.'

'Is that so?' asked Oliver. 'Then answer me this, why am I sitting here trying to talk sense into you? More, why is Deb upstairs now, *breaking her heart*? Your own words, I remind you. Why, brought down to its most basic, is my father exploring every avenue to clear your name? Why should any of us bother, if you *just don't fit*? Come on, tell me!'

Mawgan said, precisely,

'I'm off of a council estate. I didn't go to a posh school, and I left when I was sixteen to go to work – manual work, at that – not university. I keep a pub, I work in a kitchen … and you try to tell me I *do* fit?'

'God, what's to do with you?' Oliver stared at him, baffled. 'Look at yourself, for God's sake! You don't just *work in a kitchen,* you cook like the Archangel Gabriel! You're fluent in three languages, you run two successful businesses – '

'And I've been in prison.'

'Oh well, if you think that clinches the argument, there's no more to be said, of course.'

There was a long silence, but Mawgan must have set his brain to work at last, for after a while he said, as if it was forced out of him,

'You make Deb's mum sound some kind of monster.'

'My opinion exactly. Put bluntly, she likes her own way and doesn't care how she gets it.'

'All those people you said about …?'

'Dad knew her before he met Helen – my mother, you've met her.'

'Yes. A beautiful lady.'

Oliver looked surprised.

'Is she? Yes, I suppose she is … Anyway, as Nonie tells it, my stepmother worked to break up their marriage, and after she had succeeded, saw Nonie – she's my godmother, did you know that? – off as well – that one is a long story, I'll tell you some day, if we're still speaking. She tried to stop my marriage to Chel, and when she didn't succeed, took the first chance she had of trying to break that up, too. She damn nearly succeeded.'

'But you're still together,' said Mawgan.

'Yes, we ran away. An option not open to you, by the way, and in that context may I point out a couple of things?'

'Like what?'

'Apart from the fact that she loves you, which you seem determined to ignore, Deb is trying to start up a business barely a stone's throw away. How's she going to do that, if you ditch her for no better reason than you don't like being investigated? *She's* not investigating you. Then there's Chel. She loves her job with you, but how can she work here if you break Deb's heart and destroy all her plans? She can't, is the short answer. And then there's me – I live just up the road from your pub, and I'm damned if I like the idea of having to go all the way to Helford every time I fancy a drink! You say yourself that you've nothing to hide, so what's the big deal?'

Mawgan said,

'If Deb's mum wants to know something about me, and doesn't want to ask me herself, the option is open for her to ask your dad to ask me. She hasn't ... or has she?'

'Dad trusts you.' Almost true ...

'But he knew about the detective. Come to that, you all knew, Deb included. So what's she hoping to discover?'

Oliver said, apologetically,

'I think she's hoping to find you bought the Fish with Mafia money.'

'*What?*'

'I take it, you didn't, then?'

'You can take it any way you like! You mean, you all *knew* this, and none of you thought to ask me about it? What did you think I'd do, lie?'

'It wasn't quite like that,' said Oliver. 'But OK, if it clears the air, and makes you feel any better, I'm asking now. How *did* you do it?'

'Why the hell should I tell you?' Mawgan was really angry now, and it was a relief, Oliver realised. He had been too still, too quiet, too controlled. 'If you all think I've been up to some kind of scam, then think it, why should I care?'

'You should care, because this whole thing has got out of hand. We weren't accusing you of anything, we had it in mind to defend you. But of course, if you want to give in without a fight we can save our breath. Let her win, why not? No doubt Deb will get over it one day.'

Mawgan gave him a vicious look. Oliver said, provocatively,

'So do I conclude that there *is* something nasty in the woodshed?'

He thought that Mawgan wasn't going to answer, but after a moment he said,

'No. Or not for me. It was never meant to be a secret in that way.'

'It gets more intriguing by the minute. Are you going to tell me after that?'

To his private surprise, Mawgan said, after consideration,

'No reason why not. It should be obvious, anyway, I would've thought.'

'Not to me. I'm thick.'

Mawgan looked at him, for the first time, with a gleam of amusement.

'Oh yes? Well, someone came up with the money, right? That much *has* to be obvious, even to a thicko like you. So, who was I likely to know with that sort of cash lying around?'

'God knows!' Oliver narrowed his eyes. 'But if it's that obvious – you and your partner won the money. Am I on the right track?'

'Spot on. There was six of us in the syndicate, Edward and me, three you don't need to worry about, and the DJ who came in to do the discos in the ballroom Saturday nights. He was a presenter on the local radio station as well; like me, he was heading off in the hope for better things. He was a mate – a good mate, as it turned out. When I ran into trouble, he was one of the ones as didn't turn his back.'

'And he bought your partner's share of the Fish?'

'Not exactly that, no. He made me a loan. I paid interest on it, like any other loan, my solicitor arranged it all. Beginning of this year, I paid it all back, now I have a business loan like anyone else. But without him, I'd've had to sell. Which is why I don't go telling the whole world about it.'

'You've lost me,' said Oliver.

'He's a household name now, Con. He don't really need to be linked with someone who's been on trial for murder, leave out the light seasoning of incest. It wouldn't be a good way to thank him.'

'That,' said Oliver, carefully, 'is putting it a bit strong.' He thought for a moment. 'Con ... that rings a bell. Con Delaney? Outspoken Irish newcomer? A slot on Radio One in the afternoon, and a rather bizarre music programme on late night telly on BBC2? That the one?'

'That's the one.'

'You have friends in interesting places. I don't say high ones, you notice!'

'Yeah ... he was going to be best man at the wedding.'

'Hopefully, he still will. We don't have to tell him how bloody stupid you are, after all.'

Mawgan said nothing. After a minute, Oliver said, regretfully,

'My stepmother is going to be so disappointed. She really wanted it to be organized crime.'

'Some people would say being a Radio One DJ *is* organised crime.'

'That's better,' said Oliver, approvingly. 'You almost made a joke, there.'

Mawgan was instantly sober.

'It don't alter nothing.'

'You plan to serve the Dreaded Dot your head on a plate, with a *jus* of my sister's tears and garnished with broken dreams and shattered friendships?'

'Don't come clever with me!'

'Listen,' said Oliver. 'Here's what you do. Give me ten minutes to get the family off the premises, then go upstairs, take Deb in your arms, and just say you love her. Sentimental, I know, but if it's true, does it matter? And what have you to lose?' Mawgan said nothing, and after a moment, Oliver pointed out, 'Any other way, you have everything to lose, and don't try and kid me you don't know it. Stop punishing yourself, for God's sake. Pop another Prozac, and get on with it – and don't give me any backchat. I've been there too, remember.' He got to his feet, awkwardly, and realised that Mawgan was watching him. Their eyes met. 'No, it doesn't get any better. But you can't let it down you.' He hesitated. 'Chel and I think you're only now grieving. So get on and grieve, get it over. And then get on with your life. OK?'

Mawgan hesitated, but only for a second.

'OK.'

'Good man. Oh – and let Chel do the bar tonight. You look all in.'

Ten minutes later, following instructions, Mawgan went back up to the flat and found it, as promised, deserted. He went quietly to the bedroom door and opened it. Debbie was lying face-down on the bed, not moving, hardly breathing.

'Deb?'

No reply.

He sat down on the edge of the bed, and Debbie, feeling the depression of the mattress, huddled deeper into herself. She heard the double thud as he kicked off his shoes, and then felt him roll over beside her, and reach out for her, gathering her to him. Her own arms reached out almost of their own volition to slide round his neck. They lay there for a long moment, holding each other tightly, saying nothing. Mawgan spoke first, with difficulty.

'Just hold me, bird. Never let me go.' He buried his face in her neck. 'How can I apologise?'

For answer, she kissed him, his eyebrows, his eyelids, nose, and finally his mouth. It turned into a long, long kiss, mutually healing. After a while, he said,

'I'm not really like this. It's just, it's all got on top of me.'

'I know,' said Debbie.

'Will you still marry me?'

'Yes.'

'I hurt you.'

'Yes. Just don't do it again, will you? I couldn't bear it.'

'You can put money on it …' He sounded drowsy. Debbie, withdrawing her head a little so that she could look at him, saw that he was on the brink of falling asleep. She relaxed back against him, snuggling close. Truth to tell, she was hardly disappointed, twenty-four hours of non-stop drama had taken their toll on her too, all she wanted for now was to be close to him, and to feel safe there.

So they slept together, entwined on the bed, and in the darkening corners, the shadows began to beat a retreat.

XII

That Christmas turned out to be the strangest that Debbie had ever known. In place of the usual family gathering at her parents' house, with herself and Susan and Tom and the children obediently sitting around the table to eat turkey and Christmas pudding together, and open presents round the tree thereafter, events took a dive into a highly-organised spate of commercial activity. The restaurant was relentlessly busy every night with private parties, booked to capacity both on Christmas Eve and for lunchtime on Christmas Day, if she saw Mawgan at all it was at breakfast time. Otherwise, it was either as a blur passing on the stairs, or in an exhausted heap beside her in the bed when she woke up. How he had ever coped with all this and with the increased activity in the pub itself, she couldn't even begin to imagine, but it did run through her head that it was no wonder that, in February, he had taken a run for the peace and quiet of a lonely cottage on Bodmin Moor, and there suffered a near-fatal accident entirely due to neglect for taking elementary care.

As far as she herself was concerned, the only family she had close to her now were Oliver and Chel, who had never taken part in family Christmases as a couple unless, reluctantly on Oliver's part, with Chel's family. Up until the time he met Chel, Oliver had for years now made sure that he was out of the country, generally in Greece with his many friends there, when the festive season arrived. So, uncharted territory.

'What are you planning to do?' Chel asked, snatching a coffee break with her sister-in-law one morning.

'The options are limited,' Debbie replied. She took a pensive sip of her coffee. 'I can sit up here on my own, or I can help in the bar. Of the two alternatives, I prefer the second. When the kitchen is all cleared up after Christmas Day lunch, which will be quite late in the afternoon, we're going to St Austell for a couple of nights. The restaurant is closed, Tommy doesn't mind, and with you around to keep an eye on things, Mawgan might even relax a bit'.

'Does he open the restaurant again before New Year?'

'No. New Year's Eve, and then a lunch on New Year's Day, and he can start taking it apart ready for his father to move in after that.'

'You should take more than just the one whole day away, then,' said Chel. 'He's not a well man, your lovely bloke. In fact, he looks a wreck.'

'Mmm. Running on neat adrenalin.' Debbie looked quickly at Chel, and then away again. 'Well, we might have – but although things are greatly improved in that area, relations with his family are still pretty dodgy. The last thing we need to enliven Christmas is a resumption of hostilities because the unspeakable Cressida has failed to get in touch.'

'Surely, they wouldn't!'

'It isn't just the immediate family though, is it? It's a huge one, loads of aunts and uncles and cousins and things, and they all interact like the Waltons according to Anna and Allison, and of course they all took sides, and I don't really know *which* side, and neither does Mawgan. And there's a grandmother I haven't met yet, and who believes he's a bully boy who ruined little sister Cressida's life by killing her beloved husband, whereas the truth …'

'Is slightly different. Pity, though.' Chel said nothing for a moment, then added. 'Do they realise the state he's got himself into? Has he told them? Have you?'

'I haven't. I doubt that he has either.'

'God!' Chel thought about this. 'That could be interesting. Suppose they catch on? His mother, at least, is almost certain to guess, surely?'

'You see why we agreed that two nights, one full day, is enough.'

'I certainly do.' Chel paused, but there was really nothing to add to something that wasn't her business in the first place.

She said, instead, 'So the bottom line is, you're going to spend Christmas Eve and most of Christmas Day virtually on your own?'

'Give or take Tommy & Co., and the pre-Christmas-lunch drinkers in the bars, yes.'

'No,' said Chel. 'That won't do. The bar can manage without you, it always has – and Tommy says Christmas Day generally isn't busy anyway, people have other places to be. Come with us, instead. We're going to Trelewan on Christmas Eve to have lunch with our friends there, they're relatives of yours too, they'd love to meet you. In fact, they probably ought to be on the guest list for your wedding, when you stop and think about it.'

'I couldn't possibly – '

'Of course you could. I already said, they're family. And your dad is coming down late that night, and on Christmas Day, Nonie and Theo are coming over for the truly definitive English Christmas lunch, and remind me to ask Mawgan how I should deal with a goose, will you? My few recipe books are all dismissive on the subject, they prefer the idea of turkey, and so did Mum, always. There'll be plenty for you, it's more like an ostrich, and it's only fair, your dad will want to see you, too.'

If she was honest, the thought of spending her first Christmas since her rift with her mother effectively alone wasn't one that Debbie looked forward to with anything but trepidation, more particularly since the aftershock of her monumental row with Mawgan was still reverberating round.

'If you're sure nobody will mind, and I won't be intruding, that would be lovely. But I'd like to be back here on the evening of Christmas Eve – Tommy says the male voice choir will be here, singing carols round your Christmas tree you put up – he says they always used to, but they haven't done it for a few years, since … well, you know. So …'

Chel, who of course knew all about this already, nodded in agreement.

'Me too, I love listening to them, and under the circumstances, you should be here, anyway. Your Dad won't mind – we'll tell him to meet us here, unless he's very late, he'll like it too. So do we call it settled, then? I'll give Jeff and Millie a ring and tell them. They'll be thrilled.'

'It's not them I worry about so much, the Cornish seem to be endlessly hospitable whether you're family or not. But I don't want Oliver to feel I'm invading your space.'

'This may amaze you, but it's Oliver who suggested I discuss it with you,' said Chel. 'I should have thought about Mawgan being the head chef – but I've been so busy it never occurred to me.' She finished her coffee and got up to take the mugs to the kitchen. 'On the subject of which, I must get back to work, and judging by the pile of papers on the table, so must you. How's it all going?'

'It grinds like the mills of God, slowly.' Debbie got to her feet with reluctance. 'I've been getting one or two letters from people who came to us last year, it's a pity I can't tell them more yet.'

'But you are re-opening? Definitely?'

'We're working along those lines, yes. But exactly how or when is another question.'

'It'll be all right on the night,' said Chel, offering comfort.

'Maybe. But at the rate we're going, we'll be giving lectures in a tent on the lawn!'

Chel hesitated. The subject of Tim Howells was a delicate one these days, but she was interested to know if Tim's letter-writing had gone further than the all-too-obvious.

'Did you ever hear from Tim? I know you were going to write.'

'I did write. It was a pig of a letter to put together, if you want to know, and he hasn't replied.'

'Probably didn't know what to say,' said Chel, sympathetically. 'But at least you've been up-front with him. That must make you feel better.'

'You'd think so, wouldn't you?'

There was no reply to that, and so Chel made none. She thanked Debbie for the coffee and went downstairs to her office, where she sat for a few minutes, thinking. It was true that Tim Howells must have found Debbie's taking over his personal dream and making it her own hard to take, particularly as he had such a deep-rooted antipathy to Mawgan, but he didn't have a copyright in the idea. He had said he loved Debbie, had wrecked his young marriage on that very rock, he could be more forgiving towards her, surely. He had tried, and failed. It was somebody else's turn.

It would be galling for him if Debbie succeeded, and Chel believed that she probably would. She had thrown out the dead wood and kept the solid foundation timbers, Roger Hickling and herself and the simple idea of teaching sailing in this beautiful place. She had added Carl Colenso, his qualifications and his yacht, and if she played her cards right, she would yet recruit Oliver to her shore-based programme, his thinking appeared to be shifting ground. She had the co-operation of Mawgan at the Fish, which Tim had not had, and Chel's own experience of handling the public to draw on. And above all, she had capital.

Poor Tim, then.

Back upstairs, Debbie too was sitting and thinking, but not about Tim. There were a couple of things she hadn't mentioned to Chel, burying her misgivings with jolly Christmas chat about choirs and family visits. She wished now that she had mentioned them, Chel might have had something to say that would have helped. Or then again, she might not. The bottom line was that Mawgan most definitely did *not* want to go to visit his family on Christmas Day, or probably any other day, and the reasons weren't far to seek. After thinking about them for a few daunting minutes, she went downstairs to find her sister-in-law, suddenly feeling that she had to unload onto somebody, and Chel was the obvious person. Unfortunately, by that time,

Chel had left the office to go along to check up on activities in the pub kitchen, and was nowhere to be seen.

Having once decided that she wanted a sympathetic ear, Debbie realised that she wouldn't settle until she had poured out her troubles for a second opinion. They bulked too large and obscured the coming festivities like smog. For once, it wasn't raining. A walk would do her good, she concluded, and collecting a coat, set off along the foreshore to the house by the creek. Oliver had been behaving more like a proper brother of late than he had in years, and maybe his input would be more valuable than Chel's, which was probably predictable. It would certainly be different.

Oliver was absent-mindedly pleased to see her, up in his studio working on sketches for a commission. He grunted without looking up as she came through the door, apparently recognising her by instinct, and went on with his work, laying bold strokes of charcoal onto sugar paper. Debbie knew better than to interrupt until he was ready, and moved restlessly about, looking at the half-finished canvas on the big easel and the finished pictures on the walls, her brother's talent taking her breath away all over again. After a few minutes, he spoke.

'Hi, Deb. Don't often see you here.'

If that was true, it was his fault. Debbie said,

'Are you busy? Am I interrupting? Only, I wanted to ask you something – tell you something, I suppose. Talk about it.'

Oliver looked up then, and laid aside the stick of charcoal he had been using, wiping his fingers absently on a painty rag which, since the paint was wet, only made things worse.

'This is a new come-out. Since when have my views been of interest?'

'You like Mawgan,' said Debbie, because this was something that was becoming increasingly obvious. The two of them interacted in a way that neither Chel nor Debbie – nor Jerry, for that matter – had ever seen before. By this time, too, it wasn't merely from Mawgan's side, Oliver was giving as good as he got. It was, said Chel, privately to Debbie, a joy to see.

'Because I thought he'd got so that he wouldn't ever trust any friend to come that close and take such liberties,' she had confided. 'Or maybe, that he had always been that way – but against all sense, they seem to talk the same language.'

'Whatever that is,' had said Debbie, dubiously. 'Between them, they speak at least four different ones – so which one do they meet in, do you think?'

'The language of the soul,' had said Chel, and then laughed at herself. 'How pretentious!'

But that had been on another occasion. Now, Oliver gave his sister a quizzical look.

'That's true, but how does it help? What's he been up to now?'

'Being a dutiful son,' said Debbie, and made a rueful face.

'Never a good idea. Bad casting, too.' He caught her eye. 'Come on, Deb. It has to be done sometimes, even I can see that.'

'We're going to spend a couple of nights with his parents over Christmas,' said Debbie, slowly.

'So? Not the end of the world, is it? You've met them, you like them, they're prepared to meet him half-way. Given the circumstances, that's fair enough – isn't it?'

Debbie pulled out a stool from beneath the bench and perched herself on it. If Oliver was prepared to listen, she might as well be comfortable while she talked.

'For the past eighteen months, every time he's been there for more than the blink of an eyelash, Cressida has turned up and smashed the whole thing to smithereens.'

'That can't go on for ever. It's up to his family to make a stand, if they don't, they'll alienate him completely. Do you think they want to do that?'

'No, I don't. When we went over to Launceston while Anna was here, back in September, they were lovely. You could tell, they've been torn all ways, and they really love him, deep down. The only son ... even if he did turn his back on the family business.'

'I can't fault him on that one,' said Oliver. 'So, where's the problem? Now the ice has been broken, do you think they'll go back on it?'

'To be fair,' said Debbie, speaking slowly, thinking things out, 'I don't think it was ever their choice to turn him away – he went of his own accord and they didn't know how to stop him. Were even relieved, maybe. It must have been terrible, trying to be fair to both sides.'

'Then it sounds to me, that if it happens that the unspeakable Cressida gets up to her usual tricks, it's up to *you* to stop him taking off again. Do you think you can?'

'Actually,' said Debbie, 'Chel thinks she won't. She thinks ...'

'Ah,' said Oliver. He didn't ask what Chel thought, merely said, 'She's strange sometimes, is Chel. I've known her to be right in some very peculiar circumstances. If she says Cressida won't show up, she probably won't.'

'The only problem is, *if* Chel is right, she won't have sent a Christmas card, either.'

'From what I understand, that'll be nobody's fault but her own. Certainly not Mawgan's.'

'She's still their child. The baby ... little sister, come to that. And Mawgan can't help but feel responsible in a way, even if not for the ultimate reason. And how can any of them stop thinking about ... well, everything, and blaming him even if they try not to? Which brings me to another thing. And I'm not sure that it isn't the worst.'

When she didn't continue, Oliver said, eventually,

'Are you going to tell me?'

'It's the house,' said Debbie.

'The *house*?' Oliver looked blank.

'Yes. When we've visited them before, it's been in a rented house in Launceston – little sister Cress made things so unpleasant they did a runner to let the dust settle. His mother couldn't even go to the shops without someone saying something ... Allison says it was unbearable, even if it was only a few people, and Cressida having hysterics everywhere – it just seemed a good idea to lie low for a bit. I don't know if it was.'

'The incest thing,' said Oliver. 'Load of rubbish – most people know that, surely.Sheer spite on little sister's part. Silly, hysterical little witch!'

'But nasty to live with, think about it. I can't blame them, and poor Mawgan was banged up in Exeter too, and so far as the general public believe, he deserved to be. But that's the point.'

'You've lost me,' said Oliver, after a pause.

'They've gone back home. We won't be visiting them in Launceston, we'll be at their old home in St Austell ... and that's ...' She paused, and Oliver finished for her, thoughtfully.

'The scene of the crime. I see what you mean.'

'Suppose the rockery is still there?' said Debbie, blurting out her worst fear. 'He'll have to see it – it's going to be impossible. It's where Mike Stanley died, and they said it was his fault!'

Oliver didn't make the mistake of thinking that *they* referred to the family, but he looked sceptical just the same.

'It'll be long gone, surely! For God's sake, Deb, they won't want to look at it either. How could they?'

'Well, I do hope so. But even if it isn't there any more ... there's going to be a change in the familiar garden that's going to dig in the sore spot almost as painfully. I think, to be honest, he'd sooner spend Christmas in an open field than go back home.'

'It's got to be faced, Deb. He must know it himself, or he wouldn't have agreed to go. If you *don't* go, even if only for a couple of nights, you'll simply widen the breach, and he obviously doesn't want that to happen. And if you don't go, the next time – and there will be a next time – will be even harder.'

'It's a difficult thing to have to do, even so,' said Debbie. 'It's not even as if it ends there … there's other members of the family, and people who used to be his friends … he's no idea any more where he stands with any of them. You see, he's never been back.'

'Then it's probably time he found out. You never know, he may get a pleasant surprise.'

'He *may*,' Debbie agreed, sceptically.

'You don't think so?'

'It just seems to me that, if they wanted to, they've had plenty of time to say, hi, glad you're back with us. They haven't.'

'You have thought, that may be his own fault? He has rather made a habit of pushing people away since he was released from prison. You know that – even I know that, and I've only known him a few weeks. How Con Delaney got away with it will remain forever a mystery – skin like a rhinoceros, probably.'

Debbie ignored this red herring.

'It doesn't matter whose fault it is, does it? It's still a fact.'

'Even so, it seems to me you've only got two choices. Stay away, and let the whole impossible situation fossilise into rock, or go and see what happens. You say Mawgan has opted for going. On the whole, he has to be right – and rather brave, too, when you think about it.'

'Oh, he doesn't suffer from a tendency to hang back,' said Debbie, on a note of bitterness. 'Burning houses or impossible situations, he's right there in the middle!'

'If that's the way he is, and it seems to be, you're going to have to live with it, aren't you? And you wouldn't love him the way you do if he crawled away.'

'True. Knowing that doesn't make it any easier.'

'Rushing in where angels fear to tread is what got him into trouble in the first place.'

'I know, I *know!*'

'So what do you want me to say?' asked Oliver, with interest.

'I don't want you to say anything. I just wanted you to listen to me. And you have, so thank you.'

'It'll be all right, Deb.' Oliver reached out, just touched her cheek. 'It isn't only you that's in there fighting for him. There's his mum and dad, his other grandparents, his sisters – '

'Anna won't be there. They're coming over in February, for the wedding.' Mawgan's older sister lived with her husband and family in Switzerland.

'Don't split hairs.'

'I'm glad you can like him so unreservedly, in spite of everything. You do, don't you?'

'Yeah …' Oliver hesitated. 'Yes, I do. But I can't, for the life of me, see what made you choose him over all the handsome and gilded youths you've had around your feet all your life. He's nothing to look at, and let's face it, he can be rough as rats when he tries.'

'He's real,' said Debbie, after thinking about it.

'He's certainly that. Maybe you're right, a good dose of reality is what our family needs.' He grinned at her, warm and suddenly, she realised, unfamiliar. 'It's a novelty, when you think about it, to even be *calling* us a family, and meaning it.' He saw his sister's face, and on impulse, went across and put his arms round her, something else that was unfamiliar. 'It'll all be OK, Deb. All of it.'

'I don't see how it can,' said Debbie, suddenly desolate.

'Trust me. It's early days.'

'Are you going all clairvoyant on me, too?' asked Debbie, accusingly, but his arms were comforting and there was no heat in the question.

'No, it's one of life's great lessons, and believe me, I'm an expert. Summed up, I believe, as *it'll be all the same in a hundred years* – or something.'

'Oh Oliver!' said Debbie, burying her face in his sweatshirt. 'I never thought I'd sink so low as to call *you* of all people, a comfort!'

* * * * *

Debbie wasn't alone in finding the coming Christmas season a mixed blessing. Susan, too, was finding it hard going this year, although for different reasons. The abandonment of old-established, familiar and loved customs is always painful.

Oliver apart, Christmas had always been a family occasion in the Nankervis family, the one moment in the year when they all came together and pretended that all was well – not that the word 'pretence' had ever been spoken aloud, and to Susan and Debbie perhaps it hadn't even occurred. Dot and Jerry, welcoming their daughters and son-in-law and grandchildren into their home, had always managed to put on a good show, and it had always been a high point in the year. A tradition, reaching far back into the past as long as Susan could remember, altering slightly when Oliver became old enough to take himself elsewhere and then again on Susan's marriage, and when the grandchildren came on the scene, but basically remaining constant.

This year, it would all be very different.

The break-up of their parents' marriage would have made a difference in any case, but Susan felt that with Debbie's support they might have made something of it. Now, even that was to be denied. The family Christmas would this year be taking place in St Erbyn, where her father, her brother and her sister-in-law, and no doubt Debbie as well, if not Mawgan, would all foregather and, she was fairly certain, have a great time together, all the signs had been there on their own brief trip to the west. She was left alone, with her mother's bitterness and her husband's lack of interest, to do the best that she could with the wreck of an outlived tradition.

Dot, clinging rather pathetically, Susan thought, to old habit, wanted the remnants of her family to come to her for Christmas Day. Tom thought otherwise.

'It was OK with Deb around, she's good with the kids. Without her, it'll be a complete nightmare! Why can't she come to us instead?'

'She wants to keep things as normal as possible.'

'But they won't be,' Tom objected. 'They'll miss their Grandpa, they'll miss their auntie, it'll be really dismal. At least if she comes here, Maria can look after them.'

'Maria has the day off. She's going out with her friends.'

'She could go another day instead.'

Susan gave him a look.

'Right, fine. You tell her. Then you can leave me and Mum to entertain each other and slope off – to walk the dog.' The derision in her voice was unmistakeable. Tom, who objected to having his thoughts read, said mutinously,

'*Someone* has to walk the dog.'

'And you might meet someone more interesting to talk to than us,' continued Susan.

But this was open warfare.

'I just think, under the circumstances, the kids'd be happier here.'

'Then you suggest it,' said Susan, with finality. She turned away, leaving Tom glowering.

Jerry, to his annoyance, was on Susan's side.

'Susan's mother is a great traditionalist. She loves preparing Christmas for the children, let her have her fun. It's going to be bad enough for her as it is.'

'Don't you think a complete break would be better for her?' asked Tom, reasonably he thought.

'You can have too many breakages all at once in one life,' said Jerry. He was, to be honest, sorry for Dot. He had a feeling that Christmas with Oliver and Chel, although novel, and no doubt exclusively adult, would be both different and rather enjoyable, and he had been touched and pleased to be invited. Oliver and Chel seemed to know a great many people and, starting with the male voice choir in the Fish on Christmas Eve, the festive season looked likely to be a lot more festive than Jerry had become used to these days. Even the thought of eating his Christmas lunch with Nonie seemed acceptable; he and Nonie, he thought, had reached some understanding on his last visit.

If only he could do the same with Helen ...

He realised that his son-in-law had said something, he hadn't heard a word.

'I'm sorry?'

'I was thinking of the children,' said Tom. 'It won't be much fun for them.'

'I think that's rather up to you and Susan,' said Jerry.

Defeated, Tom took himself off to sulk. If the festivities had taken place in his own house, of course he would have played his part as polite host and devoted Dad, he told himself – but while Susan was messing around in the kitchen with the turkey, and her mother was there to keep an eye on the children, it would surely have been quite reasonable to slip out with Clinker and give him some exercise, get him from under Susan's feet. It would be a kindness, even. And if Elaine met him round the corner in the Black Lion, then they could have had a Christmas drink together; surely it would be unreasonable to begrudge him that much. It would be harmless enough, God knew. The rest of the day would be spent with his family, after all.

It was Susan's fault that it wouldn't happen. Susan and her inability to stand up to her dinosaur of a mother with her outdated ideas and old-fashioned traditions. He felt resentment against her, and the resentment began to colour his attitude towards the coming festivities, creating an atmosphere in the house that his sensitive young son couldn't help but feel.

'Mrs Casson, I must tell you,' said Maria, materialising unexpectedly in the drawing room, where Susan was addressing Christmas cards and wishing that it had been socially permissible to enclose them with the wedding invitations. She had already, effectively, done this job once. Perhaps it was time she became computer literate and stuck the whole boring job on a disc, or whatever it was you did. She wasn't in the mood for Maria.

'I'm busy, Maria. Is it important?'

'I think so,' said Maria. She waited. After a moment, Mrs Casson put down her pen and turned towards her with a long-suffering expression.

'So, what is it?'

'It is the little boy Sebastian,' said Maria. 'He 'as the nightmare, he will not go to sleep, he cries in the night. He is unhappy.'

Join the club, Seb!

Susan frowned.

'How long has this been going on, Maria?'

'You know, he 'as always 'ad bad dreams. But now, is every night. There is something wrong.'

Susan found herself wondering if it could be her own unhappiness rubbing off on her sensitive little son. She had tried to be her usual self, but perhaps she hadn't succeeded. She felt guilty.

'Do you have any idea what it might be?'

Maria shrugged her shoulders.

'He will not say. He just cries and does not rest.'

'All right.' Susan considered. 'I'll talk to Annabel, see if there's anything wrong at school. And the next time he cries in the night, you call me. We'll get to the bottom of it, he's very highly strung you know, I don't suppose it'll turn out to be much.'

Maria didn't agree, but she knew better than to argue with Mrs Casson and in any case, she had achieved her object. Mrs Casson knew about the nightmares, and she would do something about them, of that at least Maria knew she could be certain. She went away satisfied, and Susan returned to her cards.

This is an unhappy house, she found herself thinking. No wonder poor Seb has nightmares. How can things have changed so much just in a few months?

But it wasn't just a few months. It was a lot longer than that.

Just for a second, as she sat there with her pen poised, Susan felt as if had been for ever.

Talking to Annabel about school proved to be a non-starter. She just stood there twining one leg around the other and looking bored.

'I don't see him that much. He's only a baby.'

'You must see him in the playground. Is he being bullied? Has he friends?'

Annabel shrugged.

'I suppose so.'

'Do you see him playing with other children?' Susan pressed, but Annabel had lost interest.

'Mummy, I told you, I don't watch him. I've got my own friends.'

Defeated, Susan gave up the futile argument, as it was rapidly becoming, and Annabel went away. She went upstairs to her own room, avoiding Maria, and slammed the door, throwing herself onto the bed. After a minute or two, she picked up her old pink rabbit and cuddled him, rocking to and fro.

The one thing she wasn't going to tell her mother was that she and Seb were afraid that Mummy and Daddy were going to split up like her friend Annie's Mummy and Daddy had done, and like Grandma and Grandpa too, although they were old people. Even so, their break-up had eroded their grandchildren's security. And Mummy and Daddy had been getting angrier and angrier lately, too, she and Seb had heard them when they were supposed to be safely in bed, arguing, arguing down in the drawing-room. It usually ended with Daddy going out.

To mention her fears – and Seb's too, no doubt – Annabel obscurely felt would be to make them real. She curled herself into a tight ball and put her thumb in her mouth.

XIII

Christmas Eve dawned with a clear sky and a light dusting of frost, perfect Christmas weather. Debbie awoke early because her feet were cold, Mawgan had turned over at some time during the night and dragged the duvet across the bed, leaving them exposed to the chilly dawn. She sat up, curling them back into the feathery warmth, wide-awake. Reaching over to her alarm clock, she turned it round to see the time. Twenty past six. Early, but even so, too late to start going back to sleep. She looked at her bedfellow thoughtfully. He looked very snug, naturally enough since he now had most of the duvet, and it seemed a shame to disturb him when he could realistically sleep for another hour if he wanted to. It would have been nice to wake him, she thought, but he still didn't sleep at all well, still was haunted by too many bad dreams, he needed to get as much rest as he could when he could. She slid quietly over the edge of the bed and tiptoed to the bedroom door, collecting her dressing-gown on the way.

Their living-room was chilly, the heating didn't come on in the pub until six-thirty; she switched on the electric fire and stood there shivering, clutching her warm dressing-gown around her. Christmas Eve, but the usual Christmas tingle of excitement was missing this year, in spite of the little tree on the chest that stood between the windows, the boxes of presents for her family and for Mawgan's, and the cards on the mantelpiece and the dresser. Quite a few cards, but apart from the ones from abroad, most of them from her own friends. However had Mawgan managed to alienate everyone at home so thoroughly? Was Oliver right, and he had done so deliberately? Roger, she recalled, had once said something very similar, and one or two in the village here had let drop remarks that bore out the theory. Had disgrace really been that hard to bear, or was it sheer defiance? Or a bit of both? And how to unravel the tragic tangle he had thus created? Everyone wasn't going to be as easily won back as the villagers here; it was a sad fact that the better people thought they knew you, the more they blamed you for letting them down. It had also seemed to her, as her knowledge of him grew, that apart from celebrity DJ Connor Delaney, who for whatever reason had faced out the storm, he had turned his back on all his friends in this country, the only ones with whom he now had any contact were his old work colleagues in France, in Switzerland and in Italy, and that was very possibly because they were so far away that he couldn't quarrel with them.

Or because none of them knew Cressida … was it she who was responsible, then?

Or if not responsible exactly, at the root of it all?

Come to think of it, Con Delaney probably didn't know Cressida, either … Edward Rushton, Mawgan's erstwhile partner, on the other hand, must have known her quite well. But what would make an apparently loving sister turn on her brother so viciously? Her blood ran suddenly cold; she felt her mind reaching out after a truth, but it slipped away before she trapped it.

Debbie pushed the uncomfortable almost-revelation away, it had just seemed to her, all of a sudden, that there was a suggestion of more than thoughtless hysteria, and about that she didn't know, couldn't begin to guess, and did not even wish to think. Abandoning fruitless conjecture, she went into the kitchen to make herself a warming cup of tea.

Leaning on the worktop while the kettle came to the boil, she realised that there was another circumstance extinguishing the usual bright, childish flame of excitement. Her mother, her sister, her nephew and niece … it was going to be strange, celebrating Christmas without them. They were part of a tradition, going way back into her own childhood.

Time for a change, then, she told herself briskly. Even so, she did miss the children. Chel had made a similar comment; last year she had had her own sister and her husband and children for Christmas, it would have been interesting, Debbie thought, to see what Oliver had made of that. Chel's niece Candy was to be one of her own bridesmaids; she herself and Candy had shared that privilege for Chel at her unexpected and hasty wedding to Oliver, five years ago.

Weddings in our family, Debbie found herself thinking, never seem to be occasions for total rejoicing. That one was very strange too, and for much the same reasons, only that time it had been Susan who had boycotted the ceremony.

Susan ...

Of all the circumstances surrounding her own engagement and impending marriage, Debbie now found, Susan and the situation in which she had been placed was the one that caused the most ... not anxiety. Concern? Dad thought Susan was unhappy, although she seemed to Debbie to be her usual bossy, organising self. It was true that Susan had been placed in an unenviable position, the only one of her children to whom their mother now spoke – and Dad was only her adoptive father, too. It had never seemed to make any difference, but perhaps to Susan, it did. Perhaps that was what was making her unhappy, but if so it seemed to Debbie a waste of emotion. Dad would never abandon Susan, he had always loved her just as much as his natural children, you didn't make mistakes about things like that. She wouldn't abandon her either, and nor did she think Oliver would when it came down to it, for all their relationship had always been on the uneasy side. Families didn't do that kind of thing.

Families? They were a *family*? A real one?

Well ... yes. It was becoming all too apparent that, against all the odds, they were.

She must speak to Chel. She felt, obscurely, that they should be particularly nice to Susan. She had got the dirty end of the stick, and it wasn't fair when she was the only one of them who had been a dutiful child.

The kettle boiled at that point in her thoughts, and she made her tea, carrying the mug back to the fire. The room was warming up now, she switched on the Christmas tree lights, snuggled into an armchair and wrapped her hands around the hot mug.*My home. My life. Beyond that door, the man I'm going to marry.*

That set her tingling, no doubt about it.

Strange, the places life took you to.

Against her will, she found her thoughts turning again to her mother. Would she miss her youngest child over the Christmas period? Would she, perhaps, soften in her attitude, reopen her door and her heart, and let Debbie back in? It was a pleasant dream to toy with for a few minutes, but in her own heart, Debbie knew that her mother had never done a U-turn in her life, and she wouldn't be about to start now. She had never met Mawgan, but she despised and hated the very idea of him, and for reasons that to Debbie seemed ridiculous. Dad must have told her that the conviction was unlikely to stand on appeal, and she presumably knew nothing about the horrible things Cressida had said or she would have most certainly have mentioned them, so it could only be that this was all about the Fish, and the builders' yard, the council estate and the comprehensive school, and even more unbelievably, the career as a chef. Unreasoning prejudice therefore, and there had never been an answer to that. Where people came from, in Debbie's book, didn't matter. It was where they were going that mattered. And anyway, where Mawgan had come from was nothing to despise, he sprang from good, hard-working stock, in spite of the odd rough edge here and there he had been, quite possibly, more rigorously brought up than Debbie herself even if to a slightly different set of rules.Her mother had never even bothered to meet him. The whole rift was stupid – stupid, and irreparable, unless she herself gave in.

No way! That would only be even more heartbreaking than the present impasse. She knew that for certain after Mawgan's recent dive into despair. She hoped, very much she hoped, that he would never do that again. Particularly not over Christmas.

Debbie, her mother's daughter after all, set her jaw rebelliously. Nobody had the right to dictate to somebody else so brutally, it was a lesson that, sadly, her mother must learn. Only, she wished very much that it hadn't fallen to her lot to be the teacher.

It was ironic, when you thought about it, that she, always her mother's darling, was now less welcome at home than Oliver, whom her mother had always heartily disliked. For a moment, sitting there with the bright lights twinkling on the little tree and the cards on the mantelpiece that her mother would never see, Debbie wanted to weep.

Sounds of activity behind the bedroom door prevented her, Mawgan was awake and heading for the shower, she heard the click of the bathroom door as he went in. Pulling herself together, she drank her cooling tea and by the time he came out of the bedroom, clean, shaved and ready for the day, she was able to smile at him unreservedly.

'Hi bird! What's the problem, insomnia?' He bent to kiss her.

'Cold,' said Debbie. 'You went off with the duvet – again!'

'Oops! Breakfast?' He headed off for the kitchen, unrepentant. 'You get dressed, I'll fix something.'

'Is that a peace offering?' asked Debbie, following with her empty mug. He paused with the fridge door open, turning to gather her into his arms and kiss her again, soundly.

'No, but this is. Or shall we just go back to bed and share the duvet out fairly?'

The idea was tempting, but Debbie resisted it.

'Better not. You've got work to do, and I'm supposed to be at the creek by ten. I wish you could come too.'

'Me too, but I can't, so that's that – but it is only seven o'clock. What on earth did you think I had in mind?'

Debbie gave a spurt of laughter.

'Knowing you, I daren't even imagine!' She disentangled herself, hesitating, tempted again. But no. She very much enjoyed making love with Mawgan, a straightforward and considerate performer with no kinky hang-ups – although she did feel that when the time was right, his horizons should be widened a little – but probably now wasn't the moment. If she had the time, he probably didn't, and since he was already showered and dressed that must clinch it. 'We've all those days until the New Year when the restaurant isn't open, and we can make love all morning if we want to.'

'There's a great idea!' said Mawgan.

Debbie showered and dressed in her turn, and by the time she came out of the bedroom again, the flat was full of the wonderful smell of grilling bacon and toast. There was a lot to be said, she thought complacently, for a man who was handy about the kitchen, but she was going to have to watch herself or she would let him do it all the time, and that wouldn't be fair – or then again, bearing in mind her cooking skills, perhaps it would.

He seemed to be in an upbeat mood this morning, although she would be happy when the dark shadows had gone from beneath his eyes and the strain from around his mouth. Personal problems apart, he loved his job and the seasonal festivities had definitely given him a buzz, so that she wondered, not for the first time, what the future held for them both and found the thought exciting. She went into the tiny kitchen and lolled against the worktop so that she could talk to him as he worked.

'This time next year, I wonder where we shall be,' she speculated. Mawgan grinned.

'Save that for the New Year. But hopefully, we'll be right here.'

'I didn't mean physically, I meant … well, workwise, I suppose.'

'A little bit further on?' He began cracking eggs expertly into a gently trembling pan of water. Debbie couldn't have done it one-handed if she had been paid, and she watched in awe.

'Watching you cook is poetry in motion! If I tried to do that, I'd have a saucepan full of crushed eggshell and egg noodles.'

'Tasty.'

'I love you,' said Debbie, because it suddenly came over her afresh. Mawgan left his eggs and came over to kiss her again, thoroughly and light-heartedly.

'Good. Now can I get on with the breakfast?'

There was no way they could use the dining table, it was still smothered in Debbie's growing mountain of paperwork. They ate by the fire, with the plates on their knees, and the toast and coffee balanced among the books and magazines on the coffee table, enjoying their unusual domestic intimacy.

'I told Denise I'd do her stint on the bar tonight, if you and Chel don't object,' said Debbie, through a mouthful of perfectly poached egg. She swallowed appreciatively, her own poached eggs, done the easy way in an egg-poacher, always turned into something closely resembling half a rather resilient tennis ball. 'Her sister is having a party. She wanted to go.'

'So long as somebody does it, I don't care a toss, and I'm sure Chel won't,' said Mawgan, cheerfully. 'Will you be back in time? It'll be a madhouse tonight, I should think.'

'I'll make sure we are. It seemed a sensible idea, when you'll be working anyway.' She paused. 'I wish you weren't, but I suppose I'll have to get used to it.'

'We'll make it up some other time,' Mawgan promised.

During a whole month in Tenerife, Debbie thought, wryly. Although, it wasn't going to be as bad as she had thought. Helen had written to her, out of the blue, offering the use of an apartment belonging to some friends of her own for a fortnight, and better yet, they had a yacht in Puerto Colon which, Debbie being the sister of the great Oliver Nankervis and a qualified yachtmaster in her own right, they were prepared to loan for the second fortnight. If she let herself, she almost felt anticipation – and anyway, if it healed Mawgan, the place would have justified its existence. She wondered what he would be like on a boat, he freely admitted to being a complete tyro.

'You've gone quiet,' said Mawgan, gathering up the plates. 'What are you thinking, bird? You're miles away.'

'I was just looking forward to playing Captain Bligh on Helen's friends' boat,' said Debbie, and he laughed as he stood up.

'Am I allowed to cast you adrift in the liferaft?'

'Better not.' Debbie finished her coffee. 'I'll wash up, you got it all.'

'You will,' agreed Mawgan, glancing at his watch. 'I'm off – have a nice day, see you this evening – '

The door of the flat banged behind him. Debbie almost thought she saw a swirl of dust in his wake. Smiling to herself, she ran water into the sink and began on her usual job, that of washer-up.

Going downstairs later on, she found Chel in the office checking the post before they went off to Trelewan, she wouldn't be working again for a couple of days, although she would probably just look in tomorrow morning, and again on Boxing Day to see that all was well in Mawgan's absence.

'Hi Deb.' She looked up as her sister-in-law came in. 'Won't be a second – just let me give this lot to Shirley to deal with, and I'll be ready.' She picked up a sheaf of papers from her desk. 'I saw the Cornish hurricane passing through the lobby just now, heading for the great outdoors. On a turkey hunt, he said.'

Debbie shook her head.

'He gets bronze ones – only I think he said they're black, it sounds a bit racist to me – from someone who breeds them locally. They're better, apparently. Me, I thought a turkey was just a turkey. Did you ask him how to cook your ostrich?'

'Certainly did. And he gave me a recipe for rum and apple stuffing that sounds as if it would blow your mind – ' Chel headed for the door. 'Back in a minute. Then we'll go.'

The friends – relatives even – to whom they were going for lunch were cousins whom Chel and Oliver had first met when they came down to Cornwall eighteen months or so earlier. Millie Jackson was, Debbie thought, but wasn't absolutely sure, Jerry's first cousin, although they had never met. She had an idea that their fathers had been brothers, so that worked. Millie was married to a farmer called Jeff Jackson, they had a daughter called Judy who was married to one of the local doctors. Judy and Keith had been good friends to Chel and Oliver when they first arrived in Trelewan, and still were, although they saw less of each other these days. There was Great Uncle William and his wife Jenny, too, who also farmed, at a place called Higher Vellanzoe where, so Chel informed Debbie as they walked together back to the little creek, by coincidence, there was a cottage where Nonie's teacher, friend and lover, Matthew Sutton the well-known artist, had come to a premature and rather sticky end thirty years earlier.

'He flew a plane into the roof in a fog,' she said. 'You've been there actually, it's the one we were living in when you came last year. It was pretty terrible for Nonie. She's taken years to get over it.'

'Not too good for him, either,' suggested Debbie. She paused. 'I like Nonie. What's her connection with Dad, do we know?'

'She and Helen were students together. Actually, I don't think she and your father hit it off that well.'

'Nor do she and Helen, these days,' said Debbie. 'That night they all came to dinner at your place, it stuck out a mile. Shame.'

Chel made no reply to this. She didn't feel that it would be a good idea to tell Debbie that at the back of all the ill-feeling between the three erstwhile friends lay Deb's own mother, and the way she had manipulated a secret she should never have known in the first place. Deb's mother was a spectre at the Christmas feast already.

'Come on,' she said, instead, picking up the pace. 'Let's go get Oliver and start Christmas!'

* * * * *

Jerry was well on his way by the time his children were headed home from the Christmas Eve celebration in Trelewan, his big, powerful Mercedes eating up the miles between Dorset and Cornwall, and he was in a happy mood. He had taken time, before he left, to ring Helen – there was no harm in wishing her a happy Christmas, after all, and he wanted to thank her for her services to his daughter, among other things. It gave him an excellent excuse.

'It was good of you to think of it,' he said. 'She was over the moon when you wrote. Good of your friends too, since they don't know her from Adam.'

'Oh, I think they'd know her from Adam,' said Helen, a laugh in her voice. 'Very shapely young woman, your daughter Debbie. I gave her a good reference, that's all. They were happy to come up with the goods.'

'The yacht as well? That was gilding the lily a bit, wasn't it?'

'She's Oliver's sister, he taught her everything she knows – well, most of it. That's a good enough reference for anyone. Anyway, she's captain of a sailing school, that has to clinch it.'

'It was still exceptionally good of them. I hope she wrote and thanked them nicely.'

'Of course she did, Jerry, don't be so like a parent!'

There was a brief pause, while both of them thought about that remark, then Helen said, a challenge in her voice,

'And did you grasp the nettle and warn poor Mawgan that dear Dot was interfering in his private life?'

'I didn't have to. He already knew,' said Jerry, cringing at the memory. 'Dot wasn't exactly making it the secret of the year, and Tim Howells had already told him.'

'*Ouch!*' said Helen, thinking about it. 'So what happened? How did he take it?'

'Badly. Wouldn't you?' Jerry said.

'You already know the answer to that.' Helen waited a moment to allow this to sink in, before asking, 'So, what did you do?'

'I didn't. Oliver did.'

'*Oliver* did?'

'Debbie was in pieces, Mawgan stormed off ... no, he didn't storm, exactly. He just went, saying he couldn't damage her family, I ask you!But then, he doesn't know Dot.'

'Couldn't marry Deb, is what you're saying? Oh, poor Debbie – she loves him to bits!' Pause. '*Bloody* Dot! So what did Oliver do? I don't see him as a diplomat, somehow, didn't he make things worse?'

'Strangely, no. I don't know exactly what was said between the two of them, but the engagement is on again.'

'But did he find out the answer to the million pound question?'

'He did. And then I went to see Dot when I got back ...'

He stopped speaking. The memory of that visit was vivid in his mind. Helen said, prompting,

'Nothing she did could surprise me, so tell me anyway.'

'I told her, the money came from a legitimate source. And she laughed in my face.'

'*What* legitimate source?' Dot had demanded.

'A temporary, private loan.'

'Oh, my dear Jerry!' Her face had been full of derision. 'You *believe* that?'

'Yes, as it happens.'

'Who provided this famous loan, then?'

'That's not for me to tell you. But it's the truth, even so. And you should pay off your detective and leave it at that.'

"That's not for me to tell you!"Dot's mimicry was perfect. 'Well, for your information, I mean to find out.'

'She chose not to believe me,' said Jerry, now. 'There was no way I was giving her chapter and verse, it should have been enough to know that the money was legal.'

'Are you going to give *me* chapter and verse?' asked Helen, with interest.

'No reason why not, in your case. You won't be wanting to make trouble with it.'

'*Could* she? How intriguing! So, tell me.'

So he had.

'Did you ever hear of a DJ called Con Delaney? Radio One, BBC2, very popular with the young, apparently.'

'Yeah. I listen to him sometimes while I'm working. He's wickedly funny – and I mean *wickedly*! You're not going to tell me *he* was the mysterious benefactor?'

'He was one of the original Pools syndicate, as it turns out. Before he was famous. As a matter of fact, I believe he's tipped to be Mawgan's best man at the wedding.'

'Good heavens!' For once, Helen was silenced, leaving Jerry a space in which to say,

'Mawgan wasn't going to tell, but Oliver got it out of him. The thing is … I don't think for a moment that anything Dot could say would hurt Con Delaney, but if she found out, she might very well think she could use the threat as a lever. And even more, she might succeed. Mawgan is very sensitive on the subject of his prison sentence, maybe sets more store by it than he should under the circumstances. He might be swayed by threats to drag his friend into it … I won't say he would, but he *might*. And you never know, some mischievous journalist just might pick it up and run with it, even though I think it's unlikely. There is such a thing as guilt by association.'

'These days, I wouldn't put anything past the tabloids. Con Delaney is big just at the moment, riding the crest of the wave.' Helen sounded thoughtful. 'The higher you go, the harder you can fall. So Dot's going on digging, is what you're saying?'

'On the principle that everyone has something to hide, yes. Mind you, I think her chances of finding out that particular secret are pretty small, but ...'

'She's hoping there might be others? Sounds just like Dot!' Helen hesitated. 'What do you think? Is there anything?'

'No. I don't think there is. I think everything else is already up front.' There it was again. His voice faltered, in spite of himself.

'You don't sound sure,' said Helen, half as a question. Jerry shrugged, although Helen couldn't see it.

'I just wish she'd let it alone.'

'She loves Debbie,' said Helen, conceding a point to the enemy. 'She wants what she thinks is best for her. Mothers are like that. And sometimes, we can all get it wrong.' *I did*, she was tempted to add, but resisted the temptation. Enough was enough, and on that particular subject, probably more than enough.

'Funny way of showing it, she has, if that's so!' retorted Jerry.

For a second there, they seemed to be on opposite sides of the argument to their usual ones, and sheer surprise brought them both up short. Jerry said, abruptly changing the subject,

'I should be on my way. Have you any messages for them – the children? I'll be leaving for Cornwall as soon as I put this phone down, I'll be seeing them all tonight, there's some sort of shindig at the Fish.'

'Just give them all my love.' Helen accepted the change of subject, but still she hesitated. 'It's a bit hard on poor Susan.'

'Nothing I can do about that, she wouldn't let me over the threshold,' said Jerry. Both of them knew that *she* didn't refer to Susan. Helen sighed, audibly, at the other end of the line.

'I know, but poor Susan all the same. It won't be much of a Christmas for her.'

'Someone has to stay with Dot, or it won't be much of a Christmas for her, either.'

'Don't break my heart!'

'It's still true. I'll make it up to Susan and the kids somehow. And when you think about it, it's time we all moved on. You can't let traditions get graven in stone, they turn into obligations and anyway, it's too painful when they shatter.'

'True,' said Helen. He thought he heard a note of derision in her voice, but perhaps he was wrong for the next thing she said was, 'What are you doing over New Year?'

'Going to bed early with a good book.'

'Poor old man! I've got a better idea.' She hesitated. 'I'm having a party. Why don't you come? I could get you a room at the pub.'

These days, he seemed to spend half his life dossing around in pubs. First the Fish, now the Black Bull. He was too surprised for a moment to answer.

'Are you still there, or have you fainted?' asked Helen, with interest.

'I'm still here. Did you say what I thought you said?'

'Don't read too much into it. I just thought, since you're on your own and you've treated me to all those lunches …'

'Well, thank you,' said Jerry. 'I'd love to come to your party.'

'I'll see you, then. Eight o'clock, dress informal. I'll speak to the Black Bull. Just friends, Jerry – happy Christmas.'

He just had time to wish her a happy Christmas too, and she was gone. He stood there for some time with the phone in his hand and his mind reeling.

He would have been astonished if he had known that Helen was thinking of him, driving down to Cornwall and his family

– *their* family – and whatever unspecified shindig was taking place at the Fish with something dangerously close to envy.

* * * * *

Mawgan had been right in his prediction, with the promise of carols round the tree from the local male voice choir, even with the accompanying threat of a collection in aid of a children's charity, the bar was unusually busy, although to call it a madhouse, exactly, was probably unfair. Some, but not all of the choir's singers were regulars, and they clustered round the bar in festive mood.

'Evening, young Debbie!' Robert Pengelly, Shirley's father and one of the lead singers came up to the bar to order six pints for himself and his mates. 'Didn't expect to see you working behind the bar tonight! Where's the Tregear girl?'

'She wanted to go to a party, and why not?' Debbie answered, as she pulled the first pint. 'I wasn't doing anything this evening except being here – Mawgan is working anyway – so it seemed obvious.'

'You're a good girl,' said Robert, approvingly. He gathered the filled glasses onto a tray and paused, looking at her with a question in his eyes. 'Going through with this marriage then, are you? Seems like the two of you go well together.'

'We do.' Debbie met his eyes with a friendly smile. The relationship between Mawgan and the village had only recently returned to being anything approaching friendly, although she thought that they had always had some kind of respect for him, at least in the context of his working life. Robert nodded.

'He did good, going in after that Howells woman in that fire,' he said. 'Be in tonight, will he?'

'I shouldn't think so. He's got the restaurant full.'

'He's a hard worker, I'll say that,' Robert opined. He turned away then, carrying his tray carefully back to the table where his friends sat, leaving Debbie wondering. There had been an intention behind that little exchange that she couldn't quite put her finger on. On the whole, though, it had been friendly.

The bar continued to fill up, and Debbie, Tommy and Sunday Sam were kept busy. She saw Oliver and Chel when they came in, and a little later her father came up to say hullo. She thought, without identifying the cause, that he looked unusually happy. If it hadn't been fanciful, she would almost have said that there was a glow about him. She leaned across the bar counter to kiss him soundly.

'Hi Dad, good to see you! What're you drinking? On the house, of course.'

'Hullo there, my little barmaid.' He returned the kiss with interest, thinking it was a good thing her mother couldn't see her, on Christmas Eve too. 'Do I get to talk with you tonight?'

'Chel thought you might like to go to the midnight service at the church with her, and I'm coming too. Will that do?'

'Bit of a contrast,' said Jerry. He grinned at her, boyish suddenly. 'Just like old times, eh?' There was a momentary pause, while they both considered old times, then Debbie said, with an awkward laugh,

'Although you may have had enough carols by then. And some of the tunes may surprise you, too.' She had already found this for herself.

'Never!' said Jerry. 'It's Christmas. And mine's a pint – *that* one.' He pointed, and his daughter drew it for him, and his unlucky remark was forgotten.

It would be too much to hope for that his son would attend the midnight service too, he thought, and he was right. But it would be good to be there with two of his three girls.

He wondered what Susan would be doing.

The choir struck up at nine o'clock and sang for a full hour, gathered around the big Christmas tree, glittering with coloured lights, that Chel had had placed in the corner by the hearth – Mawgan had warned her it was too exposed on the forecourt in a big wind to put one outside, as she would have liked to do. Tommy had dimmed the lights, it was only the tree lights and the fire, and the glow from behind the bar, that lit the scene. The men sang, the firelight flickering across their brown, country faces, the wonderful music rising to the old beams. Magical! Debbie leaned on the bar, watching the singers, the rapt audience in the crowded room, the flickering lights, and her heart sang with the choir.

She had always loved Christmas. This one might seem strange now, but it was the first of many that would follow the same pattern, running on into the future. The Jacksons at Trelewan, their daughter Judy and her husband, Keith, had taken to her just as Chel had said they would, she felt that they were already friends. As she peered now into the crowd, she could just make out her own closer family in the corner, Oliver and Chel and her father, round a table with a group of their new friends. New beginnings to a new life ... the old carols made the echoes ring, the listeners becoming part of them, the familiar Christmas magic working, as it always did, in this unfamiliar setting.

Impossible to believe that only a year ago she had never set foot in here, never met Mawgan, barely seen the village, knew none of these people who were now her friends. She watched and listened enthralled, and was so ensnared by the scene that she nearly jumped out of her skin when an arm went round her shoulders.

'Sorry – didn't mean to give you a heart attack!' said Mawgan. She turned her head, and found herself looking straight into his eyes and her heart turned over.

'What are you doing here?' Debbie asked.

'Taking a break. I could steal ten minutes, I thought I'd better show my face.'

He was right, of course, it was his pub, even if Chel now ran it for him. Debbie leaned into his shoulder, enjoying the warmth and the unexpected closeness of him. Her favourite carol of all, *In the Bleak Midwinter* rose into the four corners of the room, if a single moment could be perfection, this was it.

Then it was *Hark the Herald Angels Sing*, and it was all over. The lights went on again, and the choir broke ranks, eddying purposefully through the crowd towards the bar. Robert Pengelly was once more there, in front of Debbie.

'Enjoy that, did you?' he asked.

Debbie, Mawgan's arm still round her shoulders, nodded, bright-eyed.

'It was brilliant! I love the Cornish choirs – I love men's voices when they sing together.'

Robert nodded towards Mawgan.

'You should hear him, some time. Got some good voice on him.' He looked at them both, full in the face. 'Daresay the choir'd sing for your wedding, 'f you wanted.'

Mawgan had gone still. Debbie said,

'Do you mean that?'

'Most of us reckon you earned it.' He nodded towards Mawgan. 'Brave of you, that night. Her too. You've only to ask.'

'Then we're asking,' said Debbie. 'Aren't we, Mawgan?'

'Reckon we are.' He removed his hand from her shoulder. 'What're you drinking, Robert? Barmaid here's gone into a daze.'

He drew the pints expertly and ranged them along the bar, refusing payment.

'No, on the house for you tonight.' He opened the till and removed money, notes changed hands across the bar. 'And that's for the kids. And thank the choir for us.'

'Be in touch after Christmas, tell us what you want.'

'We will.'

'Well!' said Debbie, when Robert had gone. Her eyes were sparkling. 'That was a surprise!'

'More like a shock,' said Mawgan. 'Listen bird, I must go back to my kitchen.'

'Poor old Cinderella! When will you finish? Dad and Chel and I are going to the midnight service, so I may not see you till later on.'

'Are you?' Mawgan glanced at his watch. 'What time're you leaving?'

'Service starts at eleven thirty, I should think we want to walk up there not later than eleven, or do you think earlier?'

'I'll come with you, if we finish clearing up in time – should do, we're about done serving now.' He turned her face towards him and kissed her, his mouth tasted of wine. A muted cheer went up from the choir. 'I'll let you know how it goes. Stick a ticket in the till for that, will you?'

He was gone as swiftly as he had appeared. Debbie, her evening now topped off with a cherry, turned to the next customer.

* * * * *

Another tree glittering with lights, towering up into the vaulted ceiling of a church that had stood since before the Normans came. Candles flickering on deep stone sills, catching gleams from coloured glass, dark and mysterious from the night outside. A huge congregation of people pressing round, warm and friendly at this celebration. Standing room only now, Debbie saw, and was glad, as she sat squashed between her father and Mawgan, that Dad and Chel had come up earlier and secured a pew for them all, even if only a very small one by a pillar at the back.

There was a sense of anticipation, of expectation. Friends nodded and waved to each other, people were waving to herself and Mawgan and Chel too, mouthing *happy Christmas* and smiling. She had a sense of belonging, of being stamped with a seal of approval. A miracle, she found herself thinking, and wasn't joking. A small miracle in this congregation so largely composed of decent people with narrow, hard-working lives and inherited standards. Fishermen, farmers, shopkeepers, manual workers ... village people – if you discounted the growing invasion of incomers, here as everywhere else in Cornwall. She bore a Cornish name, she would soon bear a different one, was all at once proud, and felt for Mawgan's hand to find her own immediately and warmly clasped. They exchanged a smile.

The organ ceased to play a wandering voluntary, and launched into the familiar opening bars of *Once in Royal David's City* and the congregation fell silent and rose as one to its feet as the processional began, and the pure, clear notes of a boy's voice rose soaring above the organ. In churches all over the country, the same ritual would be under way, the feeling of connection, of continuation, was strong. Debbie, who was not consciously religious but had been brought up in a rigorously Christian household thanks to her mother, felt the tug of it and against her inclinations, was deeply moved. Whatever you believed, there was something about collective worship that reached, like water in a dry spell, right down to the roots.

Young Damien Tregear, everyone in the church well knew, was a perfect terror and a perennial thorn in the flesh of every teacher at the local school, but now, walking angelically at the head of the choir, his hymn book open on his hands like a choirboy on a Christmas card, he looked seraphic. He even, Debbie noted as he passed her, had raised his eyes to heaven. Little fiend!

It occurred to her, out of nowhere, that she had never known the names of the choirboys at the big, important urban church her mother favoured, let alone their horrible antecedents, but before she had time to consider the discovery objectively, the second verse was reached and the congregation blasted out the old, familiar words – and she realised immediately what Robert Pengelly had meant. Whatever his roots or his upbringing, whatever his ambitions and whatever he had or had not done in the past or present, her future husband had music in his soul. He sang tenor, effortless and true, and without looking at the hymn book they shared, words and music together a part of him as much as hands or head or heart.

What was it Nonie had said? *Brought up a Wesleyan Methodist.* There was, Debbie opined, a lot of it about in Cornwall. It had never entered her head that with all his continental sophistication, he would be quite so simple in his outlook, and perhaps he wasn't, any more. But he had come, of his own free will, to this ecumenical service and he was at ease with it as she herself, she knew, was not; for her, it was simply a delightful festival, carnival time. And they were to be married in this church, not, like Oliver and Chel, in a register office. His choice, quite as much as hers and, she now saw, a concession. There was a Wesleyan chapel up the hill.

The things you didn't realise about people, even when you thought yourself so close to them!

Reaching this realisation, a number of other things slotted into place. The attitude of his family, for instance, particularly the older members. A certain amount of wrestling-with-the-conscience now had to enter into it, and she completely missed the first reading from the Old Testament as she tried to evaluate this in her mind. She found that she was no longer sure whose side they were actually on, if they searched their hearts. She had thought they had unfairly favoured Cressida ... but had they? Mawgan's own view of events, too, although she doubted if he was particularly devout, must have been coloured by his upbringing, and some of it must have stuck – although not an abhorrence for alcohol, obviously, and his father and sisters weren't teetotal either, although come to think, she wasn't certain about his mother. But a decent, God-fearing family, for all that, plunged wholesale into a nightmare.

Wicked! Truly wicked. Impossible even to imagine how Cressida had justified it all to herself, how she had clung so determinedly to the world's sympathy, lied for it, wept for it, whined for it ...she must have been totally self-deluding, surely. Impossible, too, to imagine how Mawgan must have felt as he was taken away and locked up. She stole a look at him now, and was conscious of a totally inappropriate wish to protect him, a man more than able to look after himself.

The congregation rose for another carol. Debbie, rising with them, put the dark thoughts away and did her best to recapture the Christmassy feeling she had had earlier. She couldn't, now, even remember exactly what it was that had sent her down that shadowy byway.

It was some time, however, before she began to feel truly warm again and had recovered her spirits.

Carols, anthems and old, familiar words; *While Shepherds Watched,* that reliable old plodder, sung to a joyous, unfamiliar tune that reverberated in the vaulted roof. *'Tis Night on the Silent Mountain,* Debbie's favourite Christmas anthem, sung by the choir with Damien and his equally devilish friends in the forefront, singing like the angels they emphatically were not. A Christmas card come to life.

Why was it, Jerry found himself asking, round about this time in the proceedings and unaware that he was almost echoing his daughter, that the Christmas service back home in the huge town church in Embridge had never had this earthy reality, this friendly warmth? A richer church, a wealthier congregation, more elaborate decorations, far more accomplished readers – but here in this Cornish village, so much more ... well, heart, he supposed. Real people, turning in an honest job before their friends. He did, he realised, rather like the Cornish accent. Dot, on the other hand, would have a fit if she ever heard Mawgan, and he was a lot less broad in his speech than many.

What had he done?

More particularly, what had he allowed to be done to his children?

Whatever it was, two of them looked well on the way to surviving, but that didn't relieve him of culpability, they had suffered – for his sins, largely – along the way. And what would become of the third? Jerry didn't know, but he spared her a thought, that adopted girl of his, struggling on her own in Embridge, with her bitter mother and her wandering husband, trying to keep the magic of Christmas alive for her children. He couldn't help her. He could only stand by her if she needed him. He hoped that she wouldn't, while fearing that she would.

And as for Helen, about her, he had no idea what to do, but every idea of what he had already done, and perhaps that was the first step along the road to – reconciliation?

It was the first time he had thought the word so specifically. He lost his place in the hymn book.

Then the service was over, and the congregation pouring out into the night. It had been cold and frosty when they went in, now there was a softness in the air, a mildness that could turn to rain.

'Never get a white Christmas in Cornwall,' said Shirley, passing them with her father and mother, her younger sister and two fisherman brothers. 'Happy Christmas Mr Angwin, Mrs Nankervis – happy Christmas – ' She smiled at Debbie as she passed. Jerry, she didn't know.

They walked down the sloping street in a wandering crowd of people, all talking, calling to each other, peeling off from the main stream to go into their homes or dive down the narrow opes that led off the main street of the village. By the time they reached the Fish, they were alone, anyone who lived beyond this point had gone home by car. In the car park behind the pub, they paused.

'Happy Christmas!' Chel kissed Mawgan on the cheek. 'Have a lovely one, when you finally get to it. See you after breakfast, Debbie. When you like.'

Jerry shook hands with Mawgan, they wouldn't be seeing him tomorrow, when he had finished work he and Debbie would be off to St Austell. He kissed his daughter, enfolding her in a bear hug.

'And you sleep well, my girl!'

He and Chel climbed into his car to drive to the house by the creek, where Oliver had no doubt long gone to bed. Debbie and Mawgan let themselves into the Fish by the back door and went slowly upstairs, arms entwined, the unfailing magic of the midnight service still ringing in their ears. In the flat, lit only by the lights on Debbie's little tree, they kissed.

'Happy Christmas,' said Debbie, when she had control of her mouth again, and giggled.

'We'll hope so,' said Mawgan. 'Did you want a hot drink, or shall we go and fight over – or even under – the duvet, bird?'

'I go with the second,' said Debbie. It seemed like a good idea. And it was.

XIV

Debbie drove to the creek on Christmas morning: the clear, frosty weather of yesterday had turned into pouring rain and a rising wind, and there was no way she intended to walk and get soaked to the skin. She found her father sitting with Oliver and the remains of a late breakfast, and Chel poking the goose experimentally in the kitchen. The house was full of delectable smells.

'Turned out nice again!' said Debbie, coming in from the porch on the wings of the wind, staggering under the weight of the box of parcels in her arms. 'Happy Christmas! It's blowing a hooley out there!'

'At least the gutter should stay up this time,' observed Oliver. 'Coffee?' He reached for the pot. 'He did a good job, your man down the road.'

Debbie lowered her box onto the sofa and came to lean across the table to kiss them both.

'Yes please, I'd love some coffee. We had breakfast at seven!'

'Toast?' asked Jerry, with his mouth full. He pushed the rack towards her. 'We laid you a place, sit down.'

Chel came out of the kitchen.

'Happy Christmas, Deb! How's things?'

The question was automatic, and so when Debbie paused before replying, all three of the others looked at her in query. She saw this, and hurriedly said,

'Yeah – fine – ' She realised she had convinced none of them, and added, more honestly, 'Mawgan's a bit twitchy this morning, to be honest. He got up at quarter to six, and he didn't need to, and I'm not sure he'd really slept at all. I don't know where he went, down to the office I think, I went to sleep again. When I woke up, he was back upstairs putting Bucks Fizz, and locally smoked salmon with scrambled egg together in the kitchen – but he hadn't been there long.'

'Whoo!' said Chel, admiringly. 'Plain marmalade is a bit of a come-down, after that.'

Debbie was grateful for the input, but thought she might as well pursue the subject to its end.

'I got to thinking ... I know it sounds strange, but when was he last home for Christmas? I think it might be rather a long time.'

'Christmas can be a funny time of year,' Oliver remarked, recalling a few under that heading.

Chel looked thoughtful.

'It's got to be at least four years, I suppose.'

'I think it might be nearer to fourteen,' said Debbie. She found that they were all looking at her again, and explained. 'Chefs are generally working at Christmas – think about it, there's a lot of eating involved. He worked abroad up until quite recently, there's no way he'd have got back. He's been home during that time, I'm not saying that – but not for the great Christmas jamboree, when whole families get together – you know, even ours does – did -' She paused in momentary confusion, and then went on, 'He's lost the habit – and under the circumstances, I think it's getting to him a bit. He hasn't said, but I think he's half afraid that it won't be so much Christmas night, as firework night. And you can see why. Allison says there's been no word from Cressida ...' She caught Chel's eye and dropped her own to the toast on her plate.

'He was in fine form yesterday,' said Chel, offering comfort. 'In fact, I've not seen him quite so relaxed, ever.'

Debbie shook her head.

'It hasn't lasted. He looks this morning as if he's not slept for a week, and you can tell, he's really working to keep the balls in the air. If he drops one, there's going to be tears before bed, I can feel it in my bones!'

'Do you have to go?' asked Oliver.

'I think we do, yes. Apart from, we've already said we will, it would only be putting it off if we made an excuse now.'

'You mean, sooner or later, the chickens will come home to roost?'

'Yes. It's just, I'd sooner it wasn't today.'

'You've met them before,' said Jerry. 'Don't you think you may be exaggerating?'

Debbie repeated what she had already said to Oliver.

'That wasn't like this. It was somewhere else, and just the immediate family. This time, there'll be a whole cast of extras, each with their own opinion. There's no guarantee who's going to say what. I *know* it's got to be faced. I just wish it wasn't at Christmas.'

'It might be a good thing to get it over,' suggested Jerry.

'Getting it over with is one thing. Sparking off a family feud is another. Little sister said some pretty appalling things, you remember.'

Chel began gathering the plates together, stacking them into a tottering pile. She looked thoughtful.

'His mother and father and Allison must have thought of all this.'

'I've no doubt they have. I doubt they're allowing for Mawgan. He's only got to hit a real low, like he did the other day, and all hell will break loose if someone so much as breathes out of place. And I just told you, all the signs are there.'

Chel continued to look thoughtful.

'I know it sounds harsh, when you'll get caught up in the middle, but mightn't that be a good thing? It seems to me that, until everything is out in the open, nothing is going to be mended. You can't just go on pasting over the cracks, something'll give sooner or later.'

'Thanks for that happy Christmas thought!' Debbie retorted.

'You're welcome.' Chel picked up her pile, but paused with it in her hands, allowing Debbie time to say, gloomily,

'It seemed like such a good idea at the time.'

'It still is a good idea,' said Chel, firmly, and headed off for the kitchen with the plates. Once there, she put them down on the worktop and considered that last remark. Did that come from hope, personal conviction, or inner knowledge? Not for the first time, she had no idea. It would be nice to think it was the last, or at a push, even the second, but she had a horrible feeling it was only the first. The one thing she was sure of was that if Debbie and Mawgan got through this, things could only get better, and they needed to. Apart from Dot, who was a law unto herself, their own family seemed united in their acceptance of Mawgan, and in their liking for him too. It did nothing to alter the fact that he was rapidly becoming very stressful to live with, and before the marriage took place that needed to change. Chel had lived through that kind of stress. You never really got over it.

Debbie came through with a fistful of mugs and the empty coffee pot. She put them down and stood there, looking useless.

'Can I do anything?'

'It's all done, if you mean peeling the veg,' said Chel, and noted the thankful expression on her sister-in-law's face, and something else too. 'Cheer up, Deb. It's Christmas, the season of goodwill! If Grannie rocks the boat, someone'll sit on her. Be sure. Anyway, surely she's not such a miserable old bat as to try?'

'I know nothing about her. She championed Cressida, that's all.'

'Well, Cressida's not here. Nor will she be. So stop thinking that she's going to turn up and wreck the festivities.'

'It would be like her.'

'She *won't* Deb, believe me. Now will you cheer up and load that dishwasher, please? You know your problem, it's being separated from the beloved object on Christmas morning! I hope he gave you a really splendid present to compensate.'

'I think he must have consulted with Allison, he gave me a bottle of my most favourite scent. He never thought of that for himself. *Or* had the faintest idea what it was. But it was a lovely gesture anyway, just going into the shop to buy it probably half-killed him!'

'Not over-burdened with imagination, then,' said Chel, and grinned wickedly. 'Deb, do you really know what you're doing? You were brought up wine and roses, from now on, it's going to be beer and supermarket carnations.'

Debbie considered this, apparently taking it seriously.

'It's probably an awful thing to admit, but I rather like beer, it quenches your thirst – and I like carnations, come to that. They smell spicy, like cloves, and they last longer than roses anyway. There you go –' She slammed the dishwasher shut. 'What shall I do now?'

'Switch it on,' Chel suggested, and they both dissolved into giggles.

'After that little pearl of wisdom from the Thoughts of Chairperson Nankervis, are you going to cheer up now?' asked Chel, and Debbie, still giggling, said,

'Yes.'

* * * * *

Christmas Day had a stickier start back in Embridge.Here, there was no smoked salmon and scrambled egg, no Buck's Fizz, and very little conversation around the breakfast table. By ten o'clock, the children, awake since far too early and already knowing that this Christmas wasn't going to be quite like others, were fractious and over-excited, and Tom had already shouted at them once, in spite of a resolution not to do so, and Sebastian had dissolved into tears, which made it worse. To his father, tears were babyish, and he allowed himself to be betrayed into an unwise comment.

'That girl spoils them,' he said, austerely. 'It's time she moved on, they're too old for a nanny now.'

328

Maria was the stable element in his children's lives, the one person who was always there when they needed her. Sebastian cried harder, and Annabel's mouth opened to allow unwise words to escape.

'That's mean, Daddy! Maria doesn't spoil us, she's ever so strict! She makes us put everything away.'

'Then you must know how to do that by this time, without being told,' said Tom, trying to backtrack with a humorous comment, but only succeeding in adding to his mistake. He smiled at his daughter, trying to make a joke of it. Annabel was unimpressed.

'Why can't Maria come with us to Grandma's?' she whined, now, pushing her luck.

'Because,' said Susan, briskly. 'Come and help me clear the breakfast things, Annabel, and don't ask so many questions.'

'It was only *one* question,' Annabel objected. 'And why won't Auntie Debbie be there?'

'Because she's in Cornwall.'

'I wish *we* were in Cornwall.'

'Well, we aren't. Poor Grandma, she'd be all alone without us.'

'She could come too. Let's put everything in the car, and go there.'

Susan pressed her lips together, and met Tom's eyes. His expression said, as clearly as if he had spoken, *now talk yourself out of that one*. It was true, Grandma was no more welcome in Cornwall than Maria was at Grandma's house, but it couldn't be said. Sebastian chose this tactless moment to ask,

'Why doesn't Auntie Debbie come home any more?'

'Why, why, why?' said Susan, sweepingly and unreasonably.

'Well, *why*?' asked Annabel, and Tom got to his feet.

'I'll give the dog a run,' he said.

No, not a good start, and Susan feared that it was probably only going to get worse. This year, there wouldn't even be a lunchtime telephone call to bring the family together, even Chel, who generally instigated it, could have nothing to say to Dot. In any case, the members of the family that Chel would want to speak to were already with her – Debbie and her father. Not *my* father, Susan thought, and then realised that if she kept on thinking like that, Christmas Day was doomed. She put on a bright face that deceived neither of her children.

'Why don't you two go with Daddy and give Clinker a good walk, while I clear up?' she asked. 'Then we can all go to Grandma's.'

'I want to stay here,' said Sebastian. 'It's dull at Grandma's without Grandpa. *Or* Auntie Debbie,' he added, and Tom slammed out of the room muttering about finding the dog. Annabel slid from her chair.

'I want to go with Daddy,' she announced, although it was quite obvious that Daddy wanted to be on his own. Sebastian jumped up beside her.

'Me too.'

But the bang of the front door announced that they were too late. Daddy was already gone.

Susan and the children were left standing in the hall, looking at each other. Annabel's face was set in a look of pure defiance, Sebastian's lip was wobbling dangerously. Susan wondered what her own face looked like and thought desperately and without inspiration for a way to retrieve the situation. Into this impasse came Maria, ready to go off to be with her friends and come to say goodbye. She stopped at the foot of the stairs, taking in the situation at a glance. Maria stood in some awe of Mrs Casson, but she realised at once that this couldn't be allowed to pass. Not on Christmas Day or on any other day. She dropped her coat and bag onto a chair and stepped into the breach.

'Come, Sebastian, this does not do!' she said calmly. She went to put her arms round him, lovingly, wiping his sad eyes with a tissue, and Susan, watching her dumbly, found herself thinking, *no Tom, you're wrong. She doesn't spoil them. She loves them. And so do I, if I only knew how.* She felt a sick twist inside her.

Maybe something of how she felt came across to the children, for Annabel suddenly rushed into her arms and hugged her, hard, and Sebastian had stopped crying. Maria sat back on her heels.

'That is better. Now, I tell you what you must do, the two of you. It is not only you who will miss the Grandpa and the Auntie. You must help your mama and make this day a joyous one. No tears. Smiles, happy, happy! You will go to your Grandma's house and be good children, and when you come home, Mama will put you to bed and read to you just like Maria, and you will see, it will all be good things.'

'Daddy said he would send you away,' Sebastian whispered.

'Well, he won't,' said Susan, with decision. How would she ever manage without Maria? She said, 'Maria is our friend.' It was a new idea. Maria stood up, and they looked at each other.

'Then that is good,' said Maria, wondering if she believed it. 'Now remember, all the three of you – happy, happy, and tomorrow is the day for yourselves. Today is for Grandma!' She picked up her coat and turned for the door. 'Now, say after me – Happy Christmas!'

'Happy Christmas,' chorused the children, and Susan added,

'Happy Christmas, and have a lovely day, Maria.'

Maria wanted to say, Mrs Casson, I think we should talk, but didn't quite have the courage. She smiled instead, and thought that she would write to her own mother at home in Poland and ask her for her opinion. Whatever Mrs Casson said, she knew that her days here were, in the nature of things, numbered. The children were growing up fast now, and they shouldn't do it without love. Mrs Casson, poor woman, seemed unable to love anybody and who could blame her with a mother and a husband like she had? Maria had no high opinion of either Dot or Tom.

She ran across the hall, suddenly wanting to get away from this unhappy house and be among people who could laugh and be at ease with themselves, and Susan and the children were left looking at each other, warily.

That told us, Susan thought wryly. All three of us.

'Come on then, let's do what we're told, shall we?' she said. 'You help me clear the breakfast table, Annabel, and Sebby can put the mats away, and when we've stacked the machine, we'll give Grandpa and Auntie Debbie a ring – and Uncle Oliver and Chel, too – and wish them all a happy Christmas.'

'And Mawgan,' said Sebastian, determined his new friend shouldn't be ignored. He had long forgotten about the ogre.

'Certainly Mawgan, if he's there,' said Susan. 'If not, Auntie Debbie'll tell him, I'm sure.' She held out her hands, and to her surprise, her children slipped their small hands into hers. Together, they went into the dining room and began to clear the breakfast.

It wasn't until Jerry rang, just as Annabel was loading the last careful plate into the machine under her mother's watchful eye – something that she was not normally allowed to do – that Susan realised she had been assuming that she and Tom and the children would be sidelined along with her mother, and was ashamed. Of course they wouldn't do that. What was the matter with her?

'I hoped we'd catch you before you left,' said Jerry, with satisfaction. 'Having a good time, the four of you?'

Tom had come home and flung himself into a chair with yesterday's paper, ignoring his children. Susan lied,

'Yes, wonderful! The children are over-excited and full of themselves, of course. Looking forward to lunch at Grandma's.'

'Huh!' came disbelievingly from behind the paper.

'That's good,' said Jerry, who knew a lie when he heard one. He felt grieved for Susan. 'Just wanted to say, happy Christmas to you all. Deb is here, and Chel and Oliver – I'll put them on.' Susan heard murmuring in the background, and then Deb's voice, happy.

'Suse! Happy Christmas!'

One by one, they came on the line, voices bright with laughter, enjoying themselves. The children spoke on the telephone, giggling at some silly joke from the other end, Tom unbent enough to have a laugh with his father-in-law. *Have a great time* they cried, and their happiness and goodwill seemed to be in the very room.

But when she put the phone down after saying a last goodbye, it was like switching off. Susan looked at her children, happy now and sitting beside the pile of presents opened earlier under the Christmas tree, and at Tom, back behind his paper, and her heart went down like a stone.

I want to be there. I want to be part of it. I want to be laughing and enjoying myself, not doing my duty because Mummy is in the wrong, and nobody else is good enough for her, and my children missing out on all the fun.

The lights on the tree twinkled over the children's heads, seeming to mock at her. She felt desolate.

I want to belong.

She put on a bright smile and clapped her hands.

'Come on everyone. Time to go to Grandma's!' and such was the impetus of the wave of goodwill from Cornwall that all three of them came without complaint.

* * * * *

In fact, Susan's Christmas turned out to be not so bad. Dot loved her last remaining child, even if in her own way, and she loved her grandchildren and had always both liked and respected her son-in-law, she had done her best to make the day a success knowing that it would take some effort, and if everyone tries hard enough, it's amazing what can be achieved. Not quite the fun and laughter of other years, but a courageous attempt nevertheless, and if the empty chairs around the drawing room couldn't help but be noticed, nobody commented. No, it was Debbie's day that fell disastrously short of the standards set by other years, and the fact that she had almost expected it didn't console her. It wasn't Mawgan's fault entirely, although he certainly didn't help. It was mainly his grandmother's.

The first part of the day went brilliantly. Chel was good at Christmas, she had grown up in a family that gave it the whole works, and the company was congenial, even Jerry and Nonie seeming to have made a move back towards friendship. Jerry was in a benign mood with his two natural children under the same roof for once, and Theo full of admiration for this, his first ever English Christmas. The goose, stuffed and cooked according to precise instructions, was perfect. If it seemed a little strange without the children around, if the absence of Mawgan was noticeable, nobody said so, and the conversation was adult and stimulating. Presents were exchanged, and Debbie's present from Oliver topped the heap, consisting as it did of a small and beautiful antique enamel box containing a note which read,

OK, you win. I'll teach navigation for you if you really insist. Love, Oliver xx

Debbie, opening it not knowing what to expect, sat with the small piece of paper in her hands and didn't know whether she wanted to laugh with pleasure or cry because she could guess what it had cost him. Looking up, she saw his eyes on her and managed a smile.

'Thank you,' she said, feeling it inadequate.

'You're welcome.'

334

Then, at half past four, Debbie's mobile rang. She was expecting the call, and had it handy, picking it up immediately.

'Hi! Everything OK …? OK, fine, I'll be back in ten minutes then … yes. No problem. See you.' She switched off and looked at the others. 'That was Mawgan,' she said, unnecessarily. 'Time to go. He's just putting the stuff in the car. Well …' She smiled around the company. 'That's it then. It's been lovely, Chel, lovely food! Thank you both – *all* – so much!'

She went out into the wet, windy dusk, leaving the lights and the laughter behind and drove her own car back to the Fish, parking it beside Mawgan's which, she could see in the light of the security lamps, was already loaded with their cases and the box of presents. She found Mawgan himself in the flat, and she realised the instant she set eyes on him that although he wasn't exactly drunk, he had certainly been drinking, which had lent him a kind of spurious cheerfulness that overlaid his obvious tiredness and that, she thought, but didn't say, wasn't necessarily a good idea. He tossed her the keys of his Volvo, carelessly.

'You're driving, bird. I've had a few.'

Good thing I haven't, Debbie thought, but then, she had half-expected it. She caught the keys and swung them from her finger.

'Come on then. Let's go.'

In the car, once they were on the road, he promptly went to sleep, which was all very well, Debbie thought, except that she had no idea where was their ultimate destination. She had never been to the family home; didn't, she now realised, want to go any more than he did. Oh well. Christmas and all that. At least she knew the way to St Austell itself.

When they ran into the edges of the town some time later, she woke him, not without difficulty.

'We've got here. Now where do I go?'

Mawgan had slid down in the seat as he slept, now he levered himself upright with a groan.

'Oh God! How about back home?'

There was very little traffic around on this Christmas evening. Debbie slowed down.

'Come on, be helpful. You've got to give me a lead here.'

Mawgan looked out of the window onto the lamplit, familiar road and felt his heart sink.

'Turn left at the next but one set of traffic lights. There's a turning takes you through a housing estate about a mile down the road. Go down there.'

'Left or right?'

'Right.' He fell silent after that, and Debbie, following instructions, drove without speaking. The left turning seemed to be leading out of town, turning into a B road leading off into countryside and darkness. The housing estate, when it came, took her by surprise with its streetlights and its tidy little bungalows.

'What – down here?'

'Nowhere else to go, that I can see. Shame.'

Debbie wanted to tell him to give over, but didn't; in this mood, she had already learned, there was no point in talking to him. She turned into the little estate and drove on. The bungalows had become neat, new houses, three up, three down, Debbie reckoned, and small, cared-for gardens. She suspected the near presence of decking and patios and probably sub-tropical palm trees, and recalling the rented house in Launceston that she had visited, was surprised.

'Left,' said Mawgan.

The houses fell behind, a rough lane crunched unexpectedly under the wheels. There was a wall on the right, dark, unlit; a barn perhaps, and a gateway. Beyond, in the headlights, Debbie dimly made out a high, chain-link fence and a sign that read **G. ANGWIN & SON Building Contractors.** They had arrived – but where?

A security light went on as they turned through the gateway into a yard – an ex-farmyard, Debbie thought, with on two sides old farm buildings, to the left the chain-link fence, and on the fourth side, the back of a big granite house. There were four cars, one with a foreign plate, and a truck parked outside the barns, or stables, or whatever they had once been, and lights shining out of the windows of the house. Debbie drew in beside the truck and applied the brake, and as she did so, a door opened and Mawgan's sisters – two of them at least, Anna and Allison – came running out.

'We thought you'd got lost!' Anna cried, launching herself at her brother and giving him a bear hug. 'Or maybe forgotten the way – ' She turned to Debbie. 'Deb! Lovely to see you again!'

'I thought you weren't coming over until February,' said Debbie, it being the first thing that came into her head.

'Oh, we thought we might as well,' said Anna, with airy unconcern. 'Give you a surprise – Christmas, and that – it's ages since we did, or Mawgan either come to that. All this foreign living, it plays hell with family gatherings.' She broke off, realising that she was deceiving nobody and that all of them knew that she and Kurt and their twin boys were here to take the pressure off. Allison, the younger, and always the quieter of the two, stepped forward then and kissed Debbie lightly on the cheek.

'Nice to see you again. Let's get the car unloaded and your stuff inside, shall we, before it starts raining again.'

Inside, the rest of the family came tumbling into the big farmhouse kitchen to say hullo, Mawgan's parents, Cally and Pip; a tall, fair man with glasses and a slight foreign accent who must be Kurt Stern, Anna's husband, and two identical little boys of about four or five who hung back on their father's hands and had to be hauled out bodily from behind him, overcome with shyness – an unusual failing in the Angwin family, as Debbie already knew.

'These are Martin and Luc,' said Anna, pronouncing the names French fashion. 'Come on boys, say hullo to your uncle and to Debbie.'

'They've grown a bit,' Mawgan commented, and instantly wished he hadn't because it gave Anna the cue to say,

'Well, they do – and you haven't seen them since their christening, after all,' and obviously wished immediately afterwards that she hadn't, either. The reason why their uncle had become a stranger to them seemed to hang in the air, written in letters of fire.

Bang! First pitfall of the holiday. Debbie winced, and thought that she wasn't the only one.

Cally stepped forward.

'Your Gran's waiting by the fire to see you both, come through and say hullo, and then you can go up and unpack, settle in while the girls and I make a nice cup of tea.'

'Good to see you, girl.' Pip kissed Debbie's cheek. 'Off you go then. I'll get the kettle on.'

'Gran' was Cally's mother, tall and thin and relentlessly ladylike, long widowed. She it was, Debbie knew, who had been responsible for Mawgan's original interest in cooking, but the relationship had deteriorated recently and, she immediately realised, to the disappointment of both parties. She didn't seem to be proud of his more positive achievements, and their greeting was restrained; almost, Debbie thought, as if Gran didn't even wish to touch her grandson, although Debbie herself rated a peck on the cheek and a stiff little smile.

Oh bugger ... Debbie thought, inelegantly, and went off to help carry the bags upstairs.

They were sleeping in Mawgan's old room, and apart from a double bed which had to be a new arrival, it contained some surprising mementoes of the boy and then the teenager he must once have been. Books – not a lot, he was no great reader, although he appeared at some point to have had an, on the

338

whole unexpected, taste for writers such as Douglas Adams and Terry Pratchett – a music centre, a lot of LPs and tapes and just a handful of CDs, it had been a long time ago, after all. A collection of classic car models set out carefully on a shelf, no doubt by his mother. A framed photograph of a much younger Mawgan before his hair began to recede and he put on a bit of weight, laughing and vital astride an old Harley Davidson with a girl on the pillion; she was tall, slim and had long legs spread out to help balance the bike, and long blonde hair. She looked very pleased with herself, about seventeen or eighteen so long become history, Debbie concluded. More surprisingly, an acoustic guitar propped into a corner, and what Debbie thought might be a trumpet, in a leather case.

'Did you play that thing?' she asked, curiously.

'Which thing?'

'Either of them.'

'Both of them. I was in the town band as a boy, and I moved on to the guitar later.'

'Well? Play them well, I mean?'

Mawgan picked up the guitar and ran his fingers over the strings, flinching at the sound.

'Ouch! Needs tuning.' He set it aside, collapsing onto the edge of the bed and resting his head against the headboard. 'This was a bad idea, Deb.'

Debbie sat down beside him.

'It would have been a worse one if we hadn't come.'

'Do you think so?' He closed his eyes. 'I can't face it – not tea *en famille*. All I want to do is sleep, to be honest.'

'Then sleep,' said Debbie, watching him. 'I'll make your excuses, and I can wake you up in a couple of hours. You'll maybe feel better able to face them then.' How much alcohol dispersed from the body per hour? She had no idea. Enough?

'Maybe. I certainly can't right now, I'm shattered. Am I ever going to bounce back, d'you think?'

'Yes, of course you are.'

'I sh'd like to know when, then. These days, I just feel permanently steamrollered.'

'I suppose,' said Debbie, trying to answer the question sensibly, 'when you let go of whatever it is that keeps you awake at night.'

'And how do I do that?'

'I've no idea,' she admitted. 'Only you know what it is you're hanging on to.'

'I aren't hanging onto anything that I know of.' He failed to meet her eyes.

'It'll be all right on the night,' said Debbie, noticing, and tried to put conviction into the comforting cliché. She got to her feet. 'Two hours then, and I'll just tell them you need some space to yourself after working all day.'

'And a right wuss I'm going to sound,' said Mawgan, but he didn't argue, and she left him and made her way back downstairs.

Her excuses for him, she thought, didn't go down too well. Anna, to be sure, laughed, and said,

'Poor little brother! He must be getting old!' but the brighter, more intelligent Allison looked sceptical, and his mother looked worried.

'Perhaps this wasn't such a good idea,' she said, in almost an echo of her son, and they all rushed to reassure her.

'No no,' said Debbie, hurriedly and, she thought, unconvincingly. 'He just needs a bit of time to unwind. He's been working very hard, today *and* yesterday.' Keep talking, Deb. You might just kid somebody. The twins, for instance.

Gran sniffed.

'Time to sober up, you mean! I could smell it on his breath.'

'Come on Gran, it's Christmas!' said Anna, smiling, but her grandmother only primmed her lips more tightly together.

340

'Even less excuse for excess, I should have thought, on the birthday of Our Lord.'

Allison caught Debbie's eye and raised her own eyes to the ceiling, but in spite of this show of solidarity, Debbie felt a small stir of anger. Mawgan was far from drunk and incapable after all, and nobody could say that he was. Cally, who was beside her, laid a hand on her arm.

'Another cup of tea, Debbie? We'll have a proper supper later on.'

Debbie was still fairly full of roast goose and Christmas pudding, but thought it might be a bad move to say so. She smiled, feeling like a guest where in Launceston she had felt accepted. The reason was this stiff, unbending grandmother, she realised. Pip's parents had been darlings, quite different. As if she had read her thoughts, Allison said,

'Nan and Grandad are coming over for lunch tomorrow.' The words fell into a pause that could be felt, like stones plopping into a pond, and were followed by a silence in which the murmuring of the twins, playing with their Christmas presents over by the window, oblivious to undercurrents in the adult world, sounded as insubstantial as the wind. Gran said,

'I wonder what has become of that poor child, and if she's having a proper Christmas,' and sighed. 'I can't help thinking of her, with us all sitting here enjoying ourselves.'

Since at that precise moment probably nobody was enjoying themselves apart from Luc and Martin, this seemed to Debbie deliberately provocative. Anna said, briskly,

'The last we heard, she'd gone off with a friend of Mike's.'

'It seems all wrong ...' said Gran. Allison jumped to her feet.

'Let's clear away, shall we?'

Gran picked up her cup, little finger elevated genteelly, and looked reproving.

'I have not finished, Allison. I think I would like another cup, Catherine dear.'

Allison sat down again. People these days didn't *flounce*, Debbie reflected, but at that instant, Allison quite definitely had flounced. To her horror, Gran now turned her attention to her.

'Of course, you have never met Cressida, Debbie dear,' she said. 'Such a sweet child. Very much the baby, of course. We all love her very much.'

Don't include me, Debbie thought, and managed a smile.

'Yes.' Gran sighed again. 'Such a shame she isn't with us today. Poor little baby duckling, she was hatched with no oil on her feathers, you know.'

Allison and Anna, who had heard this handy phrase many times before, exchanged a glance and Debbie looked down at her hands, which she found were tightly locked together so that the knuckles were white.

It could only get worse, and so it did. The interval between the welcoming cup of tea and the Christmas night supper of cold turkey and ham, salad and Christmas cake was summarily disposed of by Allison proposing a couple of rounds of one of the twins' Christmas games, but time moves inexorably on, and eventually there was no alternative but for Debbie to go upstairs again and wake Mawgan, who was so deeply asleep she nearly had to push him onto the floor to disturb him. Naturally enough, he awoke in a bad mood, dizzy with fatigue and stupid with being woken from a sound sleep, and she hadn't the heart to tell him that things were no better downstairs, crossing her fingers and trusting to luck.

Something must have been said in her absence, she realised when they arrived in the kitchen where the supper was set out, although who by, she couldn't guess. The twins were in bed by this time, and Kurt had opened a bottle of wine, Cally, Anna and Allison were actually laughing over some joke. Only Pip looked serious, and Gran sat rigidly disapproving at the end of the long wooden table. However, she said nothing, and Cally had been careful to sit Mawgan as far away from her as possible. They got through supper like that; it was hard work, with Mawgan unnaturally silent and his grandmother virtually ignoring him, but there was no bloodshed.

'We'll wash up,' said Allison, when the meal was over. 'You go and sit down, Mum, you've done enough.'

'Good girl,' said Gran, approvingly. She took Debbie's arm. 'Now, you come and talk to me Debbie, guests don't wash up in this house.' Debbie was dragged away, looking over her shoulder – to join the grown-ups, she rather felt, and firmly put in her place as an outsider. Anna, Allison, Mawgan and Kurt watched her departure, she thought, with sympathy. She would far sooner have been in the kitchen with them.

But Gran was in a gracious mood now, it seemed. She spoke to Debbie kindly about her business, asking intelligent questions as if she really wanted to know the answers, and against her inclinations, Debbie began to like her. It was, she thought, only another symptom of the havoc Cressida had wrought that relations within the family had become so strained. It occurred to her, not for the first time, that the more you loved someone, the harder it was to forgive them for disappointing you, and she began to feel more friendly towards Mawgan's grandmother.

The washing up seemed to take forever, probably they were spinning it out between the four of them; they were siblings after all, friends over a long time. Debbie felt unreasonably excluded, but it hadn't been their doing, and eventually they reappeared. Anna smiled brightly around the company.

'How about a round or two of whist? Gran? I know you like a game, come on.' She sounded rehearsed.

Gran seemed to draw herself up.

'No thank you, Anna, I must go home soon. Dizzy will need his run.'

Dizzy, Debbie assumed, was some kind of dog. Pip had a dog too, a lurcher, whom she had met on a previous occasion:

343

he didn't seem to have a name. He had slunk in behind Kurt and was now arranging himself on the hearthrug. Pip leaned forward to throw another log on the fire.

'That's all right, Allison will drive you home if you don't want to be on the road this late. We can bring your car back in the morning.'

'Thank you, Philip, but I can manage perfectly well.'

Pip muttered something that sounded ominously like *please yourself*, and leaned back in his chair. Mawgan had got as far outside the family circle as possible, in a chair by the window, he still looked shattered and Debbie thought had every intention of switching off and drifting back to sleep, which might be the safest option now she came to think about it. Unfortunately, Cally, with the best intentions in the world, said,

'Come by the fire, Mawgan darling, it's so cold tonight, you'll freeze over there!'

'I'm fine.'

Cally stood awkwardly for a moment, and then sat down abruptly.

'Well, this is nice,' she said, inaccurately, and added, even more unfortunately, 'All of us together!' She then flushed hotly, realising what she had said. She hadn't meant it *like that*, of course she hadn't, but -

'Most of us,' Gran corrected her, acidly. She sighed – she was a mistress of the significant sigh. 'I wonder, will we ever *all* be together again?'

'That'll do, Mother,' said Cally uncomfortably. Gran sat up straight. The temporary truce was obviously over, it was open season again.

'No, it will not do, Catherine! Christmas is a time for remembering absent family and friends. It seems to me that you're afraid to mention the poor child's name!'

'Mother ...' Cally stopped, helplessly. Anna leapt into the breach.

344

'Shall I make some coffee? I'm sure we could all do with a cup.'

'Thank you Marianne, but it keeps me awake,' said Gran.

Silence.

'Although it seems to me,' added Gran, without turning her head to look, 'that *some* of us could do with keeping awake. It is very bad manners, Mawgan Angwin, to sulk in corners and to go to sleep in company. And what you have to be so weary about, I cannot think! Your poor mother can keep awake, and she's been slaving away today cooking Christmas dinner for eight of us!'

Mawgan said, without obvious animosity,

'And I've done it for six times that number.'

'Huh! With a whole kitchen staff to help you, another chef, everyone, and you young and strong! That's nothing!' Gran sounded scornful, deliberately winding him up, Debbie thought, and quailed.

'You're telling me that Anna and Allison did nothing to help?' Mawgan got to his feet. 'Excuse me, I'm going to bed.'

'Mawgan – ' Cally began.

Slam! The door banged behind him.

'Oh dear ...' said Cally.

'Really!' Gran had stiffened as if she had a poker down her back. There were tears in her eyes, Debbie suddenly realised, glinting in the light from the fire although she had turned her head away. She got to her feet.

'Excuse me,' she said. 'I'll be back in a minute.'

She left the room, more quietly, and went upstairs, aware of the diminishing sound of vociferation behind her. Mawgan was sitting on the foot of the bed, one arm hooked around the old-fashioned bedpost and the other, fist clenched, at his side. He looked not so much furious, which might have been expected, as tragic. Debbie sat down beside him, and for a moment neither of them spoke. Debbie broke the silence first.

'Do you think you ought to come down and make peace with her?' she said cautiously.

'Why? She started it. You heard her, needling me.'

'She's old,' said Debbie, coaxing.

'That's no excuse. Anyway, which would you rather I did? Leave the room, or give her a mouthful back?'

'You shouldn't have risen to the bait.'

'I'm tired,' said Mawgan, and sounded it. 'Tired, and tired of feeling like this, and tired of people picking on me ... shall we just go back to the Fish?'

'Tomorrow, maybe.' Debbie risked reaching out and touching him. 'Do what you said, go to bed. We'll see how it looks in the morning.' To her relief, he let go of the bedpost and turned to her, taking her in his arms.

'Is it ever going to come to an end, Deb?'

'When it goes to appeal, they'll all have to back down.'

'If I win. It isn't certain. I wonder sometimes if it would be safer not to try.'

'She loves you. That's why ...' She hesitated. Mawgan said,

'I let them all down, didn't I? And they're right, what *has* become of Cress?'

'She couldn't face it, and ran off. But you mustn't. That would be the final straw.' She kissed him, but his kiss in return was perfunctory, preoccupied. She stood up. 'Go to bed. Tomorrow is another day.'

'Unfortunately,' muttered Mawgan. He added, 'We'll go home after breakfast tomorrow,' and Debbie didn't argue.

Downstairs again, Gran was putting on her coat ready to leave. She looked at Debbie almost pleadingly as she came down the stairs, but only said,

'It's been nice to meet you, dear. I don't suppose we'll meet again if you're leaving on Friday morning, so I'll wish you a Happy New Year.'

Debbie allowed herself to be kissed.

'We'll see you at the wedding then, if not before.'

'Maybe,' said Gran.

'Of course you'll be there!' Cally cried. Gran looked suddenly frail.

'If I'm spared. With so much to worry me, my heart, you know ... not strong.'

'Mother!'

Pip said, bracingly,

'Come on Ella, you're as strong as an ox!'

Anna took Debbie by the arm and Kurt by the hand.

'Goodnight, Gran.' She dragged her captives towards the sitting room. 'Let's go and play Happy Families, shall we, everyone?'

Allison followed them into the room, closing the door behind her.

'That wasn't the most tactful thing you ever said, Anna,' she remarked.

'Well!'

'Happy Christmas,' said Debbie, and tried to keep bitterness out of her voice. Allison looked at her.

'Mawgan all right?'

'No. Pissed off with everything and everyone, and – ' She broke off, remembering that none of them knew anything about stress, or clinical depression. 'Where are the cards, then?'

'You don't really want to play Happy Families?' Allison sounded amazed.

'What I should like to do,' said Debbie, throwing caution to the four winds, 'is to get not too slightly pissed, have a good time, and put the whole problem on the fire!'

'Then let's get on with it,' said Allison, with decision. 'Kurt, the glasses are in that cupboard. Where's the bottle opener? There's no time to waste!'

XV

Mawgan had a presentiment, the moment that he woke on Boxing Day, that it was going to be a disaster. The weight of it was on his back before he had even opened his eyes. For one thing, and probably the least of them, after lying awake for most of the night, he had now overslept, a cardinal sin in his family. And then he thought of the previous evening, and only just managed not to groan aloud. How to make bad worse – he was becoming the world's expert!

The temptation to just stay where he was and hide under the duvet, hoping it would all go away, conflicted sharply with the urgent need to escape out of this house before worse happened, and the latter won. He opened his eyes and sat up, and the familiar room leapt into focus with the impact of a punch in the stomach, loaded with the memories of happier days. All gone, blown away on the wind, and *why*? How had it all gone so horribly wrong, and what had he ever done that people should believe such terrible lies about him? His grandmother, last night, had hardly been able to look at him. Taking that as an example, beyond these walls there could be a whole town full of people who felt the same … in this room, so reminiscent of quite different times, it was almost impossible to believe that he wouldn't wake up and find it had all been a horrible dream.

Outside in the garden he could hear the sounds of the children arguing over something, and then Anna's voice, soothing and authoritative and Kurt, laughing. Life going on in the very place where death had struck so suddenly and unexpectedly. It had been a terrible mistake to come, and the knowledge curled itself into his stomach like a snake, making him feel sick. There was a sharp pain above his right eye. *Let me out of here*! He could feel a threat, like bats' wings in the corners of the room, hanging there and waiting for the dark …

A shower failed to clear his head, which had begun to thump, steadily, like a drum. Back in the bedroom, it felt stuffy and oppressive, when he had dressed he went to the window to push it wide open to let in the cold, wintry air, trying, he suddenly realised, not to look out.

This was ridiculous! If the rockery was there, it was there, and better face up to it, if it hadn't yet gone it was going to stay. He couldn't spend the rest of his life avoiding the garden, it was obvious that visits here were going to be fairly frequent. Better beat it now, before it became an obsession, but even so, it was incredibly hard to look down from the window.

There was no rockery. Where it had been there was a new shrubbery, bushes with berries or pretty winter foliage, frondy and decorative; their colours seemed to him to be unnaturally intense and bright. Not a rock in sight. He narrowed his eyes against the painfully vivid colours – migraine colours, although he didn't yet recognise them as such – and took a deep, relieved breath, but he should have known. Nobody would leave that, not after what happened.

Above the shrubbery, the big oak where the two girls had been hiding, watching, leaned over from the rear garden of one of the houses in the new estate that bounded the old farmhouse. Nobody had cut that down, but they wouldn't, would they? It had a preservation order on it, or something. He shut his eyes completely, remembering how the sound of their giggling had made him look up ... and Mike dying at his feet. He had made an odd gurgling noise at the end, Mawgan could hear it now, as against his eyelids, the scene scrolled back as if it was yesterday ... back and back and ...

'Oh *shit!*' said Mawgan, uncharacteristically. He opened his eyes.

The whole miserable business, that he was – almost – able to hold at a distance in St Erbyn, where he had other things to occupy him, was in the familiar room with him, as bitter and unbearable as if it had all been yesterday, and with it came a belated, painful realisation that hiding the facts, even with the best motive in the world, had probably been a mistake.It had inevitably tied his hands at his trial and he had been lucky to get off as lightly as he did – and now it had led to last night, and an extra, bitter punishment that he hadn't earned.

With hindsight, abruptly returned to reality, he found himself wondering what on earth had got into him?

The instinct to protect Cress and the long habit of doing so was the short answer there, and later on it had seemed impossible to change his evidence, it was that simple. He saw now that it had been a terrible mistake, and for both of them not just himself. People might still not have believed it for he couldn't have relied on Mandy to back him up, and he wouldn't blame them either, but at least it would have *been* the truth, and out in the open before Mike cut loose and met his tragic, unnecessary end. He might even be alive today, which was a bitter thought. It wasn't that he had actually lied ... but then, he hadn't had to. He had told the truth, and nothing but the truth, but he had not told the whole truth, and he was beginning to think that Jerry suspected it. It had *seemed* the best thing to do, Mike was dead and nothing was going to bring him back, where was the point in distressing everyone further? It had all seemed reasonable in the heat of the moment, but *had* it, in fact, been the best thing? For himself, for instance, or maybe even more particularly, for Cress?

Would it really have changed anything if he had acted in a different way? It could have made it all a great deal worse. If he had been believed, he probably wouldn't have gone to prison, but if he *hadn't* been believed, and it sounded fairly far-fetched after all ... well, sexual offenders had a pretty gruesome time in prison, as he very well knew. Not from personal experience, thank God, but from personal observation, certainly. And it would almost certainly have been for life. So no ... probably it had been the best thing from his own standpoint.

But for Cress ...?

At that point his knees gave way and he sat down abruptly on the bed. He had a vague idea that, notwithstanding the mess that now faced him, he had come to a decision and it was with relief. It had been a hard secret to keep all this time.

He remembered Debbie yesterday, saying that it would all be fine if he could just let go of whatever it was that kept him awake at night. But then, she had no idea what it was.

He must talk to Jerry, he couldn't handle it on his own any more, if he tried the damage would just go on and on until it destroyed the whole family. The necessity to stop it somehow now, while there might still be something to be saved, drove him back onto his feet to go and find Deb, to get out of here. It could perhaps be sorted out even at this late date if only he could talk to Jerry before he went home tomorrow, until then he had nothing to say to any of them.

Those two girls must have heard every word. What Mike said, what had made him say it, and what he had said himself in reply. What it was that had put the fatal sting into the tail of the row between them. It was even more imperative that they should now be found and made to back him up. Unless they did so, it was a lost cause, simply because nobody would want to believe him.

By the time he had reached the door, he had realised that he didn't want to face them, the family. Knowing what they must have wondered, what they might think, and what they might now have to know, going downstairs was harder than rushing into a burning building and he knew that for a fact. It took a deliberate effort to open the bedroom door.

The house was quiet. He went downstairs speedily, almost as if he was afraid of being followed, and ended up in the hall. There was the faint murmur of talk from the kitchen, the rest of the downstairs rooms were empty behind open doors. Feeling almost as if he had no right to be there, he headed in the direction of the kitchen, the only door that was closed, and on opening it found not Debbie and his sisters, as he had hoped, but his parents, sitting at the end of the long kitchen table talking seriously over mugs of coffee. So unwelcome was the sight that it took a considerable effort not to retreat and slam the door on them.

Pip and Cally broke off what they were saying the instant their errant son appeared, and in the light of what he had just been thinking, it meant only one thing, they had been talking about him – which in fact they had been, but not in the way in which he supposed. He immediately went on the defensive, and the stage was set for one of those awful family rows whose aftermath can hang around like smog for evermore.. Pip had only to say, *Ah, you're awake at last*, to set a light to a very short fuse. He said it.

'Ah, you're awake at last!' He smiled as he spoke, but Mawgan only heard the words.

'If anyone wanted me earlier, you could have woken me,' he snapped. Pip, who was facing him directly, narrowed his eyes suddenly, and was about to return a placatory answer, but Cally, still smarting from her mother's outspoken comments after the small fracas on the previous evening, jumped in first. In your parents' house, you are always to some extent a child and it makes no difference if you're rapidly rising thirty-four.

'Don't speak to your father like that, Mawgan! What is the matter with you? And I hope that you're planning to apologise to Mother for your behaviour last night!'

'Why? Is she planning to apologise to me?'

'You were very rude to her! On Christmas Day, too, where were your manners?'

Pip said, 'Cally, give over. Get the boy some breakfast. Sit down, Mawgan.'

'I'm just looking for Deb, then we're off.'

Cally, over by the stove with the kettle, paused, mouth open, and Pip said,

'No you're not, son. You're out of luck, she's gone over the fields with Anna and the kids while it's not raining. *Sit down!*'

After a brief hesitation, Mawgan sat, and Cally, without speaking, banged a mug of coffee down in front of him.

'I'll make you some toast,' she said. She sounded grudging but she hadn't intended to. It was just that she felt that this was a stranger, where back in the summer she had thought that Debbie Nankervis had returned their son to them, and the disappointment was bitter.

'Don't bother.' The very thought of it made Mawgan nauseated. His father, he noticed with detached interest, seemed to have separated into two halves, one of which was several inches higher than the other. The pain in his head was excrutiatingly familiar this time, here we go again. Migraine number two. He thought about driving back to St Erbyn, and immediately stopped thinking about it. There were odd little lines of geometric shapes hanging in the air on the periphery of his vision – entopic images, but he didn't know that – and he tried not to see them.

'That'll do,' said Pip, misunderstanding. 'Now then, what's all this about?'

'All what?'

'Something's up,' said Pip. 'Last night, maybe, you were tired like you said, although it's never been like you, but this morning you're downright ornery, and I intend to know why. We've had enough trouble and strife in this family, we don't need you stirring it up again.'

'*Showdown at the OK Corral*,' Mawgan murmured, provocatively, and the odd little shapes shimmered and danced.

'Yes, Mawgan,' said Cally, unwisely. 'We've all been through enough, surely!'

'*You've* been through enough?' said Mawgan. He took a deep breath. His mother had flung a slice of bread straight onto the hotplate of the Aga, and the smell of it was disgusting. He said, with a bitterness that shocked all three of them, 'Have you ever stopped to consider what *I* might be going through?

Nobody called *you* a murderer, nobody sent *you* to prison! *Your* family don't treat you as if you had some contagious disease, none of them believe that *you* wanted an incestuous relationship with your own sister! If you need their support, they don't turn away! So don't talk to me about what *you've* been through!' He had worked up to a shout, and as he came to the end, there was a horrible silence. Smoke began to rise from the Aga where the toast had been forgotten. Pip said, as if the words choked him,

'Is that what you think we think?' and wished he had phrased it more tidily. The line between comedy and tragedy can be a very narrow one. Cally's face was aghast, her mouth open.

'Well, don't you?' Mawgan demanded, fiercely.

'No, of course we don't!' Cally could hardly get the words out. 'It was just ... only Cress needed us ...'

'Oh, and I didn't?'

Cally opened her mouth to speak, and Pip cut in hastily, before she had a chance to make things worse.

'Her husband was dead, son, and however it happened ... well, it was you who was responsible. We never believed those other things, but you must see ...'

'I didn't kill him,' said Mawgan.

'You said ...'

'I know what I said, you didn't have to *believe* it so thoroughly. That's just how it felt when it happened. But I didn't.'

'He was *dead*!' said Cally. The horror of that afternoon was in the kitchen with them like a fog. A real fog was rising from the toast, which was now on fire. None of them noticed.

'Why didn't you say?' asked Pip.

'I thought I did. None of you listened. You only listened to Cress.'

'Oh, God,' said Cally, in a whisper. She sank down onto her chair. 'Mawgan, don't, please – we can't go back there again. Please!'

'And that will make it right, will it?' He realised what was happening on the stove, got to his feet, and slammed down the lid of the Aga, smothering the flames. '*Now* do you see why I'm going? And I'm damned if I'll bother to come back!' Standing up so abruptly had been a mistake, the room began to lurch round like a rather jerky roundabout. The smell of burning was sickeningly strong, for a moment there he was back at Seagulls with the fire raging behind him. He felt his father's hand under his elbow, pushing him back down onto the chair.

'Now what's the matter?' Pip sounded angry.

'Sorry. Migraine.'

'You don't have migraines!' cried Cally in patent disbelief.

'Now, I do.'

'Since when?' Cally demanded, shaken into being unreasonable, and Mawgan answered, literally.

'Since the end of August,' and pressed his hands over his mouth to hold back nausea.

The door opened at that moment, and Debbie came in. She saw the three of them like a tableau entitled 'The Great Family Row' and shut it behind her hurriedly before the twins came running in after her. There was an indignant shout of *Tante Debbee*! from beyond the door, and the insistent thump of small hands on the panels, but she leaned on it until she heard Anna's voice, calling the boys away. She didn't know what Anna might have seen, but was grateful to her anyway.

'I'm glad it's you, young lady,' said Pip. It sounded like a threat, he still had his hands on his son's shoulders. 'I want a word with you!' He turned to Cally. 'You can deal with this, while I find out what's really going on here.'

'What's been happening?' asked Debbie, bewildered.

'That's what we'd all like to know,' said Pip. 'I thought you might just be able to tell us.'

Mawgan raised his head and looked at her. There were two of her, which wasn't necessarily a good thing. He tried to focus, and failed. It was too much effort to go on being angry, he felt far too ill.

'Just tell him, bird. And then we're out of here.'

'You'll be no such thing!' cried his mother. 'Just look at the state of you!' Pip took Debbie's arm and took her out of the kitchen into the hall, forcing her when she would have held back.

'Into the dining room.' He was practically frog-marching her. She saw Allison's startled face hanging over the banisters and made a face back. It was like being back at school, hauled up before the headmistress.

'Sit down,' said Pip, when they were safely in the dining room, and when she had sat in the chair he set for her by the hearth, switched the electric fire on and drew up his own chair opposite. 'Now then, we thought everything was in a fair way to being sorted out. So what's the problem?'

Debbie had no more real idea than he had, but she did have a few clues.

'I think, for one thing, he was hurt by his grandmother's behaviour yesterday,' she said.

'Hurt?' asked Pip, as if the word was new to him. 'You play with fire, you expect to get burned. She's an old woman, she loved him, he let us all down. What did he expect? Absolution?'

'Just a fair hearing might have been good,' said Debbie. She shifted uncomfortably under Pip's gaze.

'There was a trial. That's a fair hearing, in this country,' he said.

'You don't believe that. You don't believe he killed Cressida's husband.'

'The jury said so,' said Pip, doggedly. '*He* said so. Believe me, we all wish it wasn't so, and we appreciate your efforts.'

'It wasn't so,' said Debbie. He looked at her, troubled.

'I know you said about an appeal, but it's best left alone. There's been things said ...'

'You can't possibly believe them, either,' said Debbie, with more firmness than she felt.

'Didn't come out of nowhere,' said Pip. He looked miserable.

Since she knew that her own father had a problem with this, too, Debbie changed tack.

'Perhaps you should try believing what Mawgan told you, in preference to Cressida.'

'Girl was beside herself,' said Pip, slowly. 'Wrung your heart, it did. And there's things he don't seem *able* to tell us.'

'But what was she beside herself *with*? From what I hear, it wouldn't have been grief,' Debbie retorted, and then bit her lip. 'Sorry. Shouldn't have said that. But anyway, he wasn't on trial for … for that. And the simple truth is that Mike Stanley fell, and it was his own fault.'

'Is it now.' Pip looked at her. 'I'd like to believe that, but were you there?'

'No. But Mawgan was. And so were two others.'

'And we all know what they say. It's a bugger, Debbie. She's our daughter, just like he's our son. What do we do? We didn't turn him away. He went on his own, we tried to be fair. If he says different, that's not true.'

Mawgan didn't, of course. But, once again, the point of view was everything.

'He went, because he didn't see it was possible to stay,' said Debbie. 'Listen, if any of that stuff was true, do you really think my father would be paying for my wedding?'

Pip shook his head. He looked as if he wanted to be convinced, but wasn't, quite.

'Didn't come out of thin air,' he repeated.

'It might have come from an over-active imagination,' Debbie retorted. 'My father says there must have been some doubt about the evidence for the judge to be so lenient.' Pip shook his head again, sadly.

'You got to prove that. Can you? Mawgan got nothing to say about it?'

'No.'

'Stand-off, then, isn't it?'

They looked at each other for a long moment. Debbie saw that Pip and Cally were doing their best. Perhaps she would see it even more clearly if she had ever met Cressida, although she thought that she probably wouldn't like her much – if at all, come to think. She probably knew Mawgan better than they did these days. She could get no further than that. Finally, Pip looked away.

'I thought we'd got through all this,' he said, hopelessly. Debbie said nothing, she could think of nothing sensible to say and deemed it best. Eventually, Pip went on, as if he was trying to convince himself as much as her. 'We'd do anything for the boy. We didn't mean for him to feel shut out of the family.' He spread his hands, in despair. 'We've had our differences, yes, no use denying it. But we're proud of him, of course we are. He's done well. It's just ...' He ended as he had begun. 'We'd do anything for him ...'

Debbie stirred on her chair, she spoke almost apologetically.

'It's got to be sorted out somehow. My father thinks he went to prison for something he didn't do, and I go with that. And the rest ... well, he denies it. Couldn't you try to believe him? Look at it that way, do *that* for him?'

'You believe him,' said Pip. It was a statement. 'Lots don't. And not just from then, neither.'

'Of course I believe him. I've said I'll marry him, haven't I? And my father hasn't put his foot down, has he?' Debbie sounded indignant. Pip gave her a knowing look.

'Your mum has, from what I gather. Perhaps we should all have another think about this.'

Debbie said, 'I don't think it has anything to do with anybody but me and Mawgan.'

'He had no right to ask – '

'If you want to know, he didn't. I did. And you don't really believe all that crap anyway, so why …?' She ended, with sudden heat, 'And if you say *no smoke without fire*, I shall – ' She broke off.

'Shall what?' asked Pip, with interest, and he looked and sounded so like Mawgan as he spoke that she answered on impulse as if it was truly Mawgan she was speaking to.

'Flatten your face!'

Pip was surprised into a shout of laughter.

'I tell you what, Deborah Nankervis,' he said. 'If he could only come up with some sensible explanation, I'd be right glad to see you my son's wife! Pax, then?'

'The thing is,' said Debbie, who, having been brought up to respect her elders, was relieved to have got away with that, 'is it necessarily up to him to come up with one?'

Although this was obviously a new idea to Pip, he looked unconvinced. Caught at an unexpected disadvantage, he changed the subject.

'That's not the problem right here and now, anyway,' he said. 'The boy's ill. I thought so when you got here yesterday, this morning I'm sure. So what's the story? And don't try and hide things from me, I've known him since a child. I don't make mistakes. Breakdown, is it?'

If she said yes, it wouldn't help Mawgan. They could put it down to remorse equally as well as to resentment of injustice, or Chel's preferred explanation, grief. Saying no would be even more pointless. She settled for,

'Not exactly, but near enough,'

'And what does 'near enough' mean?'

'It means, I hope, he was heading that way, and we headed him off.'

'We?'

'Me, and Chel and Oliver, and Tommy and everyone.'

'None of you never thought to tell us, his family?' Pip sounded hurt. Well, it was his turn.

'His choice,' said Debbie, and then saw Pip's face and wished she hadn't had to.

'I see.'

Into this impasse came Anna, with a steaming mug of tea in each hand.

'Allison and I thought you might be needing this,' she said, warily. 'What's all the fuss about? Mum's just chased Mawgan back upstairs to bed, and ordered us take the twins out of the house, so we're all taking the lunch to Nan and Grandad instead of the other way around. What's going on? Since when did he get migraines?'

'Since coming downstairs arse over tip and head-butting the newel post at the bottom, is favourite,' said Debbie. She sipped the hot tea gratefully. Anna perched on the arm of her father's chair, ruffling what little remained of his hair affectionately.

'That sounds reasonable,' she said. She looked at Debbie, apologetically. 'I thought total war had broken out this morning. All that loud, angry shouting. Is ... well, everything OK?'

Pip said, stiffly,

'Debbie and I have decided that we all need to come to an agreement.'

Have we? Debbie thought. Well, perhaps we have. Although *what* agreement, God alone knows. It looks like he said, a total stand-off, to me.

'Oh,' said Anna, as if she didn't believe in it, either. 'Well, at the risk of saying something terminally unhelpful, I don't believe that *agree to differ* is going to be an acceptable option.'

Since nobody else did either, a silence greeted this. She shrugged her shoulders and stood up again.

'Allison said she'd take you in her car, Debbie, when you're ready – unless you want to squeeze in between the boys, that is. No? Drink your tea first.'

'I'm ordered out, too?' asked Debbie.

'Seems like it. Unless you want to go all Victorian-heroine, and smooth his suffering brow, and I wouldn't, if I was you. He looked to me as if he might bite your hand off.'

Debbie decided, after only a second's consideration, that on the whole she would leave Mawgan to his mother. It might just ram home the point that she had been trying to make to Pip. She finished her tea and went upstairs to find her coat before going off, even if maybe heartlessly, to enjoy herself. It wasn't, she told herself as she ran back down to the hall and the waiting Allison, that she didn't have a pang at leaving him. It was *expedient*, that was the word, and she already knew from experience that he would survive.

Heartless or no, she enjoyed the day. Allison was the one of Mawgan's close relatives with whom Debbie found most in common, and she had a little Mazda sports car which she drove fast and furiously. They travelled to Nan and Grandad's bungalow by a scenic route that took them some miles out of their way, and arrived, windblown and laughing and the best of friends, just as Anna was beginning to speculate gleefully that Allison had landed them both in some ditch. Lunch, which Cally had packed up and sent over wholesale, was prepared by the three girls and after it had been cleared away, they all left Nan resting, Grandad reading the paper, and took the twins down to Carlyon Bay to turn them loose on the sand, where they ran and shouted and hopefully, said Kurt, exhausted themselves – whether Luc and Martin had exhausted themselves was a moot point, although Anna claimed that it had exhausted *her*, just heading them off from plunging into the freezing cold sea. Then back to the bungalow for tea for the children, and finally, back to the farmhouse, where Anna hustled the now definitely exhausted twins upstairs with promises of a story before bed, and Debbie went to see how Mawgan had fared.

'He's looking better,' had said Cally. 'Slept most of the day, which is good. He still says he wants to go back to St Erbyn, and I'm not having it.' She gave Debbie a fierce look, as if it had been her suggestion. 'He needs a proper break, if you want my opinion, which I don't suppose you do any more than he does, so off you go upstairs and talk him out of it.' It wasn't a request. It was an order.

Debbie went up to the bedroom and sat on the foot of the bed, knowing that it might not be that easy.

'Hullo,' she said. 'What's this, been giving your mum a hard time?'

Mawgan propped himself on his elbow the better to see her. He looked shattered, and her heart smote her.

'I know what she's saying. I need to speak to your dad before he goes back tomorrow, that's more important..'

'Not a problem,' said Debbie, startled at the urgency in his voice. 'He can come here on his way. Do you want me to ring him?'

'I'm not sure that's a good idea … God!' He rubbed his forehead as if it pained him. 'I wish I could think.' Debbie said,

'It might be better than rushing off now and setting off another migraine. You don't look really rid of the last one.'

'No, it's just a headache now.' He dismissed it as unimportant.

'What's it about, anyway?' Debbie asked, but he wouldn't tell her. She looked at him, worried now. Whatever it was, she realised, it had triggered both this morning's row and the migraine. She thought that he looked shocked as much as anything, and her mind whirled with speculations.

'I knew it was a mistake to come back here,' she said.

'Maybe it wasn't. I just don't know.'

'Anyway,' said Debbie, 'you're not going anywhere tonight, and that's final. Whatever it is, if it's waited this long, it can wait a few hours longer.'

He looked at her as if that was asking too much, but he seemed to see the sense of it, for he said, 'Would he come?'

'Of course he would. It's time they all met up anyway, and what better moment when Anna is here as well?'

'I'm not sure this is going to turn out to be a good moment,' said Mawgan darkly.

'I wish you'd tell me why.'

'Oh I will – when I've spoken to your dad,' said Mawgan, and she couldn't get anything more out of him.

* * * * *

It was Jerry's last night by the river, and he was actually saying that he wished he had been able to see more of Debbie and Mawgan on this visit when the phone rang.

'They'll be home tomorrow,' said Chel, getting up to answer it. 'You don't have to rush off early, do you?'

'Not before lunch, anyway,' said Jerry. He stretched out his feet towards the fire and leaned back in his chair contentedly. 'I've to be back in time for early dinner with Susan and Tom and the children.' Family life, he realised, had never been like this since Helen … but it was dangerous to think that. Chel was now speaking on the phone.

'Deb! We were just talking about you!' There was a pause, while she listened. 'What? Hang on, you'd better talk to him.' She held out the phone. 'For you, Jerry. Deb. She sounds in a bit of a tizz.'

'Hullo?' Jerry took the phone. 'Hi Deb, what's the problem?' He listened, and Chel came back to sit on the sofa beside Oliver, her hands clasped together. After a moment, she realised that he was looking at her.

'Something wrong?' he asked. Chel shook her head.

'You'll think I'm silly.'

'You know I never do. What's up?'

It was true, Oliver tended to take her more seriously than she did herself. Chel said,

'Something's happened. Some door has opened … I told you that you'd say I was silly.'

'Opened onto what? Not a dark cupboard full of skeletons, I hope.'

Chel said, slowly,

'Sunlight ...'

'That's good, then. Time something went right for Mawgan.'

She looked at him. That hadn't sounded quite like Oliver, who normally didn't care that much about other people's troubles. She said, testing him,

'I should have thought a lot of things had, come to that.'

'Not deep down. Not where it matters.'

'No ...' She was surprised. 'You really *do* like him, don't you?'

'Don't say that as if I've never liked anyone before! It makes you sound like my dear stepmother.' He was laughing at her, but Chel knew, and thought that he knew too, that even if Dot said it, it had been in one sense true. Oliver constructed barriers. Mawgan crashed them. It was as simple as that.

Jerry set the phone back on its rest and turned to them.

'Seems like I'll be leaving earlier than I thought,' he said. 'I'm invited to lunch. Deb says, get there early, Mawgan has something he wants to talk to me about.'

'Like, what?' asked Oliver.

'She doesn't know. But she thinks something happened this morning. There was a bit of a barney, she says.'

'Nice to know ours isn't the only family that can have them.'

Jerry was becoming increasingly sure that his family was a lot more normal than he had ever given it the credit for. He laughed.

'As a solicitor, I have to disillusion you. We are not unique.'

'You are going to have a day of it, aren't you,' observed Chel. 'Deb's problems for lunch, Susan's for dinner. Would you like ours for breakfast, make a complete set?'

'Susan doesn't have problems. They aren't allowed,' said Oliver, and after his unexpected perception over Mawgan, Chel felt as if she had run into a wall. Some things never changed. She got to her feet.

'I know we've been eating solidly for the last forty-eight hours, but do either of you fancy some supper?'

'So long as it doesn't involve cold meat of any description,' said Oliver.

'You'll take what you're given, and be thankful,' Chel told him. 'Jerry?'

'What? Oh ... yes. Yes. Whatever.' He met Chel's eyes. 'Sorry. Mind wandering. I was just thinking ...' He broke off with a deprecating smile. 'Sorry.'

Chel turned back from the kitchen door and came to sit on the arm of his chair.

'What did Deb say?'

'Nothing. She didn't know anything.' He looked at them both, seriously. 'I'm hoping, to be honest, that whatever it is that young man has been holding back, he's changed his mind. Because he has been holding something back.'

'He says not,' offered Oliver.

'He can say not until the wind changes, it isn't true.'

'But you don't think he did it,' said Chel.

'Did what? He didn't do *nothing*, his brother-in-law was dead.' Jerry sat up straight. 'I'll say to you what I wouldn't dream of saying to Deb. His sister is supposed to have been devoted to him. Why should she tell such wicked lies, that's what gets to me.'

'You don't believe ...?' Chel looked shocked.

'I hope I don't. But it keeps coming back to this, what do any of us really know about him, and even more, about her?'

'Nobody in the village thinks it's true. They're all disgusted with her.'

'You think they would have known?'

'Actually, I'm sure they would. You know villages.' Chel hesitated. 'You must like him. You've backed Deb from the first.'

'That's true. I just never expected him to be so ... so intransigent. People who won't give, particularly to their legal representative, have something to hide. I'd just like to know what it is, that's all.' Jerry hesitated. 'I thought he'd tell me. And he hasn't.'

Oliver said,

'Is it remotely possible that he doesn't even know? That it came as much of a surprise to him as to everyone else?'

'How, for God's sake?' demanded Jerry.

'I don't know.' Oliver spoke apologetically. 'It was just a thought.'

'Rumours like that start somewhere, and for some reason,' said Jerry, with conviction. 'And before you both jump down my throat, hold on a minute. I'm not saying it's true, if I even suspected it might be, I'd have Deb out of there in a flash, believe me. I'm just saying, it came from *somewhere*, and for *some reason*. And that I want to know where, and what. And that it worries me that he won't tell me. He *has* to know.'

'If little sister Cressida started it –' Chel began, and stopped. 'No. There's nothing in what he says about her, or about what happened, that makes that sound right. She'd need a reason, and I don't see one. She wanted out from her marriage, that's obvious ... I begin to see what you mean.'

'Well, I'm glad about that!'

'Be good to have it cleared up before she actually marries him,' said Oliver, thoughtfully. Chel looked at him.

'Do you think he'd tell *you*?'

'I think that pigs might fly first.' He hesitated. 'Chel's right, you know, Dad. The villagers here would have known. They were all a bit rough on him, but it was because a man died and he didn't seem to care. They all laugh themselves sick at the idea that he considered Cressida with anything other than rather exasperated affection – as a tolerable nuisance, even, which it seems she was. He hadn't the time for any nonsense. They all say so.'

Jerry said, carefully,

'If such a rumour arose about you and Deb, say, I wouldn't believe it. Mawgan's parents seem suspiciously equivocal on the subject. Who knows what? Why won't he come out straight and say? And that's where it sticks every time.'

'Then let's hope, tomorrow, he will come straight out and say,' said Oliver.

'Or they will,' said Chel.

Jerry didn't hold out much hope for it, but he drove to St Austell the following day trying to be optimistic. To be honest, both as Debbie's father and now as Mawgan's solicitor, he found it difficult to accept his apparent inability to tell the whole truth. Oliver's suggestion that he didn't know it was obviously ridiculous, he had to. He liked Mawgan, he liked him very much, but it was beginning to feel more and more obvious that Dot had a point, with her private detective and her intractable attitude, and perhaps he should have taken the same stance. The thought was immediately followed by the recollection of Deb's distress when Mawgan had tried to call the whole thing off because he thought none of them trusted him ... but if anything happened to Deb ...

But no. Mawgan would never hurt her. It took her mother to do that.

Debbie had given him minute directions, and he found his way without trouble. Driving into the farmyard behind the house, he realised immediately that Dot had one thing wrong, this wasn't her notion of council estate territory, this was a prosperous business attached to a respectable family home. This was a family that had done all right for itself, and wherever it had begun, it had made the most of opportunity, held its head high, and worked for what it had, which wasn't negligible. Everywhere he looked was well-kept; there was some kind of conversion going on in one of the barns, well-ordered and organised. They probably weren't in his own income bracket, but they were doing all right. He would never need to apologise for his daughter's in-laws, whatever Dot might think.

If ...

He probably shouldn't have let it all go this far. He had been swept along on the tide of the sudden change within his own family and Helen's claim that Mawgan, as well as Chel, was responsible. He thought that he had allowed it all to go too far now, but when he was in Mawgan's likeable company, he tended to forget the things he ought to be remembering as a concerned father. Charm, they called it. He, of all people, should have learned to distrust it. He parked his car beside Mawgan's and got out, not the first person in the past forty-eight hours to be wishing he was almost anywhere but here.

Debbie came flying out of the new conversion, followed more slowly by a slim, dark young woman recognisably related to Mawgan, and everything instantly changed. She hurtled into his arms.

'Dad! Lovely, you found your way then?' And then, almost in the same breath, 'This is Allison. We've just been looking at her will-be little house, do you want to see? She's going to work for her Dad but she wants to be independent – '

Jerry hugged her back.

'Perhaps I'd better meet her parents first? Hullo, Allison.' He shook hands and received a friendly smile. Charismatic family, he registered. Good news, bad news?

'Good thinking!' Debbie took his arm and urged him towards the back door.

Most of the family had concentrated in the kitchen, as was a habit with them, it was that kind of kitchen – that kind of family, come to that. The twins were roaring round the big table making *brrm brrm* noises being a Formula 1 race, Anna was setting out mugs on the worktop and trying not to trip over them as she did so, Cally brewing coffee, and Pip and Kurt sitting at the end of the table discussing football over the sports pages of a tabloid newspaper. It immediately occurred to Jerry, as he was introduced to them all, that he now knew exactly how his grandchildren were likely to look; even the little boys, with their tall, spare, fair, father had come out square, dark and determined. With Jerry himself in their bloodline, any children of Deb's and Mawgan's wouldn't stand a chance. He realised that he was once again thinking as if the marriage was a foregone conclusion, and knew that it had to do with the warmth and friendliness that had greeted him. He wanted it to happen, there was no arguing with it. He wanted all this boisterous normality, all this warmth and goodwill for his girl. He wanted it to reach out and touch his son, to bring him into line with the rest of the human race, make him all the things that his upbringing had knocked out of him. Between Chel's family and this one his children would be safe. He wanted it, suddenly, quite passionately. Straightening up from repelling a collision with a twin, he found Cally smiling at him.

'Regular madhouse, isn't it?' She poured two mugs of coffee and put them on a tray. 'You can take this upstairs to that lad of ours, have a chat in private.' She gave him a slightly defiant smile. 'I made him stop in bed. Yelling blue murder and waking the whole household at crack of dawn this morning, I don't know!'

Anna scooped up the tray.

'Come on,' she said. 'I'll show you the way.'

Jerry followed her out into the hall, but at the foot of the stairs, she paused, and looked at him beadily.

'Sort him out, will you? Mum's just realised the meaning of the word 'depressed'. She thought it meant, just not very happy. She didn't think you took pills for it, not in our family. She never thought it was a real illness.'

'I can only sort him out, as you put it, if he'll let me,' Jerry pointed out. Anna turned and led the way up the stairs.

'He'd better,' she said, darkly.

Mawgan greeted him with a deprecating smile and a slightly shame-faced explanation.

'My mum's been bullying me,' he announced. 'She says if I'm good, I can get up for lunch. I feel about eight – the bits of me that don't feel about eighty, that is.'

'Serves you right, waking the whole household, shouting fit to wake the dead,' Anna told him, firmly. She put down the tray on the dressing table. 'I'll leave the two of you to it.'

'Never let the women bully you,' said Jerry, with a smile, as the door closed behind her. 'Here – have some coffee.' He handed over a mug, and sat on the foot of the bed with his own.

'Funnily enough, it's quite pleasant,' confessed Mawgan, propping himself on an elbow to accept it. 'Nice to have someone telling me what to do for a change, for God knows, I don't know any more.'

'What's the problem? Debbie said you were insistent you wanted to talk to me.'

'You're going to think I'm crazy. Come to think, you won't be far wrong.'

'So what is it?' said Jerry, when the pause had gone on too long. Mawgan looked down into his coffee, swirling it round and round and watching it spin.

'I know you think I've been holding out on you,' he said, and hesitated.

'Ah.' Jerry waited, and then added, 'Yes, I do. Are you ready to fill in the gaps?'

Mawgan looked up, flicking him with a quick, golden glance, and then looked down again at the tiny vortex in the mug.

'I looked out the window when I got up in the morning. That window, over there. Made me start thinking straight at last. What it all led to.'

Jerry got up and walked over to the window, and looked out. If Mawgan wanted to approach by a circuitous route that was fine, so long as he got there in the end. Below him was the front garden of the farmhouse, beds of shrubs and climbers and dormant perennials, a small shrubbery, and leaning over the far corner from the garden of the house beyond, a great oak tree, perfect for climbing. No rockery.

'I take it, that's the famous tree?' he said. 'Funny ... I always imagined it as a back garden.'

'Their back garden. Not ours. Might as well be, nobody never goes past since they built the other road.'

'Whereabouts was the rockery?'

He saw Mawgan flinch, but he answered readily enough,

'Where the shrubbery is now. It weren't quite that shape – it sort of curved out, into the lawn, like a half-moon. There was a patio, and a bird bath thing.'

Very artistic, but perfect for falling onto, Jerry concluded. He said,

'So, tell me what happened. Take it a step at a time. How did it all begin?'

'What I told you was true – as far as it went.' He hesitated. After a moment, Jerry prompted him

'You had a slanging match, he told you all about what a rotten wife your sister was, and you told him what a rotten husband she said *he* was, do I have that right?'

'Pretty much. Something like that.'

'And then you came to blows.'

'No ...' Mawgan put his coffee mug down on the bedside table, Jerry saw that his hand was shaking. 'No. Look, I'm going to have to go back a bit. And before you ask, yes, I did keep this back deliberate. I just tried to tell myself it wasn't nothing to do with it. I think now, I may have got it wrong. Horribly wrong, come to that. I don't know what to do.'

'Just tell me,' said Jerry. 'We'll decide what to do after.'

'When I come back from Italy, I still had friends here,' said Mawgan. 'Good friends, the kind you keep up with ... I used to come over on Sunday evenings, when my restaurant was closed, meet up with the lads, have a jar or two ... you know how it goes. I didn't have no pub to worry over in them days, I was a lot freer. We generally used to go to the same two or three pubs ... I suppose we'd been drinking in them for years, come to that. Kev and Robbie & Co. certainly had. I'd spend the night at home, here, and drive back first thing in the morning and do the marketing on the way.'

'Go on,' said Jerry, after another pause.

'The thing is, people knew us. We grew up together on the same estate, we went to the same schools, we lived here all our lives. They might not know us well, or even approve of us a lot, but they'd nod and smile as we came in, pass the time of day – you know?'

Jerry wondered where this was leading. He said,

'I know. Casual acquaintances, we call them in more civilised parts.'

Mawgan almost laughed.

'Them, yes.But you see ... after a while, people began to turn away if I come in, barely nod to me ... one or two of them cut me dead. Robbie said I was dreaming, but Kev asked me what I'd been up to ... and as far as I knew, the answer was 'nothing'. But it went on, and it got worse. Kev said, perhaps they resented my success ... but it didn't seem to fit. We began to drink in other places, not saying anything to each other, but ... we just did. Tell the truth, I'd put it out of my mind, it was yesterday when I got to thinking about it again ... and I realised they were all friends or relatives of the Stanleys. The same people that made all the unpleasantness that drove the family away after I went to prison. And it all went together and made a horrible sort of sense.'

'You're saying,' said Jerry, working this out as it went along, 'that you think Mike Stanley, and not your sister, originally started this story going around about your ... unnatural relationship?'

'I don't think so. I *know* so.'

'That would be slander,' said Jerry, almost automatically. Mawgan grinned, but not mirthfully.

'Bit late to find out that now,' he suggested. 'He's dead and buried three year gone.'

'Let's go back a bit,' said Jerry, letting this pass. 'You're telling me, if I understand you correctly, that all this goes back to *before* your brother-in-law's death?'

'Months before, probably. You can ask Kev or Robbie if you do want confirmation.' He made a wry face. 'I expect they're still around somewhere.'

'You don't sound certain.'

Mawgan shrugged, as if it didn't matter.

'Not seen them for years.'

Jerry let it pass. He said,

'We'll check it out. And presumably, there will be people at your end who can speak up for you?'

'When Cress came over, she spent most of her time with Mandy.'

'I thought you told me she spent her time sounding off to you about her husband.'

'She did. But I didn't have that much time to listen to her – or patience, truth be told. She'd go up to the flat and chew Mandy's ear when I had to get on working.'

'So who is Mandy?'

'Mandy Rushton. Edward's wife.'

Jerry realised that there was something here that was worth knowing, one knot in the tangle that was teasing loose at last.

'So, this Mandy – she knows that there was neither time nor inclination for any funny business?'

'Nice way of putting it, but yes, she does, she and some others. Whether she'll come out and say it is another thing.' Mawgan shifted his shoulders uncomfortably against the pillow. 'She didn't like me none.' He failed to meet Jerry's eyes, and Jerry said,

'Why not?' but almost knew the answer already.

'She made a pass at me and got slapped down. I don't play games with the wives of my friends. Probably I slapped her down a bit hard ... I never had that much tact with girls.'

'I see. So what you're saying is, the best witness to your innocence is standing ready with a knife to stab you in the back?'

'It's worse than that.'

'You really are a defence solicitor's nightmare, aren't you?' Jerry spoke almost in admiration. 'I don't think I ever saw such a talent for shooting yourself in the foot!'

'Yeah ... well.'

'Let's look at it sensibly. If there is an independent witness who can say it was so much nonsense, that gets you off that hook, at least. And anyway, you were never on trial for that. So let's get back to the day of Mike Stanley's death.'

There was a long silence.

'Mawgan?'

'Only, there's more.'

'You said that what you told me was true, so where does the story diverge from the accepted version?'

'What I told you *was* true. I just didn't tell it all.'

'Ah ...' said Jerry. He waited. Mawgan shifted uncomfortably against the pillows and failed to meet his eyes, disturbingly. Finally, he said, in a rush,

'I tried to make myself think it didn't have to come out. It'd about kill 'em downstairs, that's if they believed me. Then, if they didn't ... well, it wouldn't have helped none. Just made bad worse. But I think now I should have said … at least it'd've been a straight choice then, her or me. As 'tis …'

Jerry was nobody's fool, very few solicitors are. He began to have a horrible suspicion of what Mawgan was trying to avoid saying outright and wished that he could help. But you should never lead a witness. He waited. After a while, Mawgan went on, still looking anywhere but at him.

'I s'pose in a way I ought to've seen it coming … you see, Cress'd always made up stories. About how she was some kind of a changeling, swapped over in the hospital the night she was born … she made up some tale, anyone'd tell you. It weren't no secret, she'd tell the world given the chance. It was just a tale … we thought it was. Don't really know now if she believed it herself, but I hope she did, because …' He drew a breath. 'Don't know as I can tell you even now.'

'You have to,' said Jerry. 'If it helps, I think I can guess, but you have to say it yourself.'

Long pause. Finally, Mawgan said, so low that Jerry almost didn't hear,

'You don't expect to find your own sister laid out stark naked on your bed when you knock off working.'

Jerry said, calmly because he had half-expected it,

'Tell me how it happened. You told me, I think, that she always came for the day, how did she come to stay overnight?'

'The car wouldn't start – she said it wouldn't. Some problem with the ignition, I don't know, I didn't have time to look, but Edward did. He couldn't start it neither. Man up the garage said he'd come out first thing, it didn't seem worth calling out the AA. Wish we had now, but we gave her a bed for the night instead.'

'But you were working, you say. Where did she spend the evening? In the bar?'

'In the flat, with Mandy – she and Edward lived in it then, it was their pub. I had the room at the top of the stairs as a bedsit – that half of the place was mine, 'though Mandy looked after the rooms. The room next to mine was vacant, we gave that to Cress. Time I got up there, they'd all gone to bed – I thought. Then, when I opened the door, there she was, arranged all artistic on my bed like a … like a tart. I didn't know where to look, leave alone what to do.'

Jerry had sisters of his own, trying to imagine a similar situation left him full of sympathy. He asked, with some curiosity,

'So, what *did* you do?'

'Be honest, I thought Mandy'd put her up to it to teach me a lesson, first off. I said I was going to have a shower and when I come out, she'd better be gone, and I went into the bathroom and slammed the door. But when I did come out, she was still there – and worse, she'd locked the door and hidden the key.'

'Awkward,' said Jerry. Mawgan flashed him a look, and looked away again. He said,

'She was lying there with her arms held out to me, she said she loved me and I knew she wasn't really my sister, and I told her not to talk rubbish. So she began to cry, and go on about ill-fated love or some nonsense she'd read in a book some time, and she got up off the bed and tried to put her arms round me. I gave her a shove off.' He turned his head away, reliving the moment with some pain, withdrawn into some private place where Jerry was not invited. Jerry, imagining it, could only sympathise. He said, prompting,

'So, what did she do, after you'd repulsed her like that?

Strangely, his misunderstanding of this phrase brought Mawgan back to the room, and now. He looked directly at Jerry again.

'I wouldn't say that,' he said, wryly. 'She just came back at me, clinging round my neck. I had to pick her off by force and dump her on the bed. I threw the duvet over her, and she sort of huddled under it, looking at me like I'd kicked her or something, and the tears running down her face, working herself into hysterics. I told her to give me the key right now, or I'd ring Mandy and get her to bring the master. And she said, if I did that, she'd scream.'

After a short pause, Jerry repeated,

'So, what did you do?'

'Picked up the phone, of course, and rang the internal number. She opened her mouth to scream like she said and I slapped her – hard. She shut up then and just went on crying, but quietly thank goodness. I asked Mandy to come and unlock the door and then beat it into the shower, and when I heard the lock turn, I come out and wrapped Cress in my bathrobe and pushed her out the door. But Mandy hadn't gone away. She was waiting outside and come to meet Cress and take her off, and she give me such a look … but I don't know to this day if it was a put-up job between them or just Cress losing it, and I never found the key, neither.'

'Did Mandy Rushton ever bring up the subject with you?'

'No, and I wasn't going to ask her, was I?'

Jerry supposed not. He said, because it was obviously relevant, 'And did her husband ever find out – Stanley?'

'Certainly did. She went home next day and told him as I'd made love to her. Then that's when she walked out and went home.'

'Did he believe her?'

'I don't know. He didn't tell them here, if so. Only me, when we was in the garden. In fact, he said a lot more'n that. I just hadn't wanted to think about it, be honest.'

This time, Jerry waited, and after a while, Mawgan said,

'It was when I said that Cress thought he had another woman … he said, 'Why not, when she's got another man?' and he said it with such … such *venom*! I told him not to be silly. I must be some stupid.' He brushed his face with his hands, as if he was trying to brush the memory away. 'Who was this man, then? I asked him. And he said, *You*! Be truthful, I began to wonder then if Mandy was ever behind it at all, but things was going so fast ...' He broke off.

'Take your time,' said Jerry. He sipped his coffee and nodded towards the mug on the bedside table. 'Drink that. It'll help. Not a lot, but it will.'

Mawgan picked up the mug obediently, but held it between his palms without drinking.

'He believed it, you know – not necessarily the making love bit, he must have known her by that time, but the rest. From what'd been happening round here, he'd been believing it a long time, poor bugger, that much was obvious. But I told you, there wasn't ... wasn't *room*, if you see what I mean, even if it hadn't been rubbish.'

Jerry saw. He said,

'Go over it with me again. She came over to see you. How did she come? Bus, train, did you have to collect her, drive her home, what? Something, however innocent that would involve you in being with her a lot without witnesses?'

'No, nothing like that. How could I? I already said, I had a restaurant to run. She took the early bus or the train from Liskeard to St Austell and then borrowed Nan's car, that was the one as wouldn't start that time. I had nothing to do with it.'

'Then,' said Jerry, 'I think you should be asking yourself, not why did he say that, but why did she come?'

'I done that, too.' Mawgan put the mug down again, and Jerry picked it up and put it back in his hands.

'Drink, while it's halfway hot.' He waited until Mawgan had done so, then said, 'So, what conclusion did you come to?'

Mawgan said, slowly, 'When Mike said that, well, you can imagine – I was gobsmacked. I said, are you barking mad? She's my sister, for heaven's sake! Maybe I said it too loudly, guilty conscience and that, though I'd no reason. And he shouted, *she says not*! I shouted back, what the hell was he on about? Of course she was my sister! And he hit me.'

'*He* hit *you*? You're certain of that?'

'Damn near broke my jaw, real feeling behind it. And then ...'

'You hit him back?'

'No. Far as I remember now, I never hit him at all. I threw up my arms to fend him off, and then ... I saw Cress, and it was such a shock, he got a thump in on my ribs that near knocked the breath out of me. He was crazy. He had to be. His face ...'

Jerry said, calmly,

'You saw your sister. What shocked you? It was reasonable for her to be there. She was in the house, she must have wondered what you were both saying about her.'

'It was the way she looked,' said Mawgan.

'Ah ...'

'She must have heard what I said, or maybe my face give me away ... I was horrified, if you want to know. And Mike shouting the odds about how she must be crazy ... anyway, she was looking at me as if she hated me. *Hated* me ... and sort of gleeful with it.'

'Tell me about Cressida,' said Jerry, his heart unexpectedly aching for the deceased Michael Stanley. Poor bugger indeed, if he had ever loved the girl at all, as presumably he must have done. Mawgan looked at him, his expression blank as if he hadn't understood. Jerry said, quietly,

'Just tell me what she was like. Don't hurry, think it out. Was she bright? Like the two downstairs? Like you?'

'No ...,' said Mawgan, slowly, 'No, she wasn't a bit like us. She was ... different.'

'In what way, different? *Was* she your true sister?'

'Of course she was! I remember the day she was born, and a bloody awful day it was, too!'

'Awful, in what particular way?'

'You'll have to ask Dad for details, I was only a kid. But I remember the way it seemed then, and I know now that they thought Mum would die, and the baby with her ... Christ ...' It wasn't an expletive. It sounded more like a prayer. Mawgan said. 'Cress fantasised, I told you – about just about everything. Made up stories ... she said that baby *did* die, and Mum brought back another one from the hospital. But it was all imagination, we never thought as she really believed it. How could she, she's eyes in her head – you've probably noticed already, we're all out the same mould. Her too. She was my sister, all right.'

'Maybe she did believe it. Maybe her whole life was fantasy.'

Mawgan said nothing. A series of unreadable emotions chased each other across his face, but he didn't speak, and Jerry didn't blame him. He said, after a while,

'It wasn't your fault. You'd been away for years, you came back different, grown-up, exciting, successful. In the time you'd been away, she'd grown from a child to a woman, you couldn't know it was only on the outside. So she looked at you with hero-worship and made up a story to suit, and lived it. That's how it must have been. You couldn't have known.'

'She married Mike ...' He sounded bewildered.

'Probably she knew in her heart somewhere that what she felt was wrong. He was your friend, wasn't he? Perhaps that was why.'

'Not that much of a friend,' Mawgan objected. 'I knew him, we was at school together, but he was a year behind me. We weren't never close.'

Jerry just about remembered being at school, he thought wryly. The gap between one year and the year behind was a chasm. He said, 'You see what we're getting here, I hope?'

'A real mess,' said Mawgan. He looked despairing. 'How did I get in a mess like this?'

'What we're getting,' said Jerry, ignoring this, 'is an explanation of her subsequent behaviour – after the accident, I mean, after all, her husband had already written the script for her. To put it bluntly, she was punishing you. *Hell hath no fury*, and all that. And at the same time, she was twisting it round so she could duck out herself and leave you carrying the can.'

'She can't have *believed* that nonsense?'

'Under certain circumstances, I daresay she could make herself. I had better talk to your parents, I think, try and fill in the blanks. They must know, even if they've never faced it. Didn't you ever wonder ...? Deb said that you said once that she could have been damaged at birth. Did you say that seriously?'

'I suppose I must have done ... she was always – oh, inadequate somehow. We grew up with it. We just thought she was a bit spoiled, we didn't think ...' He paused. 'We let her down, didn't we? The lot of us did, but me most of all. If I'd told them ...'

'You mustn't shoulder all the blame. Leave it now. Go on about the accident.'

'You know most of it already.'

'Tell me anyway.'

'He went on hitting me. He was beside himself. Cress had gone indoors ... for help, I thought, but I was wrong, of course. Then he got hold of me and ... we went down. I can hear the sound of his skull cracking down on the rocks now ... that was it, really.'

'If that's the truth, you must have been bruised,' said Jerry, ever practical.

'I was. Black and blue, all over my ribs and shoulders as well as where he hit me in the face. Nobody seemed that interested, and to be honest, it seemed unimportant.'

'It was very important. Didn't the police ask? Mike Stanley wouldn't be bruised, not if you didn't hit him, only where he fell.'

'He was dead. That was the clincher.'

'Well, there'll be a post mortem report on file. We'll have a look at it. So, did anyone but you know about these bruises?'

'Nan and Grandad, maybe ... I stopped with them until those girls spoke up and I was arrested. You could ask Grandad, I suppose, if it matters.'

Jerry spoke very slowly and clearly, as if to a child.

'I will ask. If you were black and blue, as you say, and he was not, and the autopsy report will tell us that, the inference is very clear. If it wasn't accident – and I believe it was – then it was certainly self-defence. And the fact that he was killed was undoubtedly an accident, even if you had shoved him away that little bit too hard.'

'And the rest?'

Jerry considered.

'You were never charged with incest. It's only of importance to your family, and I think you must tell them the truth.'

'I can't. Think how hurt they'll be.'

'You have to. Or I will, if you prefer. But they must know. If they don't, not only are they being unjust to you, but when your sister comes back, nobody will help her. Leaving you to fester with resentment will help nobody, and nor will leaving your family under a misapprehension.'

'Suppose she never comes back?'

'It won't be your fault. Believe me.' He paused. 'Are you OK?'

'Yes. Probably.' Mawgan clenched his hands to stop them shaking. 'I just wish I could hide under the pillow and stay there for ever, but I'll get over it.'

'I'm sure you will.' Jerry took the two mugs, both now empty, in his hand. 'It's going to be all right, you know. I'll speak to your parents and to your grandparents. And just in case there's any come-back, we'll get sworn statements from Amanda Rushton and your friend ... Kev?'

'Kevin Rickard.' Mawgan had buried his face in his hands. 'I expect Allison can find him for you.'

Jerry stood up. He didn't want to go so abruptly, but he didn't feel that he would be welcome if he stayed either. Mawgan had flung himself onto his side with his back to him, it was a clear enough statement. He said, with unwonted diffidence,

'Your sister can be searched for, you know. You don't have to involve the police. I'll speak to your father about it, she should be found.'

'I know,' said Mawgan, muffled into the pillow.

'I'll see you at lunch,' said Jerry.

Outside on the landing, he paused, and closed his eyes in sheer relief. Yes, it was a mess, but it was little sister's mess, not big brother's. If she could be found, she could be helped, and his own beloved daughter was safe. Everything that he had wished for her would be hers without shadow; there would be medical records, school records, family knowledge that would identify Cressida Stanley for what she must have been, interpreted in the light of present knowledge. Those concerned could be brought to admit it now that they knew how unacceptable was the alternative. No happy ending maybe, but at least they could close ranks again. And he would tell Dot to call her dogs off and leave Debbie alone, for if she chose, at her age, to marry a chef who owned a pub on the side, it was nobody's business but her own. And the sooner he did so, the better, for when the finance angle proved a dead end, Dot might dig deeper and then the fat would really be in the fire. He shuddered at the thought of her reaction if she should ever hear the word 'incest'. Thank God she had never come to Cornwall! Rumour might not be in the written record, but it was still alive locally.

So, not a bad morning's work already. And now for Mawgan's father, who must play his part or, Jerry suspected, lose the son along with the daughter.

He went downstairs to see about it.

XVI

'So, are you going to tell Mummy?' was the first question that Susan asked. Jerry looked at her speculatively.

'Would you?'

Susan looked uncomfortable, without realising it she wriggled in her chair.

'Well?'

'I think I'd say as little about it as possible,' she said, a little to Jerry's surprise. He looked at her with interest, both his natural children had displayed unexpected hidden depths, and now here was Susan doing it too. Her father had been an intelligent man, he recalled. Clever, too, which wasn't quite the same, except in the matter of Dot, possibly.

'Would you care to tell me why?' he asked, quietly.

The answer to that was *not really*, but Susan took a stab at it all the same.

'She would only say things like 'there's no smoke without fire', and 'he's had plenty of time to make up a good story',' she suggested, and added, in fairness to her absent mother, 'Both are true.'

'Superficially true,' said Jerry. 'I'm looking forward to catching up with that young woman, Amanda Rushton. I wonder if she knew exactly what she was doing? Playing with fire, I would call it. I hope the end result gave her a salutory lesson; if not, I certainly shall.'

'You think she set it up, then?'

'Almost certainly. Don't you?'

'Yes.' Susan hesitated. 'Is the tree close enough for those two girls to have heard what was actually said?'

Jerry looked at her with approval.

'Yes, it probably is. How they interpreted it is, of course, another matter, they were only schoolgirls at the time, after all. It may account for what followed.'

'Of course, you can't lead a witness,' said Susan, thoughtfully.

'Certainly not. Perish the thought!'

'Do you think they'll really let him off the hook?'

'I think that realistically they have no choice, but you never know. Justice wears a blindfold, remember.'

'It's a grim business you engage in,' said Susan, with an affectionate grin. Jerry laughed, then looked at her curiously.

'You don't still fancy it yourself?'

Susan began to answer, and then broke off as Tom came in through the door of the drawing room, carrying a tray of glasses and a bottle of port. There was no way, she found herself thinking, that she was going to discuss either Debbie's affairs or her own ambitions in front of her husband, and the realisation gave her a jolt. Hard on its heels came the unbidden thought that Tom had been her mother's choice and she winced internally. Anyway, she didn't think that she did fancy her father's profession for herself any more. Somewhere along the line, her needs had changed; she needed, she obscurely felt, to branch out for herself, plough a new furrow, not to follow her adopted father. That ambition belonged to the past, rooted, she was beginning to realise, in a need to belong. Ambition itself was unexpectedly still there. Its direction remained an open invitation to a mystery tour.

Unfortunately, the need to belong also remained. Now that she had recognised it, she knew that it was beginning to undermine her. Tom's fault? Present circumstances? Who knew. Some shrink, possibly, but she wouldn't ask.

She wondered, fleetingly, about her natural father, of whom she knew next to nothing. All her life, she had been so determined to be one of the Nankervises that she had hardly spared him a thought, that misty progenitor who had left her so well-provided for. For perhaps the first time, she felt guilty. Henry Worthington, investment broker: a shadow only, and yet the contributor of half of her genes. Curiosity, released from bondage by the break-up of the family of which she had so much longed to be a real part, turned over in its sleep and twitched an eyelid. In the hour-glass of Dot's complacency, another grain of sand shifted and plummeted downwards.

'Port, Jerry?' said Tom, placing the tray on a side-table and preparing to pour. Jerry, regarding his son-in-law with disapprobation, murmured,

'Please ...' He had less of an opinion of Tom than he had once had. In the run-up to Christmas, Jerry knew, he had been seen at least once at a party when not in the company of his wife. He had not been officially in Elaine's company, either, but she had been present and the two of them had gravitated together. Jerry wondered if Tom knew how wide was his, Jerry's, acquaintance in a town where he had been born, brought up, and spent most of his working life, or how much unwelcome attention Dot's social-climbing aspirations had attracted as she ascended over the bodies of weaker rivals. There were those who would be happy to see Dot squirm; Tom might think that his affair was well hidden, and of no interest to anyone but himself, but either he deceived himself unforgivably on both counts, or he had very little respect for Susan. He wondered if Susan had even received an invitation to that party or if she had been deliberately excluded. He knew that quite soon, if this went on, he was going to have to intervene, if only for the sake of his grandchildren, and he didn't relish the prospect. A word in Tom's ear might serve, but he had a feeling that the days when it would have been enough to put a stop to a flourishing affair had long been gone.

What a worry children were. Oliver had always been a problem, of course, but now he had Debbie with her immensely likeable, bright, ambitious but otherwise disastrous partner, and even Susan, about whom he had never had a single qualm, being swept headlong towards the weir and not even making an attempt to swim.

Or was she? Susan wasn't happy.

Jerry sipped his port and considered Susan's reply to his original question, would she tell her mother about Mawgan's surprise confession?

Yes, Susan was definitely changing. He wondered, a little apprehensively, where such a change might lead. Susan wasn't a free agent, she and Tom had two children – two sensitive and intelligent children. Jerry took another sip and felt his heart sinking.

Happy New Year … he could feel it coming on.

* * * * *

'So, taken by and large, not the most successful Christmas you've ever spent,' said Chel.

It was the morning of New Year's Eve. Debbie and Mawgan had returned to the Fish half an hour before, and Debbie, having dumped her bags back in the flat, had made her immediate way down to the office and a sympathetic ear. Chel had listened, and made no comment until the end. Now, Debbie shrugged her shoulders. Her face was thoughtful.

'Well … yes, and no. It explained why tempers ran so high, which Dad says now had always bothered him, and it certainly cleared the air, but it's going to be a while before anyone is happier for it.'

'I can see that. How did the family take it?'

'Half with relief, half with rejection. They couldn't win, you see. But Dad persuaded them that it would be better to accept the truth than go on making themselves believe … well, whatever they did believe. I don't know. They don't want to accept it, you see – Pip and Cally. About Cressida. They'd always wondered … but they never asked. They just didn't realise how dangerous it was to mix real life and fantasy like that, although of course, they all knew she made up stories. Lying, some would call it.'

'And Mawgan?'

'He's gone very quiet. He didn't want to speak to anyone, not even me. Just took himself off upstairs when Dad had gone and shut himself into the bedroom.'

'He can't blame himself.'

'No. I don't think he does, except for not doing anything about it when he realised how far she believed herself, but then, he did think it was Mandy Rushton behind it at first and later it was … well, too late. But I do think he blames his mum and dad … and so do I.'

'They should never have let her marry,' said Chel, thoughtfully.

'They thought he'd look after her. You can see their point. Nobody wants to admit their child is … different, I suppose.'

'And there's no chance it was something genetic,' said Chel. She spoke carefully, trying to make it a statement rather than a question, but Debbie shook her head with confidence.

'No chance. It was a sickly pregnancy, Cally nearly lost the baby twice, it was never right … and then a pretty horrific delivery. She just wasn't … they all knew she wasn't the same as the rest of them. Of course, there'll be all sorts of questions asked now, but it's rather late. The damage is done.'

'If Mike Stanley loved her – and I suppose he must have done, at least to begin with – surely he at least guessed the truth? He lived with her, undiluted.'

Debbie shrugged her shoulders.

'Maybe he found it charming, there are men who go for the helpless type. And maybe, while she was protected by her family, it *was* charming, their affection for her is genuine – which of course, makes it that much worse for them. Maybe she only came unstuck when she found herself having to live like the rest of us, on her own resources. He certainly doesn't seem to have tried to help her.'

Chel said, even more carefully than before,

'So what will they do now? Will they look for her?'

'Well, yes ... of course they will.' Debbie looked at her, strangely. 'You don't think they'll find her, do you?'

'No. Or not alive, anyway. Maybe not at all ...' Chel stopped speaking. Impossible to say to practical, clear-eyed Deb that Cressida Stanley had created a monster that had finally destroyed her, but the knowledge was there in the high-tech office, a weight on her spirits. She gave herself a shake, like a dog coming out of the water. She had to ask. 'So what's the position now? I was surprised, to be honest, when you said you were staying until today. We thought you'd be back on Friday.'

'Oh well,' said Debbie. She perched on the edge of Chel's desk and kicked her heels against the wood. 'Things changed somehow after Mawgan blew a fuse. It shook them all.'

'Made them stop and think, I daresay,' said Chel, wisely. 'He should have done it months back, if you ask me.' She paused there, but curiosity got the better of her. 'And Jerry? How did they all get on?'

'It was Dad who made Mawgan see that he must tell them all the truth,' said Debbie. 'I think he wasn't going to – but trying to fudge the issue was never going to help. Dad made him see that. It was queer ... after that, it was queer. Nobody seemed quite to know where they stood any more. As if someone had opened a window, and the light had shown them somewhere unexpected.'

Chel looked thoughtful, trying to imagine such a situation in her own family, and failing. It must have been equally incomprehensible to the Angwins: people like them, down to earth, practical people without an imaginative bone in their bodies wouldn't take kindly to being transported to La-la Land. That, of course, had been the problem all along. The practical explanation had to be the right one, she had never seen it so clearly. Debbie went on, hesitantly, trying to sort it out in her own mind as she went.

'When Dad came back downstairs, he went off with Pip and they shut themselves into the sitting-room. Nobody went near them, it was obvious something was up. Then Pip came and got Cally, and they were all in there, talk, talk, talk. We could hear Cally crying and the men comforting her. Kurt and I took the twins out into the garden to get them away from it all, and Allison and Anna shut themselves into the kitchen with the lunch. There was nothing any of us could do, but we hadn't a clue what it was all about and we were all on edge.

'Then lunch was very odd. Whatever they had been saying in there, they all came out friends. Dad managed to whisper to me that it was all going to be all right, but that was all, and to be truthful, I couldn't see how. Then Mawgan came down looking as if he was away on another planet and we all had a nice lunch together and talked about the wedding.' She looked at Chel, helplessly. 'People are truly weird. And it got weirder. When Dad had gone, Pip went off in his car and that was when Mawgan disappeared off upstairs again. I went to see if he was OK, but he said he just wanted to be quiet on his own. You can't argue with that, so we all took the twins out, and when we got back, there was Pip and Cally and Gran sitting around the teacups and it wasn't until then that they told us what it had all been about.'

Debbie then told her, too, one or two other things that had come out during that long, serious family discussion.

'The police were hard on Mawgan – very hard. Too hard. He said he'd done it, you see, and nobody realised that he was so deeply in shock, let alone why. And when he'd said it, they wouldn't let him unsay it. There was the evidence of those two girls. They bullied … and he wasn't sure that he *hadn't* done it, at least in one sense, and Cressida would only weep and have hysterics, and now nobody is quite sure what they were even about. Allison says she was totally incoherent.'

'And do they now accept that she was also totally away with the fairies? Because if they don't, nothing is ever going to get better – not for any of them.'

'I think they do.' Contradictorily, Debbie shook her head. 'They were stunned. Stunned to the point of not knowing which way was up – it wasn't until the twins came rushing in and saying they were hungry that anyone realised it was after seven o'clock. Then Cally went off to get some tea for everyone, and found that Mawgan had come down to the kitchen and already done it. Cooking is a sort of passion with him ... he said it helped put things into perspective. Macaroni cheese ... I never thought of it as therapeutic.'

'And did everyone eat it?' asked Chel, unable to stop herself.

'You bet we did! There's nothing like an afternoon of high drama to work up an appetite, we all found – and anyway, it was delicious. Far too good to waste. Comfort food – in every sense.'

They had needed comforting, that disrupted, kindly family. Chel said,

'And afterwards – did he disappear again? Mawgan?'

'No. He let his Gran kiss him goodbye as if she really cared about him after all, and then he went upstairs and sang *Paddy McGinty's Goat* to the twins when they were finally in bed, and accompanied himself on the guitar. Chel, he had sat up there tuning it during the afternoon – with itself, if you know what I mean, sort of occupational therapy – and when he brought it down later and did it properly with his dad's electronic organ, it was about a semitone out.' She looked at her sister-in-law, raised her eyes to the ceiling, shrugged her shoulders. 'Full of surprises, my man. He plays the trumpet too – but he left that behind, thank goodness. But the guitar came back with us. That and a load of other personal stuff he had left in his room at home when he went abroad.'

Chel looked at her levelly, thinking this out.

'Sounds like he's coming to terms with life as it has to be, then,' she said. 'Not before time. The barrenness of that flat when you first moved into it was scary stuff.'

'I know.' Debbie hesitated. 'Chel ... look, I know you're busy. But will you just listen a minute longer? If I tell you something that's going to sound ... well, silly?'

'Of course.'

'It's pretty obvious that Mawgan has had a pretty rotten time, one way or the other, the last few years, and when the pressure came off so unexpectedly ... well, it showed. His mum went into overcompensation-mode, and his dad wasn't much better. They insisted we stayed on, and it was a good idea – it made him ease up for a day or two. He slept a lot, in the daytime at least, and actually he looks a lot better for it. But it left me and Allison as company for each other, when Anna and Kurt & Co. left on Saturday, and she talked to me.'

'What about?' asked Chel, curiously, when Debbie stopped.

'Oh ... this and that. Their childhood and their friends, the things they did, filling in background, you know? But ... half the time, when she was talking about Mawgan, she didn't say *he* ... she said *they*. She didn't even know she was doing it, it came so easily ... *they* did this, *they* went there, *they*, all the time. *They.* As if ... well, as if there was more than one of him.'

'So? Didn't you ask her?'

'No. I found I didn't want to know the answer.' Debbie looked at Chel, half-apologetic, half asking some unspoken question. 'You see, I got the impression that he ran with a crowd ... that they were a gang of good mates over a long time ... and where are they? He *has* no friends of that kind. If he had, I would know by now.' She hesitated, watching Chel's face. 'I told you it was going to sound silly.'

Chel didn't think it was silly, she thought it was sad, if anything. Sad, and unnecessary. She said,

'On previous form, if they existed outside your imagination, he probably slammed the door on them himself.'

'You don't think they might have ... well, voted with their feet?'

'If they did, he's well rid of them.'

'And if they didn't?'

'They probably feel that they're well rid of him.'

'That was honest,' said Debbie, after a pause.

'Sauce for the goose, and all that.' Chel turned back to her computer. 'Look, I must get on, or my boss will catch me slacking. Don't fret about it Deb, take it a step at a time. And there's a ton of messages upstairs from Roger, he said you weren't answering his emails. I left them by your computer. About the Boat Show. Are you going?'

'We certainly are.'

'Mawgan too?' asked Chel, with interest.

'Don't know. Don't know if I shall be able to tear him away from the demolition of his restaurant.'

'He's surely going to let up a bit!'

'He says he closes in January in order to do maintenance work on the building.'

'He's going to drive you mad out in Tenerife.'

'I know.'

Chel opened a file and then paused, looking at it.

'Are you going back to St Austell before the wedding?'

'We're invited for lunch on his birthday, the last week in January, near enough.'

'So what's that – thirty-five?'

'Thirty-four. He's not that much older than Oliver after all. Not even a year.'

'Make him take you for a drink in a pub, then, and see who comes up to say hullo. Allison will no doubt be able to point you to the right pub.'

'I get the impression that even if she did, we wouldn't go there,' said Debbie.

'Sad,' said Chel, giving voice to her thoughts, but Debbie was already on her way to the door, to run upstairs to deal with her messages and resume her own affairs. In the doorway, however, she paused, looking back over her shoulder, and this time there was a laugh in her eyes.

'I didn't tell you the best bit.'

Chel's hands, hovering above her keyboard, paused. She looked suspiciously at her sister-in-law.

'What, then?'

'When his dad turns up on Friday to have a look at the restaurant job, he's going to bring one more thing on the truck ...'

'Oh, yes?'

'Mawgan bought it to get around on when he visited home from abroad. It's been in the barn where Allison is going to live.'

'And? I presume it isn't a horse.'

Debbie grinned, her expression suddenly sunnily free from care.

'*And* it's a bloody great big bike. A Kawasaki. Brilliant! A man with hidden depths, mine!' The door shut behind her. Chel looked at her monitor screen, and grinned as if it could share the joke.

'And there was me thinking he was Volvo-man – I *don't* think!'

All the same, she did wonder, and not for the first time, when all the defences came down just what would be found behind them? Trumpet playing, near-perfect pitch and big bikes were probably only the start.

Dot was going to hate it!

✵ ✵ ✵ ✵ ✵

Time moved on towards the wedding. New Year's Eve came and went. Jerry had an interesting time at Helen's party and liked her friends who regarded him with open speculation, and was allowed to kiss his hostess goodnight before he returned to the Black Bull, which was a great step forward and earned him a disturbed night. His children, two of them at least, had a riotous time at the Fish, and the third attended a party at the house of acquaintances of hers, friends of Tom's, where she didn't have quite such a good time. She wasn't sure why. Elaine was there, but she kept a circumspect distance. Even so, Susan felt an undercurrent, a vague feeling that people were looking at her, watching, and hiding smiles. She sensed sympathy and resented it. It could all have been her imagination.

'You could have at least looked as if you were enjoying yourself,' Tom told her, on the way home. He sat relaxed in the front passenger seat, it was Susan who had drawn the short straw.

'I thought I did,' said Susan, who had done her best. But nothing she could do was right for Tom at the moment. He laughed, not with amusement.

'You looked like a duchess, slumming,' he accused her. 'If my friends aren't good enough for you and your bloody mother, stay at home next time.'

'What's my mother got to do with it?' asked Susan, bewildered.

'Just look what she's doing to your poor sister!' Tom retorted. 'If Deb wants to commit social suicide, whose business is it but hers?'

'You've lost me,' said Susan. 'Are you trying to say that your friends are social suicide, or what?' There was more acerbity in the words than was probably wise.

'Of course not, but your sister's bit of rough trade certainly is!'

'I see,' said Susan. The uneasy evening, and Elaine's bright, pitying glances from time to time, and now Tom's confrontational attitude, suddenly made her angry. 'You're saying, are you, that I had better not ask my sister and her husband to any of our parties in case he lets the side down?'

'Well, come on! He's a bit of a disaster, wouldn't you say?' He used a phrase that Oliver had used in a similar context. 'Rough as rats, and probably doesn't even know how to use a knife and fork properly!'

'Don't be ridiculous! He runs a top-class restaurant.'

'He's a cook.'

'A chef.'

'Where's the difference?' Tom sneered.

Susan suddenly saw, perhaps for the first time, how some – not by any means all, but some – of her mother's friends, and also her own, might view Debbie's choice of a husband. The fleeting glimpse of her mother's point of view for some reason she didn't analyse, sent her own opinions swinging like a compass needle to the opposite pole. She had liked Mawgan, and he had been wonderful with the children – better by far than their own father. She said,

'I never knew you were such a crashing snob.'

'Not me, darling. You've seen how your mother likes it.' He paused, smiling, although in the dark inside the car she didn't see it. 'It'll bring the old cow down off her perch – if it happens.'

'Why shouldn't it happen?'

'Your mother will stop it, that's why. She's told everyone.'

'Don't hold your breath!' said Susan, furious. She added, belatedly, 'And don't call my mother an old cow.'

Tom laughed.

'If it comes off – if – there'll be people all over this town laughing themselves sick at the pair of you. How are the mighty fallen! First Oliver, and now Deb – my God, what a joke!'

Susan felt her flesh crawl on her arms. She didn't believe him, if there was anyone at all who felt like that it could only be one or two, but just suppose she was wrong? Suddenly, the wedding, to which she had been looking forward, assumed a different aspect. Not everyone had accepted the invitation; her father's friends and associates, Debbie's friends ... but her own and her mother's? Only one or two, although some of them had watched Deb grow up ...

'They're saying,' said Tom, still laughing, 'that Deb is getting married in Cornwall because your mother won't have him in the house.'

'My mother has never met him.' She took the war into the enemy's camp. '*You* have. You liked him. You said so.'

'I liked his pub,' said Tom, easily. 'That's where he belongs. Anyway, I'm only telling you what people are saying.'

Susan had been brought up to consider herself and her family as very definitely a cut above most, it had become ingrained into her over the years until she no longer consciously thought about it. Now, all of a sudden, she felt herself turning into somebody quite different. Somebody whose values, unconsciously learned from father, brother and sister, were totally in opposition to the assumptions of the years. She said, with suppressed venom,

'They'd better not say it to me!' She pushed the point home, with interest. 'You accepted his hospitality – you have no right to talk about him behind his back! It's *vulgar* to gossip behind people's backs if you won't say it to their faces – and I wouldn't advise it!'

'Oh, I wouldn't,' said Tom. 'I wouldn't dare! I don't want to end up in the morgue, believe me. And I mean that – *look out!*' He put a swift hand on the wheel, and Susan slapped it away. The oncoming car swerved back to its own side. 'Bloody drunken drivers! You think they'd learn!'

'Don't – ever – do that again, you patronising pig!' said Susan. She knew that she had let her concentration lapse, but it was the other driver who was mainly at fault. She found that she was breathing hard. Tom, relaxing again, gave another irritating snigger.

'You women drivers!' he said.

Happy New Year.

* * * * *

Now, the hangovers of New Year were but a memory. Debbie went up to the Boat Show, driven there by her partner-to-be Carl Colenso, and met her other partner, Roger Hickling, at Earl's Court, and the three of them spent two days on some useful research work, talked in the right places, placed an order for three new Wayfarers and collected a selection of brochures for the second yacht they intended to buy for instruction purposes, the latter to be talked over and a decision made at leisure. Meanwhile, Mawgan and his father and his men set to work stripping out the dismantled restaurant to see what they could find behind the walls and ceiling panels. Old beams, Mawgan told Debbie, delightedly, on her return from London. Really grotty plasterwork, it had probably been cheaper to wall them up, but no dry rot, very little worm. Nothing that couldn't be restored and renewed. Debbie, walking into the devastated space, looked with interest at the exposed walls.

'Goodness!' she said.

'It was complete vandalism!' said Mawgan, leading her round and pointing out the hidden beauties of the old woodwork. 'Look at that – look at those – beautiful old wood!'

Debbie looked at him quickly, his enthusiasm for antique beams surprised her. Perhaps he was more of a builder than he had thought?

'Has Oliver seen it yet?' she asked, curiously.

'Certainly has. Came up with some good ideas, too.'

Pip came tramping towards them through the rubble on the floor, hard hat in place and a big grin on his face.

'Debbie!' He enfolded her in a dusty hug. 'Good to see you, girl! What d'you think?'

'I think,' said Debbie, 'that if it was mine, I'd be wishing I hadn't started!'

'You just wait and see,' Pip told her.

Susan came down for a midweek visit, on her own, while the children were at school. Tom had refused to take another weekend, so it seemed to her the best option although the children had been desperately disappointed. She admired the beams and discussed the details of the wedding with her customary good sense, but Debbie thought she seemed unlike her usual self. She asked once if there was anything wrong, but Susan said no, there wasn't. It was just SAD syndrome, or something. They hadn't seen the sun for what felt like weeks, had they? Debbie didn't believe her, but didn't push it. Susan came with her for a fitting of her wedding dress, chosen in Truro with the help of Chel and Cally, and approved its classic simplicity. The bridesmaid's dresses, in a cool sea green, also met with her approval. Anyone could wear that colour, she agreed. Good choice. Details for the reception were finalised, Susan promised to give final numbers a week before the wedding … and suddenly, that wasn't so far away. Less than a month, said Debbie, suddenly quietening down.

'Not having second thoughts?' asked Susan, looking at her.

'No, of course not. It's just … I suppose it's always a big step.'

Was it? Susan tried to remember how she had felt before her own wedding, but she had been a lot younger than Debbie – in every way, now she came to think about it. And unlike Debbie, she hadn't been deeply committed. She felt envy, like a worm in an apple, nibbling at her heart and turned her face away.

What am I? Who am I? *Why* am I?

'Suse?' asked Debbie.

Susan pulled herself together.

'Sorry. Goose walked over my grave.' She smiled. Debbie gave a sigh of pure satisfaction.

'No time for that! Tell it to go away. Oh Suse, I never thought that life could be so … so *full!*'

Susan said, to hide another nibble from the worm,

'Come on Deb, down from the clouds and concentrate. Have you got the ushers sorted out? Your two sidekicks, you said, but that's not enough. You need at least two more.'

'Kurt – Mawgan's brother-in-law – and Keith, he's Dad's cousin's son-in-law. It's so strange, having Nankervis relatives instead of just Grannie's family.'

Another nip. Susan stood up briskly, there was no reason to do so, but she felt the need to make some statement of intent, even if she had no idea of what intent she was making a statement.

'Well, so long as it's all arranged. Cup of tea?' She turned away, so that Debbie shouldn't see her face, and Debbie got to her feet too, slightly perturbed but unsure of exactly why.

'No. We need something stronger. Mawgan's on the bar tonight, let's go down and have a drink and annoy him. Get tiddly and have a sisterly giggle together.'

'Fine,' said Susan. She had never had a *giggle* with her sister before, she thought confusedly as she followed her downstairs. Not sisterly or any other kind, giggling had never been on her agenda. Perhaps it should have been. Perhaps, as Tom had unkindly implied, she was uptight and stuck-up. Oliver had certainly thought so for most of his life, and made it very clear.

But I'm not, Susan thought, on the brink of an uncomfortable admission. I just don't know what people expect of me. I try to be good and everyone despises me ... well, not everyone, but the people I want to like me. Oliver, and Debbie, and Dad.

My children love me. I think they do. My husband doesn't. Maria criticises me, she thinks I'm useless as a mother. Perhaps I am.

Debbie had paused at the door to the snug, that gave access to the bars without going outside. She turned round to see if Susan was still with her, and caught an expression on her sister's face that made her reach out, impulsively.

'Suse, there *is* something wrong, I know it! Why won't you tell me? It's not Mum is it, she's not been getting at you again?'

Susan put her hand on the door of the snug and pushed it open.

'No, of course she hasn't. Come on – let's get at that drink!'

'No *of course* about it,' Debbie muttered, but she followed her sister obediently through the door. The two things, the closeness of her wedding and her mother's intractable attitude came together in her head and suddenly made her scared.

Dot never gave in. And time was running out.

Susan was right, bring on the alcohol!

The feeling of insecurity remained.

* * * * *

Dot had received a report from Andy Simpson in the new year that had certainly not pleased her. Deborah's Disaster, as she had taken to calling him to those of her intimates who listened to her, was, on paper at least, unassailable. She didn't believe a word of it. He was a consummate conman, she would give him that, but that was as far as she would go. His armour appeared to have no chink into which she could insert a lever with which to move his world, but that couldn't possibly be true. Everyone had a chink somewhere, and Dot, reading the unwelcome report, had a very good idea where to look. She was still sure the answer had to be money, still completely unaware that she had been looking in entirely the wrong place.

Money. It all came down to money in the end. Debbie had money, the Disaster had none. He was in debt – mortgages were debt, and he had two of them. Everyone agreed he had charm, the best conmen always did, that was exactly why they got away with things. Charm was a useful commodity in the profession of a confidence trickster, but only an illusion in the end.

There was only one option left, one weapon to her hand. It went against the grain, it was playing into his hands, it was sinking to his level, but it would save Deborah from a lifetime of misery and regret. Nobody could say that she didn't love her daughter, or care for her future, that was what all this fuss was about surely. She genuinely regretted the rift between them, ached with it sometimes, if anyone would believe her; certainly wished that things could be otherwise. She wanted her daughter back more than anything. Therefore, she would pick up her ultimate weapon and use it, and the final victory, as she had always known, would be hers.

Deborah would live to thank her. She was comfortably sure of it. It never even entered her head either that things could never be the same between her and Debbie afterwards, or that the daughter she professed to love so much, like the man whom she had once claimed to love, would by her actions suffer irreparable loss.

XVII

Once events start rolling in a certain direction, they can seem to develop momentum on their own, and the oddest threads start to appear in the pattern. Who would have imagined, for instance, that Mawgan's new-found predilection for driving Debbie's car – a sparkling new Golf GTI in a conspicuous shade of yellow – over his own battered but practical Volvo workhorse would have turned out to be of any significance at all in the overall design?

On this one particular cold January morning, the morning of Mawgan's thirty-fourth birthday, Debbie and Mawgan drove as promised to St Austell. They had more than one end in mind by this time, Debbie's planning permission had at last come through, and she wanted to talk the plans over with Pip and his father Garfie, whose building firm would be undertaking the work alongside the renovation of the restaurant – the latter would need to keep precedence, but it was progressing nicely, and the two jobs could overlap quite happily, particularly in the early stages. It was also necessary to discuss costs and the probable time-scale, so that Debbie, Roger and Carl could make their plans accordingly, and it seemed sensible to do this while they were heading that way anyway. Since Tommy had taken his mother on an excursion to Florida on holiday, Chel had agreed to take over the bar that evening, so there was no hurry to get back. It looked like a leisurely day out with the Angwin family, but nothing is ever that simple.

It was on the way there, right in the middle of St Austell on a Saturday morning, that it happened. They had stopped at traffic lights, in the outer lane to go straight ahead, the inner lane being for those turning left, about three cars back in the waiting line. It was the brilliant daffodil yellow of the car that first caught the eye of a group, two men and two women, strolling along the pavement from the opposite direction. Debbie, used to the often rude remarks of other people on the colour of her car, could amost have written the script for them – *Hey, get an eyeful of that, will you! Doesn't mean to be missed, does she?* – or on this particular morning, *he*. Only this time, it was slightly different. One of the women stopped in her tracks, dragging at her partner and pointing, and all four of them stopped and began to behave in the most extraordinary way, jumping up and down, waving their arms and yelling. Debbie said,

'Do you know those people on the pavement, by any chance?' and Mawgan, who had been watching the lights, took a swift look and said,

'*Shit!*' just as the lights changed and the traffic began to move again. '*Bugger!*' he added, slammed the car into gear and stalled the engine. The breathing space gave Debbie time to say,

'I think they want to talk to you.' Mawgan didn't habitually swear. His reaction had been so strong, so unexpected, she almost hadn't said it at all.

'Well, I can't do anything about it now,' snapped Mawgan, getting angry. 'Oh *hell!* There's a pub somewhere round the corner, yell as we go past – ' It was so unlike him to swear, certainly three times in a row, that Debbie didn't even argue. She wound down the window and stuck her arm out, pointing, as they moved forward, yelling,

'*Pub!*' at the top of her voice. She wasn't sure they could have heard, but they had certainly got the message. Three of them began to run, then one of the men slowed down to wait for the last woman, heavily pregnant, to catch up while the other two sped ahead. 'You're in the wrong lane,' said Debbie, unwisely.

'I know that!' Mawgan signalled to pull across to the accompaniment of the blast of several horns behind him. He swore again, under his breath, and took the left turn with less style than usual, disrupting both lanes and passing the second couple as they went. The man saluted to Debbie as they passed and gave a thumbs-up sign, but as she wound the window back up, she thought she wouldn't ask Mawgan who they were. The memory of her Christmas conversation with Allison slipped into her mind and stuck there. She held her peace.

They reached the pub first, of course, it was further than Debbie had expected, and turned into the car park. Mawgan pulled into a parking space and switched off the engine. He had had a little space in which to pull himself together, and had almost succeeded.

'Sorry,' he said.

'Nobody hit us,' said Debbie, although it had been close. Now that they were stationary, she asked, curiously, 'Who are they – those people?'

Mawgan rubbed his hands across his face, as if he was trying to rub something away, but before he could frame a reply, the first pair burst round the corner into the car park, breathless and laughing, and he shrugged his shoulders and opened the car door.

'You're just about to find out,' he said.

Debbie got out more slowly, emerging from the car just as the woman, arriving a few steps in front, launched herself straight into Mawgan's arms and hugged him, kissing his cheek with every appearance of delight.

'Mug! What a brilliant surprise, we thought we were never going to see you again!'

Who? Debbie blinked. The man, arriving more temperately, said,

'We've a very large bone to pick with you, my friend, but it's good to see you anyway!' and slapped Mawgan on the upper arm with enough force to hurt. He winced, but didn't retaliate as Debbie might have expected, in fact he bore all the appearance of someone caught at a disadvantage. The man now turned his attention to Debbie.

'And who's this, you dark horse, you? Not that we ha'n't heard rumours, of course.' He gave Mawgan a severe look. 'Wondering where our invitations had got to, we were.'

'Robbie – give over a moment.' Mawgan looked suddenly tired. 'This is Debbie Nankervis, and as you obviously already know, she's fool enough to marry me. Deb, meet Robbie Pascoe and Molly, who's an ever bigger fool because she married *him*.'

Molly said, with a challenge in her voice,

'We go back years, we were all at school together.' She added, with a swift look at Debbie. 'He was best man at our wedding, he's godfather to our son, would you believe it? And Nicky wouldn't know him now if they met in the street!'

'Moll – please,' said Mawgan. Robbie opened his mouth, but then caught Debbie's eye as she shook her head at him, mouthing the word, *don't*. He raised his eyebrows, but said,

'That'll do, Moll. It's blurry cold out here, shall we go indoors and have a drink on it? Kev and Charlie will find us OK, they'll be here dreckly.' He led the way to the door into the bar without waiting for a reply. Molly linked her arm through Mawgan's and took him with her, almost as if she was afraid he might get away, and Debbie followed on behind.

Finding a table wasn't hard, the bar was almost empty. While Mawgan and Robbie got the drinks in and wrangled over who should pay, Molly and Debbie sat down and looked at each other, cautiously.

'You must think we're all mad,' said Molly.

Debbie didn't think that at all. What she thought was that this was just another manifestation of the havoc that Cressida Stanley had wrought in her brother's life, and she was curious to see where it would lead.

'You were all close friends, weren't you?' she said. Best find out, before the others arrived and the whole thing ran away with her, she might never catch up otherwise, and from Molly's greeting, if nothing else, it was a fair guess. Molly said,

'Robbie and Kev and Mug were like those three musketeers – right from the start, when they was all at primary school, then on to the comp. Scrumping apples first, then on to swapping girlfriends, smoking behind the bus stop, underage drinking, all the rest of it … always in trouble together, always bailing each other out – only …'

'Only, in the end, it wasn't possible to bail Mawgan out?' said Debbie, and tried not to sound bitter.

'Something like that.' Molly looked at her, quietly.

'So, where did you come in?' asked Debbie, when she had found her voice again.

'I was in the year behind. Hanging round the bus stop hoping to be noticed, we all did. All us girls, well, you know how it is? They were brilliant, all three of them – Robbie all big and tall and fair and and a great sports hero, and Kev so romantic looking, thin and dark and handsome, and really clever, and Mug lived up to his name, he weren't no oil painting, but he was wicked fun. He's gone a bit stuggy now, though, hasn't he?'

'Stuggy?' Debbie queried. It was a wonderful word, but she had no idea what it meant. Molly grinned.

'Solid. Broadened out. Mind, it's no surprise, his dad's the same, and his grandad, but you know that, of course.' Her eyes took on a far-away, reminiscent look. 'Our mum used to say he had a face like the sort of monkey you wouldn't want to keep as a pet around the house.'

Debbie smothered a laugh. She looked at Molly speculatively, it occurred to her that here might be a source of information to fill in a number of yawning gaps in the record.

'I suppose you knew them all – Anna and Allison, and so on?' She couldn't quite bring herself to name Cressida and Mike Stanley, but Molly was bright. She gave Debbie a sympathetic look.

'Anna was two years ahead, almost a grown-up, and Allison a year behind, just a kid. Charlie could tell you more about Cress, they were the same year but I can tell you for free, she didn't think much to her! Mike Stanley was my year, we went around together for a while. He was all right, nothing to shout about. Most of the time. Bit of a hanger-on, fancied himself one of the Gang. Good looking, if you think that kind of thing's important.'

'Ouch! That was a bit damning,' said Debbie. She hesitated, but then decided to say it anyway. 'And what about the rest of the time?'

Molly shrugged her shoulders.

'He had a jealous streak, wide as the A30. Lost his cool if I so much as had a joke with the boys. You've got to be a lot of fun for people to stand that for long. And he was one of those, he couldn't never be wrong. If you caught him wrong-footed, it was always because of something *you*'d done. I stood it for a bit, then I moved on.'

Debbie sat very still. Two more pieces of the jigsaw slotted easily into place. Mike Stanley wouldn't be in the wrong. When he found himself another woman, it was because Cressida had another man ... and if the only candidate was her own brother, that would do. And in a bizarre twist of events, he had been almost right. Had he really known? For his sake, Debbie hoped not while fearing the opposite, for surely he must have to be so spiteful.

Before Molly had time to notice her silence, Mawgan and Robbie arrived with the drinks. As he pulled out a chair to sit down, Robbie said,

'And what part of Cornwall do you come from, Debbie Nankervis? Are you a St Erbyn girl?'

'She doesn't, she's a horrible emmet,' said Mawgan, instantly.

'With a name like that? Never!'

'My father's family come from down in West Penwith,' said Debbie. 'I'd never met them before this Christmas, although my brother had. I'm afraid that rather puts me beyond the pale, I was born in Dorset.'

'Never mind, my bird, it's still almost the west country,' said Robbie, consolingly. 'We'll soon make a proper Cornish maid of you.'

'Time's running out on that one,' said Molly. There was a brief silence, into which she added,

'We were just talking about the old days.'

'She said you'd gone stuggy,' said Debbie, to Mawgan, and he laughed, ruefully.

'Runs in the family, Moll, and the job doesn't help.'

'Should've stuck to the day job,' said Robbie, and grinned.

'Did it surprise you, when he chucked building and went off to be a chef?' asked Debbie, curiously. She had no idea why these two, on the whole rather pleasant, people were no longer on Mawgan's Christmas card list, although she could take a guess, and she didn't want anyone to ask. It was necessary, therefore, to keep the conversation rolling or the subject would inevitably come up.

'Not so much as it surprised his dad,' said Robbie, grinning even more broadly.He took a substantial gulp at his pint, reflectively. 'He was always handy around the kitchen. More like a girl, we used to tell him. Blame it on his Gran, she was the sort teaches a kid to make gingerbread men in the cradle.'

'You might as well, the family does,' said Mawgan.

The occasion might have then turned into a harmless game of 'Do you remember?', had not Kev and Charlie, arriving belatedly as predicted, pushed through the outside door at that moment. Kev was made of a different metal from the amiable Robbie, and he, it became clear very soon, wanted answers. Stopping only briefly to get drinks from the bar, he headed across the room towards them, Charlie at his heels. He placed the two glasses on the table, and leaned forward on his hands.

'Well, good morning, Mr Angwin! And where have you been all this time?' He then smiled at Debbie. 'Kevin Rickard.'

He held out a hand, and Debbie took it and had her own firmly grasped. 'Pleased to meet you. This is my wife, Charlie.' He raised his eyebrows, and Debbie said, as Mawgan didn't introduce her this time,

'Debbie Nankervis. Hullo.' She smiled at Charlie, who smiled back. Charlie was much her own age, the other three all older. It must have made a bond, for Charlie slipped onto the bench beside her, with a friendly smile.

'Hi.'

Kevin Rickard didn't immediately sit down. He picked up his pint and stood for a moment, looking down at Mawgan. He spoke slowly, as if he had been choosing his words with care and wanted to give them weight.

'I can see why you might not have wanted us to come visiting, but you could have written. We did.'

Mawgan looked up, meeting his eyes squarely but saying nothing, and Kev went on.

'We were supposed to be 'best friends' the three of us, I thought. Known for it, in fact, over a long time. Even ordinary friends stick by each other, I always supposed.'

'It just seemed easier.' Mawgan shrugged. 'What was there to say, anyway?'

'Quite a lot, actually,' said Molly, taking a hand. 'Like, thank you for sticking by me, how's my godson? Things like that.'

Mawgan got to his feet.

'Come on, Deb. We should be getting on.'

Kev caught at his arm.

'Oh no, you don't, you bastard!' he said.

Nobody moved for a minute, not even Debbie, then Kev slowly dropped his hand.

'Sorry. You want to go, you go. But as an alternative, you could trust us. We never believed all that crap anyway. Your sister Cressida was way out of order, and anyone said different, he ended up spitting teeth.' Mawgan said nothing, and Robbie said, quietly,

'That's true, and no need to go punishing yourself, neither. We aren't the only ones, and that you can believe, too.'

Mawgan slowly sat down again, and this time, Kev sat, too.

'If your family had stayed around, you'd have known,' said Molly. 'It was only a few, and stupid Cress playing to the gallery, having hysterics all over the place – it blew over. There's nobody I know as isn't glad to see your mum and dad back home, and those that aren't, don't matter.'

Kev said, rancorously,

'We'd have come looking for you, when you got out, if we'd thought you wanted us. You made it clear you didn't. That was your choice. Not ours. Remember that.'

'It wasn't that – ' said Mawgan, and stopped.

'Then what the fucking hell *was* it?' shouted Kev, so loudly that he made the others jump.

'Work it out for yourself!' snapped Mawgan.

It was Debbie who stood up this time. She jerked her head towards the door.

'You, Kev, or whatever your name is. Come for a walk in the car park.' She moved away without waiting to see if he'd follow, and after a startled moment, he picked up her drink and his own and followed, leaving the remaining four in an uncomfortable silence.

Outside in the car park, Kev found Debbie leaning against the wall, waiting for him.

'So, what's all this about?' He raised his eyebrows. 'Sounded a bit like pistols at dawn back there. Here.' He handed her the glass. Debbie took it, but didn't drink. She wasn't yet ready to drink with Kevin Rickard.

'Ease up, will you? What did you think you were doing in there? You can't have a showdown in public, not unless you want to end up with an undignified scene! How do you think he feels? Use your imagination – or perhaps you haven't any?' Debbie could be rancorous, too.

Kev frowned at her for a moment, before saying,

'Mug was always tougher than that.'

'He still is, over most things. But not over that, it was too humiliating. And undeserved. And complicated. You do realise that the whole thing was an accident anyway?'

'*Was* it?' Kev stared at her. He narrowed his eyes at her. 'Drink with me, Debbie Nankervis. I think we're going to be friends.'

'Don't bet on it!'

'I'd stake my mortgage, and that's a hefty sum!' He held out his glass, temptingly, and after a moment she clinked her own against it and drank.

'But I still haven't forgiven you, wading in like that with all guns firing.'

Kev leaned against the wall beside her.

'So tell me. Having a funny five minutes, is he, our Mug? I thought he looked a bit strung out.'

Debbie said,

'Since he came out of prison – seriously depressed, should you be interested – just over eighteen months ago, he's had at least three potentially fatal accidents and ended up in hospital twice. Does that answer your question?'

'A not-so-funny ten minutes, then.' He drank, pensively. 'Depression, eh? Well, poor old Mug. But he could have come to us. We never listened to that stupid sister of his anyway.'

'He didn't know that.'

'Well, he should've. Silly bugger!' Kev sounded angry. Debbie said,

'Don't take it personally. She loused things up so much for him, he seems to have decided to deal with everyone by either ignoring them, or if that wasn't possible, pretending that nothing had happened. It isn't just you, it was the same in St Erbyn.'

'Mug by name, and mug by nature,' Kev observed.

'He'd just as soon nobody mentioned the word *prison* to him ever again.'

'I can see that. Uh-oh – ' He broke off. 'Here he comes now. I will be good, I promise.'

'You'd better,' Debbie muttered, and then Mawgan was with them.

'Sorry, mate,' said Kev, instantly. 'I wasn't trying to pick a fight.' He put his arm round Debbie, giving her a brotherly hug. 'Deb here has just been tearing me off a strip. I think we were about to kiss and make up, but you've gone and spoiled it now.'

'Well, fine, but it's time we were moving on.'

'No it isn't.' Debbie came to a sudden decision. She planted a kiss on Kev's cheek and disentangled herself from his arm. 'There! It's time we went back inside and bought another round. I want to get to know your friends.'

'Good girl!' said Kev. He put a hand on Mawgan's shoulder and turned him round. 'Time to dig the dirt, my friend. I bet she doesn't know the half of it!' He gave him a shove. 'Move along, there!'

When the three of them came back in together, the others looked astounded. They had had their heads together, Debbie had noticed as they came back through the door, and appeared to be on the verge of quarrelling. They sat back when Kev, Mawgan and Debbie rejoined them and looked embarrassed.

'Right,' said Kev, sweeping the empties into a cluster in front of him. 'We've changed the rules. We've declared a moratorium on the last three or four years, and we don't want to talk about them. But before, and after, that's open season. Who wants what?' He gathered up the glasses, three in each hand, and waited for replies.

Debbie wondered if he knew the exact meaning of the word *moratorium*, or if Mawgan did, come to that, it was a word often carelessly used. She held her peace.

Mawgan, since he was already standing, went with Kev to the bar to bring back the fresh round, and Debbie slipped in beside Charlie again. Charlie budged up to make room for her, giving the table a push to make space.

'Anyone would think this was twins, at least,' she grumbled.

'Quads,' said Robbie, grinning, but Debbie noticed that he gave the table a further tug in his direction.

'When's it due?' Debbie asked, and added, because the next step was obvious, 'Not at the beginning of February, I hope.'

'That's when the Big Day is, is it?' asked Molly, smiling at her. 'Is it a date that's going to make any difference to us?'

'I should hope so!' Debbie smiled back. 'For heaven's sake, you don't have crises like that over people who don't matter!'

'What a wise girl you are,' said Robbie. 'Mug's a lucky man.'

'Why *Mug*?' asked Debbie. 'He's no beauty, of course, but it seems a bit harsh.'

'He's grown into his looks, well, as far as he could he has, but he was like something off of a church gutter as a small boy,' Molly explained. 'We'll show you some photos, if you'd like to see them.'

'Maybe that's where the word *guttersnipe* came from,' Charlie speculated.

'I'd love to see some photos,' said Debbie. The group was relaxing, the first, dangerous step safely behind them. They were happy to bring out all sorts of scandalous tales for Debbie to laugh over, extending her knowledge of the man she had agreed to marry into a wider landscape. Charlie, so much the younger, had little to contribute, but the tales were obviously familiar, and that in itself was interesting. They must have often talked about their absent friend. Missing him, Debbie concluded, and if Chel was wrong and Cressida wasn't already dead, she would be happy to wring her stupid little neck for her!

'Remember Riley Craddock?' asked Molly, at one point, and Mawgan said,

'Must we?' while Robbie and Kev guffawed with laughter. Molly turned to Debbie.

'She was American, over here 'doing' Europe, you know like they do? In the space of one summer, she had all three of them.'

'Excuse *me*!' said Kev, indignantly, but Robbie looked sheepish. Mawgan looked at Debbie enigmatically and made no comment.

'She was a right little goer, she was,' said Robbie reminiscently, and Molly dug her elbow into his ribs before continuing.

'We girls hated her of course, she was all slender and slinky and sophisticated. Horrible!And moving in on our territory, too! Anyway, after she'd worked through Kev and Robbie, she went for the hat trick – Mug took her out a couple of times, but then he said she had to go.'

'She did, too,' said Mawgan, with feeling. 'Most expensive girl in Cornwall, she was, and me only an underpaid apprentice.'

'So what did you do?' asked Debbie, with interest.

'He had a motor bike,' said Molly, before anyone else could reply. 'An old Harley, it was, all noise and smoke, but she fancied herself riding on the back. Got to be better than Robbie's pushbike, and Kev was still catching the bus. But then, he always was a cut above the rest of us, Mug, soon's his family moved off of the estate.'

'I hope you're not using that old bike to make your point,' said Robbie, grinning. ''orrible old thing, that was!'

'Not as 'orrible as Dad's old truck,' said Mawgan, with retrospective satisfaction. 'Mind you, you've to hand it to her,

416

she took it on the chin.' He turned to Debbie, grinning. 'We was all going to a dance, and there she was, all dressed up to the nines, when this dirty old heap of scrap turns up to pick her up. At least the old bike was clean – *ish*, anyway.'

'White trousers, she had on, as I remember,' said Kev, reminiscently. 'Well, they was white when she started out. She never went out with him no more.' He paused. 'What'd been in that old truck then, Mug? I never asked. Never liked to, be honest.'

Mawgan laughed.

'Don't remember, but it didn't come off easy. She made me pay to get her stuff cleaned, but it was worth every penny.'

'Oh well,' said Molly, carelessly. 'I'm sure her mum had warned her not to play in the gutter, she should've listened. She was some posh, not our sort at all.' She looked at Debbie, apologetically. 'Not that there's anything *wrong* with posh.'

'Well gee, thanks,' said Debbie. They exchanged a smile. Debbie said, 'Actually, I think I've seen her photograph – he had it in his bedroom at home.'

The others hooted, and Mawgan said, with assumed dignity,

'That was a picture of the bike, not her. And it was my mum, not me, as left it there.'

Debbie grinned at him.

'Forgiveness'll cost you.'

'Later on,' said Mawgan, and returned the grin.

'Remember the fair?' Robbie interrupted. 'That was Riley too – that was in Kev's turn – ' They were off again, talking over each other, contradicting each other, not so much strolling down Memory Lane as running full pelt, shouting and pushing each other. Finally,

'Wonder what became of her?' Kev mused.

'No good, I wouldn't wonder, if she went on the way she started,' said Mawgan. There was something in the curve of his smile that set Debbie wondering, but it was old history and no business of hers. She contented herself with saying,

'I should laugh if she turns up in your restaurant one day, posher than ever and married to a millionaire, and comes nose to nose with *you*!'

'At least her third millionaire, by this time,' said Kev. 'And talking of marrying …'

A sudden hush fell on the company. Mawgan broke it.

'Well, that shut everyone up. Noon, second Saturday in February, the Anglican church at St Erbyn. You'll all be there, kids too, we hope. Don't we Deb?'

'Shan't do it without you,' said Debbie, firmly. 'And there's a party in the evening, at the Fish. We want you there, too. *And* for the lunchtime reception, although Susan'll do her nut when we upset her table arrangements.'

Kev twisted his glass round and round, watching the liquid swirling inside it.

'Had an arrangement ourselves, we three,' he said. 'Robbie got married, he had to toss up which of us was best man, so we decided it should go alphabetical – Angwin for Pascoe, Pascoe for Rickard, Rickard for Angwin. Guess by this time, my job's taken?'

''fraid so.' Mawgan said. 'Never thought this was going to happen … but you damn well better be around when we have a christening.'

'Just glad to know you've one good friend left, is all,' said Kev, and sounded as if he meant it. Robbie picked up his empty glass.

'Another one, everyone?'

'Shouldn't.' Mawgan glanced at his watch. 'And I'm driving, too.'

'Another one won't hurt you, and we've got a lot of drinking to catch up on.'

'Oh, go on then – but only a half, thanks. This can't turn into a session, we're expected for lunch.'

Robbie went off to the bar, and Charlie turned to Debbie.

'You and me, we can't play this memory game, shame isn't it?'

'Instructive to listen to,' said Debbie.

'You can say that again.' She looked sideways along the table. 'I saw Mug around of course, when I was a kid, but I was so much younger than them. I never met him properly until now. Never thought I'd end up marrying Kev, neither. You don't, do you?'

'Have you been married to him long?' Debbie asked.

'Near enough two years. I reckon he'd have dragged Mug to the wedding by the scruff of his neck, if he hadn't been still inside, and no argument about it. Might have been a good thing.' She paused, and looked down at her hands. 'Kev proposed a toast to *absent friends*, and you could see what he was thinking – in fact, I thought he was only just not crying, but maybe I imagined that, there'd been a fair bit of drink going the rounds by then. Still – that was then.'

'Molly said you were at school with Cressida.' Debbie didn't make it a question, but Charlie took it up as she had hoped.

'Daddy's little princess? Yes, I was.' There was scorn in her voice.

'What was she like?'

'I thought she was awful, but they three – ' she jerked her head towards Kev and Mawgan, and by inference, the still absent Robbie '- they was still a legend, you know? So, she was Mug's little sister, although they was all long gone of course – Mug gone abroad, by then, even – and she was quite popular because of that. But she was a pain, just the same.'

'In any particular way?' queried Debbie.

'Spoilt brat. Spiteful, too, if she didn't get her own way. But she could smile like the sun coming out – as I see he can, too, now he's begun to ease up – and she was some pretty. She got away with murder.' She winced. 'Sorry. Didn't mean that.'

'Was she bright? The other three are.'

'Reckon she was standing behind the door when that was given out,' said Charlie, dismissively. 'Got away with that too, though – everybody's pet, she was.' She gave a snort of derision. 'Silly little witch! She told lies, too – made things up as she went along, like there was no tomorrow!'

'You didn't like her,' diagnosed Debbie, and they exchanged a grin.

'You could say that. Waste of good space, she was.'

Interesting, but not that much of a surprise. Debbie sat back then and listened to the conversation, bubbling around them again now Robbie had returned with the fresh round balanced on a tray. She had never, she realised, seen Mawgan so relaxed and animated since she had known him, nor heard him reverting so resoundingly to his roots; she could only understand about half of what they were all saying. Her mother would have a fit at the company she was keeping today, and yet she felt at home, at ease with them all. They were real friends, their pleasure at making contact at last with their missing partner-in-crime as transparent as water. She thought about what Charlie had told her about *absent friends*. She could believe it of Kev. They were all very close, that was obvious, but in any group of three there will be inequality. Big, fair, amiable Robbie was the odd one here.

Stupid little bitch, Cress!

When Kev called another round, it had to be time to go, although Debbie, and she thought Mawgan too, would have been happy to stay. But his family would already be wondering where they had got to, and all six of them piled out into the cold January air to speed Debbie and Mawgan on their way. It was too much to hope that the yellow car would escape comment.

'What d'you call this, then?' Robbie asked, banging its roof. 'Real posemobile you've got here, mate! Spotted it a mile off, but never thought it would be you! Not your colour, I'd've thought.'

'It's mine,' said Debbie. 'What's the matter, don't you like it?' She opened the nearside door and prepared to get in. Kev was there, holding it ready to close after her. He grinned at her.

'Like to be seen, do you, Deb Nankervis?' He looked at the black and yellow leather seats and blinked. 'Regular wasps' nest, isn't it?'

'Be grateful,' said Molly, pertinently. 'If it'd've been dark blue, or black, we'd never've looked twice.'

'True. Yellow is good, if you look at it like that.' Kev shut the door and looked over the top of the car at Mawgan, just about to get in. 'You go careful, mate. No more accidents.'

They were all standing there, waving frantically, as the yellow car turned onto the road again.

For a while, they drove in silence, then Debbie said, reflectively,

'Mug ... I like it.'

'Just don't tell me it fits me. I know what you're thinking.'

'No, you don't. I was thinking how nice they all were, and that that was probably why ... but you aren't contagious, you know. You wouldn't have contaminated Molly and Robbie's kids. And you can hurt your friends.'

'I know, I *know*!'

Debbie sat back in her seat then and held her peace. There was no point in starting an argument while they were driving along, two and a half pints was quite enough, although he was probably still just about under the limit. Even now, with his sentence at an end, he couldn't afford not to be. Any more, though, and she'd be the one driving home.

Just as they were turning into the road through the estate, Mawgan said, unexpectedly,

'I'll tell you something, bird, because you deserve it. This morning is the first time for ages that I've felt as I might be a proper human being again one day.'

Debbie was so taken aback by this that, before she could find a reply, they were driving into the builders' yard and the moment was gone.

They were nearly late for lunch. Cally came bustling anxiously out of the kitchen as soon as she heard the front door open.

'So there you are! We were beginning to think something had happened to you.'

'You could say it did. We ran into Robbie and Kev,' said Mawgan, throwing the line away like a pro as he gave his mother a quick kiss. Debbie had often heard the phrase *double take*, but she had never seen one before. Cally said, weakly,

'Well, that explains it, I suppose ...'

Allison appeared in the kitchen door. She was smiling broadly.

'It always did before, I don't see why anything should have changed. How are they?'

'I don't know. They looked fine to me.'

'Mmm.' Allison exchanged a look with Debbie, raised her eyes to the ceiling. 'Now you *are* here at last, I'm going to dish up. Can you find Dad, he was in the office talking on the phone last time we checked.'

Mawgan went off to do this errand, and Debbie went into the kitchen with Allison and Cally.

'Can I do anything?'

Allison picked up the carving knife and hefted it in her hand.

'I shouldn't have sent him away. Oh well.' She set about the leg of lamb with more enthusiasm than skill. 'You can pass me that pile of plates. We're not waiting for him to come back, I'll pass out from starvation.'

'I'm sorry,' said Debbie, fetching the plates. 'We did try to get away once or twice, but ...'

'You don't need to tell us, we've been there before,' said Allison. She flipped a slightly ragged slice onto the top plate. 'Tell us, before we say the wrong thing – are we allowed to talk about it, or is it another dead end?'

'Didn't look like a dead end to me.' Debbie set the top plate aside and held out the next one. Cally, busy with the vegetables, was listening, she could see. She went on, 'It got off to a sticky start – well, you can imagine, can't you? – but it soon degenerated into a serious do-you-remember session, and I think, it cleared a bit of space.'

'Room to manoeuvre now, you mean?' said Allison. 'Well, jolly good – give that plate back a minute, I'll put a bit more on it.' She paused, resting the carving knife and fork on the joint, her face serious. 'I tell you what, Deb – ' She broke off, as the bang of the front door announced the arrival of Pip and Mawgan. 'No, never mind. Tell you later.' She carved another hefty slice.

'Nan and Grandad not joining us today?' asked Debbie, pushing the next plate in Cally's direction.

'Not this time, they thought we'd like to be on our own for once. But they'd like you to go round for tea before you go.' Cally slapped a spoonful of carrots onto a plate with perhaps unnecessary force. 'Nan's bothered there's been no word from Cress. And so am I.'

'Cress is just getting at us one way, when she finds she can't the other any more,' said Allison. She sounded as if she had said it too often before. Cally slapped out another spoonful of carrots.

'She may've behaved bad, but she's still your sister Allison.'

'Well, you know what they say – you choose your friends, but your relatives you just have to put up with.'

For a moment the air simmered between mother and daughter, but then Pip came in, headed for the fridge and the beer and they looked away from each other. The next spoonful of carrots landed on the plate more gently, and Allison laid aside her knife to help with the vegetables. Pip gave Debbie a slap on the rump in passing.

'Hey girl, you're looking tasty!'

Debbie jumped in surprise at the unexpected assault, but she was getting used to Pip by this time. She grabbed him.

'You want one of those back, or are you going to say hullo nicely?'

Pip's grin was so like Mawgan's when he was up to mischief that Debbie kissed him with extra warmth, and he looked pleased.

'Hullo, nicely,' he said, and went for the beer. His square back, thus presented to her, reminded Debbie of Molly's word, *stuggy*, and she found herself wondering how it originated. She was about to ask if anyone here knew when she found herself with a hot plate in each hand.

'Just take those through now,' said Cally. 'I've laid it in the dining room, as it's an occasion. Come along, Allison.' Debbie meekly did as she was told, but Allison held back

'Just going to put some cream on my hands, won't be a minute.'

'Huh!' said Pip, with a fiendish grin in her direction. 'Only brickie I know, uses handcream! You wait till the boys hear!'

'Might catch on.' Allison squirted handcream into her palm, and rubbed her hands together. 'Anyway Dad, you needn't think you're going to economise on sandpaper using my skin!'

'He's never got you bricklaying!' exclaimed Debbie, as they headed for the dining room.

'Says, I want to run a building firm, I've got to know how to build,' said Allison, but she sounded pleased. 'Beats being cabin crew by a mile! I've never had such fun.'

'Would that be anything to do with the rest of the gang being blokes?' Mawgan asked, as they sat down to the table, and Allison grinned.

'Could be. They tried that old *fifty pee's worth o' skyhooks* on me, the very first day. Don't know where they think I grew up! I soon sorted *them* out!'

'Tough cookie!'

'Ho!' she retorted. 'Better than being a big girl's blouse, like you, brother!'

'Role reversal is carried to ridiculous lengths in this family,' Debbie remarked, and they all laughed.

My sister-in-law is a bricklayer. That wouldn't go down a storm with her mother. Debbie found herself wishing with unexpected force that Dot would look at *people*, not just at social class. She missed such a lot of fun. Life was about more important things than what people did for a living, or what they earned – and in that last respect, she was coming to realise, the Angwins were doing very nicely, thank you. It was simply that their values were different. They wouldn't know how to put on airs about it if somebody offered them their heart's desire to do so.

Which they couldn't.

Cress back in the family circle, reconciled to Mawgan? Fat chance!

It was a lively meal, Mawgan and his parents at last beginning to relax and rebuild their relationship, and Allison was in fine form, another one in the family who had belatedly begun to find her way. Mawgan, not-so-innocently asking which of them had to watch out for their foundations, himself or Debbie, sparked off a sibling wrangle, which ended in Allison collapsing in helpless mirth over the trifle that finished the meal.

'You can bet your boots – or even *my* boots – that if it's raining, Dad'll put me on the outdoor shift,' she said, when she had recovered her poise, and turning to Debbie added, 'And then you'll be the only person in history to have a weatherbeaten brickie for a bridesmaid! Should I wear my smart steel-capped footwear, do you think?'

'You children!' said Cally affectionately, getting up to clear away. 'Will you never grow up? Now, you men get out from under our feet and go and talk your business in the other room, and we'll bring in some coffee when we're done. Shoo, away with you!'

But when they came into the sitting room with the coffee mugs, the washing-up done, it was to find Pip looking through Debbie's plans, and Mawgan fast asleep, sprawled in an armchair.

'Dear of him,' said Allison, putting the tray on a handy table. 'Should we wake him up, do you think?'

'No, leave him,' said Debbie, instantly protective. Cally looked at her severely,

'He won't sleep tonight if he sleeps all afternoon.' She might have been talking about a very young child.

'Actually, he probably won't much anyway. He's loads better, but not too good in the dark yet,' said Debbie. Allison giggled.

'I'm glad to hear it! And you not even married!'

'What do you mean?' asked Cally, almost as if she was accusing Debbie of something.

'Nasty dreams,' said Debbie, and didn't add that they were, on the whole, waking dreams. 'But it *is* getting better,' she added, seeing Cally's face. 'Truly. Since the restaurant closed and he's not so spaced out on adrenalin. He'll be human by the time we come back from Tenerife, you see.'

Pip looked up from the plans with a grunt that was meant to conceal his own concern.

'Going for a month, you said.'

Debbie took the mug that Allison handed her and wrapped her hands round it as if to comfort herself. The continuing bad dreams worried her, she had hoped they would go away after the events of Christmas but they hadn't done so. She wasn't going to say that in front of Cally, she worried enough already.

It seemed as if getting *into* a state was easier than getting out of it.

'Some friends of Oliver's mother have lent us their apartment in Los Cristianos for a fortnight,' she said. 'It's a great place apparently, right by the beach and with a wonderful swimming pool. We can chill out there in style. And the second fortnight, they said we could take their yacht, so I'll be giving him a bit of occupational therapy, teaching him sailing.'

'Sounds as if that should sort him out, then,' said Pip.He returned his attention to the plans. 'Now then, young Debbie, I've been giving this a look.'

Debbie took her coffee and perched on the arm of his chair, looking at the plans over his shoulder.

'I'm longing to see it started.'

'We'll just get the boy's wall up, and knock through into that outhouse for him, and then I'll set the team on your job. You won't be wanting the carpenter or the plasterer for a while, we can put them into the Fish. Reckon maybe a fortnight, that do you?'

'So the answer to the million pound question is, you *both* have to watch out for your foundations!' said Allison.

'Thank God, mine are already there,' remarked Mawgan, without opening his eyes. Allison gave him a scathing look that was wasted, as his eyes remained closed.

'Oh, back with us, are you? That's nice. Coffee? It'll keep you awake.'

Before Mawgan could come up with a suitable reply, they were interrupted by the ring of his mobile, which he had left balanced on the edge of his father's electronic organ. Allison, who was nearest, picked it up and passed it across, and Mawgan, yawning, took it.

'Angwin ... oh, hullo Chel. What's up, problem?' He paused while Chel apparently was saying something at length, and then said, '*What?* You're joking! When ...?' Another pause.'Yeah, I'll talk about it, but no promises ... what ...? Yes, I know that. Who told them, anyway ...? Yes, that works, it had to be, didn't it? I – ' He broke off, holding the phone away from his ear and making a face at it before cautiously replacing it. 'Have you finished? Good! No, of course I wouldn't do that ... yes ... yes ... if they must. You fix it, I'll go with the flow. But they keep to the point, OK? Otherwise I'm not playing.'Bye.' He switched off the phone and laid it on the arm of his chair. 'Well, well ...' He looked pensive.

'So what was all that about?' asked Allison, when it seemed as if he was just going to sit there and not tell them. 'Good news? Bad news? Come on, give!'

'I'm not really sure ...' said Mawgan. He looked up, caught sight of their faces, and burst out laughing. 'All right, all right, I'll come clean. Just give me some coffee, I think I'm still dreaming.'

Allison picked up a mug and held it just out of reach.

'Start talking first.'

'All right, all *right*! You're getting worse than Anna! What's happened, somebody in the village – favourite is that Marie Tregear who used to work for you at Seagulls, Deb, via her daughter who works for *me* – '

'Come to the point,' said Allison, but took pity on him and handed over the mug. 'Talk while you drink.'

'What – lit'rally? I'll choke.' Mawgan grinned at her. 'Anyway, she talked to the local radio station about the alterations to the restaurant, and the name, and why we're calling it that – '

'Why, what are you calling it?' Pip interrupted.

'*An Rosen Gwyn.* Deb's choice.'

'After a fishing boat that sailed out of St Erbyn in the war,' Debbie enlarged on this. 'The crew were St Erbyn men. Heroes.'

Pip nodded.

'Good idea. How do the locals feel?'

'Very happy, it seems.' Mawgan took up the tale. 'There were two Tregears on board when she went down, one of them was Marie's grandfather which maybe explains it. Anyway, the local radio rang just after we left, they want to do an interview, but more than that ... the West of England TV want to do a feature too, as part of a local-interest programme. The TV lot came into the bar at lunchtime – combining business with pleasure, presumably – and poor old Chel had to explain I wasn't there.'

Debbie pulled a face.

'Has anyone told them about Oliver and the mural?'

'Oliver has already dropped himself in it, asking round the village for input.'

'Oh ... I don't know if I mean *oh dear*, or *oh good*.'

'And will you let them do it?' asked Cally.

'So long as I can prevent them digging up old bones,' said Mawgan, carefully. 'Free publicity never hurt no-one, that I know.'

'Dad'll stop them,' said Debbie, confidently. 'There's an appeal pending, that'll shut them up. Talk to him before you talk to them, have the block in place.'

'Wow!' said Allison. 'So everything's coming up roses at last!'

'White roses?' Mawgan raised his eyebrows at her. 'Don't count your chickens. There could yet be a great big snake in the undergrowth.'

'Don't be such a pessimist!'

'There's always one more river to cross.'

'Then just hope it isn't a water snake that's after you,' said Allison.

* * * * *

Back at the Fish, Chel walked with the media men to their car, waved goodbye as they drove away, and then went slowly back to the office where, although she was officially off duty, she sat for some time staring into space. Wheels had been set in motion, she could almost hear them turning, but to what purpose? She had never managed to tune into her gift on purpose with any great success, but she felt excitement, rising like a spring inside her and hanging trembling on the air around. The next few years of Mawgan Angwin's life were going to be amazing.

Unless ...

Dot came into her head only a second later, and with Dot the recollection of a hard-learned lesson that nothing in this life is graven in stone. Chance, not a pre-ordained path, governs existence, the road has turnings, forks, crossroads. She had passed them herself, and knew that there were more ahead.

But Dot couldn't hurt Mawgan, had already hurt Debbie as much as it was surely possible. Dot was no threat, how could she be?

* * * * *

Far to the east, in Embridge, Dot sat down at her elegant writing desk and began to draft a letter. It wasn't easy, it had to strike exactly the right note: it had to tell the recipient, in no uncertain terms, that she was onto his game and he had no hope of winning. It had to deal a body-blow that would leave him reeling, while at the same time tying him with immovable knots so that there was no come-back. It had to finish him, so far as Debbie was concerned, for ever. And if it cost her, as it would – well, her daughter's happiness was worth the price.

* * * * *

Not that far away in actual distance, although a million miles in mood or intention, Jerry was on the telephone.

'Helen!' he cried, when she picked up her phone.

'Oh, it's you! What is it this time? It's getting to be a habit!Don't build too much on New Year, I was only sorry for you.'

Jerry was almost beginning to believe that she was lying, but a solicitor doesn't abandon caution easily. He said,

'I hoped that, as a return for your hospitality, you'd let me take you to the theatre. They're putting on a production of *Cats* at the Winter Gardens, and I know you love it.'

Helen said nothing. Jerry went on, a note of desperation creeping into his voice,

'It's nearly sold out, but I've been able to get two seats right in the middle of the front circle for Thursday.'

Still no reply.

'Helen?'

'Hush. I'm thinking this one out.'

Jerry waited. After a while, he said,

'Well?'

'I couldn't get home unless it was a matinée.'

'It isn't,' said Jerry. And waited again. Helen said,

'This isn't another of your cries for help, is it? I told you Jerry, I won't be involved, and I mean it. I will not be caught up in Dot's insidious toils a second time in my life, it only leads to grief.'

'I promise, this is a simple return of hospitality that I thought would give you pleasure.'

'Solicitor's honour?'

'Solicitor's honour. My children's names will not be mentioned unless by you.'

'How is Deb?'

'Deb, when I spoke to her last, was fine. Will you come?'

'I shall have to book a hotel,' said Helen, thoughtfully. 'Can you get me a room at the Langland, do you think?'

'You could have my spare room,' said Jerry, and held his breath.

'Jerry! As if I would ... *dare!*' Helen sounded shocked, but was probably laughing, he thought.

'I would promise to be on my best behaviour. And there's a key.'

'That doesn't bode well for best behaviour. What will dear Dot say?'

'Do you care?'

'Do you?'

'So will you come? I'll treat you to dinner at Mario's beforehand.'

'Now there's temptation! I love Italian food. Is Mario as good as Mawgan?'

'Honest opinion?'

'Jerry, you're a solicitor! Of course, honest.' That time, he heard the laugh, she made no attempt to disguise it. He grinned to himself.

'Then possibly not. But good, all the same. There's a lot of leeway, after all.'

'All right, I'll come. But I'll look after the key.'

Jerry swallowed. All at once he felt like a seventeen-year-old contemplating his first date ... or no, more like that twenty-five-year-old Jerry who had escorted twenty-year-old Helen Macken and her friends to the pantomime at that same Winter Gardens. That hadn't been a matinee either, he remembered. Himself, Helen, Nonie Fingall, and inexplicably at the time, Matthew Sutton. Up the ladder and down the snake, throw a six and start again.

'I shall look forward to it,' he said, and heard his own voice, unsteady.

'Good,' said Helen. 'I'll meet you after you finish work, shall I?'

'Come here. I'll get back early.'

'Good.' She rang off. Jerry sat there, the phone in his hand and a silly smile on his face, wondering. Was he making a fool of himself?

If so, bring on the clowns!

* * * * *

Tim Howells was speaking to his friend Jake, who crewed for him during the sailing season on his Flying Fifteen, and who had inadvertently gone off with Tim's key to the club boathouse. Jake, whose father ran the Crown & Anchor in Embridge, was one of the few people who didn't tiptoe round him these days and talking to him was a relief.

'I'll leave the key in the bar,' Jake was saying. 'I've to be up in town a couple of days, I won't be back until late Friday. Is that all right? Do you mind calling in for it?'

'Just so long as nobody says anything clever,' said Tim.

'Spit in their eye! Anyway, you need only duck in and out again. Leave it late enough, most of them'll have gone home unless it's the weekend.'

'OK then. Tell your father I'll be in.'

'No problem!'

* * * * *

So, all the pieces were in place, balanced, ready to fall into a new pattern. When they fell, the road would lie clear ahead, open and free to walk. But not for everybody.

Winners and losers, they're always there.

XVIII

The media were back on track by Thursday morning, this time on the phone. Whatever the redoubtable Mrs Tregear had told them had caught their imagination, they were determined that there was a programme here, and maybe, their spokesman said, dangling a carrot, a follow-up when the restaurant opened. The intervening time, he had told Chel, had been occupied in getting clearance from the boss, finding a slot in the schedule, and drawing up a story board to work from.

'It's not a story,' Chel objected.

'Same difference. Is Mr Angwin available to talk to, today or tomorrow? We want to get this show on the road!'

'In principle, he's available,' said Chel. 'You have to catch him first.'

'Bit of a live wire, is he? We had heard that,' said the spokesman.

Chel didn't answer immediately. It was her considered opinion that Mawgan was coming a bit loose since Christmas, and even more since his momentous birthday, and the jury was out at present as to whether he was untangling or unravelling. He was certainly on a high, which the work involved in the rapidly approaching wedding wasn't doing anything to help. There was beginning to be an uncomfortable feeling of an accident waiting to happen about him, and Mawgan's interpretation of an accident tended to be liberal right now.

'He's very busy,' she said, cautiously.

'It's in his interests,' said the persuasive voice on the line. 'And what about Oliver Nankervis? Will he take part in the programme, do you think?'

'You are a glutton for punishment, aren't you?' said Chel, admiringly. 'You want *both* of them? One is a handful!'

'Well, good. Makes good television, that kind of thing.'

Chel had been taken aback by Oliver's surprisingly ready acquiescence, not realising that both Nonie and gallery-owner Gifford Thomas, who handled a lot of his pictures, had given him a heavy lecture on media relations, but she still didn't trust him to behave. Or Mawgan either, for that matter. But that was the television company's headache. She said,

'Oliver will appear in your programme, but not to the extent of a preview of his design for the wall. You can look at the material supplied by the village, that he's working from.'

'Fair enough.'

The office door swung open, and Mawgan came in, shouldering his way through with a large box in his arms, which he dumped, predictably, on the corner of Chel's desk rather than on his own.

'Mawgan – '

'Half a sec. Let me get rid of this.' So it wasn't going to stay on her desk, Chel was relieved to see. Mawgan began clearing a space on his own, but was immediately side-tracked by the post, which Shirley had left lying there and Chel had been interrupted before she could sort. He picked it up and flicked absently through it. Chel said, into the phone,

'He's just come in – my boss. If he stops still long enough, I'll put him on in a minute. Is there anything else I can help you with?'

The spokesman began to talk about his plans, and Mawgan dropped most of his post back onto the desk and picked up a paper knife to open a letter. Ignoring Chel, who was trying to attract his attention, he began to read the single sheet of paper the envelope contained.

He went very still. Chel had a sudden, unreasonable conviction of overwhelming fury, although he gave no sign.

'*Mawgan!*' Chel said urgently, waving to attract his attention. 'This way, boss! The telly man wants to speak to you!'

Mawgan looked up slowly. He seemed to have gone a long way away, Chel thought.

'Deal with it yourself, can you? Or get rid of him. I've got to go out.' He cast about looking for his car keys, and Chel tried to remonstrate with him.

'It won't take you a second. It's important.' He wasn't listening, she saw. She said, hopelessly, 'It's the television people. Free advertising – remember?'

'Tomorrow,' said Mawgan. He had found his keys and turned round with them in his hand, pushing the letter and its envelope into the back pocket of his jeans, reaching for his leather jacket that hung on the back of the door almost in the same movement. He looked at his watch, visibly calculating. 'Tell Deb I'll be back this evening sometime, will you? I'll give her a ring – got to go – sorry.'

'Mawgan!' Chel dropped the phone and made a dash after him. 'Stop a minute – where are you *going*?'

'Got a problem to see to.' He was already half way to the rear entrance. 'Tell him I'll ring tomorrow.' Bang! The outside door swung to behind him. Chel almost ran after him, but knew it was useless and turned back to the office. She picked up the phone again.

'Sorry about that. I warned you you'd have to catch him first!' She made herself laugh, including the spokesman for the TV company in the joke. 'He says he'll ring you when he gets back tomorrow. I'll see that he does.'

And what had that all been about? she wondered, as she put the phone back on its rest. The vibrations it had left behind it still shivered in the room.

Well, he was a grown-up. He would have to get on with it whatever it was, as he obviously intended, on his own. She looked at her own watch, pushing apprehension out of her mind. Debbie, she knew, had gone up to the boathouse to have a preliminary look at the work that needed to be done on the boats she had bought, indirectly, from Tim and Lesley.

436

She wouldn't be back for ages, and no point in bothering her. No point in bothering her anyway. What was going to happen was already under way, and no stopping it now.

She got to her feet with a sigh, and made her own arrangements about the re-siting of the large box, which she discovered, contained a new and sophisticated printer for the computers.

* * * * *

Mawgan's Volvo flew east along the A30, going like the wind.

* * * * *

Unfortunately for her, Dot drove into her driveway, after being out for most of the day, when it was already dark, and the security lights came on to illuminate a strange car parked by the door. She switched off her lights and studied it for a moment, but it was nobody she knew. A white Volvo estate, not in the first blush of its youth, she had never set eyes on it before. She hesitated a moment before getting out of her own car, you never knew these days. She took a good grip on her rubber torch before opening the door and stepping out. As she did so, the door of the Volvo also opened and a man got out. They met at the foot of the shallow flight of steps up to the front door.

'Good evening,' said Dot. She wasn't sure why, but his presence made her nervous. He wasn't particularly tall, but he was broad across the shoulders and there was something inimical in his attitude. Silhouetted against the light on the corner of the house, he had a round, cropped head, set on a powerful neck; a Neanderthal, she thought. She felt threatened, and tightened her grip on the torch. 'Can I help you?'

'Angwin,' he said.

'Ah,' said Dot. Her heartbeat, which to her annoyance had accelerated on seeing him, began to slow. 'You'd better come in. We can't talk out here.'

He followed her into the hall, close on her heels, crowding her uncomfortably and without speaking – in fact, she realised, apart from telling her his name he had said nothing at all. Overawed by the house, she decided, he wouldn't have been anywhere like this before. When the door had closed behind them, she said,

'I don't know why you should have bothered to come here,' in a dismissive way that was designed to make him abashed. It failed.

'You wrote to me,' he said. Just the simple statement.

'I know that. I presume you've come for your money? You could have saved yourself the journey, I would have sent the money. We need not have met.' She sounded contemptuous, she would have preferred it that way. Her hearer noted the disdain in her voice, and her careless words, and his intentions imperceptibly shifted, not entirely for the better. Dot, encased in her own self-satisfaction, had no idea. The only light in the hall was from the stairway, so that he was still in shadow, and standing between her and the light switch. She should have put on the light as she came in, but with him so close behind her, she ... well, she hadn't. There was something in his stillness now that made her suddenly remember that this was a man who had killed somebody, spent time in prison. She swallowed, unaccountably nervous. She hadn't thought he would be so bulky, just a skimpy little cook. But he wouldn't hurt her. She was doing him a favour. He said,

'A quarter of a million pounds, not to marry your daughter.' Again, a simple statement. Dot began to feel flustered, without quite knowing why.

'Since you're here, I can give you a cheque now, if that's what you want. Post-dated, of course. I want the wedding stopped and Deborah home with me before you cash it.'

'I see.' Heartless, self-satisfied cow! He hadn't wholly believed in it. His mistake.

Dot opened the drawing room door and switched on the light, immediately she felt better. Going over to the table under the window, she opened her handbag and took out her cheque book. The warmth of success was spreading through her now she was in the light, she had known that she was right. She had known him for a fortune-hunter the moment she had learned of his existence, that showed how shrewd she was. Poor Jerry – taken in as always by all this talk about love and other rubbish, just as he had been over Cheryl. It was lucky that Deborah had a mother, at least, who knew the ways of the world!

'And to whom should I make it out, Mr Angwin?' She made the courtesy into almost an insult.

He hadn't meant to take her money at all. He had intended to reason with her face-to-face, persuade her, not because he cared himself one way or the other what she thought of him, but for Debbie. Debbie did care. His revised intentions, barely recognised, hardened.

So, *Blackmailers, inc.?* He nearly laughed, but it wasn't funny.

'M.G. Angwin will do nicely,' he said.

She wrote the cheque, turned with it in her hand. He had moved into the doorway and the light fell now across his face. A dark, pugnacious face, with amber eyes like a lion's, and thick, black eyebrows.Not, she found herself thinking, a face she would want to argue with. Not handsome, as she would have expected. Strong. The word came into her mind and stayed there, like a stone in her shoe, digging in. His mouth was hard, angry. Anger beat off him like an electrical field. He didn't like being caught out. She smiled with patronising kindness as she held out the cheque.

'I'm glad we understand each other,' she said. 'You will see from the date that you may cash it the day after the wedding should have taken place. You see, I am not a fool.' She waved the cheque at him. 'Take it, then. And remember, if you try to double-cross me, I shall put a stop on it and let Deborah know exactly what has taken place between us. Either way, she won't be marrying you. It makes no difference which.'

She had to walk over to him, holding it out. He took it then, twitching it from her fingers and folding it without looking at it, pushing it into his back pocket. She had an impression, which she didn't like, that he had deliberately avoided touching her fingers with his own.

'I don't think,' he said, 'that we understand each other at all, Mrs Nankervis. *I* might understand *you*. That's one thing.'

'What do you mean?' She stared at him, taking a step back, not knowing why.

'I shan't be cashing it. Do you want to know what I shall be doing with it?'

Dot wasn't sure that she did, suddenly

'Don't be foolish!' she cried. 'That's a great deal of money! Of course you'll cash it.'

'Is a quarter of a million the value you put on your daughter? I value her a good deal higher'n that.'

'Now listen – ' Something had gone wrong. Her heart, which had steadied, began to thump, too fast.

'No. You listen. I want to see you at your daughter's wedding. I want to see you, and I want her to see you smiling, as if you're happy about it. In the church, if you please, I don't care where. If you want to hide at the back, that's fine, just so long as she sees you. You needn't stay for the reception, I don't want you on my premises.' He paused, and the scorn in his eyes shook her. 'And if I don't see you, lady, shall I tell you what I mean to do?'

'You can't do anything!'

'You think so? Then let me tell you. I shall fax your letter, and your cheque, to the editor of your local paper. Is that clear?'

Dot swallowed. Her voice wasn't quite her own, her throat unaccountably dry.

'You wouldn't dare!'

'Really? Don't put money on it, I can be some nasty when I'm in the mood.'

Her heart was hammering in her ears now. The worst thing about him was, apart from taking the cheque and putting it in his pocket, he hadn't moved. He just stood there, propped against the doorframe, broad and menacing and – she had to face it – scary. She said, trying to put authority into her voice.

'That's blackmail! I most strongly advise you to give that cheque back at once!' She held out her hand. For answer, he smiled at her. His face fell easily into laughter lines, but there was no genuine laughter there. If there had been, the smile would have been blinding. Dot swallowed again, although her mouth was dry.

'D'you want to take it by force? It's the only way you'll get it, lady.'

'I must insist! Or do you want me to send for the police?'

He laughed outright at that.

'Giss on! When you wrote me that letter? It's hardly theft, or demanding money with menaces.'

Silence. He was looking at her, she thought, as if she was something nasty from beneath a stone, but there was nothing she could do. Menaces ... she wished he hadn't used the word. She couldn't take the cheque back from a man with shoulders like a wrestler. She could, it flitted through her mind, provoke him so that he manhandled her and then scream for help, land him in real trouble – but then she knew, she didn't dare. He was an ex-convict, a demonstrably violent man, and suppose nobody heard? The houses in this street stood in spacious grounds. In her own brightly lit, elegant drawing room she was scared to the point where her stomach churned, and she took another two steps back. She held his eyes only with an effort.

'You really would be wise to give it back.' Her voice was unmistakeably shaking now.

He only grinned at her, and she found she had backed into the window until the table dug into the small of her back.

'Furthermore,' he said, and he didn't look or sound a bit like a man who knew words like *furthermore*, which made it worse, somehow. 'Furthermore, there's going to be contact in the future. Birthday cards, Christmas cards, that sort of thing? *Love from Mum*, and a few kisses, maybe? I won't insist on letters, that's up to you. Maybe she won't want them none. I wouldn't, you treated me the way you treat Deb, but that's for you. Understood?'

There was only one thing to do. Dot nodded, speechless. He pushed himself away from the doorframe and took a step towards her, casually. The table was cutting her in half.

'That's good then. Oh, and one last thing.' He paused. 'I've known some beauties in my time, lady, but I've been around your family long enough now to know you're top of the heap. There's not a one of them that's come near, you haven't hurt. What makes you think you're so entitled, to run other people's lives? You got a direct line to God, or something? So get this through your head. The day I marry Deb, they're my family too. So if you once more hurt Deb, or Chel, or Oliver, Deb's dad or Oliver's mum, or Susan and her kids, or Oliver's godmother come to that – well, you know what's coming. Just don't never bloody forget!'

Dot couldn't help it, the words spoke themselves.

'Will you tell Deborah?'

He flicked her with a searing look of consummate scorn.

'No. I wouldn't never hurt her so. If she ever learns, it's down to you.'

He left after that, turning abruptly on his heel without goodbye. The front door slammed behind him, and a moment later she heard the engine of his car, roaring away down the drive. Then, and only then, did she move from the table and collapse into a chair.

She sat there for a long time, while her pulse steadied and her heart rate dropped to a more normal pace. Her thoughts were in turmoil, flying this way and that.

He wouldn't do it. He wouldn't dare!

Don't put money on it. No, she couldn't call his bluff. *She* didn't dare. He was an alien, from another world, who knew what such a person was capable of?

She could tell Jerry. Jerry would have to do something.

Did she want Jerry to know that she had tried to buy that man off? Offered him two hundred and fifty thousand pounds to ditch Jerry's precious daughter almost at the altar?

No, she didn't.

See another solicitor, get him warned away?

Jerry apart, did she want *anyone* to know what she had tried to do? Things had a way of seeping into the pool of common knowledge in this town, so -

No, once again, she didn't.

She could cancel the cheque, but it wouldn't help. It would still exist. For him to cash it would be to kill the goose that laid the golden eggs, he would lose Debbie and her fortune ...

There was no way she could bribe or persuade the editor of the *Embridge Herald* to bury a story like that. These days, he was a young man called Jonathan Holmes, and yet another chicken that was now coming home to roost. He was a friend of Cheryl's, once much more than a friend. She flushed hotly at the very thought of approaching him.

So, another dead end.

Dot sat on, in the brightly lit room, coming to terms with the bitter knowledge that she had let herself be outsmarted by a Cornish yob off a council estate, and for the simple reason that that was exactly what she had thought he was. And he wasn't. Or if he was, she had been making some serious misconceptions throughout her life.

Exactly what he was, she didn't want to think. She recognised that she had no weapon to turn against him, that she couldn't manipulate him in any way, that he would stand in her path, obstructing her, for as long as it took, or forever.

He held the ultimate deterrent, and he didn't care a toss for anything she chose to do.

So, like it or not, he was going to become her son-in-law, this Mawgan Angwin. And he was always going to know exactly what she had done.

She found that she was not just hot, but sweating, prickling all over with an unusual sensation which, after a few moments she identified, correctly, as shame. Out of it grew some uncomfortable reflections. They took the form of a list. She shivered as a chill ran over her skin. A list of friends, of children …

Jerry and Helen.

Poor Henry.

Matthew Sutton.

Nonie Fingall.

Oliver.

The Wainwright girl

Susan.

Had she hurt them?

No, surely not! It had been for their own good, all for the best. They needed guidance from somebody with a head on their shoulders. She had meant to make them happy.

Had she? The sheer ambiguity of the question set her mind reeling.

And Debbie. Had it been for Debbie's own good, all for the best, to make her happy?

If so, she had failed. Debbie would marry that … that *terrible* man with the pub, because …

Because, Dot told herself, with unusual and shaming honesty, quite simply because, he wasn't vulnerable. Mawgan Angwin carried no emotional baggage that she could forcibly access in order to make him do things her way, or if he did, she had been looking in the wrong place. He quite simply didn't care what she did ... how she let herself down.

Forcibly? She had never *forced* people.

Dot sat there for a long, long time.

Be sure your sins will find you out.

But I didn't mean to sin. I didn't.

She looked around the expensively furnished, luxurious room, in the beautiful house in the very best area of town. She felt the rich warmth of silk against her skin, her hands rested, limp and sparkling with precious stones, in the lap of her exclusive and costly designer skirt, and she thought,

This is all I have. Unless I change.

✻ ✻ ✻ ✻ ✻

Mawgan, meanwhile, his mind all over the place and not on what he was doing, had turned the wrong way on hitting the main road, and instead of finding himself heading west along the A31, became inextricably involved in the complicated one-way system around the centre of Embridge, finally escaping from it, cursing, on the east side of the town with no idea of where he was. He had the sense to realise that he couldn't go on until he had given himself time to calm down, or who knew where he would end up, and seeing the Crown & Anchor conveniently on his left, pulled into the car park and went into the bar to have a quick, reviving pint and to ask his way.

The landlord was a friendly soul, the pub not overly busy on a weekday in February. He was happy to draw a map on the back of an old envelope showing how to regain the dual-carriageway out of town without having to go back through the town centre, and a second pint naturally followed. The discovery that the lost stranger was also the landlord of a pub led inevitably to a third, and the evening began to settle down. Others had drifted in from the cold, wandered over to the bar, joined in the talk. Five pints down the line, Mawgan belatedly realised that wherever else he was going tonight, it wasn't Cornwall, and he had better phone Debbie and let her know; unfortunately, the sixth pint intervened, and it was at that point that his besetting demon reported for duty, and he began to slide downhill into bleak depression.

What the hell had he done? How on earth was he ever going to look Deb in the face again? He must have been out of his mind!

He saw Deb's mum as he had left her, backed so far into the bay window that she was practically through the glass, her face a study in pure shock. She had looked like a woman who had never been challenged in her life before, although surely that was impossible, and moreover she had looked scared shitless.

By him?

Mawgan had to admit that there was nobody else around who could be held responsible.

Bugger!

'My round,' said somebody, cheerfully. 'Another one, squire?'

'Yeah, why not.' Mawgan moved his glass – miraculously empty again – across the bar counter, and while the order was being filled, felt in his pocket, drawing out the folded letter and the crumpled cheque. He held them for a few minutes, not unfolding them but simply feeling them between his fingers.

He couldn't. He realised he had known that all along, and so if Deb's mum worked it out too, well, what did that change? There was no way he could tell the whole world – and by definition, Deb too – that her mother had tried to buy him off. He couldn't do that to Deb, not in a million years. He took the two folded pieces of paper and rolled them together into a fat cigarette shape. He looked at the man next to him.

'Got a light, mate?'

'Yeah, sure.' The man produced a lighter, and Mawgan, taking it, set the tiny flame to the end of the little cylinder and watched it burn away until it nearly blistered his fingers. Dropping it into a handy ashtray, he crushed it to ash with his fingertips and handed back the lighter.

'Thanks.'

'"Dear John" letter?' asked the man, pocketing his lighter with a sympathetic grin. Mawgan wondered what he would say if he answered, *No, just a cheque for a quarter of a million*, but didn't try it. He shrugged his shoulders instead, dismissively. 'Here,' said the man. 'Get this down you. They're none of them ever worth it.'

The convivial group had gone, calling cheerful valedictions, and Mawgan had gone on to whisky, and mentally into some very dark territory, before his guardian angel took a hand. The landlord had moved away to serve some new customers, when Tim Howells pulled up in the car park outside on his way to retrieve his key. He meant only to dash in and out, he tended to keep apart from people during this miserable period when he was awaiting a date for his fate to be decided in the courts. The last days of his freedom, he cynically considered them, and tried not to think about what came after, and what life would be like in the more distant future. He had, after all, seen what happened to Angwin. The good people of St Erbyn had been busily engaged in trying to freeze him out.

He noticed the Volvo. For various reasons, white Volvo estates always caught his eye these days, bringing back fresh battalions of miserable memories. This one, he noted, had a Cornish number plate, and it included the word OAF as that bloody Angwin's had done, appropriately enough he had always thought, which was just about the final straw. In only ten days, Deb was going to marry that bastard, and there was damn all anyone could do about it, least of all him. He went into the pub and there was bloody Angwin, propping up the bar and looking, not only like death, but bloody dangerous with it. Tim brought up short.

'What the *hell* are you doing here?'

'Well well.' Mawgan looked at him, with lazy detachment. 'Of all the bars in all the whatever it was, you have to choose this one.'

'It's my local,' snapped Tim, which was accurate enough in the past. 'Which doesn't explain *you*. What are you doing in Embridge?'

'Off limits, is it?' said Mawgan. He pushed his finger aimlessly round a pool of ash in the nearby ashtray. It looked like burned paper. He said, casually, 'Me, I've just been adding blackmail to murder. You know what I'm like.'

At that point in the conversation, Tim realised, as the landlord so far hadn't, fully, that bloody Angwin was paralytic. He remembered Deb, and he remembered the car outside, and he said,

'Are you staying overnight?' crisply.

'What, here?' Mawgan looked at him out of darkly shadowed eyes. 'Nah. I'm going home in a minute. Have a drink.'

Tim hesitated, but Angwin was obviously well past the reasonable stage.

'Yeah, why not? I must just make a phone call, but mine's a pint.'

Drinking with Angwin was something he had never imagined himself doing, certainly not in this pub of all pubs, but it would keep him here, hopefully, for long enough. He went to the pay phone, and, not knowing Deb's dad's number these days, rang Susan.

'*Mawgan?*' said Susan. 'Get away with you, Tim – why should Mawgan be in the Crown & Anchor?'

'I have no idea, and I'm certainly not going to ask him, but I suggest you get down here pretty damn quick, because I won't be held responsible. He's pissed out of his skull, and talking about driving to Cornwall.'

Susan had just been going to bed. For once, Tom was home and she had hoped without hope that there might be a chance, in the dim quietness of their familiar bedroom, to talk sensibly for once, if he couldn't escape into a book, or the television. She looked at her watch.

'It's after ten, Tim,' she objected.

'People can be killed in road accidents at any time,' Tim pointed out, brutally. 'Not just bloody drunk drivers, innocent people just quietly going home. You come and get the sod, and do it quick. I can only hold him here so long, he doesn't even like me, and that's before you even start on my feelings towards him.'

Susan still hesitated, but only for a moment.

'All right. You keep him there, I'll be right down. It'll take me at least a quarter of an hour, even at this time of night.'

Tom, when she told him, gave an elaborate sigh.

'You and your family! Last time, I seem to remember, it was Chel, about Oliver, in the middle of the night – can't they manage without you?'

The thought that perhaps they couldn't was a new one, and Susan found that it warmed her chilled heart a little. Nobody could call Tom's expression disappointed. He looked, in fact, like a man relieved he was headed for an undisturbed night's sleep. Perhaps, she thought bitterly, he needed one; no doubt extra-marital sex took it out of you. She said,

'I don't suppose it'll take me long. I'll be back.'

'Oh, right. Well, don't disturb me. I'll be asleep.'

'You could come with me. Give me a hand.'

'I've better things to do than start wrestling with drunks at midnight!' Tom retorted, and didn't add that Deb's intended was built like a brick shithouse, and he *certainly* wasn't tangling with him while he was under the influence. 'You'll cope,' he said, now. 'Oh – and you'd better not bring him back here, you don't want to wake the children. Like you did last time,' he ended, pointedly.

Susan gathered her car keys and her mobile phone from the hall table and stalked out of the door without replying.

* * * * *

Jerry put down the phone and pensively regarded his house guest, sitting comfortably on his sofa with her feet up and an unromantic mug of hot chocolate in her hand.

'Well, that's thrown a spanner in the works,' he said.

'Really? What's happened now?' Helen raised her beautiful eyebrows, and his knees turned to water. 'What's up Jerry? You've gone all enigmatic at me.'

'That was Susan. It seems you have competition for my spare bedroom.'

Helen turned her wrist, lazily, and looked at her watch.

'It's only just after eleven. I expect I can still go to the Langland. Or your unexpected guest could.'

'I don't think so,' said Jerry. He sat down in one of the armchairs, and elaborated. 'Well, you could, if you wanted to, but from what Susan said, they wouldn't want Mawgan.'

'*Mawgan*?' Helen sat up, and set her mug aside on a small table. 'What's Mawgan doing in Embridge?'

'Your guess is as good as mine. Tim Howells apparently came across him, rat-arsed in the Crown & Anchor. Susan has got no sense out of him – out of either of them. Tim is doing a Pilate, and washing his hands of the whole thing, and Mawgan doesn't even seem to know for sure who either of them is. Or care, which is more disturbing.'

'Oh dear,' said Helen, inadequately. She swung her feet to the floor. 'And Susan is bringing him to you?'

'She can hardly take him home with her, not in that state. Think about it.'

Helen stood up. There were two things she could do, she realised: stay, or go. Staying would be a conscious decision that might – no, *would* have far-reaching consequences. She had already expended some thought on it, although without expecting to be faced with it so soon. Now, in the event, it was being taken out of her hands. Go with the flow, then.

'Then I'd better collect my things out of your spare room,' she said, without heat.

Jerry's heart began to thump against his ribs, hard.

'Would you like me to phone the Langland? Check that they've a room available?'

'Of course they have,' said Helen, smiling. 'It's barely February.'

'To expect you, then,' said Jerry. He thought that Helen must be able to see the vibration of his ribs, if she looked. Her eyes, however, were fixed on his face, coolly.

'Are you trying to get rid of me, Jerry?'

'You can't sleep on the sofa. It's only a two-seater.' Jerry's sofa, like most of the rest of his furnishings, had been part of the deal. He hated everything about it, but he was about to learn to love it.

'I wasn't planning to.'

'N-neither can I. Damn!'

Helen was smiling. The smile reached right up into her eyes.

'I wasn't planning on that, either.'

'Oh, my God!' said Jerry. Helen patted his arm gently on her way to the spare bedroom.

'Ring your other daughter. She must be out of her mind with worry, she may not even know where he is.'

'Oh, my God!' said Jerry, in an entirely different voice, and grabbed for his phone.

Debbie disclaimed any worry, but he could hear it in her voice and knew that Helen had been right, and he should have thought of it for himself.

'He phoned about six and said he'd been delayed, but he didn't say where he was,' she said. Jerry heard the quiver in her voice and, for the second time that he recalled, was actively annoyed with his future son-in-law. Thoughtless oaf!

'Well, he's here – or he will be, quite soon. He's staying overnight, it's too late to get back to Cornwall now.'

'But what's he *doing* there?' asked Debbie, worry beginning to give way to indignation. Jerry, who had no idea of the answer, said ambivalently,

'I expect he'll tell you himself when he gets back.' He didn't know Mawgan's reasons, but he did know of one which would serve in an emergency, thank goodness.

'Chel said he had a letter and went off like a rocket without giving any reason,' said Debbie. 'Just that he had to sort out a problem. He took the letter with him, so we have no idea ...'

'Yes, well, he's had a lot on his mind, darling.'

'That's why I've been worrying,' said Debbie.

'Well you can stop worrying now, and go to bed. He'll be back with you tomorrow.' Not too early, though, from what Susan had said. Of course, she could be exaggerating, but it sounded as if Mawgan had been on a bender of some dimensions. He didn't say that to Debbie. He didn't enter into any explanations at all, it was no good making things up when he was in a state of ignorance as total as her own. He said goodnight as Helen reappeared with her overnight case and headed for his bedroom. He nearly fell over his own feet in his eagerness to help her.

'I'll carry that for you.'

Helen relinquished her case without comment, but said, as she preceded him into the bedroom,

'I wonder if Dot is OK. Should you give her a ring and check, do you think?'

'*Dot?*' said Jerry, dropping the case in his agitation. He had been trying not to think about Dot.

'She can't help coming into my head,' said Helen, half apologetically. 'Not that I give a monkey's if she's lying battered in a pool of her own blood, but perhaps it might be as well to just make sure. One way or the other.' She gave him an enigmatic look.

'You can't think that he ...' Jerry stared at her in horror.

'No. I don't think so for a moment. But Dot's gunning for him, and we all know that. I just think it might be wise to – well, check.'

'Oh, my God!' chanted Jerry, like a mantra.

'Or I'll do it, if you want,' said Helen, obligingly. 'If I use my mobile, she won't know who rang even if she dials 1471, she'll just think it's a wrong number. I needn't say anything, we only want to know she's there, and functioning properly.'

Jerry covered his eyes. His voice rose almost to a sqeak.

'*Oh, my God!*'

Helen took her mobile out of her bag and waited expectantly. As Jerry told her the number, as if the digits choked him, she entered them and listened. After a short pause, she gave a brief nod and switched off the phone.

'She's there. She sounds her usual snotty self, let's not worry about her. No sirens wailing in the background, or policemen answering the phone. If there was a confrontation, she came off all right. And Jerry, if you say 'oh my God' once more, I shall ...'

'What?' asked Jerry, unsteady with both relief and further apprehension.

'Kiss you,' said Helen, and suited the action to the word. Jerry's response, understandably, was distracted.

'Oh, my poor Deb!' he groaned.

'It needn't have anything to do with Dot. Tim Howells is another one with links to Mawgan, and we know that *he's* around, if he rang Susan. And there's awful little sister, too, coincidences happen. Don't buy trouble, Jerry.' The entry-phone buzzed. 'That'll be Susan now. You'd better go down and give her a hand.' She met his eyes, a smile in her own. 'I'll go to bed, out of the way. There's enough confusion around here for one night. And don't worry, Jerry darling. We'll get to the bottom of it in the morning.'

* * * * *

The first thought that went through Mawgan's head when he awoke in the small hours was *God, not* another *migraine!* before he recognised the more familiar symptoms of a first-class hangover. His skull felt as if it was held in an iron clamp, and his stomach lurched at the bare thought of moving. He would have liked to go back to sleep, but it wasn't an option, unfortunately. He lay where he was ... and then found himself wondering where that was. Only a very dim recollection remained in his mind about last night, it seemed to him, bizarrely, that it had included Tim Howells, but surely that was absurd? Trying not to move anything but his eyelids, he opened his eyes and took a careful look at the world.

God almighty! He closed them again, hurriedly, but the fleeting glimpse had been more than enough. He appeared to be lying in a horribly frilly room that he had never seen before, with flowered wallpaper and co-ordinating curtains covered with pink flowers, unknown to any botanist. Even the dressing table had worn a frill.

Maybe it was the frills and the rampant floral vegetation that did it. The urgent necessity to find a bathroom *now*, wherever he was became imperative. Fortunately, it turned out to be *en suite*, and somebody had kindly left the door open and the light on – it was that which had illuminated the frills, but maybe that was a small price. Crawling back to bed a horrible interval later, he collapsed under the frilled duvet, relieved to find that he had no company in the matching divan alongside, and effectively passed out. Frills or no, he didn't care. If there was some female spider lurking in this web, he simply didn't want to know.

Some hours later, Jerry Nankervis dragged himself reluctantly from his ex-wife's loving arms and began the day. When he was shaved and dressed, he dropped alka-seltzer into a large glass of water, poured a cup of tea, sugared it, and carried both in to his unexpected guest. He found Mawgan sitting up with the frilled duvet pulled around him, contemplating the room with lacklustre eyes. He obviously felt just as bad as he deserved, and the relief on his face when he saw Jerry was almost laughable.

'Hullo, good morning,' said Jerry. He looked at his guest more carefully. 'Well, morning, anyway. Here. Get this down you.' He handed Mawgan the glass and put the mug of tea on the bedside table.

'Thanks.' Mawgan drank, thirstily, and after a pause, went on. 'And thank God it's you – I couldn't think where I was, it looks like a ...' He broke off, embarrassed.

'A tart's boudoir?' asked Jerry, grinning. 'Fear not, I took it over complete as it stood – it was the show flat. Tasteful, don't you think? This is the spare bedroom, you should see the master.'

That explained one thing. It was the rest that still escaped him. Mawgan said,

'What am I doing here?'

'A very good question.' Jerry looked at him pensively. 'Susan and Tim dumped you off, late last night. Don't you remember?'

'No.' No, he certainly didn't remember Susan. Just Tim Howells ... *why* Tim Howells? He must have had a real skinful.

'She scooped you up out of the Crown & Anchor,' said Jerry, helpfully.

The Crown & Anchor ... well, it was obvious that there had to be a Crown & Anchor in there somewhere. Mawgan almost shook his head, and stopped, hurriedly. A wave of no doubt deserved nausea began to creep from his stomach to his throat. He rested a clenched fist against his mouth and tried to put his mind into gear. It would do no more than make the equivalent of a horrid scrunching noise.

'I think I'll sign the pledge,' he said. Jerry laughed.

'Serves you right,' he said. 'I'm not giving you any sympathy, my son, I hope you feel terrible. You should have seen the state of you last night! Get yourself a shower and a shave, and come and have some breakfast. You can tell us what all this is about over the toast and marmalade. I put a disposable razor and a new toothbrush by the sink, and I'll bring you your shirt when it's ironed.'

Mawgan looked at him with the amazed admiration of an only son with three sisters, a loving mother, and two doting grandmothers, plus an efficient and partisan housekeeper and the sort of job that requires constant laundering. Ironing had never figured largely in his life. Jerry saw his expression, and grinned. He picked up the empty glass and headed for the door.

'Don't look at me as if I had three heads – Helen's doing it.'

Helen. Oh well. On balance, that was almost as unlikely.

Mawgan got up – very slowly and carefully – and took his headache to the bathroom. It was, he decided ten minutes later, almost a pity that the shower cleared his head. He still had no recollection of Susan and only the haziest of Tim, but everything else was horribly and abundantly clear.

Emerging from the frilly bedroom, he found himself in a huge living area with big windows opening on a balcony and overlooking a spectacular view. There were signs that here, the frills were in process of subjugation. Jerry sat in an armchair, reading a newspaper, he looked up at the sound of the door.

'Oh, there you are. Well, I won't say you look better, exactly, but I expect you'll live.'

'I need to phone Debbie,' said Mawgan. 'My mobile's got no signal. She'll be worried sick – I was going to be back yesterday evening.'

Jerry folded his newspaper.

'Oh, Debbie knows where you are. We phoned her last night.'

'That must have given her a surprise …' said Mawgan, slowly. He held out the mug of tea. 'What shall I do with this? I'm sorry, my stomach wouldn't look at it.'

'I've already told you that it serves you right, so I won't repeat it.' Jerry got to his feet and took the mug from him. 'You might do better with coffee. Black. Sit down, I'll get some for you.'

Returning from the kitchen, where Helen was busy burning toast in the old familiar way that made his heart turn over, ridiculously, he found that Mawgan was still standing by the window, lost in thought.

'Problems? Here – ' He put the fresh mug in his hand. 'Anything we can help you with?'

'What exactly did you tell Debbie?' asked Mawgan, because this was most immediately important.

'Not a lot we could tell her, was there? We said you'd explain when you got back today. I presume you will be explaining?'

'The thing is,' said Mawgan, slowly, 'I didn't mean her to ever know I was here … which makes it difficult.'

'Ah,' said Jerry. Helen came out of the kitchen, bearing the toast rack in one hand and a *cafetière* in the other. She looked very much at home.

'Morning, Mawgan! How're you feeling? Or shouldn't I ask?' She put the things down on a table already laid for three and, to his surprise, came over and kissed his cheek. 'You certainly add fresh colour to this terrible family! So far as I know, none of us has ever had to be carried home before, or not since college days, anyway.' She sounded as if she found it funny, which was a relief. He gave her a rueful grin, and she patted his arm. 'Breakfast. Something in your stomach will make you feel better. I imagine it's pretty empty by this time.'

Repellent though the idea had sounded, toast, and even more the black coffee, finally finished what the shower had started, although he found it necessary to pass on the butter and marmalade. Mawgan was by this time painfully aware that he was, to put it vulgarly, right up Shit Creek, and had nobody to blame but himself, so that when Jerry said, towards the end of the meal,

'Do you want to tell us what all this is about?' he only hesitated for a second. It was completely obvious that he would have to tell Jerry, at least, because the repercussions could quite simply be too dire and he might end up, yet again, requiring the services of a good solicitor.

'I think I've got to, if you've time to listen. But shouldn't you be in your office, or something? I'm sorry ... I'm being an all-round nuisance, aren't I?'

'About par for the course in our family,' put in Helen, and Jerry said, while quietly relishing *our family*,

'I phoned my secretary and said there was a family crisis. Is there?'

'I don't know,' said Mawgan. 'I think I might have got myself into more trouble.'

'Have some more coffee,' said Jerry, pouring. 'Get it off your conscience, and take heart, I've heard it all before.'

'I doubt you've heard this,' said Mawgan. He looked at Helen, and she made to get to her feet.

'I'll go and wash up,' she said, reaching for the plates, but he stopped her.

'No, you might as well hear it.' It went through his mind that perhaps she had a right to hear, although he couldn't pin down quite why. 'Just never let Deb know. You must promise.'

Helen slid back into her chair, exchanging a glance with Jerry. If a mind could boggle, whatever boggling was, hers was doing it now. The possibilities were endless. Mawgan said,

'I had a letter from Deb's mum.'

'Ah,' said Jerry, after a long and pregnant pause.

'Shit!' said Helen, conversationally. She didn't sound surprised.

'You could say that. She offered me a quarter of a million to ditch Deb.' He hadn't meant to say it quite so abruptly. Helen's eyes opened very wide, and Jerry said nothing. A nerve twitched beside his mouth, that was all, and his whole face seemed to tighten. After a pause, Mawgan went on,

'I was angry – no, there isn't a word for how I felt, so *angry* will just have to do. After all she's already done to Deb, and her prying into my private business and everything, it was just one thing too much. It was as if Deb was a *possession* to wrangle over, not a person in her own right, no concern for her feelings, her business, nothing! I told Chel I had to go and sort something out, and to tell Deb I'd be back in the evening … and I got into my car and I headed off to have it out with her. Not a very clever idea, I know that now.'

'And did you have it out with her?' asked Jerry. Dot had been *her usual snotty self* last night, but maybe they had misinterpreted the significance of that. He caught Helen's eye, and knew she was thinking exactly what he was thinking, had Mawgan thumped Dot after all? And if so …?

'I'm not quite sure what I did,' said Mawgan. 'Oh, I know what I *did*, of course, but …'

'Tell us,' said Jerry, when the silence had gone on too long. 'You have to, you know, or I can't help you. I presume I'm going to have to?'

'To be honest, I don't know that, either.' Mawgan pulled himself together, seeming to come back from a far distance. 'What I meant to do, was to put it to her that the only person who was going to be hurt if she carried on like this was her, and hadn't she better just give in. I thought she might be … well, reasonable, if she knew there wasn't anything else to do. Deb's her daughter, for God's sake!'

'This is Dot we're talking about,' said Helen, bitterly. 'The word *reasonable* isn't in her vocabulary.'

'I realise that now. I didn't at first. That's why ...' He broke off. This was turning out more difficult to explain even than he had expected. 'First thing, she wasn't home, which threw me. Some cleaning woman she had there told me she'd be back in the evening, around six. That meant straight away that I wouldn't get back to Deb until late, but I thought, I could ring her when I left here and make up something, tell some story, I had all afternoon to make one up ... but it didn't work out like that. For a start, she didn't get back until near enough seven o'clock. I was parked on the drive by that time, waiting for her.'

'That must have given her a surprise,' said Helen.

'I dunno – actually, I got the impression it frightened her to death.'

'Good!'

'Helen ...' said Jerry.

'I told her who I was, and she asked me in, said we couldn't talk outside or something, and then ... well, she just assumed that I'd come for the pay-off. And I ...' This was where the story became slightly questionable. Mawgan hesitated.

'Go on,' said Jerry.

'I was so bloody teasy by this time, I let her,' said Mawgan.

There was a silence, while Jerry and Helen appeared to consider this in all its aspects. Helen said,

'So what did she do? Did she give you a cheque then and there?'

'Post-dated, of course.' He sounded sardonic. Jerry said,

'And you took it.' A statement, not a question.

'I did. And then – God, I don't know what got into me! I behaved like some total yob from the rough end of town- I even sounded like one. I started threatening her – I was so bloody *furious* .' He put the palms of his hands over his eyes, leaning forward to hide his expression. 'You should just of heard me! My mum would have been dead ashamed – '

'Threatening her with what, exactly?' asked Jerry. He sounded merely interested, but bearing in mind Mawgan's turbulent history, and how little, in sober fact, they really knew about him, apprehension stirred beneath his calm.

'I told her,' said Mawgan, still not looking up, 'that if she didn't turn up at the church with a smile on her face, I'd send the cheque, and the letter, to your local newspaper. I don't even know what it *is*!'

'She fell for it?' asked Helen, her eyes sparkling.

'What, with me standing there like the wrath of God? Of course she fell for it. She wriggled a bit, but she believed me. I think she believed me. Whether she'll do it, after she's time to think it out, is something else.'

'So then, you left,' said Jerry, hopefully. Bad enough, but containable.

'No' said Mawgan. 'I went and told her, that wasn't the end of it. That she'd to lay off the lot of you, or else. And *then*, I left.'

'Bloody hell,' said Jerry, without meaning to. Helen looked awestruck.

'That sounds like pretty wholesale blackmail to me,' she said, reverently.

'Me, too,' said Mawgan, unhappily. Jerry said, levelly,

'And will you? Publish if she doesn't turn up?'

'Of course not, how could I do that to Deb – to any of you, come to that? Anyway, I can't. I burnt the cheque, and the letter, in that pub. Truth to tell, I was sick at myself. Only she stood there, so smug and sure she'd got me bang to rights, not caring a toss how Deb might feel – she *asked* for it.'

'She always does,' said Helen. She paused. 'I have to say, though, that she's never actually *got* it before. As a matter of fact, I don't know quite *what* to say.'

Jerry was thinking all round the problem, swiftly and thoroughly. If there was a way for Dot to recover and get back at Mawgan, she would do it – but was there? She didn't know the papers were burnt. She wouldn't risk the story getting out, surely. It looked to him uncommonly as if Mawgan had painted her into a corner. The cheque, after all, would never be cashed, she already knew that. She would have to live with the fact of its existence, even if it didn't actually exist any more. Just so long as nobody told her that. Mawgan wouldn't. He wouldn't. Helen certainly wouldn't.

It was, of course a crime, if you chose to look at it that way, and this time, a crime of which Mawgan couldn't claim it was an accident. On the other hand, the pure justice of it was so artistically correct that he could only admire it. It would very probably work, too. Dot would look after that herself, her own silly conceit and pride would see to it. The really brilliant thing was that only an outsider would have done it – and she had relegated Mawgan to the outside herself, learning nothing about him that might have given her a real weapon, just as if he didn't matter. Contemptuous. She always was.And the most beautiful part of all, when it came down to it, was that unless Dot chose to produce the cheque stub, Mawgan himself had destroyed the evidence, and without the cheque, or evidence that Mawgan had received the letter, there was nothing to say she wasn't making up the whole thing. It was a lovely job. He had only admiration.

'I think there's only one thing to be said,' he said, with quiet satisfaction. 'Nice one, Mawgan. Well done!'

It took a second for that to sink in. Mawgan looked up, shocked.

'What?'

'I think you may have just done what none of us ever had the guts or the means to do. Put her back in her box and slammed the lid down permanently.'

'That's not right. You could have, if it hadn't been other people involved.' Mawgan was clear on that. 'I just got lucky. That's not the same. Anyway, she was scared of me, I made damn sure of that. She's been watching too much telly, that one.'

Helen got up then, and put her arms round him, hugging him.

'Mawgan, you are wonderful! If ever Jerry had any doubts that you're the right man for Debbie, I hope he's buried them now!'

He had, Jerry realised. However unadmirable Mawgan's behaviour, it had proved one thing beyond doubt, Deb would always be safe with him. She wouldn't even be hurt by it, if they were careful now. It might be deplorable, but it was brilliant too.

'Right now,' he said, briskly. 'Let's work on the cover story. Deb knows you're here, so we must work out just *why* you're here, and come to that, totally rat-arsed in a pub. Fortunately, there is an explanation that will serve.'

'There is?' Mawgan looked surprised – no, startled was a better word, Jerry decided. Helen sat down again.

'I feel like a conspirator,' she said. 'Not a very able one, actually, because I can't think of a single thing that would be convincing. Jerry? The floor is yours.'

'I was going to get in touch with you,' said Jerry. 'Probably not write, but Deb isn't to know that. You see, we've located Angela Bartlett.'

'Who?' Mawgan stared at him. The name was familiar, but this morning he couldn't place it.

'Angela Bartlett. The younger of the two girls who got you convicted. She's seventeen now, and living with some man in Plymouth.'

'Hope he beats her, then,' said Mawgan, shocked. 'She and her mate nearly got me a life sentence.'

'It'll come as no consolation to know that she says she's sorry about that.'

'I'll clear away,' said Helen, and this time, nobody stopped her. When she had gone,

'*Sorry* is easy,' said Mawgan. 'Is she going to take it back?'

'We're working on it. I think, however, that she'll be glad to get it off her conscience.'

'Nice for her.'

'She was only a child, Mawgan. That's no excuse, I know.'

'She and her friend loused up my career, ruined my reputation, and sent me to prison. So no, it's no excuse.'

'Stick with that attitude, and it'll more than explain last night,' said Jerry, almost with satisfaction. 'And no – before you say anything, I'm not blaming you.'

'And the other little cow?'

'We haven't traced her yet. Bartlett reckons she's gone abroad.'

'Safest place for her.'

'Mawgan ...' said Jerry, and paused. 'Perhaps we'll discuss this when you get back from your honeymoon. There's no hurry.'

'What you mean, is, I might be halfway reasonable by then,' said Mawgan, with a ghost of a smile. 'OK.'

'Right.' Jerry looked at his watch. 'Now then, I must go, I have an appointment I can't miss, even for you. I'll just slip into the kitchen and say goodbye to Helen.'

Helen wasn't doing anything, he recalled that she had never been too hot on the washing up. She was leaning on the draining board, looking out at the sunlit spread of the harbour, pensive and still. Jerry went up to her and put his arm round her, drawing her to him. She moved into his embrace without speaking.

'Helen?' said Jerry. She let out a long sigh of contentment.

'Will you tell her you know, Jerry – tell Dot?'

'Certainly not! It would defeat the whole object.'

'And will it work – do you think it will stick? Will she leave us all alone?'

'With only a very little luck, yes. Will you marry me again, if it does?'

'No.'

'Oh, Helen – '

'You don't really want me to. And I don't want to marry again, either.'

'Then will you live with me?' asked Jerry, gently. 'Can you ever trust me again?'

Helen said, precisely,

'I don't want to be put in a position where I have to. Yes Jerry, I'll live with you – when it suits us both. I've missed you.' He would never guess how much, she would never give him the satisfaction of hearing it from her. She said, businesslike, 'We can work something out. But only if Dot comes to Debbie's wedding, then I'll *know* that we're safe. I can't go through all that again'

'I loved you, you know. Always.'

'You had a very funny way of showing it.'

'I didn't understand you.'

'And we both know why.'

'Did you love me?' He was suddenly very serious.

Helen looked up, deep into his eyes. For a long time she said nothing at all, and when she did speak, he could have considered it a disappointment. She pushed herself away from him.

'Go to work, Jerry. You're late already.' She smiled. 'Last night was good, wasn't it?'

'Last night,' said Jerry, fumbling for words to express what he felt, 'was water after drought, spring after snow, rest after a long struggle …'

'Nobody ever said anything prettier to me,' said Helen.

Reluctantly, Jerry prepared to leave.

'Stay with him,' he said. 'I don't like to ask, but he shouldn't go back quite yet, I don't think, and I don't think he should be alone.'

'Of course I will. Don't worry, Jerry. I'll help you keep Deb's happiness intact.' She leaned across, not touching him with her hands or body, and kissed him lightly on the lips. 'Go.'

Jerry went back into the living room, wondering if she would be there when he got home that evening, and found that Mawgan had gone out onto the balcony into the fresh air, leaning on the rail and, like Helen, looking down on the harbour. He looked, Jerry thought, utterly destroyed, and deserved to, but at the same time at peace, as if the events of last night had, however unfortunately, vanquished some monster that had ridden on his shoulders for too long.

'Nice view, isn't it?' said Jerry, going quietly to stand beside him.

'Not bad. Not home, though.'

'Go back there,' said Jerry, gently. 'This afternoon. I reckon you're probably still over the limit now, so wait until lunchtime, will you, before starting off? Go for a brisk walk, would be good, and Helen'll drive you to the Crown & Anchor to pick up your car. And I'll see you in just over a week.' He held out his hand, and Mawgan took it, finding his own warmly gripped. 'And don't worry about Dot. She had it coming, and if you want my view, she may call your bluff – in the end, anyway – but she won't make a court case out of it if nothing happens. She hasn't really a leg to stand on anyway.'

'I feel a bit ... brutal,' said Mawgan, returning the grip firmly.

'Don't. That's her line. You've vindicated a long line of victims, if you want to know. Drive carefully. And, Mawgan ...' It maybe wasn't his business, but Jerry was going to say it anyway.

'What?'

'Don't let alcohol become a way of escaping from life's problems. It's a very easy trap to fall into, if you're inclined that way.'

'You mean, I am?'

'I just mean, watch it. You'll be a better husband for my daughter if you can face things without it.'

'Yeah … I know. I'll watch it.'

He would, Jerry thought, as he drove to his office. When he remembered, he would. He was no fool, he was very ambitious and he genuinely loved Debbie. But it was ironic that the one person who had had the guts to slap Dot down now felt guilty about it. Dot, sadly, would never appreciate the irony. He wondered if she would say anything, and decided that he wouldn't give her the opportunity. Let her stew! And as for Mawgan, well, he recalled what Susan had said, so unexpectedly, the night she had told him about the detective.

He's probably capable of things that we are not. If he's pushed, he'll push back …

Well, he certainly had done that.

But he did wonder if Dot would appear at Deb's wedding, and if she did, where would his own life go thereafter?

XIX

The clock was counting down. The car park at the Fish had virtually disappeared beneath a huge, fancy marquee and the restaurant kitchen, shut down over the past month, was up and humming with activity once more. The wedding cake had been iced, unexpectedly and beautifully, by that same Marie Tregear who had told her grandfather's story to the media, and now waited, safely boxed against accidents, beside a swirling contemporary tiered cake stand in the comparative safety of the office. In various places around the Mediterranean, the Swiss Alps, the south of England and Cornwall, people were beginning to shake out their wedding finery and take suitcases out of cupboards.

Into the sheltered mouth of St Erbyn creek, completing a brisk and wintry passage under sail from Falmouth, a sleek white Feeling 326 with a light drifting of snow on her deck crept under engine and picked up an empty mooring under the windows of the village, and Debbie's two partners, looking unlikely ushers, scudded ashore in an inflatable dinghy in search of showers and beer, not necessarily in that order. They would remain there now, living on board, until the season started, working on Debbie's behalf and seeing to her business affairs while she was away on her extended honeymoon. Pip Angwin and his men worked on in the sealed-off restaurant, stepping on and around television camera men who were trying to make their short documentary before their quarry skipped to warmer climes and getting under everybody's feet as they did so. Con Delaney, celebrity DJ, was heard to make a suggestive joke on the radio about seeing a friend safely onto the road to ruin at the weekend, and predicting a serious hangover by Monday. Lighthearted and apparently taking his listeners into his confidence, he somehow omitted to say exactly who, when or where. The television anchor man, preparing to include the event as the wind-up to the documentary, and feeling that Oliver

Nankervis was enough cream to put on the top, had no idea of the extra dollop that was about to come his way.

'I *can't* go away and leave it all for a month,' said Mawgan, pleading for mercy.

'Oh yes, you can!' cried Debbie and Chel, in chorus. It was pantomime time in the village, it tended to be infectious.

'And we don't want to see you again until we can reckernise you, neither,' Pip added, severely. 'Poor Deb here, she don't even know who she's marrying!'

Up the road at Seagulls, the wintry weather had brought a temporary stop to work, allowing Allison time to get her nails back into shape for her appearance as a bridesmaid.

In a studio in St Ives, Nonie Theodorakis, after long and careful thought, summoned the courage to make a phone call.

'Helen,' she said, when the call was answered. 'Nonie here.' There was a silence, so long that Nonie added, 'Are you there?'

'Yes, I'm here,' said Helen. 'What may I do for you?'

'Come off it, Helen,' said Nonie, while acknowledging the justice of Helen's reaction. 'I just got to thinking, Deb wants you at her wedding, but it might be a bit awkward for you if you stay among the family, with Susan there and everything. I thought you might like to stay with us. We're going too, and it would give you a … a place.'

Since this was a problem that had occupied Helen's thoughts on and off for some time, she was conscious of a strong feeling of reprieve. But she couldn't just grab at the offered lifeline, there was too much baggage to carry around … or maybe, just abandon. The thought, light and soft and pure as the snowflakes that blew about in the wind outside, floated into her head, spun around and spiralled down gently to settle. She said,

'Well …'

'We aren't young any more,' said Nonie, understanding perfectly. 'If age has one compensation, it has to be the learning of wisdom. Why throw a perfectly good friendship out of the window for something that by this time can't be helped? It happened, we can't alter that ... but can we forget it, Hel? Or no, not that, but put it behind us? Get it into perspective? Start afresh?'

The old name slipped out. Nonie bit her lip, but didn't make the mistake of trying to correct it. Far away in Surrey, Helen hesitated.

'We can never get back to how it was,' she said.

'Who wants to? We're different people now. And I do rather resent, when I think about it, that we let Dot Shipham shoot us down.'

Helen had already relinquished her resistance to Jerry, and she knew that whether Dot came to the wedding or not, there was no going back from that. It would be good too, she suddenly realised, to be able to call Nonie her friend again unreservedly.

There was no telling whether Dot was really disarmed, but as Nonie said, they were older now. She could only hurt them, had only ever been able to hurt them, if they themselves allowed it.

'Actually,' said Helen, coming to a decision, 'I should like that very much. If you're sure.'

Nonie took this as ambivalently as it was meant.'

'Well, that's good then,' she said. 'See you on Friday?'

'I don't,' said Helen, finding it suddenly both strange and unacceptable, 'even know where you live. It isn't still in the old studio.'

So Nonie told her, and gave directions, and Helen put the phone down and stood there for quite a long time, thinking that she knew now exactly how the Prodigal Son had felt when he came home after his years in the wilderness.

Outside the windows, the sky was the colour of wood ash, and flakes of snow fluttered fitfully down, not settling seriously, but persistent. It looked as if it might turn out a white wedding in every sense, had said Chel, but the forecast was clear skies at the weekend. Hope on!

* * * * *

Closer to the heart of the family, things were not so happy.

Dot had still come to no decision as to what she was going to do, or not one that she would admit to, at least. She had told nobody, certainly not Jerry, about her frightening experience with the bully-boy from the boondocks, as she thought of him, trying to minimise his effect on her by pouring scorn. Only, it wasn't working. The memory of that night hung about in the back of her mind like a thundercloud, although the moment of self-perception that had followed it had been conveniently filed away and forgotten. Whenever she thought about him, standing there solid and inimical in his black leather jacket with *that* look on his face, she felt cold. Whatever could Deborah see in him? He was nothing but a thug!

A dangerous thug, who knew too much about her and had no reason to want to keep it to himself.

Dot opened her wardrobe door and peered inside, then closed it again with a bang. Whatever was she thinking of? She wasn't going to put on wedding garments and dance at her daughter's wedding to that ... that *yahoo*!

If she didn't, Jonathan Holmes, editor of the *Embridge Herald*, would take great pleasure in crucifying her. Private humiliation, within the family, would be marginally better than public humiliation outside it, but even so, a bitter pill to swallow. She could almost feel herself choking on it, even just thinking about it.

Still she hesitated, unable to make up her mind. He was obviously a nasty bit of work, but would he really do what he had said? Could she risk it?

Don't put money on it.

The clock ticked on.

* * * * *

'Do you think,' said Tom, approaching the subject with caution, 'That Deb would be very upset if I couldn't make it to her wedding?'

'What?' Susan stared at him.

'Well, it isn't as if we're that close,' Tom continued, over-explaining. 'It's you and the children that she really wants. You see, there's an audit overdue, and old Hetherington is beginning to rumble. I ought to get it sorted out as soon as possible.'

Susan sat very still. A horrible feeling that the room and its furnishings were crumbling around her kept her speechless for a moment. When she did speak, it was in a voice she didn't even recognise.

'You can't do that.'

'But you won't miss me,' Tom persisted. 'You're standing in for your mother, you'll have your father there.' He smiled at her, persuasively. 'You know I wouldn't ask, Susan, if it wasn't important. This is a big client we're talking here.'

Susan said, through stiff lips,

'They have no right to give the work to you, not at the last minute like this. This few days off has been arranged for weeks. Months, even.'

'That's the way the cookie crumbles,' said Tom, with a fatalistic shrug of his shoulders. 'We've had one or two off with 'flu, things get behind, you know how it goes.'

'I'll talk to Uncle Alex,' said Susan. Tom's boss had been a friend of her natural father: he knew her mother, which was how she had met Tom in the first place. He was one of her trustees; she had known him since childhood, and spoke with the deliberate intention of calling her husband's bluff, the only thought in her mind being to escape humiliation in front of everyone at the wedding. Tom might think her a fool, she wasn't. Tom's easy manner, she thought, so reasonable, so calm, betrayed his true intentions, it would have been more clever to seem upset. Fighting back was a natural reaction, but as she spoke she knew that it was provocative. Even so, his counter reaction astonished her.

'You can't do that!' he cried. Susan looked at him in apparently genuine astonishment.

'Why not? It's a long-standing engagement, he must see that. You can't have explained properly.'

'You'll make me look a fool,' said Tom. He went on, working himself up, 'You and your mother, both of you, you're so *arrogant*! You think you can run people's lives!'

'I thought it was your boss who was doing that,' said Susan. She narrowed her eyes at him, she had him on the run now. 'This isn't about work at all, is it? It's about you sneaking off for a weekend with Elaine. When the cat's away, the mouse will play. *That's* why you don't want me to talk to him.'

Perhaps she should have avoided that word, *mouse*, on reflection. She waited.

'Susan!' Tom was instantly full of righteous indignation. 'How could you think such a thing? You know I love you!'

Months of hurt feelings suddenly crystallised into rebellion at the bare-faced lie..

'Oh, are you telling me there isn't a precedent?' Susan flashed.

Tom went red, with shame or with anger, who knew? He said,

'Oh, if you're going to take that attitude, there's no use in talking to you!' He turned away to the door.

'Don't you *dare* run away!' said Susan. 'Let's have this out, *now*!' Immediately she had spoken, she could have bitten her tongue. Confrontation was what she had promised herself to avoid, now here she was, lighting the fuse herself.

Tom took his hand from the door handle and turned away from the door, not realising that he had left it ajar, and walked back towards her. She had never seen his face so angry.

'All right, since you insist,' he said. 'Yes, this is about Elaine. She's young, she's lively, she's sexy, she's fun. You aren't. Are you going to argue with any of that?'

Susan went white. She said,

'Tom ...'

'Don't pretend you only just found out!' said Tom. 'One of your nosy friends must have told you by this time. So, what are you going to do about it?'

Susan's momentary loss of control was over – well, almost.

'I think it's more, what are *you* going to do about it?' she suggested. 'Our home, our children, our friends – even if you don't care about me –' the words almost choked her. She ended, on a pitiful note that shocked her, never mind Tom. 'You must at least care about the children.'

'Of course I do. Why do you think I'm still here?'

Beyond the door, Annabel stood transfixed, her ear to the crack, hardly daring to breathe. Her heart thumped hard against her ribs. She was scared, without fully understanding exactly why.

'I thought,' said Susan, through stiff lips, 'that it might have been because Elaine was only a bit of fun.'

Tom laughed.

'Oh, come on Susan! When did you last look in the mirror? Your main attraction has always been your money, you're hardly a sex-object. You must have known that! I'm sure your manipulative mother did. She bought me, Susan, waved your great fortune under my nose. Face up to it.'

Susan heard someone wailing, and realised, with a shock, that it was herself. Beyond the door, Annabel winced and put her hands over her ears. Tears stole down her cheeks, her safe world began to disintegrate around her. She wanted to run, but where was there to run to? She stayed. The horrible noise stopped as suddenly as it had begun.

Susan stood, with her hands folded over her mouth, unable to believe that she had done that, and Tom stared back at her in a similar state of shock.

'Look, Susan,' he said, suddenly wishing back the last ten minutes. 'We must talk. We should have talked ages ago.'

Susan removed her hands.

'I don't think there's anything left to say,' she said. The simple statement hung in the air almost solidly. Tom said,

'I won't leave the children, you know that.'

'Do I? But you won't give up Elaine either, is what you're saying.'

'Well … yes.' He had the grace to look uncomfortable. 'But we can work something out, I'm sure we can.'

'And where will that leave me?' asked Susan, not wanting to hear the answer.

'Well … I'll still be living here, the children won't suffer, they won't even know.'

'Don't bet on it.'

'I can sleep in one of the spare rooms, if you like.'

'And what do you suppose Maria will make of that?' asked Susan, caustically.

'Maria is only a servant. It doesn't matter what she thinks.'

'To you, maybe.'

Tom shrugged his shoulders.

'It's up to you. I can move out, if you prefer, but then everyone will know, the children will suffer. Do you want that?'

Susan closed her eyes, trying to contain pain.

'So what you're saying, is you'll stay with me for the sake of the children, but continue to see Elaine, and I can just put up with it and be on my own?'

Tom fidgeted.

'Come on, Suse, it won't be like that.'

The use of the friendly family diminutive was just too much. Susan felt another howl pressing against her teeth and clenched them to hold it back. When she could speak, she said,

'Yes Tom, it will be like that. I need time to think.' *I can't bear to hurt the children, I can't let the family break up, I can't, I can't, I can't! I don't want my marriage to end in a divorce. I can't face this awful loneliness. I can't.*

She had nobody to turn to. She couldn't confide this humiliation to any of her friends, it was too bitter, too shaming. She couldn't confide in her mother, who would tell her to make the sacrifice. Her sister was too busy preparing to make a very different marriage to her own. She might once have confided in Chel, they had almost become friends at one time ... but, she had alienated Chel herself. Chel, who might have been the only safe repository for her secrets if she herself had been less ... yes, Tom was right. *Arrogant.* But she hadn't meant it.

'Take as much as you like,' Tom was saying, and her thoughts had ranged so far and so fast that it didn't make any sense to her. She pulled herself together. Time to contain the damage, until she had had a chance to deploy her arguments and fight for what she wanted, not necessarily for herself, but for Annabel and Sebastian, whom she was determined were not going to be the children of a broken home.

'Let's go a step at a time,' she said, trying to keep her voice steady. 'First thing, you can't duck out of Debbie's wedding. You know that.'

'If it ever comes off,' said Tom, smiling nastily. 'Your mother still has time to stop it, you know.'

Susan did know, but her mother had gone suspiciously quiet on the subject just recently. She was no more stupid than Helen, and she could add two and two. She did wonder ... but her mother hadn't said anything, and nor had her father. She couldn't even face the possibilities at this precise moment.

'If it doesn't, that'll be another thing,' she said, amazed at the calmness of her own voice.

'She'll leap up in the congregation and say she knows a just cause and impediment,' said Tom, only half-joking.

'She can't. There isn't one.'

Outside the door, Annabel had removed her listening ear and leaned against the doorframe, her eyes tight shut and tears squeezing out under her lashes and running down her cheeks. It was going to happen, she knew it. Everything was going to go awful, just like it had in her friend Annie's home, shouting and screaming and rows, and then everything different and horrible, and Mummy and Daddy not being together any more, and she and Sebastian being batted back and forth like two tennis balls, that nobody cared about if they fell on the ground and got hurt and kicked around. Perhaps they would be sent to live with Grandma, that had happened to one of her friends when her Mummy died. She cried harder, too miserable even to move away from the door, although she knew that if Daddy caught her listening, he would be very, very angry. It was here that Maria found her.

Beyond the door, Tom was saying,

'And if I do that?'

'Not just that,' said Susan, pushing home an advantage. 'Every other family occasion in the future. Make it look right for the children.'

It would never work, she knew it. The children weren't babies, and they were both intelligent, but it was all she could think of for now. If they were going to do a trade, it must be equal on both sides. It must protect the children.

A thought crept into her head and out again. *And Tom will have Elaine, and the only person who will be paying will be me.* The children, she must protect the children. She couldn't think any more.

'Take it or leave it,' she said.

Tom thought of Elaine, and then of his own comfortable lifestyle. He looked at Susan, drawn with shock and unhappiness and looking ten years more than her age. Elaine was twenty-two. He thought of his children and, like Susan, knew that they would never buy the package, so was it worth even trying? He was already much shaken by the devastation that he had caused, didn't know how it had blown up out of a clear sky and a reasonable request – well, an unreasonable request framed reasonably, anyway – but there was no going back now. He did the best he could, for himself, for the children, who knew?

'All right. We'll leave it like that for now. Talk after the wedding.'

'And you're coming to it.' It was a statement, not a question. Tom didn't reply. He went over to the door, opened it fully, and passed through into the empty hall. He would have to explain to Elaine and just hope she understood that it had been a good idea that just wasn't going to come to anything.

Susan sat down abruptly on the nearest chair.

She was still sitting there when Maria came in half an hour later. Sitting there motionless, as if she was afraid that to move would shatter her into pieces all over the carpet. Her face, Maria thought, was frighteningly blank. She went over to her and without speaking, put her arms round the redoubtable Mrs Casson of whom, to be truthful, she stood a little in awe. Her mother had been right in her letter, she thought. Her mother was a wise woman of great experience. She held Susan in her arms and let her weep until she was exhausted, allowing her silent sympathy to work its comforting magic until the storm was over.

'Now then,' she said, when she thought that Mrs Casson was listening. 'That is enough. You go now and wash your poor face, and Maria will make you a nice cup of tea.'

Susan thought she ought to be ashamed of crying on the *au pair*, but for some reason, found that she wasn't. There was something about Maria's calm acceptance that steadied her.

'I'm sorry, Maria,' she said. Her voice was hoarse with crying. 'You must think me a fool.'

'No, Mrs Casson, I do not. But when you are feeling better, may I speak with you?'

'Oh no – ' Susan didn't want to speak with anyone, ever again.

'I am sorry,' said Maria, and sounded as if it was true. 'Annabel was outside the door, she heard what was said. I have calmed her, but it cannot be left like this.'

'Did you hear?' asked Susan, meeting her eyes.

'No. But she has told me. That is why I must speak with you.'

Cold water splashed onto her hot face and sore eyes, and a hot cup of tea in the friendly warmth of the kitchen restored some of Susan's self-possession. She had rejected the idea that Maria brought the tea to the drawing room, at that moment she didn't care if she never set foot in it again. It also allowed time for Maria to find the right words. Even in Polish, she thought, they would have been impossible. In a foreign language whose deeper nuances she hardly understood, it was beyond impossible, but still, her mother had insisted, it had to be said. For the children's sake, and, she suddenly knew, for Mrs Casson's sake too. Mrs Casson was a strong, brave woman, who, left to herself would make a senseless decision that would ruin her own life and do nothing to help those of her children. From what she had been told, Maria's mother had been certain of it.

'Mrs Casson,' said Maria.

'You want to speak to me,' said Susan, tiredly. 'Maria, I *will* listen, but does it have to be now?'

'I think, yes it does. Annabel is distressed.'

'Yes.' Susan sighed. 'I'll go and talk to her, of course. When my face has cooled down. I can't go like this.'

'It is not only today,' said Maria. 'It is many days, now. The little Sebastian and the bad dreams, Annabel's defiance.

When I bring them from the school, the teachers say, are they happy at home? I cannot answer, I tell them, but I know. No, they are not.'

Susan buried her face in her hands, her elbows on the table. She felt suffocated already with shame and misery. She didn't need this from Maria.

'Maria ...'

'Listen,' said Maria. If she didn't say it now, she knew she wouldn't. 'It is not good for children, it is not good for you, to be so unhappy. I know what you will say, they need their father, and it is not for me to tell you different.' She paused, then, as Mrs Casson said nothing, she went on. 'Children always know when things are not right, they are like little animals. Things are not right in this house since a long time. It is not my business, you say.'

'No, it isn't,' said Susan, muffled.

'Somebody must make it their business,' said Maria, stoutly. She quailed for a moment, but then she seemed to hear her mother's voice, urging her on. 'If you and Mr Casson can arrange your disagreement, then that is good. But to be unhappy yourself because of the children is not good. They will not be safe, they will know it. And they will feel that it is their fault.'

'So what are you saying?' asked Susan. She couldn't look at Maria. She felt as if the whole foundation of her life was shaking irretrievably.

'I cannot say for you,' said Maria. 'It is for you to make your mind, but this I say. If you decide that you and the children will be better on your own, then I come with you, if you wish, until the children are settled. And if you and Mr Casson are again happy, then I stay until all are happy with you. That is all.'

'Maria ...,' said Susan. She screwed up her fists and pressed them to her eyes against the too-ready tears. Maria understood her to say, *you are good*, but wasn't sure. She reached out and touched Mrs Casson's wrist, sympathetically.

'My mother say, you prepare for the worst, it do not happen,' she said.

Susan twisted her hand so that she could clasp Maria's. Beneath her closed lids, more tears slid silently down her face. She had never felt so defeated, while at the same time never having felt so ... comforted? And in such an unexpected quarter, too. Maria pressed a tissue into her hand.

'Now, there is no need for this, Mrs Casson. Dry your eyes. Your children need you to be strong, and you must go to them. You must tell that all will be well, that you will make a good thing for them, that they must be patient and help you. They are good children. They will trust you and understand. They will feel better if you will say there is problem, and they can help you, it is the not knowing that is so bad. So Annabel tell me, and I believe her.'

There was a sound from the door, and Maria, looking up, saw the children there, huddled together and looking frightened. She beckoned them in.

'Come, your mother is sad. You must help her. All will be well, believe Maria.'

Sebastian ran forward to hug his mother, Annabel followed more slowly.

'Daddy drove away,' she said. 'He was angry, you could tell. He always drives like that when he's angry. Little bits of gravel going everywhere.'

'He'll be back.' Susan pulled herself together and returned Sebastian's hug. She held out her hand to Annabel. 'Come here. It's all right. It'll be all right.'

Annabel came forward slowly and allowed herself to be drawn close. She said, in a whisper,

'Is Daddy going to go away?'

'Not from you. Never from you.' Susan hugged her children tightly. 'We won't let you be hurt, promise.' And what an empty pledge that was.

'You and Daddy are always fighting now,' said Sebastian, in a very small voice.

'Yes, and we must talk about it, but between ourselves. You mustn't worry about it. You'll be all right.'

'We won't have to live with Grandma,' said Annabel, anxiously.

'No darling. You'll always live with me, and Maria will be there, and Daddy too, but maybe just not like we do now.'

Sebastian said, in a whisper so quiet it could hardly be heard.

'Can we go to Cornwall and all of us live with Auntie Debbie?'

Susan laughed. She made herself, although she thought her heart would break.

'I think Auntie Debbie might have something to say to that.'

'Sebastian, you are silly!' said Annabel, sounding more like herself.

They were cheering up already, Susan realised, at her own assurance and with the calming presence of Maria, and also with the childish certainty that grown-ups could make everything right, that they were not yet old enough to have seen for the fools' gold that it was. She loved them more than she had ever thought she did, she realised. She loved them to the point where she would suffer anything to keep them safe, but Maria was right, if she lived with Tom in a marriage of convenience – his convenience, of course – they would know. There was no easy way. But a way there must be, for all of them.

The hurtful things that Tom had said to her, that surely nobody could live with after they had been brought into the open, she pushed to the back of her mind, she couldn't face them right now. Just let them get through Debbie's wedding and then they could talk it out. Maybe Tom would be sorry he had gone so far, when he had calmed down and thought about it, and they could reach an acceptable compromise. And if they couldn't?

Then they would find the way that would hurt the children least, and they would take it.

She and Maria, her unexpected ally.

She hoped so much that it wouldn't come to that, while knowing in her heart that from some events there is no going back. Rejection burned into her, changing her perceptions. Only her children wanted her, needed her. Not her husband, not her adoptive father, not her half-brother or her half-sister, not in the way that she wanted them to do. Her mother cared, but only in her own way: her daughter's divorce, if it came to that, would be seen as an unforgivable failure that she would never be allowed to forget, in spite of her mother's own legal separation, Susan knew that all too well. That being the case, she wouldn't let her children down. And if they were on their own, then so be it.

Her heart misgave her then. She didn't want to be on her own.

If Tom backed down on this one it would be for her money, not for her. In the future, there would be other Elaines. Could she face that? Really?

There was a phrase that covered it, Susan thought wryly. *Small choice in rotten apples.* Then she looked up and met Maria's encouraging smile. Lucky Maria, no money, no husband, no problems. The words welled up out of her subconscious and nearly brought the tears back.

All I wanted was a man who would love me the way Oliver loves Chel, the way Mawgan loves Debbie, someone I could love in return. Was it so much to ask? Why does this have to happen to me?

But answer came there none.

* * * * *

'This feels odd,' said Helen, standing at the window of Nonie's tiny spare room and looking out at the shining sea beyond the cliff edge.

'Just odd, not wrong?' said Nonie.

'Certainly not wrong.' Helen spoke without looking round. 'Its oddness lies in its familiarity. I used to come to stay with you, in the old days. In the studio.'

'You did.'

Helen sighed.

'They were good days, while they lasted.'

'Yes, they were. Some of them, not all.'

'Do you think,' said Helen, turning away from the view and coming to perch on the edge of the bed beside her erstwhile dearest friend. 'Do you think that it *is* ever possible to go back?'

'No,' said Nonie. 'And neither do you.'

'You always were swingeingly honest,' said Helen, ruefully.

'Is this about me? Or about Jerry? Or Oliver?'

'All of you, I suppose.'

'Well then,' said Nonie. 'It's true, you can't wipe out what's happened in the past and be back where we were thirty years ago. But I suppose a second chance isn't ruled out. To make something new of it, but in the now.'

'Oliver and I will never achieve a mother/son relationship. He's too old, he's been through too much. And he's against mothers on principle.'

'I can't say that I blame him. Can't you settle for friendship?'

'I would, if he'd allow it.'

'He will, if you give him time. If ...' Nonie paused, then got to her feet. 'Come downstairs. We'll have a drink, shall we?'

'Good idea.' Helen stood up and followed her to the door. 'Where's Theo? I expected him to be here, to be honest.' Had hoped for it, if truth were told, to help to break the ice.

'He will be. He flew into Exeter, ooh about ...' Nonie glanced at her watch. 'Half an hour ago, if the plane was on time from Athens.'

'It's very strange, being here with you, and all that age you lived that I know nothing about. Marrying a Greek! I'd never have seen that for you.'

'Me neither, if you really want to know,' said Nonie, but she smiled as she said it.

'Are you happy?' asked Helen, as they went downstairs.

'Yes.' Nonie led the way into her sitting room; blazing log fire, deep, comfortable sofa and chairs, old wood. 'This room always reminds me of that cottage you and Jerry had when you were first married,' she said, with intent. Helen looked sad.

'Me too. It was the first thing I thought when I saw it.' She added, for the second time, 'They were good days.'

'Don't get sentimental,' Nonie advised. 'Sit down, get warm, it's freezing outside, you must be perished. Usual dram?'

'Please. Nothing changes, in that respect at least.'

Nonie poured the drinks and sat down in the opposite armchair by the fire. She leaned forward to throw on another log.

'So, Debbie is going to marry her chef in spite of Dot,' she said. 'She didn't give in to coercion, then? I have to say, I've been on tenterhooks this last few weeks. It isn't like Dot to be defeated.'

Helen hesitated. Nonie's ability to keep a secret had lain at the root of the break-up of their original friendship, and was therefore in no doubt. She thought, it would be interesting to hear her views. She put out a cautious feeler.

'Did you like him – Mawgan? When you met him?'

'Goodness, there's a question! I don't know him that well, we've only met about twice. He seems an unlikely choice for Debbie on the face of it, but I suppose it's the attraction of opposites. They will certainly never be dull together!'

'No.'

'And what about you and Jerry?' asked Nonie, directly. 'He still loves you, you know. He says he does.'

'I know,' said Helen. She fell silent. Nonie watched her for a few minutes, sipping her whisky with her face turned away, towards the fire. The firelight played on the fine bones of her skull, on her still-perfect skin, and threw shadows into her wonderful dark blue eyes. Helen would still be beautiful when she was ninety. No wonder Jerry still lusted after her. Silly man!

'Are you going to do anything about it?' she asked.

'Maybe – if – ' She broke off.

'If what?' asked Nonie, curiously. 'Come on, Helen, what's up? You aren't still afraid of Dot, are you? After all this time?'

'Not for myself, no. For what she might do to Jerry, maybe yes.'

'I would have thought Jerry was bombproof. The very model of an upright solicitor.'

'I have a feeling Dot might know where one or two bodies are buried. They've been married a long time, and whatever else she is, she isn't stupid.'

'Really?' Nonie sounded interested. 'You don't think Jerry *is* an upright solicitor?'

'Only so far as any of them is.'

'You old cynic, you!'

'I'm not saying,' said Helen, 'that there *are* any bodies, only that if there are, she will have sniffed them out. I wonder if that may be why Jerry hasn't divorced her. And I don't want to make him vulnerable, even if he might deserve it.'

'Sounds like a Mexican stand-off,' said Nonie, sceptically. 'Do *you* love *him*? It sounds as if you might, to me.'

Helen looked at her helplessly.

'Yes. Fool that I am, I don't think I ever stopped. Oh, I didn't swear a vow of celibacy or anything, any more than he did, but ... well, there was always Jerry, there in the background. I couldn't help it,' she pleaded, as if Nonie was blaming her.

'Oooh dear!'

Helen came to a decision. She hadn't actually been sworn to secrecy, and it would be interesting to hear Nonie's forthright views.

'As a matter of fact, it may not be *oh dear* at all. If I tell you something, will you swear on darling Matt's grave never to tell a living soul?'

'Cut my throat if I lie! What have you been up to?'

'Not me,' disclaimed Helen. 'It all began one night I went to the theatre with Jerry – '

'Well, that was a step forward!'

'Hush. Listen.' She leaned forward. 'We'd just got back to his flat. I was spending the night – in his spare room, before you say anything – and then, the phone rang, and it was Susan ...' She recounted the tale, and Nonie sat there listening, round-eyed. When it was over, Nonie said, awestruck,

'And do you think Dot will give in to such blatant blackmail?'

'I think she might. You see, whether he intended it or not, and I don't suppose he did because he doesn't know her like we do, Mawgan found her Achilles heel. She couldn't bear public shame.'

'Who could?' asked Nonie, rhetorically. She added, 'And do you think he has the steel to carry out his threat?'

'He can't. He burnt the cheque and the letter in the pub. But I do believe he has the steel to make her believe he will, and to make it stick. As he might say himself, he's some formidable when he gets the bit between his teeth, is Mawgan. I wouldn't like to cross him, I tell you for free. Particularly not at the moment, when his brakes are half-off. Dot didn't know that. Her problem.'

'He seems so pleasant,' said Nonie, objecting.

'He *is* pleasant. Pleasant, fun, easy-going on the surface. He's of a generous spirit, and would do anything in the world, probably, for Deb, lucky girl. But even so, don't jostle him in a doorway on a bad day. Personally, I think he's a star. Literally, probably. But then I may be prejudiced in his favour.'

'Goodness! So you don't envisage any dramatics at the altar tomorrow?'

'No,' said Helen, with quiet satisfaction. 'No. I think he got her bang to rights, she'll leave us all alone now. But whether she'll actually be there is another question altogether, and remains to be seen. If she is, then we can be sure.'

'And what then?'

'Then the case of Jerry Nankervis *versus* Helen Macken will be re-opened,' said Helen, with quiet satisfaction.

'I take it then, that you didn't spend the night in the spare room after all?' said Nonie. They exchanged a smile.

'No, how could I? We had to put Mawgan in there, Tom had told Susan she couldn't take him home with her, and on the whole, he was right. My God, he'd had a skinful! I don't think he remembered a thing about it the next morning! To be honest, I don't think he could even *think* for a while, and serve him right!'

'*God moves in a mysterious way,*' observed Nonie, apparently guilelessly.

'Yes. *His wonders to perform,*' said Helen, looking into the flames with a quiet smile.

Nonie hesitated, but she had to ask. 'And if she doesn't come? Dot?'

'I may tease Jerry a bit – he deserves it, after all, but I shall probably, in the end, put my trust in Mawgan. He's rock.'

'Marry him again? He'll have to divorce Dot first, she won't like that.'

'Nor did I. But no. Live with him. Love him. Not trust him, maybe, one hundred per-cent, but be happy anyway. If I'm free to walk, he's more likely to wish me to stay.'

'You always were wise,' Nonie remarked. They exchanged a smile. The years rolled back. Nonie raised her glass.

'A toast. A tripartite one,' she said.

'To what?'

'To our old friend Daniel Peachey, may he rest in peace.' The glasses clinked. 'To Matt.' Clink again. 'And to us, and the future.'

They drank, and the firelight flickered, amber, on the spirit in their glasses and the dawning new friendship in their eyes.

XX

Debbie woke up on the morning of her wedding with butterflies in the stomach and a headache. The headache was due partly to the – fairly moderate, in fact – consumption of alcohol the previous evening, but mainly to not having slept very well in a strange bed, general opinion having insisted that it was unlucky for the bride and groom to see each other before they met in church, which precluded her usual cosy night in Mawgan's bed at the Fish. Since they had been living together for five months, there was no need for the butterflies, but there they were, fluttering about more like great vultures, she thought, and making her feel rather sick. She sat up.

In the other narrow bed against the opposite wall of the small bedroom, her friend Lindsey yawned, turned over, and opened her eyes, blearily.

'Hullowazzatime?' she mumbled. Debbie picked up her watch from the chest between them and peered at it.

'Seven. Almost.'

'Urrrrgh!' Lindsey closed her eyes again. 'Aren't you supposed to be getting your beauty sleep?'

'We always wake at seven,' said Debbie. 'Earlier, sometimes.' She heard the argumentative pitch to her voice, and bit her lip.

'Don't you pick a quarrel with me,' said Lindsey, without animosity. She sat up too, and yawned. 'Would your sister–in–law kill me if I went down and made us a cup of coffee?'

'Brilliant!' Debbie threw back the duvet. 'I'll go. I know where everything is.'

Lindsey didn't move, but she did say, without enthusiasm,

'It's my duty as your bridesmaid, isn't it, to see you get a lie-in?'

'I don't do lie-ins these days,' said Debbie. She was already halfway to the door. Lindsey fell back onto her pillow. She was asleep again before Debbie reached the top of the stairs.

In the kitchen, not much to her surprise, Debbie found her brother already busy with the *cafetière*. At the point where Susan, together with Chel's sister Tracy, had gone back down to the Fish and she and Lindsey and Chel had finally retired to bed, Oliver and Jerry had not returned, but nevertheless, Oliver looked bright-eyed and wide awake.

'Hullo,' he said, predictably. 'I thought you were supposed to be slugging in bed, preparing for battle.'

'Load of balls,' said Debbie, crudely. She pulled out a chair and sat down at the table. 'Pour me one, while you're at it. I need it.'

Oliver looked at her sympathetically.

'Bad attack of the jangling nerves?'

'You could say that.' She accepted the mug he handed her, and took that first, reviving sip. Oliver sat down opposite to her with his own mug. 'Who invented this barbaric institution anyway?' she continued.

'Search me. So long as the jangles don't take the form of second thoughts, you'll be all right.'

'No, they don't do that. I just wish we could fast-forward the next few hours and be on that plane.'

'Not flying out until tomorrow evening, are you?'

'A very *long* fast forward. Did Mawgan survive last night?' She spoke with a certain amount of anxiety. Last night at the Fish hadn't been an official stag night, but there was no doubt that it had almost certainly got out of hand before the end. Most of the village, Debbie knew, had been planning to be there and the beer had inevitably flowed, quite possibly in all directions. Oliver, however, only laughed.

'Mawgan should be fine. The best man was taking his duties seriously, and protected him from himself with great efficiency. Unexpected, in an Irishman, but there you go. Life is full of surprises.'

'What's he like?' asked Debbie, curiously, for Con Delaney had not yet put in an appearance when she reluctantly withdrew from the Fish.

'Wild! He and Mawgan make a great double act. You should await his speech with apprehension, God alone knows what he'll come out with.' A silence fell between them, comfortable and peaceful. Oliver broke it, speaking thoughtfully. 'There was a crowd in from St Austell. Mawgan's father and one or two of his mates, and what I take to be some of Mawgan's old cronies. Two of them were asking after you – Kev and Robbie? Does that sound right?'

'Sounds excellent to me.'

'Seems that some of them are part of yet another choir, Cornwall must be lousy with them! They were insisting on doing a spot in the evening, since the locals have hijacked the ceremony.'

'Inter-choir rivalry?' Debbie raised her eyebrows.

'Not a full choir this time, just a spin-off group hunting a piece of the action. They all got together, they and the locals, and sang some rather unexpected songs, Chel's mother blushed! I imagine there's a rugby player or two among them ...' He let the pause speak for itself. 'They got Mawgan singing too, when he was sufficiently mellow, but I won't tell you what he sang. I can't think where he learned a song like that.' He grinned, wickedly.

'So long as he didn't play the trumpet,' said Debbie, but moodily, not returning the grin. She curled her hands round her mug, warming them. 'Oliver ...'

'What?' asked Oliver, when she didn't immediately continue.

'How would you feel if ... no. I shouldn't ask.'

'You can't go that far, and just stop,' Oliver objected. 'How would I feel if, what?'

Debbie said, not meeting his eyes,

'If Dad and Helen got together again.'

Oliver sat back in his chair. His hands, resting on the table, were relaxed and still.

'Why should I feel anything?'

'You *should* feel something,' said Debbie, believing it to be true.

'Like what? Resentment? Can't be bothered. Delight? Not that involved. Happy for them? Well that, maybe, if it's what they want. What do you think I should feel?'

'I don't know, that's why I asked.'

'How would *you* feel?'

Debbie thought for a minute.

'Happy for Dad and Helen. Sorry for Mum. Uneasy about Susan.'

That time, their eyes did meet, locking across the width of the table. Debbie, to her surprise, read the same concern in Oliver's as must show in her own.

'Ah yes ... Susan,' he said.

'Susan isn't happy.'

'Families are a great responsibility,' said Oliver, and his sister laughed.

'As if you cared! Come on, Oliver, don't be so hypocritical!'

'Oh, I care. Susan is my sister, I don't enjoy seeing her hurting. And she is.'

Debbie said, not pretending to misunderstand,

'Shall I get Mawgan to punch him on the nose for us?'

'Tempting, but better not. Perhaps your two partners in crime could rough him up a bit? They've a better chance of getting away with it. They were there last night, by the way.'

'I can imagine,' said Debbie. Roger and Carl, since their arrival in St Erbyn Creek, had swiftly made the Fish into their second home.'Susan hasn't said anything to me,' she added.

'Nor me. But then, she wouldn't tell me anything, anyway.'

Debbie nodded in agreement.

'No. Too much pride, not enough confidence to confide in either of us. I wish she would.'

'Tom is a total wanker,' said Oliver. 'If he can't see that he's got a prize, he needs his eyes tested.'

Debbie blinked.

'I didn't expect *that* from you!' she exclaimed, before she could stop herself. Oliver gave her what could only be described as a strange look.

'We may not see eye to eye on everything – no, make that on *anything* – but that doesn't mean that I can't see what she is. Or to put it more accurately, what she could be if she was left to get on with it without interference. Chel has opened my eyes to that, even if I couldn't see it for myself.'

Debbie's own eyes dropped to the dregs in the bottom of her mug. She didn't pretend to misunderstand him.

'People are as they are,' she murmured, defensively. She wasn't necessarily speaking of Susan.

'Yes. Selfish, unforgiving and bigoted,' said Oliver. He didn't mean Susan, either.

There was no future in that line of discussion. Debbie said, reverting to her sister,

'She was so happy on her wedding day. It makes you think, doesn't it?'

'You're not marrying a Tom,' said Oliver. He added, deliberately, 'Your rough diamond Cornishman couldn't care a toss if you have one pound in your pocket, or one million in the bank. He's marrying *you*. I don't think Tom was marrying Susan, I didn't at the time. He only talked himself into believing he was. It was a great big flashy wedding, yes, whereas yours is going to be a simple village affair, but there's more genuine love and commitment in your simplicity than in all Susan's pomp and ceremony, and you'd better believe it.'

'Susan was considered to be making a 'good' marriage,' said Debbie. 'I'm not. I know it, and I don't care.'

'You may be surprised,' said Oliver. 'Anyway, how do you define *good* in that context? I didn't make a good marriage, in that sense, either – but I tell you this, I've never regretted it for even one moment. And that's enough sentiment for one morning. More coffee?'

The door from the living room swung open at that point, and Chel came in, yawning and tousled from her bed, in search of coffee. She seized on the *cafetière* and it wasn't until she had the mug of coffee in her hands that she spoke.

'You're supposed to be relaxing in your bed, waiting for breakfast on a tray,' she told Debbie.

'Bed was lonely.'

'I know what you mean.' Chel yawned again. 'Lindsey awake?'

'I doubt it. Lin can snore for England.'

'I'll get breakfast then,' said Chel, apparently unaware of the *non sequitur*.

'Wake up first,' advised Oliver, with a grin. He got to his feet. 'I'm off to have a shower while there's still some hot water.'

When he had gone, Chel wandered sleepily over to the Rayburn and looked at it as if it was a stranger to her.

'Perhaps I'll leave breakfast until I've had one, too,' she said, doubtfully. She turned, and leaned her back against the rail. 'Feeling OK, Deb?'

'Butterflies. Those big ones, that they have in South America.'

'Ah. I know the ones you mean.' Chel nodded, and pulled herself up with a jerk as she nearly nodded off. 'Did we drink a lot last night? I feel strange.'

'Lin brought champagne. I think we killed it all.'

'Explains it. What time is Susan coming up with the kids?'

'She said after breakfast. That could mean any time after half-past eight. The Fish runs on oiled wheels when there are guests in.'

'I know. I oil them these days.' Chel yawned again, and finished her coffee. 'Hope that Con Delaney can get Mawgan out of his kitchen in time.'

'I made Tony and Jack promise they'd throw him out, if it became necessary. Do stop yawning, Chel, you've got me at it now!'

'Go back to bed then.'

'Can't. I feel sick.'

'Have a biscuit.' Chel groped on a shelf. 'I'll make some more coffee.'

The morning stumbled on sleepily until Susan's arrival with Tracy, Annabel and Candy while the five members of the household were still sitting over breakfast.

'The others will be up later on,' she said, blasting through the morning calm like a hurricane.

'Others?' Chel yawned.

'Your mother and father and the Toms – mine and Tracy's – and the boys, when it's time to go up to the church. Have the flowers arrived yet?'

'No.'

'I hope they aren't going to let us down. Deb, you were supposed to stay in bed and rest!'

'I couldn't.'

Susan gave her a glance of sympathy, and said, unexpectedly,

'Know the feeling. Mummy made me, and I missed out on all the excitement. Just keep from under foot, then, while we sort out these kids. Is Mawgan's sister here yet?' Allison was going to drive herself over in the Mazda, and spend the night in Deb's vacated bedroom with Lindsey.'Ought we to change the sheets?'

'No,' said Debbie, firmly. 'I only spent about seven hours in that bed, and I'm perfectly clean.Anyway, we'll be sisters by then. Have some coffee, Suse, and ease up. Allison won't care. Have you seen Mawgan this morning?'

'No, but he was around. I heard him holding forth out in the marquee with that Tony. You'd never believe it was his own wedding day.'

'He's a perfectionist where his job is concerned,' said Debbie, feeling unreasonably that she needed to excuse him.

'So it seems.'

The morning went on, gaining momentum as it went. The flowers arrived before Susan had an excuse to put a rocket under the florist, and the house by the little creek gradually filled up with people as time went by. Oliver and Chel were to take Chel's parents to the church, and the Toms – Tom Casson and Tom Harrison – arrived with Sebastian and Micky to collect Tracy. Debbie, fleeing the excitement in a sudden access of pre-wedding nerves, took refuge in Chel and Oliver's *en suite* bathroom and locked herself in. She was to dress in that room, her wedding dress hung ready against the wardrobe, fine creamy wool, smooth and soft as the silk that tied in a formal, long-tailed bow behind the waist, and simply elegant. Blondes, had said Susan, should avoid dead white: maybe she was right, she generally was. She lay in the hot, fragrant water and felt the world regain its equilibrium.

This time last year, almost to the day, she had set out to drive to Cornwall with a bad weather forecast, got caught in a blizzard on Bodmin Moor, and found herself knocking on the door of an apparently deserted, isolated cottage, and it had changed her life. Trickling bubbles through her fingers, she considered that momentous day. She had found Mawgan on the kitchen floor, injured and unconscious, never realising that in twelve months time she would be preparing for her wedding to him. Ain't life a gas? she thought irreverently.

A knock came on the bathroom door.

'Deb? It's Susan. Are you OK?'

'Fine. Just taking five.'

'You should think about getting dressed. Time's getting on. Dad's started to look at his watch.'

'Just coming.' Regretfully, Debbie pulled out the plug with her toe.

All the time that she was drying herself, applying make-up, and allowing Susan to help her into her dress, she was aware of a painful reservation in the back of her mind. This shouldn't be Susan's job, she knew that Susan was aware of it too. As she sat in front of the dressing table for Susan to place the heart-shaped crown of pearls and diamanté on her blonde hair, their eyes met in the mirror.

'Suse ...'

'Don't think about it,' said Susan, with sympathetic gentleness. 'You mustn't cry now, Deb, your make-up will smudge.'

'I'm not crying,' said Debbie, swallowing a hard lump in her throat.

'Get you!' Susan twitched the veil into place and leaned forward, kissing her sister's cheek. 'There – you look lovely! Here's your bouquet. Go downstairs when we've all gone, you don't want those over-excited children leaping all over you. Dad's waiting.'

'Oh, Suse!' Debbie got to her feet and flung her arms round her sister. 'I do love you.'

Surprised and touched, Susan returned the hug.

'Idiot! Now, remember what I said. No tears.'

She was gone, running down the stairs, leaving Debbie alone with her uncomfortable thoughts. Her mother had made so much trouble over this wedding. It wasn't like her to back down, but what could she do, now, at this eleventh hour? Debbie felt her heart thudding under the silky wool, banging against her ribs, nervous. To calm herself, she turned to look at herself in Chel's long mirror, assessing the fall of the long, elegantly draped skirt, the tiny waist emphasised by the close cut bodice, the long, tight sleeves, the overall unfamiliar elegance of her reflection. The point of the heart-shaped headdress sat on her forehead making her face seem to reflect its shape. She looked like somebody else, not herself at all. Some stranger, going forward to an unknown future.

I wish Mum was here to see me.

Car doors slammed below the window, engines coughed into life. She heard the excited squeals of the children. The wedding cars must be waiting at the top of the lane to come down, there were sounds of people hurrying each other along. Nearly time ... nearly.

She waited until she heard the children being hustled into the waiting limo by Susan, Allison and Lindsey, and then walked downstairs, serene and beautiful, to join her father.

* * * * *

Although she had tried to kid herself, Dot had always known that she had no choice. Not only did she have no doubts that that awful man meant exactly what he said, but on another, completely different level, she knew that to boycott Debbie's wedding could be considered unforgivable. Not only by others, she might well come to feel it to be so herself. Whether she would have come to this conclusion without Mawgan's intervention, not even Dot could have said with any certainty. He had simply made it inevitable.

Even so, she had no intention of making a production of her capitulation. It was necessary for Debbie to know that she was there, but as few other people as possible were to share in her defeat, for such she felt it to be. To this end, she planned carefully, choosing from her extensive wardrobe an outfit that, while elegant, was also to a certain extent disguising. Elegant winter dress, and shoes with matching handbag, but to complete the outfit, not a coat, but a swirling black cloak with a big hood that she could pull over her head to hide her. She didn't need a hat with this outfit, which smacked faintly of fancy dress but was unmistakeably classic. There was no need to let the side down, after all, she told herself to keep her courage up.So she drove alone to Truro to spend a lonely night in a hotel before leaving for st. Erbyn, where, arriving deliberately one of the first, she parked it in the frosty field that served as a car park for the little village church, and walked, alone and upright, to the church door.

It was a beautiful day, clear, cold, and blue, with a light sprinkling of snow still lying in the hedgerows, and the view across the Helford River from the churchyard was spectacular, but Dot hardly noticed.A tall, thin, fair man with glasses and a foreign accent, whom she had never seen before, thank goodness, presented her with a silver-embossed order of service and tried to show her to a pew in the middle of the flower-decorated church, but Dot insisted that she should be right at the back, near to the door where Debbie and her terrifying husband would have to pass close by. She sat there, half hidden in the shadows, with her head bowed as if in prayer as the church gradually filled up. It wasn't until she felt the congregation to be of some size that she lifted her head and, pulling her hood forward to shield her face, for some of these people would know her, looked around her.

The bridegroom had already arrived, she saw. He was standing by the altar with another man, presumably the best man, beside him, talking to the vicar, who was not yet robed for the service. The three of them seemed to be enjoying a joke, most unsuitable in church. It was the first time she had seen the man in daylight, he looked slightly less intimidating, she had to admit. She deplored the cut of his good dark suit, which was undeniably continental, but he looked almost respectable

– if you discounted a reprehensible grin, that was, and the general air of irreverence. But he was still too broad across the shoulders for comfort, and even with laughter lightening his face, he still had that strong, blunt, bullet-headed shape to his skull. She still didn't feel like calling his bluff. The best man was around the same not-very-impressive height, but slighter, with dark wavy hair, very good-looking. Too much so for his own good, or anybody else's probably, he looked to be full of himself.She looked down again hurriedly to her order of service as Chel and Oliver, together with Chel's parents, came in through the door, with closely behind them, Tom Casson and Chel's sister and brother-in-law and the two boys, Micky and Sebastian. They went up the aisle in a group, escorted by another of the ushers, a pleasant-looking, tall man with a tight mass of light brown curls. Roger, had she but known it. He seemed to know them well, Dot thought, and felt a small pang in this church full of strangers at her daughter's wedding. Her favourite daughter's wedding. She dropped her head lower, as if by doing so she could hide her feelings from herself.

On the groom's side of the church, the pews were also filling. His friends and relations looked quite ordinary, smartly dressed like guests at any other wedding, the men in tidy formal suits, the women with pretty hats; provincial of course, but on the whole a pleasant surprise. Most of them seemed to know each other, she heard them chatting happily with the same regional accent that she so deplored in that mannerless brute. Dot wasn't quite sure what she had expected; chimpanzees, possibly? She heard a burst of excitable Italian passing her ear, and at another moment, French. These, too, were headed to the groom's side. At least one of them had a face that, to her astonishment, she thought she recognised as a famous continental restaurateur from Milan. It would be too much to say that Dot began to feel small, but she certainly became a little thoughtful.

She heard a laugh that she recognised, and hid her face again as Helen Macken, that dreadful Anona Fingall, and yet another obvious foreigner that she didn't know went past her in a group. *They* wouldn't have been here had she had the arranging of the wedding, that was for sure!

The bridesmaids had arrived, she could hear the children giggling in the church porch, and a moment later Susan, looking superbly elegant, walked down to the front of the church escorted by the man with the glasses to take her place beside Tom and Sebastian, with the space on her right for Jerry. Susan knew how to dress, Dot thought complacently, it was a pity she was so dumpy. She had been conceived, not in love so much as in a desire to be upsides with Helen with her gorgeous little son, and had proved a disappointment, so solemn and commonplace. And a waste of effort too, since Henry had died and never seen her, and she herself had eventually married Jerry and produced beautiful Deborah ... but a good girl, nevertheless. A good, obedient daughter, a credit to her upbringing. Susan would never kick over the traces and marry a highwayman. She would always do her duty.

A lot of men, looking slightly uncomfortable in their best suits, had assembled in the choir stalls. Referring to her order of service, Dot discovered that the St Erbyn Male Voice Choir was to sing a choral arrangement of the Lord's Prayer followed by Andrew Lloyd Webber's *Love Changes Everything* during the signing of the register. How rustic! thought Dot, superior as ever. Some people only ever learn the hard way.

And now the organ had changed its improvisation to the opening notes of Pachelbel's immortal *Canon*, and the bridal procession had begun its journey down the aisle, and Dot found herself looking at Jerry's square back, and Debbie's slighter one with her blonde hair misty under the cream-coloured veil, going away from her towards the altar, followed by a clutch of bridesmaids in pale sea green; Annabel and Candy, Debbie's best friend Lindsey, and a dark girl who could only be the groom's sister.She was startled as much as anything to find that there were tears in her eyes, and blinked them away angrily.

The procession came to a halt by the altar and Jerry stepped back, leaving his daughter standing beside her bridegroom.

Debbie had been in some turmoil during the drive to the church, not simply because the great moment had finally arrived, but privately distressed by her mother's continuing intransigence, but as she turned and looked up into Mawgan's face, the turmoil evaporated. He smiled at her, she loved that smile, and leaning forward, whispered quietly in her ear.

'Are you warm enough, bird? You look beautiful.'

'I've got my thermal long johns on underneath,' Debbie whispered back, and saw his eyes light up with laughter. She caught the best man's eye, just behind Mawgan's shoulder. He was looking at her with open admiration, and when he saw she had caught him at it, gave her a brilliant smile. They hadn't met yet, Con Delaney had arrived after her departure from the Fish. He looked fun, she thought, and when the chips were down he had proved a good friend to Mawgan, so she smiled back at him with approval. Then she handed her bouquet to Lindsey and turned to face the altar.

The marriage took place, the register was duly signed, the choir sang beautifully and movingly, and Dot, hidden away in the back pew, thought her own private and bitter thoughts. Then the organ burst into The Entry of the Queen of Sheba and the bridal procession returned up the aisle, this time with Deborah on the arm of her ... her husband. That gorilla.Dot bit her lip, summoned her courage, and prepared to face her humiliation.

Mawgan saw her first, Debbie was too busy smiling at everyone, her happiness shining around her like visible light. Their eyes met, but to Dot's relief, he didn't smile in triumph, but just gave her a brief nod and drew Debbie's attention with a touch on her hand. Debbie turned her head in question, and found herself looking straight at her mother. For a second, she seemed frozen, and then her face burst into a smile of such pleasure and love and relief that Dot's heart turned right over. Then they were past, and she dropped her head hurriedly so that she shouldn't meet the eye of Jerry, close behind the bridesmaids and the ebullient best man, with a tall, slim, elegant lady on his arm who surely couldn't be that Neanderthal's mother?

They were safely past, and the wedding guests were piling out after them. Dot slid to her knees, letting the dark hood fall forward to conceal her completely, and openly, and for once honestly, wept for all that she had thrown away.

* * * * *

Wedding receptions are wedding receptions countrywide, universally cheerful occasions with speeches of varying quality, and the wedding reception of Debbie and Mawgan was no different, distinguished from any other village wedding only by the quality of the food, the wine, and the service. Oh yes, and by the more-or-less discreet presence of the television crew, who had promised Debbie the wedding video to end all wedding videos.

'You must have put the fear of God into your staff, or is it always like this?' said Susan, smiling at her new brother-in-law.

'Fear of me, more like,' he answered, with a grin. Mawgan was by this time just slightly drunk, relaxing into a huge wave of relief that he hadn't bothered to analyse or identify. It had something to do with Debbie, something to do with the unmistakeable goodwill of the gathering, something to do with Kev and Charlie, Robbie and Molly and the children, seated round a table with Chel and Oliver, and with Deb's new cousins, Keith and Judy Old, all of them obviously getting on like a house on fire. Susan's deliberate arrangement, he knew, and inspired. The grin held real warmth, and Susan felt warmed by it, although her feelings generally, on this occasion, were equivocal. She was happy for Debbie, taking pleasure from her sister's obvious delight in the day, while on a more private level grieving for the breakdown of her own marriage and concerned with the problems that now faced her. Tom, sitting beside the best man's delectable girlfriend, wasn't even bothering to spare her a glance, as she sat here beside Mawgan's father on the top table. He was far more taken up with his companion, who was a clone of Elaine. The best man didn't seem to care one way or the other, raising his glass to the girl in a careless toast across the gap between them, and smiling merrily.

More food, more wine, speeches. Jerry rising to his feet to make a sentimental tribute to his daughter and to welcome his son-in-law to the family; Mawgan, betraying an unexpected streak of off-beat humour and an unsuspected, to most people at least, linguistic skill, making jokes in three languages and thanking Susan and his own staff gracefully for their efforts, before praising the bridesmaids to the skies; Con Delaney, more wickedly clever in person even than on the radio or the television, replying on their behalf and dropping his old friend right in it with several surely apocryphal stories of their time spent working together in the Bristol hotel where they had first met. Everybody laughed heartily, champagne flowed freely, and the wedding cake was cut to cheers of approval, the bottom layer being saved for a repeat performance that evening, when still more friends and family members were expected to a big party with buffet and disco, and some singing in the middle from the St Austell choristers to help the food go down. Susan, recalling her disparaging remarks about the local discos, almost blushed, *would* have blushed if she had had any way of knowing, at the time, that the best man would be one of the country's top DJs.

Debbie, radiant with happiness, came up to her sister when the reception was over and gave her a big hug. The hidden presence of her mother in the church was a secret that she treasured to herself, but Susan deserved her thanks. She had done a superb job.

'Suse, that was brilliant, you did wonderfully!' she said. 'Thank you, thank you, thank you!'

'The caterers were pretty good, you know,' said Susan, deprecatingly, but Debbie only laughed.

'You arranged it all, you chose it all. Blokes are no good at things like seating plans and flowers and ... and *ambience.*

Don't try and kid me. Did you see Mum? She was right at the back and she smiled – ' She broke off. Dot hadn't appeared at the reception, perhaps a good thing but a disappointment even so.

Susan, more pleased than she let her sister see by the genuine thanks, smiled without answering and went off to retrieve her family.She hadn't seen Dot, but she knew she had been there for Jerry had been watching out for her and had passed on the news, thinking it would please Susan – as it had, of course. Only, her credulity wouldn't stretch to encompass her mother's having given in just like that, and not knowing exactly what had taken place that night in Embridge allowed her imagination free rein She had very mixed feelings on the subject but since nobody had taken her into their confidence, didn't quite like to ask.

Chel's nephew Micky, she found, had taken Sebastian under his wing, fortunately since his father seemed more taken up with Deb's friend Lindsey now, competing for her favours with Debbie's partner Roger. Tom, Susan thought miserably, was punishing her for having made him come. Annabel had vanished somewhere with Candy; probably, with the rest of Chel's family, gone off to the house by the creek with Chel and Oliver, her own father, Helen, Nonie and Theo. Left thus on her own, and unaware that Tracy was searching for her to go with them all, Susan went upstairs to her bedroom, kicked off her shoes and lay down on the bed.

Utterly lonely. Utterly miserable.

* * * * *

The evening party, bigger, more informal, bade fair to be an equal success. The marquee was seething with happy people enjoying themselves. Debbie, standing at the doorway with her husband to greet the guests, reflected that Mawgan might, indeed, have lost some friends thanks to his little sister and her husband, but he seemed to have retained a fair number just the same, and his family, which appeared to be endless, had rallied to the flag in droves as soon as the news of his probable innocence had got around. Her own friends, piling in from London, from Embridge, from yacht and sailing clubs scattered throughout the country, almost outnumbered them. It was a huge, happy gathering. The restaurant staff, going around with trays of drinks, were smiling with everyone else. It was perhaps the first time that Debbie had been fully aware of the popularity that Mawgan had once enjoyed, the discovery was bitter-sweet. The shadows, she knew would never quite leave his mind, the harsh experience would always colour his outlook. Clinical depression stayed with you, she had been told it even had she not known it from Oliver's experience. The man he had been, she would probably never know. Watching him as people ebbed and flowed about him, she was unaware that shadows had gathered in her own eyes too, until an arm came across her shoulders, comforting and friendly, and turning her head she found herself looking into the smoky blue, Irish eyes of Con Delaney.

'Life's a sod,' he said, reading her thoughts with uncanny correctness. 'Don't grieve, little one. He's a survivor, your nice new husband.'

'But he's gone – hasn't he? The man you knew in Bristol.'

'Happens to us all, one way or the other. I believe it's called 'growing up'.'

'You were good to him,' said Debbie, hesitating, wondering if she might be speaking out of turn. 'He appreciates it – and so do I. I'd like to thank you, if you don't mind.'

'A dirty job, but somebody had to do it.' Con grinned at her, brilliantly attractive and well aware of it. 'That wanker Edward Rushton really dropped him in it. Strange, isn't it, how one person clobbers you, and all of a sudden it's open season?' He gave her shoulders a squeeze. 'Take care of him, Debbie. He's a worthwhile person, in spite of all. And now, I suppose, I'd better get this show on the road for you.'

Con Delaney was good at his bizarre job, which of course explained his spectacular success. Good-looking, charismatic, and undoubtedly having kissed the Blarney Stone, he was irresistible, the ultimate loveable rogue, although Debbie, after that brief exchange, found herself wondering how much was real, how much a front. Working in partnership with the local DJ whose equipment they were using, he very soon had the party in full swing, the dance floor, laid over the tarmac of the car park, crowded with people enjoying themselves. Susan, seeing that the party didn't need her help, danced without heart with her husband and then, without surprise, found herself deserted in favour of one of Mawgan's attractive young cousins. A look around to check that all was well with the children found all four of them, together with two more, slightly younger, that she thought might belong to one of Mawgan's friends called Robbie, or something, solemnly dancing in their own corner under the eye of Mawgan's elder sister. Balked yet again of something constructive to do, she sat down at one of the tables to watch the dancing, unreasonably depressed, surely, for somebody at a wedding, and trying to pin a smile to her face.

After a while, she became aware that she was being watched, and looking up with the sudden wariness of someone who had thought they were unobserved, she found herself being carefully scrutinised by a stranger. A man. One of the ushers, she thought, one of Deb's partners, the older one, late twenties, a journalist or something, he wrote for the yachting press and lived on his boat. Another Cornishman, with a weird name that sounded more Spanish or Italian than Cornish, Carl something ... Colenso, that was it. He was a little like Mawgan to look at, she had noticed it at the church; a little taller, a little less burly, not quite so bullet-headed, but the same basic type, with close-growing dark hair, although in his case thick and probably curly, if he would let it be. Blue eyes, not golden. Better looking, but at the same time, less blindingly attractive, not necessarily a bad thing. He had no right to be staring at her like that, almost as if he *pitied* her. Unconsciously, her chin went up, and he immediately looked away.

That fixed him! Susan thought indignantly. How *dare* he look at her like that, as if he knew exactly how she was feeling? She got up and moved away, out of his sight unless he followed her, and was immediately accosted by Tracy's Tom, holding out his hands for her to dance with him.

But the malaise didn't leave her, indeed, it got worse. By the time the interval for the buffet arrived she wished that she could slip away and just go to bed and cry herself to sleep. Tom – her own Tom – had virtually ignored her, she thought that it must be becoming obvious to everyone. Chel's mother had been *kind* to her, for heaven's sake, not that she wasn't always, but more pointedly so, and Chel had come to sit beside her, talking cheerfully about the success of the party which could very well have waited until tomorrow, and even Helen, whom she thought, wrongly as it happened, didn't even like her much, had sought her out to congratulate her on the arrangements. Helen, with a brilliance about her that Susan suspected, had spent much of her time this evening with Susan's own father. Just one more nail in the coffin of her party mood.

While the buffet was being laid out on the prepared long table and served to the guests, the maverick splinter group of choristers from St Austell sang. They sang wholeheartedly, old Cornish folk songs, secular in content and obviously familiar to a lot of the guests, who joined in with the choruses. *Lamorna*, and *Little Lise* and *Up Camborne Hill* and such as these, and in special tribute to the groom, *The White Rose*.

'You should make Mawgan sing something,' Anna called out from one of the tables, a sleepy twin on her knee.

'Good idea – where's he gone?' Robbie looked about him, and Kev, diving into the crowd, towed their hapless friend out into the limelight.

'Your turn,' he said.

'I'm not drunk enough,' Mawgan protested, and a chorus went up from the choir,

'Give the man another beer!'

'Sing *Evergreen*,' Kev commanded. 'Where's Deb? Come here, Mrs Angwin!' Debbie, stepping obediently into the circle of her husband's arm, was laughing.

'Don't remember the words,' said Mawgan, but they weren't letting him get away with it.

'Just get on with it,' Robbie commanded.

Susan winced. She knew of three versions of *Evergreen*, each one worse than the last, given the way she was feeling. The keyboard player, who had brought his own instrument to the party, played the introduction to the very worst of them, the schmaltzy Roy Orbison number.

She knew, as soon as she heard the first notes, that she couldn't bear it. Mawgan sang like an angel, he would sing those words to Debbie, safe in the curve of his arm, and she, Susan, would be unable to contain her tears. Knowing it was the only way possible if she wasn't to make a prize fool of herself, she got to her feet with a quiet apology to the people round her and slipped away. Chel, who was one of them, watched her with a frown. Susan's unhappiness was like a wall, shutting people out. There was no climbing it, no way through. She was hiding herself away from them. Susan, hurrying now, didn't even notice her concerned look.

She walked through the tented passage that led into the inn, not knowing where she was going, only knowing that she must get away, running now, but you couldn't run from yourself. Straight through the hall she ran, and out onto the forecourt. There were tables there, deserted now on this cold, dark winter evening. Susan sat down abruptly on a bench, hugging herself against the frosty air. There was no wind, the harbour lay like a sheet of polished jet reflecting the stars. She shivered. Her heart was too full, it would break apart, loaded with jealousy for her sister, despair for herself, fear for her children, misery in an all-pervasive, general way that she couldn't share with anyone. She didn't belong, she wasn't necessary to any of them any more. Her father would go back to Helen, her brother had never needed her, her sister was more happily married than she herself had ever dreamed of, her husband despised her and called her unattractive and sexless, her children depended on Maria for their security, her mother cared only for outward appearances. If she threw herself into the river now, nobody would even miss her until morning, when they gathered to go home. Tears gathered in her eyes, trembled, fell. She sniffed, and wiped her fingers across her cheek, sniffed again. Shivered.

'Here,' said a voice. Something warm and woolly went about her shoulders. 'You'll catch your death out here. What's the matter, can anyone help?'

It was him. Carl whatsisname, Deb's partner. She looked at him angrily, tears sparkling on her lashes.

'No. Thank you.'

He tucked his fleece-lined sailing jacket more closely round her shoulders, and sat down beside her anyway.

'Then I'll just sit here with you and say nothing, until you feel better,' he said gently. She wanted to tell him to push off, but he did as he said and simply sat there beside her, and it suddenly felt ungrateful even to think of it. He had brought her his coat, after all.

It was that unexpected kindness that tipped the scales. All of a sudden, her head went down on her arms and she wept, uncontrollably, as if her heart would break, just as she had in front of Maria, and for a similar reason..

After a little while, Carl took her in his arms much as Maria had done, because it seemed a useful, even desirable thing to do, and held her as if he was trying to make her safe.

'Come on,' he said, after a while. 'That'll do. Here – ' He took a clean handkerchief from his pocket and pushed it into her hands. 'Blow. That's better.' He released her from his embrace, while keeping one arm around her shoulders. He had an undirected feeling that she needed human contact. Susan looked down at his handkerchief in her hands.

'There's a cliché, if you like,' she said indistinctly.

'My world-famous romantic novel impression,' said Carl. 'No – you treasure it. That's in the script too.'

Susan hadn't thought that she would laugh ever again, but she did, a smothered giggle that turned into a sob and wrung his heart. He removed his arm.

'You sit here. I'll go and find us a drink. I won't be long.'

The assurance was vaguely comforting. Susan sat there with his warm coat about her shoulders, drying her tears on his handkerchief and regaining control of herself, and after a while he came back and set a glass down in front of her before seating himself again and placing a pint on the table.

'Your sister said that brandy was your favoured spirit, so brandy it is. Now drink up, and if you want to tell me, I'll listen, and if you don't we can discuss the wedding. Been great, hasn't it? Debbie looks to be on cloud nine.'

Susan looked at him. A lamp on the corner of the Fish cast a muted light across his face, he looked kindly and she felt his sympathy. She needed somebody, she realised, she needed them desperately, but how far could she trust a journalist? Even just a yachting journalist? She said, testing the water,

'You're a journalist.'

'I'm a writer. There's a slight difference. And at the moment, I'm embarking on a new career as a sailing instructor in order to be able to eat. So you needn't fear me. I'm safe, I promise. But don't feel forced.'

'I don't,' said Susan. She hesitated. 'Why did you follow me? You were staring at me earlier.'

'I know. I ought to apologise. Only you're so different from Deb, I could hardly believe you were her sister.'

'Yeah ... I know. Deb's beautiful.'

'That isn't what I meant,' said Carl. His hand came over to cover hers, comforting and warm. 'Deb *is* beautiful, and she's full of ideas and energy, she sparkles like a firework in the dark. But much as I admire her, it's from afar. I couldn't live with her, she's got too much drive. Mawgan Angwin is welcome.'

'So, what did you mean?' asked Susan, when he didn't say any more.

'I'm not sure I should tell you,' said Carl. His fingers caressed her rings, consideringly. 'You're a married woman, *my sister Susan*, and I don't even know your married name.'

'Casson.'

'And I'm Carl Colenso, we haven't been introduced.'

'I know who you are,' said Susan, and added, with a sort of desperation, 'I just wish I knew who *I* was.'

I'm losing it, Carl thought in amazement. I'm dicing with disaster here. I should just shut up and talk about the wedding, the weather, *anything*. Not this. He said,

'You're the sister of Deb and of Oliver Nankervis, your father's daughter, your husband's wife, your children's mother. I presume you have, or have had, a mother of your own, although I don't see her today. Unless she's the lady with the wonderful eyes, sitting with your father?' He didn't think she was. Although, in an odd sort of way, she did resemble Oliver, Susan had taken the bride's mother's place herself.

'No,' said Susan. 'No to almost all of that. My mother is holding a grudge back in Embridge, she didn't like the idea of Deb marrying Mawgan.'She took a breath, impelled to continue. 'I'm only Deb's half-sister, no relation to Oliver nor to Daddy. No blood relation.I'm not sure about being my husband's wife any more, and my children – ' Her voice broke. Carl removed the brandy glass from her hand and gathered her into his arms again. She said, muffled, 'I don't belong *anywhere*!'

He could have guessed it, Carl thought. Deb, Oliver, Deb's father, were all cast in a different mould from this one. Oliver, as well as Deb, was beautiful. Susan was pretty, or she would be if she was happy. She had a charming face, a sweet expression, warmth and kindness, and she was obviously capable and sensible. A woman who deserved better than to sit and cry on her own on a winter's night, and at her sister's wedding, too. The sort of partner that a man could rely on, a friend. A lover, in the right hands, although he felt a tension in her that spoke of more than outward unhappiness. Damn, damn, damn! What had happened to this pleasant and attractive woman to make her into such a mess?

'But you do have a husband and children,' he reiterated, moving out a careful pawn across the board. He had seen the husband. A yuppie oaf, with a good opinion of himself. Deb's friend Lindsey had come close to landing him a slap in the kisser, she had said, in his hearing, to Roger. They had laughed about it. Poor Susan.

He understood her to say, through a fresh burst of tears, that her husband only cared about money. Her money? Deb, he knew, had enough to start a sailing school from scratch, so it was easy to put two and two together. He began heartily to dislike Tom Casson. Susan, her face now buried in his chest, told him what Tom had said to her. She shouldn't have. It just came out, without her meaning it, and she wept again, harder.

Carl sat there, containing his anger, holding her in his arms. He had a choice, he realised. At this moment, he had a choice. He could dry her tears, take her back into the marquee, restore her to her family, to Chel and to Oliver, and the rest of them. It wasn't his business. He didn't need to be involved.

'So let's see if I've got it right,' he said, knowing that he should shut up and get out of this, for his own sake if not for hers. 'Your Dad is the father of Oliver and Debbie, but not of you? No ... that doesn't work. Oliver has to be older than you, you're too young for him and too old for Deb – ' He broke off, feeling deep waters sucking at his feet.

'I'm thirty,' said Susan, defiantly. She sat up.

Carl was twenty-seven. He rubbed his nose, thoughtfully.

'You'll have to explain,' he said.

Susan said, succinctly,

'Mummy and Daddy were both married to other people. I'm Mummy's daughter, Oliver is Daddy's son, Debbie is their daughter.'

So the lady with the wonderful eyes is possibly Oliver's mother, although that makes things rather complicated, doesn't it? Carl didn't give voice to this conclusion. Instead, he said,

'Well? Sounds to me like the makings of a good family.'

'It's the makings of a disaster,' said Susan, more tartly than she had intended. She went on, forcefully, as well be hung for a sheep as a lamb. 'Oliver and Mummy hate each other – no, I'm not joking, before you interrupt. He doesn't like me, either. Deb just melted away as soon as she could. Daddy is going to go back to his first wife. My husband despises me. *I don't know what to do*, nobody wants me, I'm only adopted!'

'Don't cry again,' said Carl. He looked at her speculatively. 'Your father adopted you? What happened to your natural father?'

'He died. Before I was born.' She choked on a sob.

'Hmm. And did your mother adopt Oliver in the same way?'

This brought Susan up short. She had never considered it before but no, Mummy hadn't adopted Oliver. Of course, Helen might have had something to say but even so, she had never even heard the possibility mentioned that she remembered.

'No,' she said, and heard her own surprise in her voice.

'Well, there you are then,' said Carl. 'You have to care about someone before you adopt them. So you're luckier than your brother, in that respect.'

'I suppose. I never thought about it like that.'

He smiled at her. He had a nice smile.

'So, what else haven't you thought of? Deb thinks the world of you, and I don't get the impression that Oliver doesn't like you, to be honest.'

Loyalty kept Susan from saying, *it's Mummy*, she had already given away quite enough. She placed the heels of her hands over her eyes and leaned forward over the table. Carl picked up the brandy and touched her arm with the glass.

'Here. Drink. What about your natural father's family? Surely they must love you too.'

'I never met them,' said Susan, muffled. 'I don't know who they are.'

'Perhaps you should find out. It might give you a sense of identity.'

'How?' she said. She raised her face to look at him, taking the glass. 'Anyway, they've never made any attempt to find *me*. Maybe they don't even exist.' She sounded angry.

Carl was becoming curious, perhaps it was the journalist whose existence he denied in himself.

'Haven't you even wondered about them, not ever? I would have done.'

Susan thought about it.

'They were never mentioned. And I suppose, I so much wanted to belong ...' She let the sentence tail away.

'You do belong. Believe me.'

She shook her head.

'You don't know.' She believed what she said, he saw, and was sorry for it. Whatever had happened in her family to make her like this, so insecure? Deb wasn't insecure. Oliver gave no appearance of it, although Carl didn't know him well and wouldn't have liked to be dogmatic on the subject. He was certainly an over-achiever, if that was any guide. He looked at Susan thoughtfully. Talking about her natural father's family had engaged her interest, he saw, calmed her. Her relationship with her husband was nothing to do with him. *Nothing to do with him.* Remember that, Colenso.

'There are ways of finding out,' he suggested. 'I presume you know his name?'

516

'Worthington. Henry Worthington. He was an investment broker, a good one.' She didn't feel it worth mentioning that he had been so much older than her mother. 'He died the week before I was born.'

'How sad!' He sounded genuinely sorry. 'Accident?'

'Heart attack. Executive stress. I honestly don't know anything else about him. Mummy showed me a picture once, a long time ago. It didn't mean anything. I wanted Daddy to be my father.' She hesitated, curiosity, for the first time that she could remember in a long while, raising its head. It had never seemed worth being curious about a dead end before. '*How* can you find out?'

'Official records. Electoral rolls. Marriage certificates, death certificates, birth certificates. Church registers. Where did he work? Someone may remember him, you're not that old. All sorts of ways.'

'Maybe ...' said Susan. She paused. Maybe if she knew where she came from, she would feel more confident. Maybe roots were what she lacked. She didn't think so, but anything was surely better than doing nothing in the present circumstances. She needed a base from which to stand and fight back, maybe Henry Worthington, her unknown father, her children's grandfather, would give her one? 'I don't see how it would help me,' she said.

'If it doesn't, you won't be any worse off.'

'Suppose I found out that all my relatives were dead, too?'

'What, *all* of them? Unlikely, I would have thought. Just about everyone has too many cousins, for instance. And even if you did, you'd still *know*, wouldn't you? He's half of you. You should know. I could help you, if you like. I know people who will find out things like that for you, if you give them a starting point. Confidential, obviously.'

'What, like detectives?'

'Sort of, I suppose, only they call themselves researchers, or family historians, usually, and charge less.'

'I'll think about it.' Better than thinking about Tom. She found that she was feeling better, and realised that he had deliberately changed the subject to help her, tactfully shelving her personal affairs. She must have embarrassed him horribly. She smiled at him. He thought she had a lovely smile, and how could her husband say that she was plain and uninteresting, the moron? 'Thank you. You've given me something new to think about.'

'Don't let it be the only thing,' he said. His eyes met hers, seriously. 'You're a lovely woman, Susan Casson, don't let anyone tell you different. People will say anything to justify themselves, just don't buy it. Promise?'

'I'll try, anyway.' She managed another smile.

'Good girl.' He smiled at her, friendly and undemanding, a kind stranger who had been there when she had needed him. She felt herself unwinding, for what felt like the first time for years, and a restful silence crept in around them, in which the washing of the tide, rattling the shingle of the foreshore sounded unreasonably loud. He said nothing further, and the peace and the quiet and his undemanding company began to work their healing magic. Her tears had dried.

* * * * *

In the marquee, the guests had gathered to witness the cutting of the final layer of the wedding cake, a speech from the bridegroom had been called for and made, when unexpectedly, Dr Billy Pollard banged on a table for silence. When he had everybody's attention, he spoke.

'Nobody asked me to do this,' he said. 'I make that quite clear, and if you all want me to shut up, I will, I pinched this slot off the best man, who we all know is an inspired speaker, right out of my class. But there's something I feel needs to be said, and I'm the best person to say it. Now seems a good time.' He paused. 'Any dissenters? No? Are you all sitting comfortably? Then I'll begin.' He smiled at the assembled company, at Mawgan's suddenly apprehensive face and Debbie's smiling one, and took a sip from his wineglass.

'There's one or two things that many of you here today perhaps won't know. What we are celebrating today is the marriage of two people who are not just special, but extra special. Yes, both of them. We wouldn't be here at all, for instance, if Debbie had not been so level-headed and courageous.' A murmur ran around the company, some knew what he meant, more perhaps did not. He took another sip and went on. 'This time last year, all of us who live here in Cornwall will remember, we had a week of freak weather. Bitterly cold, blizzards on the moors, lines down, power off – you name it, we got it. In the middle of the worst of this, in an isolated cottage on the moor, a man who should have known better – '

'Been taller, you mean!' interrupted a voice which sounded suspiciously like Robbie's, and everyone laughed. Dr Billy grinned in the direction of the voice, and went on, as if he hadn't been interrupted.

' – climbed onto a chair to check his trip switch and fell off onto a stone floor: in doing so he suffered a serious injury which, while not life-threatening under normal circumstances, was certainly life-threatening under these. Indeed, as I have said, we might well not be here, enjoying this wonderful party, had not, a while later, another person who should have known better driven off the main road in a white-out and ended up in a snowdrift right outside the cottage where this accident took place.' He paused here for effect, and a mutter of interest ran around his audience.

'Debbie, we have to admit, at the time was no first-aider, although I understand she's done her homework since.' Laughter. 'Even so, she managed to do most of the right things, and in a moment of inspiration, struggled out into the snow and wrote the word HELP onto the blank surface of a field, thus bringing assistance in time, in the shape of Cornwall's

Air Ambulance, and saving the life of the man she has today married. They might never have met again at that point, but unknown at least to Debbie, although the jury is out as to what Mawgan knew on their first meeting – ' More laughter, and a couple of ribald remarks from the floor. Dr Billy smiled. 'Well, we'll pass over that, shall we? What I am saying is that fate would bring them together again, here in St Erbyn, and in that regard, the rest is history.' Cheering.

'But the story doesn't end there – indeed, it doesn't *begin* there. The last three or so years haven't been good for Mawgan. We all know why, and I won't go there now. Accidents happen. Tragic accidents, as in this case, might as easily happen to you and to me any day, and I, and I hope you too, shall not sit in judgement. But what was no accident was this same Mawgan going into a burning building to rescue a woman trapped inside.' In the pause that he made for effect, a pin could have been heard as it dropped. 'Thus risking his life once more, but this time knowingly and without hesitation. This is the man we would judge? I think not – ' He broke off to an unexpected wave of cheering and applause. When it had died down, he resumed, speaking levelly to hide his own emotion. 'Fortunately for him, Debbie had gone with him and once again, he lived because of her, and because of Lesley Howells' husband who came back to help. All three of them came out of that inferno alive. I do not know which of them to call the bravest.'

He paused here, and his audience waited, hanging now on his words as the climax to his speech arrived.

'There is another side to this story – to this man. One that is very personal to me. I'm not going to embarrass you, Mawgan, but I wish to say this, that kindness and generosity are virtues all too easily overlooked. When my beloved wife, Rose, was nearing the end of her life, this man did something for her that was so spontaneous and generous that, for her last few days on this earth, it isn't too much to say that it changed her world. When she died, not a week later, the happiness that he had given to her was still in her heart. This gift was beyond price, yet so simply given that it was made to seem the merest commonplace. It isn't putting it too highly, I believe, to say that the whole of the remainder of her life was encompassed in a song. I therefore ask you all to join with me in raising your glass to this remarkable couple, and to wish them, with me, a generous slice of that same happiness in their life together, and that their lives, too, may be encompassed in a song. Debbie and Mawgan!' He raised his glass and the company responded with wholehearted warmth, followed immediately by a buzz of talking.

'Con,' said Mawgan, turning in desperation to his best man. 'Do something!'

Con gave him an odd look, but responded to the plea with aplomb.

'More music,' he said, immediately, and turned away to see to it. Debbie slipped her hand through her new husband's arm.

'He was right, you know,' she murmured. 'Dr Billy. People forget too easily. He's made sure now, that between that and the origin of *An Rosen Gwyn*, they never will again. You can live here and feel among friends like you did before.'

'And that'll do,' said Mawgan, with finality. 'And if Connor Delaney plays something stupid like *Hanging out for a hero*, I warn you, I will slaughter him and it won't be no accident, neither!'

* * * * *

From behind the Fish, the sounds of the disco starting up again came faintly, the buffet was obviously over and in the chilly night air, Susan shivered a little. They had been here for long enough, it was time to rejoin the celebrations.

'You've been very kind,' she said. 'I'm sorry I was such a watering can.'

'Think nothing of it. I hope you weren't hungry. We seem to have missed out on the food, but I expect they could find us something.'

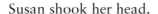

Susan shook her head.

'We had a huge lunch, quite late. And anyway ...'

'I know.' Carl touched her cheek, holding his breath, knowing a sensible man wouldn't touch her at all. 'Come along, Mrs Casson. We should go back in the warm.' He gathered up the empty glasses, and rose to his feet, holding out his free hand to her.

'Come and dance,' he said.